Dear Reader,

It is hard to believe that a month has passed since I last wrote to you. I do hope that you have been looking forward to reading this new batch of *Scarlet* titles as much as I have enjoyed selecting them for you.

Do keep those questionnaires and letters flooding in, won't you? It is extremely useful for us to receive feedback on how you like the mixture of books we present, whether you are finding them easily in the shops each month and so on. It is only by hearing from *you* that we can be sure *Scarlet* continues to please you.

I know that authors, too, like to have readers' comments on their work, so if you wish to send me a letter for your favourite *Scarlet* author, I'll be happy to pass it on.

Till next month,
Best wishes,

Sally Cooper

SALLY COOPER,
Editor-in-Chief – *Scarlet*

About the Author

Anne Styles started writing as a teenager – writing wicked stories starring her friends at school. She then stopped for years and grew up! Anne has two grown-up children, three and a half grandchildren and four step-children. This leaves her with no time for pets, but she does make and collect doll's houses and works for Cancer Relief. As a result, Anne says, 'I start writing at midnight!'

Anne used to be a costume designer in TV and films for many years before turning to interior design. One of her favourite memories is of chasing David Niven around his dressing room trying to cut holes in his costume! There are not many stars the author hasn't met at some time or another in a state of undress!

*Other **Scarlet** titles available this month:*

SECRETS – Angela Arney
THIS TIME FOREVER – Vickie Moore
THE JEWELLED WEB – Maxine Barry

ANNE STYLES

THE SINS OF SARAH

SCARLET

Enquiries to:
Robinson Publishing Ltd
7 Kensington Church Court
London W8 4SP

First published in the UK by Scarlet, 1996

A copy of the British Library Cataloguing in
Publication data is available from the British Library

ISBN 1-85487-730-5

Printed and bound in the EC

10 9 8 7 6 5 4 3 2 1

Dedicated to the man in my life who made this book possible.

CHAPTER 1

She couldn't put the chocolate in her mouth again; she was sure she couldn't! Her stomach heaved just at the thought of it, her skin felt itchy and hot from the lights and the layers of make-up caked on it, and her scalp ached from the constant fussing of the hairdresser's brush over her hair. All this anguish just for a chocolate commercial! It hardly seemed worth it to the tired star. Why, oh, why, she wondered, did they always leave the close-ups until the end of the day, when everything was at its worst?

The small studio, apart from the island of tranquillity created by the sofa where she and her co-star were lying, was total chaos, with the detritus of the day's shoot littered all over it. Discarded polystyrene cups, stubbed out cigarettes, unwanted props were scattered everywhere, and the crew and agency personnel lounged wearily on any available perch. It was near the end of a very long and exhausting day for everyone, and it showed. Even the director, normally a cheerful, ebullient type, drooped as if he had had enough.

'Just once more for luck, dears,' he coaxed, trying not to see Sarah's anguished look. 'We were just a *fraction* off.'

'Sorry, Sarah,' her co-star apologized. 'It was me that time; I missed my cue.'

Sarah did her best to be her usual calm self, and submitted to the make-up girl yet again.

'I'll throw up all over you if I have to do it again after

1

this time,' she told him sweetly, however. 'So you have been warned!'

'And I thought you were such a well brought up girl!' He grinned at her, totally unabashed.

'So I am, normally.' Sarah, one of the newer stars of children's TV, smiled the charming smile that had made her such a favourite with colleagues and viewers alike, and settled back to try to reproduce the same enthusiasm for the chocolate all over again. Somehow she marshalled her brain into gear as the studio quietened and the familiar 'Speed – mark it – action!' call rang through the set.

This time they got it totally right, and they all heaved a sigh of relief as the director called, 'Check the gate,' thanked them and told them that they could go, forgetting them immediately as he shouted for the pack shot to be set up.

'Thank God for that!' Robin sighed as they made their way to their dressing room. 'I was beginning to buckle at the knees! Shall we go for a drink to recover?'

'Sorry, Robin, I can't.' Sarah sighed. She had known this was coming – it usually did after a shoot. It never ceased to amaze her how the men she worked with seemed to think she was available to them just because they had spent the day with her. 'My boyfriend wouldn't like it, and anyway if I hurry I can just make it to Sally Jacques's ballet class at the Dance Centre.'

'A ballet class?' Robin stared in amazement. 'Heavens above, woman, you started work at seven this morning – haven't you done enough for one day? Your body looks in good enough shape to me!'

'That's because I work at keeping it that way.' Sarah shrugged. 'Just so that I can go on earning a living. Anyway, I'm doing a fitness video over the weekend for Sally – I have to turn up tonight.'

'Don't you ever stop working?' he demanded sulkily, eyeing her with some regret. He could think of a far better

2

exercise routine for her body than Sarah could at that moment.

'My modelling life-span is much shorter than yours,' she reminded him tartly. 'I'm twenty-four; I'll be over the hill before I know it. I just pray I'll get a real acting job soon, instead of all this bimbo stuff. I'm beginning to get really fed up with modelling, but, as I'm leaving *Do or Dare* after this series, I need every penny I can make right now just in case!'

'I don't think you'll have very much difficulty finding work, my darling,' Robin assured her. 'Once the word gets out that you're available, that is. You've had a fantastic amount of exposure with that programme.'

She grabbed a handful of tissues and began energetically to scrub off her make-up. 'Yeah! But only if directors watch kids' TV – and even then they might only think I can race about and do stunts! Still, my agent is working on it; don't you worry.' She laughed. 'That's why I got that magazine cover this month. I just hope it leads to something other than chocolate or shampoo ads, that's all. I didn't do eight years' training just for that, I hope.'

She hoped! It seemed ages since she had done a really meaty drama, like the police series she had been so proud of last year. Bits and pieces were all she seemed to have been doing for months, besides the programme, despite all Oscar's efforts on her behalf, and she was bored with all of it.

Wearily, she dragged on her familiar jeans and sweat-shirt, rammed an old baseball cap over her hair and, after polite goodbyes to the crew and agency personnel, made her way out. The Soho streets were crowded with office workers going home and theatre-goers on their way for an evening out as she slipped through them on her way to the Dance Centre in Covent Garden. All she really wanted was to go home and sink into a hot bath, but the discipline formed by long years of training drove her to push for that

3

little bit of extra effort from her tired body that evening – as it did most days.

Sheer determination got her through the hour of gruelling ballet, leaving her sweating and exhausted as she changed again later, in the crowded changing room that smelled of too many hot bodies and discarded old socks. She was comfortable, though, with the crowd of dancers there, many of whom she knew. It was one reason she had opted to come to that class, since Sally only taught chosen pros and Sarah was not likely to be an object of curiosity as she often was in more open classes.

They gossiped cheerfully afterwards in the coffee-shop, about who was auditioning for what show, what Andrew Lloyd Webber was rumoured to be doing next and, most importantly, who was sleeping with who – a constant source of interest to them all. Amongst them, Sarah was well liked for her quiet friendliness, despite her TV contract which made her better known than most of them. The other dancers teased her unmercifully about her TV work rather than envying her, and in their company she relaxed for once as they pored over the evening newspaper, with its banner headlines about an actress's horrific car accident.

'She was going to play the lead in Nick Grey's new film,' Sarah commented. 'Now, *that* is the kind of part I would kill for,' she added wistfully.

'Well, she won't be playing it now, unless they postpone for months, and I can't see them doing that somehow.' Another girl grinned cheerfully. 'You look a bit like Harriet – why don't you get your agent to put you forward for it?'

'I wish!' Sarah groaned. 'I don't have the prestige or the experience that Harriet has. All I'm known for lately is kids' stuff.'

'You have two years of RADA and countless TV dramas to your credit,' Polly pointed out. 'Stop selling yourself short, Campbell! You're a bloody good actress – we all know that, damn you. Go for it!'

4

'Profit from someone else's misfortune? I'd rather not!'

'You're far too soft-hearted for this business,' Polly retorted. 'Do you really think Harriet would hesitate to whip the part from *you* if it were the other way round? Of course she wouldn't!'

'Yes, well, I'll wait for Mr Grey to ring and beg me,' Sarah said with a grin. 'Anyway, you know what his films are like. They may well be good box-office, but the leads usually have at least one nude scene, and that's not my idea of being a star. I prefer to keep my clothes on, thank you!'

'He's one of the best, though,' Polly reminded her. 'Does it really matter that much? I know I'd strip off for him – personally, anyway. He's gorgeous! Far too sexy to be behind a camera! I always did go for the dark, brooding type.'

'It matters to me.' Sarah stood up. 'Anyway, it's hardly likely to happen, is it? I'm off – I'm not sure I'll even stay awake till I get home, the way I feel. Bye, girls.'

Her flat in Oakley Street had been paid for with the legacy she had inherited on her parents' death, and it was cherished by Sarah and furnished with her favourite pieces from the family home. She paused on her way through the living room as she always did when she went in, mentally saying good evening to the oil painting of them that hung over the pink and blue sofa, a happy reminder of the days when they had all been together, and then she sank finally into a long and very welcome bath.

There had to be more to life than this, she thought bitterly to herself as she soaked in the steaming water and sipped at the one glass of white wine her fitness regime allowed her. All she ever did was work and then struggle to keep her body in the top physical shape that the programme demanded.

Tomorrow, she decided. Tomorrow she would persuade Peter to take her out after they'd finished the programme, instead of simply going to the health club to work out as they normally did. He needed a break from

5

routine just as much as she did. He liked to call himself her boyfriend, after all, so let him behave like one for once! Decision made, in a slightly more cheerful mood she climbed into bed and switched on the news – so much for the glamour of an actress's life, she grimaced, and was asleep even before the first commercial break began.

Two days later, oblivious of the people around him in the busy club foyer, a weary Nicholas Grey stood transfixed by the photograph on the magazine cover. Honey-coloured hair was flung out to the wind, and the girl's huge hazel eyes sparkled straight at him, challenging him as he stared at it. 'Change of direction!' the cover shouted, *Do or Dare* star Sarah Campbell moving on!'

'Not quite your usual scene, Mr Grey.' The RAC club porter smiled at him as he picked up the magazine to pay for it.

Nick smiled back in agreement. He usually bought car magazines on his way in and out of the club when he went for a swim or to play squash. 'Maybe not,' he agreed. 'But just this once it may be exactly what I need!' He glanced at his watch and suddenly realized how late it was getting. He would be cutting it pretty fine if he was going to go back into the office before he went home, and now he knew he had to. 'Any chance of a taxi, Harry?' he added, knowing it was pouring with rain but totally confident that he would be successful.

Over six feet tall and well-built, his dark hair thick as it curled on his jacket collar, at thirty-nine, Nicholas Grey exuded a strong masculinity and an unmistakable air of power. Frequently bloody-minded, to the point of down-right rudeness, he did, however, command total respect from every crew member of his units for his dedicated attitude to his work – even if they were always wary of his periodic outbursts. He was already tapping his foot impatiently as the harassed porter came back to report – thankfully – that he had a taxi for him.

'Last one in London,' he quipped as Nick dropped a tip into his discreetly extended palm and swept out into the pouring rain

'NGA in Wardour Street,' he snapped at the driver as he pulled away from the kerb. 'Please?' he added, slightly sarcastically, as the driver glared.

'You'd be quicker walking, mate,' he commented, equally sarcastically.

Nick looked down at his cashmere jacket and expensive American shoes and decided to stay put. 'Do your best,' he said, for once biting back his desire to snap. 'I'm on a deadline.' And he flicked open the magazine to find the article about the beautiful Miss Campbell, reading it with growing excitement. He was getting desperate, he thought ruefully, if he was resorting to a lightweight children's TV presenter to replace an established star.

It wasn't as if they weren't trying. Since Monday afternoon, as soon as they had realized that Harriet was out of the running, he and Caroline, the casting agent, had searched all the London and provincial agencies looking for her replacement.

From the very start Abigail had been a nightmare part to cast. To find a girl who looked young and innocent but had enough screen presence to carry the technically difficult later scenes of the film had proved almost impossible the *first* time round. This girl, he thought with growing optimism, as the taxi driver battled through the rain, might well be his last hope. Please God, he prayed, let her be able to act as well as she looked.

Do or Dare was an incredibly popular children's programme that had been running for two years, in which the two young presenters worked alongside animal puppets to explain and promote sporting challenges. He knew his own daughter watched it when she was home from boarding-school. This girl had been on TV twice a week and he had managed to miss her!

She was leaving now, after a year's stint, and the

7

magazine was obviously doing a selling promotion for her, as it reviewed the catalogue of her talents used to the full on the programme. He only spotted the drama still that confirmed she was also an actress as the driver finally pulled up outside the office-studio complex in Wardour Street which was the headquarters of Nicholas Grey Associates, his successful commercial-making operation.

He had fully intended to collect his car and go home at a reasonable time for once, because of an academic dinner his wife was involved in, but the excitement of his find suddenly took precedence over his social life. Protecting the magazine from the rain, he flung in through the front door – to the consternation of his staff.

'Is Caroline still here?' he demanded of the startled receptionist. 'If not, find her!' he ordered over his shoulder as he ran up the stairs to his office.

Sandy grabbed the phone, sensing the urgency in his voice.

Jane Brough, his long-time assistant, looked up in surprise as he swept in, throwing his sports bag onto a chair. 'Nick, for heaven's sake,' she protested. 'I promised Diana! You swore you'd play squash and go straight home!'

'Never mind Diana's bloody dinner,' he answered, pulling a copy of *Spotlight* from the shelf behind his desk. 'I think I may have found Abigail!'

Jane gave a shriek of glee and forgot about Nick's wife for a moment as she watched him leafing through the industry's bible listing actors and actresses.

Thank goodness she was listed – not in "Leading Actresses", where they had been looking, but under "Juveniles" at the back. It was a tiny picture, too, not a bit like the magazine photographs.

'Sarah Campbell,' exclaimed the casting agent as she came in. 'Cradle-snatching from children's programmes – are we that desperate, Nick?'

'Yes, we are!' said Nick. 'Charlie and I had a very nasty

8

meeting with the distributors at lunchtime. Caroline, just look at her – she's fantastic! Like a Rossetti painting – perfect period face and that has to be the sexiest mouth I have seen in years!'

'I know of her,' Caroline said cautiously. 'She's an actress, certainly, and I agree she's lovely, but I don't know if she would do those nude scenes. She's been known to turn them down in the past.' She reached over and checked *Spotlight* then picked up the phone to dial. 'She's got a tough agent; he's going to want big money for her to do those anyway, because it would screw up her children's stuff.'

'If she does *Home Leave* she won't need to do children's stuff again,' Nick said firmly. 'And Harriet was costing a bloody fortune anyway. Sarah Campbell is fairly new – at least she won't demand the residuals that Harriet wanted.'

'Oscar, darling,' Caroline said sweetly into the phone. 'It's Caroline Geddy – how are you? Listen, sweetheart – Sarah Campbell. What's her availability? Great – fax me over her CV, would you? Nick Grey may be interested in her . . .'

While they waited for the fax to come in Caroline filled them in on the rest of her conversation with Oscar Venner.

'Has he got a showreel?' Nick was still transfixed by the photograph, still unable to believe they could have over-looked this girl.

'He's getting one sorted out.' Caroline made a gesture of impatience. 'He'll make sure he's got the right stuff on it before he sends it – you know Oscar.'

'Fairly typical of him, I agree,' sighed Nick. 'I'm surprised he hasn't been on to me before, but he's a good agent. *She* must be good.'

At that moment Sandy brought the fax sheets in. 'These came in from Oscar Venner for you, Nick,' she said, and dropped them on his desk.

Nick flicked through the sheets quickly. She was taller than he had expected, at five feet eight, and at twenty-four older than she looked, but dancing in clubs, TV plays and commercials added to her *Do or Dare* stint made impressive reading.

'She's got guts as well,' Caroline commented, reading her stunt list. 'Anyone who can hang-glide has got to have plenty of those!'

Nick laughed, and read over her shoulder, impressed, despite himself. 'Even *I* would draw the line at that,' he commented drily. 'I think I'd like to meet this young woman – out of curiosity if nothing else!'

Jane, worrying about Diana, slipped out of the office to go and phone her. She knew it would be hopeless nagging Nick to go home now. She was fond of Nick's wife, even if Nick wasn't particularly, and did a great deal to keep their complicated lives running smoothly. Luckily, the bike messenger arrived with Oscar's package at that moment, so she had the package in her hand when she went back into the office, disguising her mission beautifully. 'He must have had a biker waiting!' she laughed as she tossed the envelope to Nick. 'Talk about service!'

Nick shook the photographs out of the packet and leafed through them, whistling with delight. 'Get Oscar back,' he ordered. 'Set up an audition time. Jane, what's tomorrow like? Is there a studio free?'

Jane reached for his diary. 'The ad agency at nine; Accounts here at ten-thirty,' she reeled off. 'Lunch with Charlie Hastings, and the small studio is free until two o'clock.' Charles was Nick's associate producer on this film, as well as his long-time friend and partner in NGA.

'Make her eleven o'clock, if you can, and get James in to do the audition with her – I really do have a hunch about this one. Christ . . .!' And he held out a sheaf of photographs to Jane as Caroline pressed the redial button on the phone. They were a collection of fashion shots – outdoor shots taken on a beach. Fresh air and sunlight obviously suited her, and the camera patently adored her.

There was one shot particularly that caught his attention. She was leaning against a rock, eye-catching legs stretched out in front of her. Nick had always been a leg man, but it was the expression on her face that caught him. Dreamy, innocent, and yet with a mocking look in her eyes that simply said "Abigail" to him.

'Look, Nick, I'll call you at home,' Caroline was saying as he jerked his attention back to the office with a start. He had not felt that flash of sexual excitement for years – especially over a photograph. 'Oscar has to check with Sarah, and they're just finishing transmission at the studios.'

'I know.' Nick sighed. 'I must get home. You women do gang up on me! It's only a bloody academic dinner, and I didn't want to go to it in the first place.'

'But it's important to Diana!' Jane said. 'Don't be mean, Nicholas!'

'We'll get the showreel over to the flat,' Caroline promised. 'I'll wait for it to come and bring it myself. Go on,' she urged. 'Go home and make your wife happy for once!'

'As if anything will satisfy my wife!' Nick shrugged, and picked up the file and his briefcase before fishing in his pocket in panic. 'Where the hell did I put my car keys?'

Jane found them and threw them to him. 'Stop fussing,' she laughed. 'Go on – leave it to us!'

Nick smiled as he crossed the entrance foyer with its display of the many awards the company had won over the years; it never failed to cheer him. In a couple of hours he had gone from despair to elation, but he wasn't out of the woods yet. He had to wait and find out if the girl could really cope with the part in the morning.

Normally Nick lived alone in his flat in the Nash terraces in Regent's Park. His wife, a part-time lecturer at an Oxford college, prefered to live in their Oxfordshire farmhouse with their only daughter most of the time. They commuted in and out of each other's totally oppos-

11

ing worlds – aided by Jane's efficiency – and had done for years, managing to astonish their friends, and Diana's disapproving family, by somehow staying married for fifteen years.

If Nick strayed occasionally, Diana confidently lived with it. She was secure in the knowledge that it was *her* he was married to, and that whatever happened she was going to make sure it stayed that way. As a Catholic, divorce was not something Diana had ever dreamt of considering, and Nick respected her beliefs. She was also well aware that, although Nick was no longer in love with her – if indeed he ever had been – he still had a great deal of loyalty towards her, and was far too attached to their daughter, Charlotte, to risk rocking the boat too much.

Pleasure at the thought of seeing Charlotte quickened his step as he parked his classic Porsche 911 and ran through the lobby and up to the flat. Nick had driven one for years, long before they were fashionable, and clung to it defiantly, despite the teasing he sometimes got for his loyalty to the model – the first exotic car he had been able to treat himself to when his business had taken off.

Charlotte had come up with Diana for the last few days of the Easter holidays, and as he unlocked the front door she rushed into the hall, hurling herself at him and talking nineteen to the dozen at the same time.

'Mummy's cross with you, Daddy,' she chided. 'You're late.'

Nick sighed, and, rescuing the file that had hit the floor under her onslaught, braced himself as they went into the living room. He was sure his daughter grew several inches every term; at only fourteen, she was certainly taller than Diana.

For once Diana Grey swallowed her temper and presented her husband with as serene and genuine a smile of pleasure as she could manage as she crossed the room to him. Quietly elegant rather than pretty, she was always beautifully groomed, and tonight was no exception. He suddenly felt guilty that he had not been out to their Oxfordshire farmhouse for weeks, and to hoots of derision from Charlotte he kissed her with as much warmth as he could manage.

'Sickening how these old people carry on,' exclaimed Charlotte, laughing, happily taken in by his display of affection – though Nick knew by Diana's cool reaction that *she* wasn't.

'Less of the old!' retorted Nick. 'I really did mean to get back early, but . . .'

'Tell me while you change,' Diana chivvied. 'Bill will be here in a minute to pick us up.'

While Nick showered she looked at the file of photographs with a distinct feeling of unease. This girl was lovely, and Nick would be on location with her for several months. The budget was fairly low, by Nick's usual standards, but at least he was saving on enormous studio costs by shooting most of the film at Hastings Court in Wiltshire, which was Charlie Hastings' home.

Charles had, like many of Nick's other friends, been hit by Lloyds, and Nick, being anxious to help him out, had decided that Charlie's home would be a perfect location. He also had the distinct advantage of knowing the estate well himself, since he had almost been brought up there by Charlie's parents while his own Army parents had been stationed abroad.

'What do you think?' Nick asked, coming back into the bedroom, rubbing at his wet body furiously.

'Stunning,' Diana said reluctantly. 'If she's going on location I think Charlotte and I may just come down very frequently to spoil your pitch! How old is she?'

'Twenty-four.' He grinned, unabashed. 'Bit young for an old man like me! She's far more likely to be swept off her feet by James Willoughby, particularly since – if I employ her – they'll have a lot of fairly steamy scenes together. And you know what James is like!'

'I certainly do, and I hope you're right!' Diana flicked a

brush through her dark hair and repaired the damage he had done to her lipstick. Already half dressed, Nick came behind her to drop a kiss on her bare shoulder.

'Why should I bother with Beaujolais Nouveau when I have champagne at home?' He knowingly recognized and soothed her fears.

'Bill's here,' Charlotte called through the door as he was tying his bow tie.

'Told you I'd make it!'

'By the skin of your teeth, as usual!' Diana retorted, and picked up her bag and coat.

Following her, Nick was issuing instructions to Charlotte about Caroline's impending visit and where to put the precious tape. 'I'll ring you during the evening,' he promised. 'Be good and don't open the door to anyone but Caroline!'

Diana added other strictures, and she groaned at the stream of instructions with the weary boredom of a know-it-all adolescent. Nick laughed indulgently at Charlotte's resigned face.

'You do look very handsome in a DJ, Daddy,' she said adoringly. 'Not old at all!'

CHAPTER 2

In the club at the television studios, the *Do or Dare* party were on their second bottle of champagne – reckoned to be the best bargain around – and were just getting into their noisy stride. They were a young group – the only one over twenty-six was Paddy Brennan, their director/producer, an old hand in his fifties who looked after his 'children' with a benevolent fatherly air.

Retreating to the club after transmission was a regular winding down habit, and Sarah thought suddenly how much she would miss everyone if she didn't renew her contract. Paddy wanted her to stay, and had already offered her a considerable rise to do so, and he and Peter Lyngard, her co-presenter, made a very polished duo, the best the programme had had in its two years; they complemented each other – both blonde and athletic young people, his cheeky style a perfect foil for Sarah's easygoing charm. They had an enormous following of young fans, who followed their supposed off-screen romance avidly.

Now they were laughing and teasing her, because the tannoy had just called her to the phone. It was a familiar joke amongst the club regulars that actors got themselves noticed by being paged in the club bar. 'It's far too early, Sarah,' joked the researcher. 'All the important people are still at their desks!' Sarah took it all in her stride, as she usually did, and meandered across to the desk, with the swinging walk of the dancer she was, to take her call.

'Who was it?' Peter teased as she came back with a stunned look on her face. 'Hollywood?'

'Not quite! It was Oscar. *Nick Grey* wants to see me tomorrow. He wants me to audition for *Home Leave* the film Harriet Barrington was going to do!' After the discussion a few days previously, she could hardly believe it had actually happened!

'Well, well, there's nothing like starting at the top!' Peter, though completely without any ambition, was just a little jealous. 'He's certainly the best director this country has.'

'I did some commercials for NGA before I came here,' said Paddy's assistant, and shuddered. 'He's a vicious bastard when he gets going!'

'Very good-looking, though,' sighed another of the girls.

'But old – and married,' said Sarah firmly. 'However, guess who the male lead is going to be?' She paused for dramatic effect. 'Only James Willoughby!'

'Fastest trouser-dropper in the business!' Peter said sourly, painfully aware of Sarah's excitement.

'What a way to go, though!' laughed Polly. 'He's been married twice, hasn't he? Wasn't he married to Tamzin Carpenter at one time?'

Sarah let the gossip float over her and struggled not to let her excitement show too much; she could see that Peter was not taking the news too well. But at last, despite her misgivings, she could see a light at the end of her particular tunnel of boredom. Choosing her moment carefully, she got to her feet.

'I think I'd better go,' she said, forgetting her resolve to go out that evening in her new excitement. 'They're sending me a script to read, and if I drink much more I won't be fit to drive home let alone learn any of it!'

They all hugged her for luck. Sarah firmly told Peter she was going home alone, and almost floated out of the building to her car. Singing loudly to the radio, she sailed fearlessly around Shepherds Bush and down through Holland Park in her XR3i, hardly aware of other traffic on the wet roads, anxious to get home to see what the script would be like.

Yes, the doorman had her package. 'Just come, miss.' He gazed at her with his usual wistful admiration. 'The boy said it was important.'

'Could be my future!' Sarah told him gaily. 'I'll let you know tomorrow.' And, clutching the precious bundle, she ran up the stairs to her second floor flat – too impatient to wait for the lift.

A few minutes later she was curled up on the sofa, shoes kicked off, with a carton of yoghurt and a glass of mineral water. Caroline's friendly note was clipped to the top page, confirming her eleven o'clock appointment and asking her to prepare two scenes for her audition.

Home Leave was a tense, exciting story about an Edwardian family, and she read with growing delight. Abigail, the heiress daughter of the family, was in love with the young, local doctor, but was forced to marry someone else chosen by her bullying father. It ended on the battlefields of World War One, with Abigail reunited with her doctor.

It was a wonderful part, and by far the biggest in the film, Harriet Barrington must be really cursing that she couldn't do it, Sarah thought, gleefully turning page after page of glorious dialogue. Surely there had to be a catch. Then she found it, just as she had predicted.

She stopped reading in horror. They couldn't really be asking *her* to do love scenes like that – but Nick Grey had not only written them he had surpassed himself! She was quite adamant that she couldn't cope with exposing that amount of her flesh in front of a film crew – even for him. She had heard enough jokes and stories about nude scenes, even working in children's television, and knew all about the unused clips of them that were shown at Christmas parties within the industry.

In a fury, she dialled Oscar's home number and demanded of him whether he had read his copy of the script.

'I skimmed it quickly,' he admitted, annoyed to be interrupted in the middle of a dinner party.

'I couldn't do those sex scenes. They're awful! I've never done them! I *won't* do them! I'm *not* doing them for Nick Grey, great part or not!'

'Sarah, dear,' he tried to calm her, 'This is not your average British film director. This is the best. Whatever the script says, it is hardly going to be pornographic! Nick can be explicit, I agree, but he is a professional; he would never go too far. He has a reputation to consider, after all. You'll be fine – he'll handle it beautifully.'

'I don't care how professional he is; I'm not doing it!' Sarah shouted at him. 'It may be the part of the century, but tell them tomorrow that I'm sorry but the answer is no!'

'Like hell I will!' Oscar rejoined. 'You, young lady, will be at Nick's offices tomorrow with me at your elbow. You are not turning down a chance like this just because of a few hours of exposing your body to the camera! You did that shampoo commercial, remember, and the ice-cream one, and I don't remember you making a fuss about that!'

'I did have some clothes on for those,' Sarah objected.

'They probably suggested far more than these scenes will,' Oscar said firmly. 'Now, do as you're told for once! Wear a skirt *and* your hair loose. Abigail may have her moments, but she's meant to be a lady.'

'You could've fooled me!'

'Oh, and another thing – don't wear high heels. James Willoughby is just about six foot; you don't need to be on eye-level with him.'

'I'm five foot eight, Oscar,' she reminded him. 'Not six foot.'

'No more than an inch of heel,' Oscar reminded her. 'Now let me get back to my dinner – tomorrow at eleven!'

Sarah slammed the phone down in a filthy temper and

swore furiously at it, and at Oscar. Almost in tears, she stamped around the flat.

Reading the scenes again didn't help.

It would be just her luck to get the part, she thought furiously, when it was the last thing she wanted. Sarah Campbell worked hard on her body to keep it looking good but she was paranoid about displaying it naked – even to Peter, who complained bitterly and frequently about her refusal to go to bed with him. But Oscar had been her agent since he had seen her in a RADA production and she knew she was very lucky to have a good one like him. No way would she go against his wishes – and he knew it.

With a sigh of defeat, she went back to the script to prepare the scenes that Caroline had asked her to do, and tried to work on a way out of it – maybe they wouldn't want her at all . . .

For the sake of peace, Nick made a tremendous effort to be sociable at the kind of event he rarely found very interesting. With an Oxford degree himself, he was the intellectual equal of most of their table, but he had never been able to get excited over some of the more obscure topics academics happily spent hours discussing.

Luckily, he found himself seated next to the young American wife of Diana's immediate superior at the college, and she quickly had him laughing and joking. A pretty girl, with a delicate, elfin face, her dark hair cut wispily short, she was lively and full of fun, and, being a second wife, was relatively unknown to the rest of the group. Madeleine had spent most of her working life as a secretary in Los Angeles, a city Nick knew and loved and indeed had a home in. Her father, he soon discovered, was an executive at NBC, so she knew the film and TV world well, and they were soon exchanging Hollywood gossip.

At last, when they were finally free to go, Nick hastened Diana into her coat, much to the amusement of the others.

'I assume it's the tape that you're rushing back for?' she asked sarcastically as they walked out to the car.

'Too right it is,' he said. 'There's a lot of money riding on getting that part re-cast, and Charlie and I will lose a great deal of it if I don't cast it soon.'

'Well, in that case, we'd better hurry!'

Impatient as he was, he still exchanged his dress suit for a terry-cloth robe before he went to the study and dropped the tape into the VCR – formal suits were Nick's idea of punishment, and had been since his Canterbury school-days. He leant back in the comfort of the leather armchair and poured himself a glass of his favourite malt as Sarah Campbell's tape came up on the screen.

There were about twenty minutes of an enormous variety of work, including several commercials, most of which he realized he knew well – good production company bosses always knew what the competition was doing – and he kicked himself again. One that he particularly liked, and hadn't seen before, was an American shampoo job, where she was swimming underwater then rising from the sea clad in a very brief bikini, leaving him in no doubt about the slim waist and full, firm breasts that the swinging curtain of golden-brown hair failed to hide as it swung around her shoulders.

But, even more important to Nick, that was also a scene from a modern police drama. Sarah played the victim of some attack, being questioned fairly aggressively. The camera stayed relentlessly on her face, watching her crumble and finally weep under the barrage of questions. It was one take and her performance was superb, her air of vulnerability collapsing into panic as the questions grew nastier.

He played it back with a sense of relief that she really could act, and then he ran through the rest of the tape. When Diana came in he was staring incredulously at a montage of her *Do or Dare* stunts.

'How the hell can she do all that and not have muscles

like a wrestler?' she demanded, laughing. 'It's hardly fair! I suppose she can act as well?'

'Watch this!' He rewound the tape back to the police drama.

'She's a better actress than Harriet, that's for sure,' she commented at last. 'Are you happy now?'

'Better than I was,' he admitted. 'Just pray she really is right for it. I need the luck!'

CHAPTER 3

Neither composite nor tape had really prepared him for his first sight of Sarah Campbell. For a few seconds he simply froze as she walked into his office. Her swinging, easy walk and the confident set of her shoulders made her appear taller than the five feet eight her composite claimed, and said immediately that she was resigned to the world staring at her open-mouthed, as James Willoughby and Chris Howard, his line producer, were doing at that moment.

She wore a silk shirt and a longish wrap-around black skirt that clung to her dancer's body as she moved; her hair was in a long golden-brown plait, falling over one shoulder. Her whole appearance radiated a wholesome innocence, her wide hazel eyes holding his as they had in the magazine photograph as he, too, stared, noticing as she came closer the creamy clear skin that owed nothing to make-up, with just a light dusting of gold freckles.

Pulling himself together, he rose to his feet, and Sarah found the hand she offered clasped in his firm grip. Nick was astonished to find her hand trembling in his. She was actress enough to present an untroubled exterior.

'I'm Nick Grey.' He smiled at her, and Sarah relaxed. 'Thank you for coming at such short notice, Sarah.'

Sarah thought she should be thanking him as she was introduced to James and Chris, and Nick held a chair for her. Relieved, he suddenly noticed she was wearing fairly high-heeled shoes – Sarah's 'anti' gesture to Oscar. *He* had already made her change from her habitual jeans into a skirt when he had collected her, as he had demanded the night before.

They sat in comfortable chairs around a low table to which Jane brought coffee. Nick didn't believe in interviewing from behind a desk, unless he wanted to intimidate the interviewee. Now he sought to put the girl at her ease, and was sensitive to her nervousness as he explained the plot of *Home Leave* and the filming schedule he planned for it, giving her chance to relax in their company.

'OK . . .' He paused. 'I'd like to hear a little about you, Sarah,' he said, putting her firmly on the spot, and she smiled suddenly at his challenge.

'I'm not too interesting, really,' she confessed. Her speaking voice was clear, with a pleasant pitch, he noted quickly, ideal for film sound. 'A normal Home Counties girl, I suppose – dancing classes, pony club, that kind of thing. My family are all the super bright types. Daddy was in the City, Mummy was a solicitor, my brother is a tax lawyer. I was what Daddy called his "surprise package",' she laughed. 'My brains are in my feet, so I was packed off to stage school, since I was so useless at school. I'm good at scuba diving and abseiling down rocks, thanks to *Do or Dare*, but I can't add up.'

'Neither can my wife, and she's an Oxford lecturer,' commented Nick, drily. 'But it's not the end of the world.'

'Unless it's alimony,' added James, to shouts of laughter from the other two, and he smiled sympathetically at Sarah. 'Cheer up, sweetheart,' he counselled quietly. 'They won't bite!'

Nick leant back in his chair, studying her carefully. 'Would you unplait your hair, please, Sarah?' he asked at last. 'I'd like to see how long it is.' Oscar had been right, thought Sarah, wryly as she obediently untwisted the plait and shook the curtain of hair free, letting it tumble around her waist. Loose hair annoyed her normally, and she preferred to wear it up or plaited. The plait was her programme trademark, and both Paddy and Oscar refused to allow her to cut it off. 'Now,' he instructed, 'stand up and take your shoes off. I'd like to see you and James together – please, James.'

James laughed, and held her hands as they stood together. 'He'll count your teeth later!' he told her cheerfully, and Sarah smiled gratefully up at him, forgetting the scrutiny they were under. He really seemed to be the charmer she had heard he was. Though neither as tall or as Latin-dark as Nick Grey was, he had a ready warmth and the kind of caressing brown eyes that signalled his sympathy for her nerves without the need to say anything.

In fact there was a great deal more to James than his pretty-boy looks suggested. An intelligent and multi-faceted actor, his last film had catapulted him into the higher league of the industry, and Nick knew he was lucky to get him at the rates he had. James, unlike many in the business, had a great sense of loyalty to the man who had given him the first big break of his career.

Nick studied the two of them carefully, his fingers drumming together. Only Caroline knew he was pleased by the momentary glance they exchanged as she came in. Then he too stood up.

'Right, let's go down and try the video,' he suggested. 'But before we do, I'd like a private word with you, Sarah. You two go down; we'll join you in a minute.'

He drew Sarah aside as James and Chris left them and gestured her to a chair again alongside Caroline. 'Don't panic.' He smiled at her. 'I simply want to talk to you without James listening. Look, Sarah, you have read your script carefully, I suppose?' She nodded, knowing what was coming. 'You do realize we would be asking you to do two fairly explicit love scenes, don't you?'

Sarah bit her lip, and she concentrated on the straps of her shoes as she put them back on. 'Yes, I do,' she said finally, in a low voice.

'Are you happy about that now you have met James?' he asked, worried by her discomfort. More than ever, he was sure she was right for the part.

'No, I'm not happy,' she admitted. 'I've always refused to do anything like that before, but I do realize that it's part of the contract.' She knew she was giving way to him with hardly a fight, and she hated herself for letting ambition win over her better judgement. Oscar had given her a hard time all the way over about it, but face-to-face there was something about Nick Grey that made her feel instinctively that she could put her trust in him – as Oscar had wisely pointed out.

'We'd make it as easy as we could,' he said gently. 'I wouldn't try to exploit you, Sarah, I promise.'

Sarah kicked at the floor in a panic. How could she possibly admit to Nick, of all people, that she had only once been to bed with anyone, so she had no real experience to call on when simulating lovemaking in front of a camera – apart from reading about it in the odd blockbuster! 'As long as you know I'm probably not going to be much good at it, that's all. I accept that I'd have to do it,' she muttered finally.

'James will help you, I'm sure,' he tried to reassure her. 'He can be a cheeky sod, but he's actually quite sensitive under all that blarney!'

'He certainly seems nice,' she allowed, and then lifted her eyes to his. 'I'd just have to get very drunk to do it,' she tried to joke. 'And go on a diet!'

It was Nick's turn to smile. 'That's something you certainly don't need to do! I've seen your showreel; I'm well aware that you have the perfect body for this job!'

His frank admiration made her blush a deep crimson as she followed him down to the studio. It was no more than she was used to from the men she met, but somehow, from this powerful man, it seemed to mean so much more.

Caroline smiled sympathetically and wished her luck, then went off to talk to Oscar, fairly certain that she could discuss some preliminary terms with him. She had not missed the relief in Nick's eyes as he had talked to Sarah.

While Nick and his cameraman set up lights James carefully went over the scenes with Sarah. He knew well enough what Nick wanted, having done the same scenes with Harriet eight weeks before. 'We'll do eighteen first,' Nick told them, and Sarah's heart sank. It was by far the most difficult of the two – a sharp exchange of words, highly charged with emotion, hard enough to do at the best of times. But she had reckoned without the experienced James.

'Give us a few minutes,' he said to Nick as he set their positions to camera, again making Sarah take off her shoes. He bent close to her ear so that Nick could not hear them.

'Concentrate,' he urged her. 'Close your eyes and concentrate on hating me.'

He was gripping her wrists and hurting her deliberately. He held them, twisting his fingers into the flesh, so that when Nick said, 'Action', she sprang furiously from him, launching into the scene with flashing eyes, spitting the words at James, who reacted beautifully to them out of nowhere, turning in an above average performance – much better, Nick thought happily, than he had with Harriet.

'Not bad,' he conceded. 'Now try it again.'

He made them do it four times, deliberately testing Sarah's patience, changing lines, changing movements, assessing how well she could follow directions – after seeing the showreel he knew she could act – noticing quickly how intelligently she interpreted his instructions. James *knew* what he was doing, and cautioned her furious tongue when she was tempted to lash out at him.

When Nick pronounced his satisfaction, and switched them to the shorter, easier scene, James hugged her to him, laughing. 'Well done, sweetheart,' he soothed her. 'You didn't let the bastard wind you up!'

'He speaks well of you too!' Sarah retorted. 'But thank you, James, you were a great help.'

'I'll get my reward now.' He grinned at her.' I'm going to enjoy kissing you!' Sarah had dreaded that on the way over; now she decided that it might be rather fun.

After only a few minutes, she was half under James's spell. It was a short scene – a few gentle lines and then a kiss. To her surprise, James kissed her each time with a fervour that made Nick and Chris smile with amusement, but the rapport between the two was immediate and obvious.

Afterwards, Nick suggested that James took her back upstairs for a drink while they looked at the tapes. Caroline joined them while they played them back and then compared them with Harriet's tapes. A few minutes later they were hugging each other, laughing with delight as Nick – for once – let his enthusiasm bubble forth. 'We've done it!' he cried in relief. 'At last! We've got her! Now all you have to do is sort Oscar on money!'

'And billing!' sighed Caroline. 'And the TV people. They're not going to release her from *Do or Dare* early. You're going to have to reschedule the first two weeks.'

'It'll be worth it. She's so much better than Harriet, and stunningly pretty,' he assured her.

'I'll try and talk to Paddy Brennan – we're certainly going to need a lot of her time for fittings and press calls anyway,' Caroline suggested as they made their way back upstairs. 'I know him from way back. He's pretty amenable, or at least he was.'

'Offer him some filming opportunities,' Nick suggested. 'It might work.'

'As long as it's not during one of the heavy scenes! Not quite children's hour stuff!'

They were both laughing at that thought as they walked back into the office. Nick went straight over to Sarah, who was sitting talking to James and Jane, her drink untouched.

27

'Congratulations, Miss Campbell. I'm making a very swift decision for once, but the part is yours, if you want it.'

Sarah seemed truly astonished. Having done the difficult scene so many times, she had decided he really didn't like her performance at all – even though both James and Jane had tried to convince her that Nick had probably been winding her up, to test her nerve more than anything. Her mouth was smiling as she stammered her thanks to him but he could read the sheer panic in her expressive hazel eyes as she did so.

'Is there something else worrying you, Sarah?' he asked, suddenly concerned, but she shook her head vehemently.

'She's probably waiting for you to live up to your revolting reputation,' James said with a grin. 'Don't worry, he won't start throwing things until you've signed your contract!'

'Ignore that!' Nick was in such a good mood he could even forgive James for teasing him. 'Now, let's celebrate and go to lunch. Chris and I are meant to be meeting Charlie at Neal Street. We'll surprise him. How about it – Sarah, James?'

'Love to,' said James. 'I can chat up my new leading lady.'

Sarah could hardly believe what was happening to her.

She had really half hoped he would turn her down, and now she was being whisked into a car to drive the short distance from Wardour Street to Neal Street, being treated as the star of the film and feeling terrified of the responsibilities suddenly thrust upon her. It began to dawn on her that there was no way out now. She was going to have to do those scenes.

As she busied herself replaiting her hair in the back of the car she watched Nick surreptitiously when he turned from the front seat to talk to Chris Howard. He really wasn't at all what she had expected from her friends' descriptions of him. Certainly he wasn't the kind of man you could easily ignore, with his hard, austere face, long, slightly hooked nose and those sharply intelligent blue eyes with their heavy brows above high, well-defined cheekbones. True, there were fine lines at their corners that betrayed his age against James's gilded youth, but that only seemed to add strength to his attractiveness. James had hinted at his temper, but he had been quite charming most of the time. She had only found him difficult when he had changed his instructions during the first scene, but she realized that she had done everything he had asked of her without question – even giving in over the nude scenes.

She knew then that it was his sheer ability that made him so frightening. He controlled so many lives with his powerful talents.

He also had immaculate manners, she realized as he helped her from the car, held her chair, assisted her with her jacket when she made a movement to take it off. 'Snap!' He smiled, indicating the Ralph Lauren label on his own jacket. 'We have a tailor in common.'

'The only one I have,' she told him. 'It came from a commercial.'

'I bet it wasn't an NGA one,' joked James. 'They make you give everything back!'

'No, it wasn't, but I still had to pay for it at Polka Dot,' Sarah retorted, wondering if she should mention a rival production company.

'Rob Lomas is a man after my own heart!' laughed Nick, and ordered champagne as he looked round. 'Where the hell has Charlie got to?'

'He phoned to say he'd be a few minutes late,' the head waiter told him as he took the order.

'Typical!' Nick shrugged. 'Well, we'll order. Everyone else is starving, I'm sure.' Sarah was surprised to see him use glasses to read the menu, it seemed a sudden admission of weakness, but at least he appeared more approachable. 'Penalty of old age,' he said with a conspiratorial wink as he caught her looking at him. 'Oh, there's Charlie at last.'

Sarah suddenly connected 'Charlie' with Charles Hastings, a baronet and businessman of some repute. Nick introduced him as 'my old friend Charlie Hastings', but Sarah had seen his photographs enough times in the papers, and read enough of his background to be very much in awe of him.

Charles Hastings himself was totally floored by Sarah Campbell, and he was smitten from his first glimpse of her. He and Nick were the same age – had grown up together, gone to Kings Canterbury and Oxford together – but he looked much older. He was lightly bearded and his sandy hair was thinning slightly on top, and his body was certainly heavier than Nick's well exercised one.

'Wonderful, isn't she?' James was laughing, completely at ease with Charles as he was with everyone. 'Put your tongue back, Charlie, it's hanging out!'

Nick raised his glass. 'A toast to our new leading lady!' The other three followed suit. 'Now just be careful how you drive for the next few weeks, Sarah!'

'Driving's no problem,' Sarah told him with amusement. 'My work schedule next week is hang-gliding and a parachute jump!'

'The hell it is!' Nick suddenly looked angry. 'I'll speak to Paddy. We can't take that sort of chance now!'

'Don't worry,' Sarah soothed. 'I've done it before – it's a doddle.'

'Christ! What else can you do?' demanded Charles. He didn't watch children's programmes, so he had never seen Sarah perform. 'Do you ride?'

'Yes, I do, and I tried to get out regularly until about four years ago when my job started to get in the way,' she replied.

'I've got a stable full of horses at Hastings – you can get a bit of practice in while you're down there,' Charles suggested.

'He's got etchings as well,' murmured Nick, grinning at

30

Charles. He hadn't missed Charles's attraction to Sarah. 'I meant what I said about that jump. We can't let you do it,' he added, frowning.

'That's between you and Paddy,' she said. 'I'm sure you'll persuade him.' Like hell he would, she thought to herself. The imperturbable Paddy would suck on his pipe and ignore him.

'Can't you teach the kiddies something gentle instead – like tennis?' suggested Chris.

'You haven't seen me with a tennis racquet. I'm anything but gentle!'

'An all-round sporting challenge!' Charles was laughing. 'I'm going to enjoy having you as a house guest.'

'Might get some of that flab off,' teased Nick. 'You could be just what he needs, Sarah!'

He didn't know how right he was, thought Charles, his eyes on the beautiful girl opposite.

It was like being part of a special club, thought Sarah happily. They were the focal point of the restaurant, she noticed quickly, as much for the presence of Charles and Nick as for herself and James. She listened avidly as the three producers discussed budgets and distribution deals, talking in millions quite casually.

Nick explained to her how they had arranged their foreign sales by selling the rights independently to individual countries. 'It takes longer to arrange,' he told her, 'but it's worth it in the end. We've pre-sold the US rights for cinema, but we're still talking US TV rights.'

'I never realized it was so complicated.'

'Neither did I, really,' he told her. 'I always relied on the producers to do it for me. Now I'm a producer as well, I'm finding out just how difficult it is. Raising finance is a whole new world. I'm lucky to have such a good relationship with my old partner, Seth Waterston, and his distributors to finance this one, even though none of them were too keen to start with. This is a decidedly English film, and there were some doubts as to its suitability for

31

the American market – and that's where the real money is made on a film.'

'Luck is nothing to do with it,' Chris put in. 'They know they'll get a bloody good product from us.'

'No one can really know that until it's made,' Nick corrected him. 'However good the script is, the finished product is down to me and the actors.'

Oh, God, she thought, I hope I can cope with this. It was a lot easier just doing two *Do or Dares* a week! Caroline joined them then for coffee, with a triumphant grin. Oscar had bargained hard – he knew they were in a tight spot – but Nick was still paying less than he would have done for Harriet.

'An all-round good deal for everyone,' he commented quietly to Chris. 'Well done, Caro!' He turned to Sarah. 'I think you'll be pleased with Oscar.'

It seemed like Monopoly money to Sarah. She hardly heard the conversation going on round her. After her TV salary it was a little like winning the pools, and, as Nick had said, this was only the beginning. She swallowed her doubts about the love scenes and put them to the back of her mind. Above all, Sarah was a realist, and James was so nice maybe it wouldn't be quite so bad after all.

The party was beginning to break up. James had an appointment with the costume designer; the others were rushing back to the office. Nick offered to get a cab for her, but Charles stepped in quickly; he had already discovered where Sarah lived. 'I'll give you a lift,' he said firmly. 'I'm going roughly in that direction.' He wasn't, but anything to prolong the time with her. Nick gave him an amused look. He knew where Charles was heading, and it was not Chelsea.

'Well, I suppose you'll be safe enough with Charlie,' he commented. 'He's not usually known for pouncing on ladies in the back of cars!'

'He'd probably be mown down by a karate chop from what we know of this one!' put in James. He had no

32

reticence whatsoever about kissing Sarah firmly on her mouth as a farewell gesture. 'We're going to have real fun, sweetheart, I promise you.'

Chris and Nick were more restrained; they shook her hand politely. Caroline smiled, and promised to be in touch later that afternoon, as Charles shepherded her out. She was not sure what to expect, but she was pleasantly surprised to find a chauffeur-driven Jaguar at the kerbside. Charles handed her into it himself, as if she were a precious piece of china, not waiting for the chauffeur.

'I'm going to wake up in a minute,' she told Charles wistfully as the car pulled out into the traffic. 'And I'll find everything is a dream!'

'No way!' he said firmly. 'This is real and everyone's delighted.'

'What if the money men don't like me?'

'Nick has full casting rights,' Charles assured her. 'The decision is his and his alone, and for once I think he's made the right one. I never liked Harriet.'

Charles Hastings sat riveted to his seat and knew at that moment that he was looking at the biggest challenge of his life. He knew he wanted this girl as he had wanted no other, and Charles was ruthless under his amiable façade. He was determined from that moment on that Sarah would be his – as he had been in the heady days of wresting his first wife away from Nick in their university days.

It had been the longest-lasting quarrel that he and Nick had ever had in their long friendship, that one over Natasha. Nick had hated him for that manoeuvre for months – a hatred that had lasted until Natasha's death less than two years after her marriage to Charles. But Hastings needed another chatelaine, and in just a few moments Charles had decided he wanted this girl to be the one. Young as she was, in his eyes Sarah would be the perfect replacement for Natasha as she was still young and malleable enough to adapt to his needs.

For her part, Sarah was still very much in awe of him. Baronets and City businessmen did not figure largely in her life, as they did in her brother's, but by the time they reached her flat she had decided that she quite liked him. She had the intuitive feeling that Charles would be a good friend to her, and her smile was genuinely warm as she said goodbye to him. To her surprise he kissed her hand in farewell. It was an old-fashioned gesture, but beautifully done, and she gulped back the temptation to say something flippant.

The phone was ringing as she unlocked the door. It was Caroline, with a list of appointments for interviews and photocalls. Five minutes later Cressida Blake, the costume designer, called to arrange fitting times, followed then by the faithful Peter.

'Meet me at the club,' Sarah suggested. 'This phone is driving me mad and, I need a swim to burn off all the lunch I've eaten.'

'Good, I was going to suggest that. Shall we eat out to celebrate, or stay in?'

'I think I've probably eaten enough for today,' she laughed. 'But perhaps we'll go for a pizza.' She remembered her resolve of the day before. 'To hell with healthy living for once!'

They were happy that evening. It didn't turn out to be the quiet evening Sarah had planned it to be, but then their rare evenings out hardly ever did. 'A quick drink at the pub', in Peter's words, turned into a party. Several of their friends drifted into the bar a few minutes after they arrived, so, naturally enough, Sarah's new job had to be celebrated and discussed. They were all actors, and Sarah giggled with delight at the salacious stories they could all tell about the cast and director of her new film.

'James already thinks I'm into karate,' she told them, laughing.

'Keep it that way,' advised Johnny. 'Get Bruno at the

club to update you on a few judo throws as well, in case Mr Grey cuts up rough!'

'Can you imagine me throwing a guy his size across the floor?' Sarah demanded.

'You did it to me once. Don't you remember?' Peter put in.

'That was different; it was all organized.'

'I still got dreadful bruises on my backside.'

'Well, we'll all look out for press pictures of Nick Grey on crutches, then. If she can throw Peter, she can throw him!' Suky chuckled. 'Did you hear the story about Judy Abbott catching James screwing Tamzin?' she added. 'Talk about fight!'

'Oh, God, yes!' cried Johnny. 'She caught them at it in his dressing room at Shepperton,' he explained to Sarah, 'and blacked his eye so badly that he couldn't work for two days!'

'She divorced him for it as well,' Peter added. 'And the poor guy got landed with Tamzin.'

'That lasted all of six months,' Suky said. 'Christ! What a bitch she is! I can't imagine why he married her.'

'I rather got the idea today that James is still paying for it,' Sarah confided, remembering the laughter when James had mentioned alimony.

'Knowing Tam, I wouldn't be a bit surprised.' Johnny grimaced. 'Talking of bitches, the one you need to watch out for is Mrs Grey – the elegant Diana.' He stretched the name to make it sound like a dirty word.

'Why on earth should I worry about Nick's wife?' Sarah wanted to know.

'Because, my darling, she gets very protective over her husband,' Johnny told her. 'Don't even *try* and get close to him. It doesn't pay to upset Diana Grey.'

'I think he'd be very difficult to get close to,' Sarah suggested mildly. 'Anyway, I didn't fancy him at all. He's very nice, but terribly . . . old – and upper class, *and* he wears glasses to read!'

35

'He *is* very upper class,' Suky said. 'I looked him up in *Who's Who* this morning. Daddy was a general, no less, and Mummy is a bishop's daughter. Bags of it there!'

'Better stick to good old working-class me!' Peter teased. 'Now let's go eat. I'm starving!'

A pizza and a bottle of wine later, Peter and Sarah walked back to her flat, joking and teasing, happily arm in arm. The doorman called to her as they went in. 'These came for you, miss.' He indicated a huge basket of white flowers behind his desk which Peter had to carry, they were so enormous. Sarah ripped open the card on their way up in the lift. It said simply, 'Welcome aboard!' and was signed by both Nick and Charles.

'How sweet of them.' She smiled, but Peter was a little more cynical.

'Payment for pain to come!' he mocked as the scent of the flowers filled the flat in minutes.

Sarah fingered the card as she waited for the kettle to boil, then slipped it into her desk while Peter's back was turned. She didn't really want him to know she valued it. She had even carefully hidden her script so that he couldn't read it, well aware that, like her, he wouldn't like the idea of the love scenes. Since she refused point-blank to make love with him, she knew only too well that he would find it hard to take that she would be doing it on screen with someone else. That made her shudder violently, though whether it was pleasure or horror at the thought, she wasn't sure.

Even though he was touching her only lightly then, Peter felt it as he attempted to kiss her.

'My God! Reaction! What did I do right?' he teased cheerfully.

Sarah laughed and kissed him back. 'That would be telling! I think it's time you went, Lyngard. I'll see you tomorrow.'

It took her a little persuasion and a cup of coffee, but in the end he went, disgruntled as usual.

36

She was not in love with Peter – far from it in fact. They worked together in easy harmony, but, if she was truly honest, she had drifted into the relationship needing friendship more than anything. Peter protected her from the attentions of the other men around her, and she was fond of him, but that was all.

Pondering over her new job, she made her way to bed. But now, too excited to sleep, she half wished she *had* asked Peter to stay. Her thoughts surprisingly turned to Nick Grey instead. There were so many taboos against him he was beginning to sound almost attractive. And Sarah loved a challenge – whether it was a parachute jump or a person . . .

CHAPTER 4

Her life was certainly different from then on. There just didn't seem to be enough hours in the day to satisfy all the demands on her time, and in the constant battles between Nick and Paddy she began to feel like a mere pawn in their games.

Nick had been adamant about the jump, and any other stunts on her schedule that he considered dangerous. Paddy, as Sarah had guessed, quoted her contract to *her*, and reminded him that the television company had first call on her time and services. Sarah, herself, was totally on Paddy's side.

'Nick has no right to tell me what to do!' she stormed at Paddy. 'My contract with him starts in six weeks' time, not now. Any time he has from me at the moment is because I'm prepared to do it. Just don't tell him, and I'll do the filming, Paddy. If I break my neck, it'll be my fault, and I'll worry about that if it happens! Just reschedule showing the worst stunts for the last programme, then by the time he finds out it'll be too late. I'll teach the bastard to boss me around!' He was certainly losing his charm in her eyes with his arrogant demands.

However, Nick did back her up with the hairdresser. She met up with Ronnie at his offices and listened with horror as he discussed wigs and wig fittings. 'No!' she exclaimed. 'Why on earth should I need wigs? What's wrong with my own hair?'

'She's right,' Nick said firmly. 'I know it's more time-consuming, Ronnie, but it's crazy to cover up all this. She hasn't even got a fringe.' He surprised Sarah by sweeping up her hair and twisting it expertly into a knot, regarding her critically in the mirror. 'It's absolutely perfect!'

Ronnie stood, hand on hips, his lips pursed, as Nick and Sarah exchanged a conspiratorial glance through the mirror. 'Continuity will be hell,' he pronounced. 'And the lacquer is going to play havoc with it.'

'So, I'll wash it every day.'

'It's a lovely colour,' he admitted grudgingly. 'Is it natural?'

'Do you want me to prove it?' she demanded. Ronnie was beginning to really irritate her. She could feel Nick's hand shaking with the effort he was making not to laugh.

'No, dear.' Ronnie grinned at her. 'It wouldn't do much for me, anyway, but it might give our Nicholas a heart attack, and we don't want that, do we?'

Nick really began to laugh then. 'Just don't start complaining when he calls you an hour earlier than the others!' he told her, still smiling. He was beginning to really like this girl.

'You have permission to bawl me out if I do,' she promised, grinning back at him.

He was so much nicer when he relaxed a little, she thought.

'Don't worry. He'll do it anyway when he gets my overtime bill,' Ronnie assured her. 'Now, sir, how do we want it for this photo session?'

'Up,' said Nick. 'Not too much make-up, Patti,' he added to the make-up girl.

'Loads of eye-drops,' Sarah interrupted. 'I'm shattered, and it shows.'

'You should go to bed earlier,' Nick retorted. 'And alone!'

James appeared at that moment. 'You mean I have a rival?' he asked, sprawling into a make-up chair.

'Chance would be a fine thing! Peter is always complaining that I'm too busy to see him. Ouch!' She winced as Ronnie twisted a curler too tight, distracted by James's handsome face and the wicked grin James flashed in his direction. 'Which dress, Nick?' She indicated the two dresses that Cressida had left out for her.

'Oh, the blue, I think.' He got up to go. 'Come up for a drink, you two, when you're finished.'

The photo session with James proved to be great fun, even though she was tired. He was professional, full of ideas and they rattled through it. He made her laugh and relax, and she enjoyed his company. Her solo session had been much more difficult, though the press office had been delighted with the coverage. These were a follow-up set, extending the '*Do or Dare* girl grows up' theme.

'Anyone would think I was fourteen, not twenty-four!' Sarah complained as they made their way upstairs afterwards.

'It makes a good story, though – let them play their games. It makes our life easier to ignore it,' James counselled. 'Fancy a curry after we've seen his lordship? There's a great Thai place round the corner.'

'As long as that's all! Sure, why not?' Sarah had learnt to take a very firm line with the charming James. After numerous evenings spent rehearsing with him and Nick in NGA's deserted studios, she was beginning to get his measure, and they were becoming good friends, often sharing meals together after rehearsals.

'Cautious lady! I promise not to lay hands on you – tonight, anyway. But I'll get you in the end – even if it's on the set, in front of Nick!'

'You wouldn't dare!'

'Don't bet on it!' he teased. 'I love a dare! We used to play that behind the bike sheds at school.'

'Did you go to a real co-ed?' she asked enviously.

'The roughest comprehensive in Yorkshire,' he said. 'But I did get to university, Miss Home Counties, and I

40

did get a First – which is more than our Nicholas did, if you must know.'

'What in?'

'Biology.' He grinned. 'What do you think? My mother still thinks I ought to be doing a proper job and be a teacher.'

'With your libido? Is she mad?'

'I think I would've made a good teacher,' he said modestly as they walked into Nick's office.

'Like hell you would!' Nick had overheard him. 'Biology has to be taught, James, not demonstrated. You wouldn't have lasted five minutes!' He had Cressida with him, and costume sketches all over the desk, and the quick drink turned into dinner for all four of them. Cress and Nick were old friends, and she certainly brought out the best in him. Sarah was quite sorry when dinner was over and James took her home.

From the first moment they met, Sarah had adored Cressida Blake. Pretty, plump, dark-haired and always cheerful, Cress was ever resourceful and never at a loss for words – with language, according to James, that would strip paint. She had an Oscar to her credit from the same film that had earned Nick his, and the two had worked together on several films so he trusted her implicitly. Sarah quickly began to look forward to her sessions at Cosprops with her.

Between them, they sorted out which of Harriet's costumes might work and which were hopeless. 'There simply isn't enough time to remake everything,' Cress had said reluctantly, but somehow she managed to alter a great many of the ones she had to keep. The whole appearance of a dress seemed to change as she produced a new collar, or a stunning piece of old embroidery, ferreted out of the antique markets she and Jenny, her assistant, haunted.

The new designs that she fought Chris and Nick over until they agreed to pay for them had Sarah in raptures.

Edwardian shapes certainly suited her. 'You're going to look wonderful,' Cress assured her. 'Now breathe in!'

For a short girl she had immensely strong wrists to pull in the laces of the corset she was hauling Sarah into, and Sarah complained. 'You'll get used to it,' she added, without a shred of sympathy.

'Never! How the hell did Edwardian ladies get up to anything, trussed up like this?'

'Why do you think they had so many tea-gowns and all that gorgeous dishabille? That reminds me.' Cress rummaged through the chaotic pile that always seemed to accumulate around her on the fitting room floor. 'I found some super petticoats and camisoles in Alfies the other day for that love scene. Look, aren't they pretty?' She held up an armful of chiffon and lace.

'God, it's so thin!' Sarah fingered the fabric doubtfully.

'Well, considering it's going to come off in a few seconds anyway, it doesn't really matter, does it?' Cress said practically. 'Oh, don't look like that, Sarah. Very few actresses like doing nude scenes, but they seem to be part and parcel these days! Just be glad you've got James to do it with. At least he's young, and pretty with it!' She was so matter-of-fact that Sarah had to laugh.

'That's what James keeps telling me!'

'James would, randy beggar!'

It was to Cressida that she turned to for help with her own clothes when she was faced with a cast dinner that Nick was giving. 'What the hell do I wear for that?' she wailed. 'I've only got two dresses, and I hate them both. The rest of my stuff is pretty casual, nothing like smart enough.'

Like many actresses, Sarah lived in jeans, sweatshirts and her inevitable baseball cap. Her better clothes were a jumble of ex-commercial garments or clothes bought for a specific job – none of which matched the others. She rarely shopped willingly for new clothes, and relied totally on stylists and designers to turn her out correctly for a job.

'Never fear,' Cress said airily. 'I'll take you to see my friend Catherine. She'll sort you out for Nick's dinner, and if you need anything else we'll toddle round Harvey Nicks. But I'll take a look at your stuff first, see what we can use.'

She was as good as her word, and spent an evening at Sarah's flat, giggling and laughing, sorting out her clothes. Approving of some, tossing others aside, she was a godsend. Over a bottle of wine they made a list of what was needed and talked long into the night.

In a few short weeks the two girls became firm friends. Sarah *had* to trust her, since Cress was the only one of the crew to see the bruised ribs left by a day on the Marines' assault course. 'Nick'll kill you when he finds out!' she told Sarah, staring with genuine horror at her purple and yellow ribcage. 'That will take weeks to disappear!'

'It will *be* weeks before we do that scene,' Sarah assured her. 'Anyway, he's not to know when any of that film was shot.'

'He knows what he told you not to do. Don't underestimate him, Sarah, and don't make an enemy of him, for heaven's sake!'

'I have no intention of it. Believe it or not, Cress, I quite like the arrogant so and so. I just won't let him boss me around, and neither will Paddy.'

Cress sighed. 'You've got a lot to learn, sunshine. Chris and Nick are not producers you can manipulate at will, like you obviously can Paddy.' She stood back and looked critically at the Bruce Oldfield dress Sarah had on. 'That might do for Conor Blair's show next week. It's smart, but it doesn't show too much.'

'In that case, sold!' Sarah unzipped it. 'I'm punch drunk with shopping, and we still have to fetch those dresses from Catherine.' Catherine Jayson had made two beautiful dresses for her, totally unlike anything Sarah had owned in her life. She hadn't been able to choose between the two designs, so she had ordered both. Her brother, who handled all her financial affairs, had nearly fainted when she had asked for the money from the account he kept for her business expenses.

'You could buy a car with that amount of money!' he had protested.

'George, I'm moving up a league now,' she had argued. 'I need new clothes, and I haven't bought anything but jeans and the programme jumpsuits for years.'

He'd had to agree. 'I suppose that's true. I'll transfer some of your trust money. Get what you need, and *save all the receipts*!'

Sarah and Cress had done just that – and even Cress was drawn into the spending spree when they got to the lingerie department. 'Well, you never know.' She smiled. 'Anything can happen on location, and I never could resist La Perla!' She held up a lacy black body. 'How about this?'

'It's gorgeous,' Sarah agreed. 'Do you suppose it's tax deductible?' She was ever mindful of George's training.

'Not a chance! Unless you want to seduce your taxman. But I wouldn't mind letting James rip it off if I was wearing it; it would certainly justify the cost!'

'James? Do you really fancy him?' Sarah asked, rather relieved.

Cress laughed. 'I've fancied James for years! Mind you, this is the first time we've worked together and he hasn't been married, so this is my chance to pin him down. I've given up on married men – too many problems!'

'Well, in that little number he won't stand a chance!'

It was all the encouragement Cress needed. Loaded with shopping bags, they got a taxi to Catherine Jayson's showroom before they spent any more money.

'Can I have a G and T, Daddy? Just for tonight?' Charlotte wheedled, watching Nicholas pouring his own drink.

Nick gave in, put a teaspoon of gin in a glass and topped

it up with a lot of tonic. 'Don't let your mama catch you.'

'She's too busy fussing over the table plan,' Charlotte assured him. 'Do you like my dress? Do you think *James* will like it?' Her father's look of horror told her that he most certainly would! Nick was sure Diana knew nothing about the skimpy little number their daughter was almost wearing!

He and Diana traditionally gave a black-tie dinner party for the cast before he started a film in England. It helped him to relax his cast, and Diana loved the opportunity to play the director's wife. Charlotte was there for the first time, having wheedled and persuaded until Nick had given in.

'You are putty in that girl's hands,' Diana complained vehemently. 'I really don't want her sitting there making eyes at James and Ben all evening!'

'She's got to start some time,' Nick said reasonably, surprised at his own tolerance, but knowing inside that he could deny his precious daughter nothing; he saw little enough of her as it was. 'And James and Ben are well aware of the limits. She might as well practise on them while *you* are watching!'

'They had *better* be aware of the limits!' Diana retorted coldly, and swept out to deal with the two friends of Caroline's, who were cooking dinner. Nick's heart sank, and he cursed inwardly. She was not in the best frame of mind for a cast dinner, he realized, and he mentally braced himself for a difficult evening, wishing he had asked Jane to come and help out. Jane could always be relied on to look after things and keep everything calm.

James and Sarah, fortified by a drink with Conor Blair after the show, arrived last. Sarah had changed into Catherine Jayson's black chiffon dress, the low-cut bodice displaying her beautiful breasts, the skirt clinging to her sheer black tights. She wore perilously high heels, chosen by Cress, making her height on a par with most of

45

the men in the room, bar Nick, and the effect, as Cress had predicted, was enough to stun the entire room into silent admiration – including Nick.

'I bet you had trouble with this one on the way over!' Nick said, nodding at James and smiling as he finally pulled himself together.

'I was strong-armed into behaving,' James assured him. 'Though it took a great deal of control on my part!'

'I'm sure it did. It probably would have done on mine as well! I hope you realize the damage you could be doing to some senior's blood pressure, Sarah.' Nick took her arm. 'Let me introduce you to everyone. James, you know most people?'

'I will allow you to steal her for a few minutes,' James grinned, and went off to greet Ben Todd, one of his best friends.

Every actor and actress in the room was a well-known face – people that Sarah had known on cinema screens since she was a child – and suddenly she was overwhelmed by them. Totally awestruck, she felt as if she should be asking for autographs. Strangely, the touch of Nick's hand on her arm, or lightly on her back, was immensely reassuring. He seemed aware of her uneasiness and didn't leave her until he was sure she felt comfortable. At least she wouldn't have trouble remembering names that evening.

James brought Ben Todd over to her. 'He's playing your nasty bullying brother,' he introduced. 'But he's quite harmless, really.'

'And this is Tony Fletcher, the man you're supposed to marry!' added Ben.

'Any time you like!' laughed the thickset and very familiar-looking actor. They were enjoying teasing her over their instant relationships, and Sarah relaxed with them and gave back as good as she got until, feeling more at ease she wandered away to speak to Charlotte, the one face that she couldn't place.

She needn't have worried. Charlotte pounced on her, introducing herself, chattering easily about the programme, and plying her with questions about James. Smiling, Sarah introduced her to the three men, as she had been angling for, and walked over to look at a painting over the fireplace that had caught her eye. The beautiful flat had many impressive modern paintings, in keeping with the mix of antiques and classically modern furnishings.

'Peter Blake,' Nick said quietly behind her. 'I bought it to celebrate *King's Daughter* getting an Oscar.'

'It's lovely,' she said admiringly. 'My father was a great fan of his work; he would have loved your paintings.'

Nick topped up her glass. 'Would have?' he enquired, handing the bottle back to the waitress.

'My parents died in an air crash four years ago,' she told him, her voice breaking slightly, and she bent her head to hide her pain.

Nick was startled by her sudden desolation. 'I'm sorry,' he said. 'I shouldn't have asked.'

Sarah hastily took hold of herself and looked up, reassuring him. 'You weren't to know, don't worry. I just don't broadcast it because it's taking a lot of getting used to.'

He smiled gently back at her. 'You will – eventually. I did when my father died, but then I didn't see as much of him as you probably did of yours.'

'I was very much the baby of the family,' she admitted. 'George is fifteen years older than me. It just seemed so unfair to lose them both when I still needed them so much. Mummy would have been so proud of all this happening.' She spread her hands, encompassing the whole room. 'Mind you, she would definitely have categorized James as NSIT.'

'What on earth is that?'

'Oh, it's an old phrase from when she was a deb. Iffy escorts were coded by the mothers as "not safe in taxis"!

Somehow Daddy managed to make himself acceptable to Granny, even though he was a disreputable Guards officer at the time.'

'He didn't stay in, though?' Nick remembered her conversation at the audition, but, coming from an Army family himself, he was intrigued.

'No, he became a stockbroker long before I was born.'

'Mine was a career officer. He was a general by the time he retired,' Nick admitted. 'I was born in Malaya. I think I lived in six different countries before I came back here to school, and I was only eight then.'

'Is that why you spent so much time with Charles, then?' Sarah remembered snatches of the conversation in Charles's car the day of her audition.

'Our families were close friends. Our mothers still are.' He laughed. 'And they still scare the pants off us!'

'I thought *you* were the one who frightened everyone else!'

'You haven't met my mother – or Lady Hastings!' Nick suddenly realized his mistake. 'Oh, I'm sorry, that was insensitive of me. I'm not usually so tactless.'

'Not at all, it makes you seem more human somehow! I can't imagine you would be frightened of anyone!'

Nick knew he was neglecting his duties as a host, but he suddenly wanted to stand there talking to her for ever. He wanted to know so much more about her.

Sarah, herself, was beginning to feel very guilty about defying him over the stunts. He was being so nice to her. Now she didn't want him to be angry with her, as she knew he would be.

'I think your wife needs you,' she pointed out, reluctant to move away but painfully aware of Diana's angry eyes suddenly on them.

'She's probably ready to start dinner.' Reluctantly, Nick tore himself away. 'We'll talk later, Sarah, I hope. I'd like to show you some of the other paintings.'

Diana discovered as their guests were being seated that Charlotte had craftily changed the place settings around, seating herself where Sarah should have been, next to James. It did nothing to improve her temper, since to move her would make more difficulties. So she had to let it go and furiously watch Charlotte flirting outrageously at the opposite end of the long candlelit table, well away from any parental control.

Sarah found herself between Sir John Redman, who played her father, and Tony, with Nick opposite her. It would have been a safe haven for Charlotte, Diana thought wistfully, as the girls served the first course.

The fact that Nick was paying a great deal of attention to Sarah Campbell did nothing to enliven her mood. The girl *was* lovely to look at, she thought bitterly, and she knew his weaknesses only too well. Luckily for Sarah, Sir John was wonderful company. Champagne had sharpened his wit, and, though Nick noted with amusement that he never took his eyes from Sarah's breasts, he entertained them all with stories of his early TV and theatre days. The laughter at their end of the table was beginning to rival that at James and Ben's end.

'You are going to need a horse-whip for those two,' Diana told Nick grimly.

'Don't I always, with James and Ben?' He looked down the table. 'However, I might need it here later!'

Sarah saw the flash of warning between him and Charlotte and it made *her* shiver – though it hardly daunted Charlotte at all. *She* pouted back at him without a care in the world, secure in the knowledge that Nick could easily be manipulated. Sarah knew her own father would never have allowed *her* to wear the dress that Charlotte had on, when *she* was fourteen. Not that she would have had the nerve to try!

Nick sighed. 'I might just as well spit in the wind!' he commented resignedly.

'Oh, she'll get worse than that!' she told him cheerfully.

'You should have seen me in Aylesbury on Saturday afternoons when I was a teenager!'

'Pure jail-bait, I should think.' Tony smiled. 'Knowing some of the stage-school girls we had on a show once.'

James obviously thought the same about Charlotte too. As they moved around the room after the meal he shot over to Sarah. 'I can't cope any more!' he wailed at her. 'She is definitely after my body, and that one is *definitely* a no-no!'

'What did you tell her, then?' Sarah laughed at his discomfort. The evening was teaching her all sorts of things. The powerful Nicholas Grey was an over-indulgent father, and James could be intimidated by the same fourteen-year-old. James looked slightly uncomfortable with her question.

'I told her I screwed you three times a night, and I was too worn out for anything else.'

'You idiot!' Sarah whispered sharply at him. 'God knows who she'll repeat that to!'

'The way Diana has been glaring at you, it might be a good idea if she does tell her,' James told her. 'Now be a good girl, pretend you're madly in love with me, and I'll take you to Tramp as soon as we can escape. Ben's meeting his girlfriend there.'

Sarah's eyes lit up. 'OK, you're on'. 'I've never been to Tramp.' And she took pity on him for the last half-hour, staying with him, to Nick's annoyance. He was surprised to feel a real surge of jealousy when they left and James announced where they were going.

'Oh, lucky things!' cried Charlotte. 'Daddy, I don't suppose . . .?'

'*No way!*' said Nick and James, in unison.

James felt quite safe now. He brushed Charlotte's cheek lightly. 'We'll all be queuing up on your sixteenth birthday,' he promised. 'As long as your dad isn't around!'

'Dream on, Willoughby!' Nick assured him, seeing the teasing look turn to relief in James's eyes. 'Goodnight,

Sarah.' He hardly needed to bend to kiss her, following the lead James had given him with Charlotte.

His mouth was surprisingly soft and warm as it lingered gently on hers. Light though the contact was, the effect on them both was like an electric shock, and they drew back, staring at each other for a second in surprise. In six weeks he had never done any more than shake hands with her, which was unusual, to say the least, in the film business – the most tactile industry in the world, in her experience.

'Have fun, children,' he said – rather wistfully, Sarah thought. 'Remember NSIT, Sarah,' he added as she moved away.

'What on earth did he mean by that?' Ben asked as they went down to the waiting car.

'Oh, I'll tell you some time,' she told him sweetly. Her mind was still on the gentle kiss Nick had given her. Why on earth had it affected her so much? she wondered in amazement. It was just a kiss, after all, and a light one at that.

Nick was pensive that night as he joined Diana in their wide bed, long after the party was over. He had been restless, and in no mood to sleep, and had spent time trying to unwind playing the piano, as he often did when he was unable to sleep.

Diana was still awake, however, when he finally came to bed, and surprisingly moved into his arms – something she rarely did these days. For a few moments he lay still, hoping she wouldn't make any other demands. The days when he had been eager to make love to his wife were over, and Diana had ceased to really welcome him from the moment she had become pregnant with Charlotte. But tonight she moved impatiently against him as he tried to move away.

'What's the matter, Nick?' She was furious, because he was behaving as if she were not there.

'Nothing's the matter,' he said slowly. 'I'm tired, that's all.'

51

'You're never tired when it comes to sex with other women,' she almost jeered at him. 'What's the matter, then? Have you got that wretched child on your mind still? I might have known you'd chosen her for more than her acting ability!'

'Stop that!' He pushed her back onto the pillows and rolled away from her, but Diana, furious at his rejection when she had made an effort, swung a fist at the side of his face, catching him unawares. He grabbed at her angrily, twisting over her. In one movement he wrenched her nightdress up and off, uncaring that it tore in his hands.

For long minutes they fought a vicious, desperate battle, and then Diana changed her mind, suddenly afraid of the temper she had released in him, knowing just how strong he was when he lost control. Nick was simply angry that she had reminded him of the girl he had kissed earlier, whose soft mouth was probably still imprinted on his, however much he had tried to push her to the back of his mind.

He was uncharacteristically rough and uncaring as he finally gave in to the need inside him that he knew Sarah Campbell had evoked, forcing Diana's submission until she wept with pain and humiliation. Then, at last, his better nature took over, and he was filled with real remorse.

'Darling, darling,' he whispered. 'I'm sorry – I'm so sorry. I didn't mean to hurt you. Put it down to too much champagne.' But it wasn't champagne, and they both knew it.

Diana huddled miserably in the circle of his arms and tried not to let her tears betray her sudden and overwhelming fear. Nick lay breathing quietly, feigning sleep but feeling like a complete heel.

Diana, he knew, was the perfect wife for him. In all their years of marriage she had never complained about his appalling working hours, or the months he spent away from home on location. She was an ideal hostess, an incredibly good mother to Charlotte, and he never had to worry about domestic details in any of his homes.

So why, for heaven's sake, was he thinking as he was, about a young girl of twenty-four? From what Charlotte had confessed of her conversation with James, she was probably already sleeping with James anyway, and, knowing James as he did, Nick knew it was more than likely.

CHAPTER 5

It was hard to believe this was her last *Do or Dare*, and even harder to concentrate after the wild farewell party the night before. Paddy clutched his head in his hands as she messed up an introduction for the umpteenth time that morning. 'Tell her Nick Grey will be a doddle compared with what I am going to do to her in a minute!' he roared into the mike connected to the floor manager's headphones. He yelled so loudly that Sarah could hear it through the cans. Rob raised his eyebrows at her.

'Buck up, Sarah,' he chided quietly. 'We are getting our knickers in a twist!'

'And don't sympathize with her!' Paddy rejoined in his ear. 'Too many late nights, that's her trouble!'

Sarah smiled sweetly into camera one. 'Sorry, Paddy, darling.' She disarmed him completely, and proceeded to do it perfectly. At that moment, more than one hardened stage-hand thought regretfully that *Do or Dare* would not be the same from then on.

They watched the cut-together film of the session with the Paras, complete with the jump, and Sarah worried anew about Nick's reaction. They had added in her falls on the assault course, but edited out the language. 'Too late to worry now,' Paddy told her wryly. 'You wanted to do it sweetheart.'

He was right. She shrugged it off and got on with the job like the pro she was, though it hurt to introduce the new

54

girl presenter. She tried to like her, but she did rather resent the easy way Philippa fitted in.

'Don't tell me you're jealous!' Peter teased, when they had retired to her dressing room in the break between dress rehearsal and transmission.

'Of course not!' Sarah bent to the mirror to hide her face from him, but she was jealous, and he knew it.

'You wanted to go off and be a film star!' he reminded her brusquely. 'Life has to go on here the same without you, whether you like it or not!'

She thought about that, and everything else, as she drove down the M4 after the show. She caught all the rush hour traffic as she left London, and was almost at the Reading turn-off before she could put her foot down. The top was off the XR3i; it was a warm evening for mid-May, and it helped to let the air blow away the misery that had been building up all week. Even the crusty old gate man had wished her luck as she had left, and there was a pile of farewell bouquets on the back seat from friends and fans alike. She was really proud that she had got through the show, and the day, without bursting into tears. Now she had the agony of a new job and a new crew to get used to.

Coming in after the shoot had started was not going to be easy – friendships had already been formed, alliances made. She was the outsider, and not even first choice. Even though Nick and Chris had said they preferred her to Harriet, the crew would be comparing them, and she knew full well that she did not have Harriet's camera experience, or her reputation in the industry.

It was nearly seven when she drove into the gates of Hastings Court. Nick had suggested that she stay there the first evening so that he could go over the script and generally update her on the shoot, a suggestion backed up enthusiastically by Charles. She had turned down his offer of a guest suite at the house full-time, preferring to stay with the unit at the nearby hotel.

After having lunch with him one Saturday, she had

decided she liked him, and could not fault his manners, or behaviour, but that she preferred a little distance between herself and Charles Hastings' obvious adoration. He had astonished her by whisking her off to lunch in the helicopter he mainly kept for his own use, though since his Lloyds problems it had been used more and more for his business.

'I do own an air charter company,' he had said casually as she had voiced her surprise. 'Among others, of course!'

His admiration for her was open and constant, and, though she was sure he would never press her if she was unwilling, she preferred not to take the chance. Peter was upset enough as it was, about the pictures of her with James outside Tramp.

Carefully she pressed the code she had been given into the control pad by the electronic gates and then drove distrustfully through them as they opened. The road to the house was gravel, winding through woodlands still full of bluebells, giving them a misty haze of blue, and then she gave a gasp of amazement as the trees petered out and the house came into view.

She thought she would never forget that first sight of Hastings Court. From a distance the mellow-bricked Queen Anne mansion looked like a perfect dolls' house in the soft evening light as the sun dropped behind the woods that filled the horizon. The road curved over a wide stone bridge, spanning the lake in front of the house, which in turn spilled into a weir across the river that the lake led to. Across the lawns stately cedar trees seemed to curtsy in the gentle breeze as she drove past.

Unsure of what to expect, she stopped her car on the gravelled forecourt of the house and got out. Even as she did so Charles's assistant, Bernard, came out to greet her. She had met him a couple of times at NGA and smiled with relief at a familiar face. He took her overnight bag from her.

'Leave the keys in,' he said. 'I'll put it away for you. Welcome to Hastings Court, Miss Campbell.' He led the way in. 'You are a little earlier than we expected. Sir Charles is down at the stables, and Nicholas *was* having a swim. I'll let him know you are here after I have shown you your room.'

She followed him through the stone-flagged entrance hall, with its beautiful Brussels-weave rugs, and up the spectacular sweeping staircase that split into two as it reached the first-floor landing. A high glass dome lit the carved plaster ceilings, the last of the evening sun lighting the dark peachy walls to a warm glow. Sarah marvelled at the paintings between the arched alcoves.

'It's fabulous!' she breathed as Bernard showed her into her bedroom. He was indicating the bathroom, and other essentials, but she was hardly listening.

'If you're ready, come down in about twenty minutes,' he suggested, smiling at her wonderment. Hastings had that effect on most visitors. 'They will be in the drawing room to the left of the front door.' Discreet servant that he was, he left with no sound at all.

Over-awed, she wandered around the beautiful room with its cream and green silk-hung bed, and breathed in the scent of the yellow and white spring flowers in bowls around the room. Even the bathroom was huge. She glanced at her watch and decided to have a bath there and then, laughing as she poured in the Floris oil she found beside it and slid into the scented water. She determinedly relaxed while she tried to decide which of the two outfits she had brought with her to wear.

Nick had said, 'Don't dress up', but she finally plumped for the more formal of the two outfits – the wrap skirt she had worn for her audition and a new white cashmere sweater, well aware of the way it clung to her body. Flat shoes and loose hair, she decided, for Charles's benefit. She needed him on her side that evening.

However, Nick was alone when she finally walked into

the drawing room. Her heart sank, for he was obviously in a bad mood. He was on the phone, pacing around the room, arguing about money, but he paused in his stride long enough to indicate for her to sit down and pour her a glass of wine. Nervously, she sipped the wine and waited for him, wishing Charles were there.

The minute after he finally threw the receiver back on its base with an exclamation of disgust, he strode across the room to her. 'OK,' he said grimly, his eyes dark with anger. 'What the hell were you playing at?'

He picked up the remote control and flicked on the VCR. She watched the sequence in silence, shrinking back into the corner of the sofa. Cress had said he would be angry, but she hadn't expected anything like this icy fury.

'When was that recorded?'

Sarah shrugged. There was no point in lying to him. It was obvious from the greenery around the course that it was recent.

'Four, five weeks ago,' she admitted.

'After I told you, and Paddy, that I didn't want you to do it?'

'It was my decision, Nick,' she told him. Her voice was so low it was almost a whisper. 'I didn't want to let Paddy down.'

'It wasn't necessary to do it, and you knew that! Did it ever occur to you what it would have cost if you'd had an accident at this late stage, doing those stupid stunts? We would be talking millions, Sarah, not to mention forty-odd people out of work! It was difficult enough replacing Harriet, and I had six weeks to do that!'

'I didn't think of that. I'm sorry.' She bit her lip to stop herself from crying.

He could see the fear in her eyes, but he chose to ignore it. Leaning over her, he was so close she breathed the tangy scent of his aftershave.

'It's time you did learn to think, then,' he snapped. 'Remember this. From now on you are under contract to *me*. You disobey me – just once – and I'll put you across my knee. And that's no idle threat, believe me! You behave like a child, I'll treat you like one. I've had enough practice with my own daughter.'

The tears did slide down her cheeks then. She had been so emotional all day that they had always been close to the surface.

'Don't try conning me with tears, either!' His voice was hard, and cold.

'I'm not.' Sarah wiped her hand over her eyes. 'I *am* sorry, Nick, really. It's just been a bad day all round, and I knew you'd be mad. It didn't help.'

Nick managed to find a clean handkerchief and dried her tears, feeling genuine remorse then. 'For Christ's sake don't cry every time I yell at you,' he said, 'or you'll never stop! Now please stop, or Charlie will think I've been beating you already.'

'If it's any consolation to you,' she said, calmly lifting her sweater to reveal the still yellowing bruises. 'The bruises I got still hurt.'

'I'm delighted to hear it.' He was totally unsympathetic on that score.

Charles breezed in at that moment, and if he sensed an atmosphere between them he gave no sign of it. 'The new foal is just fine,' he announced to Nick cheerfully, and kissed Sarah's cheek. 'We'll take a look at him after supper, if you'd like to?'

'I'd love to.' Sarah fluttered her eyelashes cheekily at Nick. 'If Nick will allow it?' She felt safe now Charles was there, and Nick knew it.

'I swear, I'll swing for you before this shoot is over,' he sighed with exasperation. 'Come on, let's eat.'

Over supper Sarah entertained them with tales of the hilarious wind-up dinner and the gorilla-gram the boys had organized for her. 'They even gave me a chastity belt!' she giggled.

'Far too late, if I know James Willoughby!' Nick

59

commented with a wry smile, and began updating her on the shooting schedule.

Afterwards, when they went back to the drawing room, he kept her hard at work, only softening when he realized that she was totally on top of the script and had a firm grasp of Abigail's character. 'Right,' he relented at last. 'I'll show you where everything is, and if you still need some exercise Charlie can walk you down to the stables.'

They walked out to the old kitchen quarters, which had long ago been turned into storerooms. The unit had taken them over and turned them into make-up and wardrobe rooms, with the upstairs area taken up by the accounts and production staff. 'Six-thirty hair call,' Nick reminded her.

'Plenty of time for a swim first,' she told him blithely.

'Ronnie will *really* love it with your hair full of chlorine! I bet you don't get up in time.'

'Oh, I will. I'm going to need the exercise. I usually work out every day, and I always eat too much on location.'

'I'd better show you the pool, then,' he suggested.

He walked her through the house, talking easily about the building he had been familiar with since he was a child and obviously loved. Sarah was still inclined to be wary of him, he noted with some amusement, but he could see her visibly relax when they met up with Charles at the stables, and she was amongst the horses.

Recognizing a fellow enthusiast, Charles happily walked her around the whole yard, introducing her to his ponies, watching her obvious delight in them and smiling indulgently at her raptures over the tiny staggering foal.

Nick wandered out to lean on the paddock gate. To him, horses were for riding, not fussing over. He listened to their laughter, and the snorts and whinnies of the horses as they vied for attention and the Polo mints the two were feeding them.

Over the last few weeks he had been left in no doubt that Charles was dangerously besotted with Sarah Campbell –

her name was rarely far from his lips these days. He certainly needed another wife, but whether Sarah was the one, Nick was not at all sure. Charles's circle of older, aristocratic friends would be hard on her, and he was certain their mostly frowsty wives would hate her bright young beauty.

He *was* curious, however, about her relationship with James. Peter he dismissed from the picture. Somehow, her references to 'my boyfriend' did not have too much sincerity in them, but James was older, and used to getting his own way – though Nick still doubted Charlotte's disclosures had much substance. Sarah had been far too doubtful about the love scenes to capitulate to that extent, he was almost sure.

Was it an urge to protect her from both of them for her sake, he wondered, or for his own? He remembered the surge of jealousy he had felt when James had taken her off to Tramp after his party, the fury he had vented on Diana, and in the darkness he shuddered at the emotion the girl could rouse in him. '*You* are turning into a dirty old man,' he told himself firmly, turning as they came across the yard towards him.

Sarah was only an inch or so shorter than Charles, and he had her arm in his to guide her over the unfamiliar pathways. She would certainly make a very decorative addition to his life, Nick thought sourly, watching them as they walked back to the house, deep in conversation about horses and riding, as if he were not there.

Only when they reached the house did he assert his authority. 'Time you went to bed, Sarah,' he said firmly as they went in. 'I don't want a leading lady with bags under her eyes.'

'Charming! Nick, it's barely eleven,' she protested.

'What did I say about disobeying me?'

She had the nerve to laugh at him. 'You never know, I might enjoy it!'

Her eyes sparkled with challenge, but he noticed she ran

61

up the stairs pretty quickly when he took a step towards her.

'You're bullying her already,' Charles grumbled as Nick turned towards the gun room they had turned into their office for the film.

'She's got the hardest twelve weeks of her life ahead of her,' Nick snapped. 'And late nights will *not* help! If you want to pay court to her, Charlie, you can do it on Saturdays! Or come home early for a change. I notice you managed it tonight!'

Sarah awoke to the roar of a helicopter on the lawn outside her window – Charles going off to London, she told herself sleepily – then shook herself awake. She might as well fall into the pool, she decided, since she had been so adamant to Nick that she would. It was so close, and as it was only six there would be no one else about.

Hastily pulling a tracksuit over a white bikini, she ran down through the house to find it, built into a huge conservatory on the side of the house. Only then did she discover that Nick had beaten her to it, and she was forced to share the pool with him, much to his amusement.

Ronnie sighed as she unveiled her wet hair and reached for a hairdryer. 'Don't think flashing your tits at Herr Director is going to give you an easy ride,' he told her with a knowing grin. '*It* has been a real shit all week!'

'I've got more sense than that, Ronnie,' she assured him. 'And anyway, he was yelling at me within five minutes of my arriving.'

'Cress said he would do.' He finished drying her hair and began to work on it. 'Joanna,' he called to the dresser. 'Is the coffee on yet? I'm desperate – I don't know about madam, here. Have you met yet?'

He introduced them just as Cress arrived, with Jenny and James. Predictably, once Cress got going, things started to move. Joanna brought coffee to revive all of them and Cressida's laughter filled the make-up area as she flew around, chatting to everyone. That morning she had all the principals in at once, as well as a crowd of extras to deal with. The first couple of hours in the day were always the busiest for her, yet of all of them she was the coolest there.

Unlike the old-style, grand film designers, Cress was a hands-on type, bred, like Nick, by television's faster pace. She was quite ready to do up buttons and laces, adjust ribbons and fasten jewellery, chivvying along both artistes and staff at the same time. The runner was already asking for an exact time when the actors would be ready, and annoying her.

'Always the same,' she moaned, yanking at Sarah's corset. 'Lighting can take all the time in the world, but costume has to be ready before all of them! Joanna, get Sarah's dress, I'll see to Mariette.'

Joanna buttoned the tiny silk-covered buttons down the back of Sarah's dress. The corset was already beginning to irk her, and she wriggled continually. 'Lean into it,' she was advised. 'Don't tense up or it'll hurt even more. Put your foot up, and I'll do your boots.'

Cress whisked back and pinned a cameo to the neck of the chiffon and lace dress. Sarah was exhausted already.

'You'll do,' said Cress, standing back critically. 'OK, I'll knock off some Polaroids and Nick can have you. They *won't* be ready – lighting never are – but at least you will be.'

Joanna led the way from their dressing room area to the morning room, converted for the film into a drawing room because the French doors opened onto the garden terrace. Carefully, Sarah picked her way over the lighting cables and assorted equipment towards Nick and Alex, the first assistant director, as they stood talking over the script. To her relief, a slow smile spread over his face.

There had been no time for costume tests or parades in

the rush to get everything made; he had simply trusted his judgement and Cress's expertise from the sketches and fabric samples. For him, suddenly, after months of anguish, and battling over the script, Abigail had come to life. Sarah's height gave her the elegance of the period, and the ruffles of creamy lace and blue chiffon against her soft golden hair gave her the fragile air of innocence that he had searched for for so long.

'Perfect,' he breathed. Mindful of her make-up, he kissed her cheek lightly. 'Well done, guys,' he acknowledged. He was hard on his crews, but he was always ready to praise where it was due. 'OK, children, let's get moving!'

It was the last pleasant moment of the morning. By lunchtime, Sarah hated him. It seemed she could do nothing right for him. The corset was digging into every rib, but she dared not hold everything up while Joanna fixed it. Yet when they broke for lunch Nick turned to her with a charming smile and said, 'Not bad!'

Sarah stalked off to her dressing room in exasperation.

'I believe everything James said about him,' she sighed, sinking down into a chair carefully.

'Oh, that's nothing!' Cress assured her. 'That niggling is standard behaviour. Wait till he really gets going. Feelings don't come into it!'

'I'm not sure I can cope with it.' Sarah moaned. 'Or this damn corset!' Cress unfastened her dress to find her ribs red and sore on top of the bruises.

'Ouch!' she exclaimed with feeling. 'You should have said something! I'm amazed you got through the morning. I'm sorry, Sarah, I'll loosen it.'

'Maybe I can eat now!' Sarah joked, but she was too nervous to do more than pick at a salad, which was not like her.

'It gets easier,' James comforted. 'No point in wasting away, sweetheart.'

'I feel like the new kid at school,' she confessed sadly.

'Well come out and play after school,' he invited. 'We've found a good disco in Swindon, believe it or not!'

'I don't!'

'We're all going tonight – even Ronnie,' Cress put in.

'OK, you're on,' Sarah decided. It beat Nick ordering her to bed at eleven o'clock.

The afternoon went far better for her. Nick seemed calmer with her, as if he had wound her up to keep her on edge and try out her nerves. Now he relaxed with her, once he had set the limits for that day.

CHAPTER 6

Even though she often joined James and Ben in the hotel gym, and swam with them afterwards, Sarah frequently went up to Hastings Court early, to swim in the privacy of the pool there. Inevitably, it seemed, Nick joined her, and she quickly grew used to his company as they raced up and down the pool.

If the atmosphere had been difficult on set the day before, they hardly spoke at all; at other times they invented crazy games to play. Both highly competitive, each always had a sharp urge to win. Nick beat her on speed, but she frequently beat him on diving skills or underwater. It seemed an unwritten rule that they didn't discuss work. Occasionally he would ask what she had done the night before, and gradually she grew to trust him enough to tell him. He didn't always approve – she could soon tell that from the frown that quickly appeared – but she always told him the truth.

Some mornings she felt his eyes on her body, admiring her, she knew, yet she took care not to flirt, knowing instinctively that he would hate it. Always she kept her distance from him; always she left the pool in good time for her hair and make-up call.

Ronnie got quite used to drying off her hair when she got to him. He was the only one in the unit to know of the early-morning ritual, but, unusually for a born gossip, it went no further. If any of the others knew about it they said nothing to Sarah, and no one would dare tease Nick about it.

After her initial irritation with him, Sarah had been unsure of Ronnie, but as they got to know each other she had discovered he could be a loyal friend. Outrageously camp, with blond curly hair and a wild selection of earrings, Ronnie was over forty, a seasoned veteran of the business, and had soon taken Sarah under his wing.

'Now, don't tell me you let that big butch he-man take advantage of you, dear,' he admonished as Sarah waltzed into make-up one morning, singing cheerfully. 'You've got that look in your eye!'

'Rubbish, Ronnie. I've just got an easy day today, that's all.' Sarah poured herself some coffee from the pot he had put on when he came in.

'I wouldn't blame you if you did, though,' he rejoined. 'I was always partial to running the old hands through a bit of chest hair, and for all his faults that Nicholas certainly has a lovely body! Shame it's wasted on women!'

Sarah giggled. 'Ronnie, you're terrible! Anyway, I don't fancy Nick. I'm sorry to disappoint you. He's nice enough, but not for me.'

'Nice! He's bawled you out rotten for three weeks!'

'He's surprisingly nice first thing in the morning,' Sarah corrected him. 'Anyway, he may yell, but he would have thrown me off if he didn't like my work'

'You're right there! But he made one of his worst enemies ever doing that. Ever heard of Max Moreton?'

'The film critic on the *Unicorn*?' Everyone knew of Maxie; he was a hated slimeball.

Ronnie nodded. 'Nick threw his girlfriend off a shoot once, she was so appalling. Maxie never forgave him for that. He's sworn to get even, and the sod will – one of these days.'

'Poor Nick! It's enough to make him look over his

shoulder a great deal.' Sarah had several friends who had suffered from Maxie's poisonous pen.

'It certainly makes him a bit more careful who he jumps into bed with nowadays,' Ronnie said waspishly, securing her topknot with endless pins. They were doing an outdoor shot that morning.

'I didn't think he had much time for that,' Sarah teased, and shielded her eyes for the inevitable torrent of hairspray.

'He's always made time for it in the past. You just ask Cress – she knows all his little secrets. He *is* said to have had a thing with her once, as well!'

'Cressida? Are you kidding me, Ronnie?' Sarah spun the chair round to face him with incredulous eyes.

'Loves 'em and keeps them loyal, that's our Nicholas. She certainly had a thing for *him*, that I do know! It took her years to get over it. That stuck-up little wife of his must have something, though, since he always goes back to her.'

'Well, you learn something new everyday on this unit!'

'Laugh a minute!' he agreed. 'Did you also know our Nicky has his fortieth birthday this week?'

'Oh, gosh, no! Shall we get him a cake?'

'With forty candles? Rather you than me! He would probably hit you over the head with it for reminding him.'

'I'm sure he wouldn't.' Sarah was already planning it.

Both Cress and Alex looked doubtful when she mentioned it. 'No one has ever done that for him before,' Alex said. 'Could be dangerous ground, Sarah.'

But Sarah had made up her mind, and was feeling recklessly cheerful that morning. *Do or Dare* were coming down to do an interview and take some shots of the filming, so she would be seeing Peter and Paddy. The only drawback was that the loathsome Philippa was coming too, to interview James. Nick had very reluctantly agreed to an hour's break for them to do it, he was still sore at Paddy over the stunts, and Sarah was sure he had scheduled a kissing scene to remind Paddy who was the boss now.

She ran out to talk to the caterers before they began shooting and made swift plans with Karen and Joe, collecting a breakfast roll as she did so. Her appetite had come back, sharpened by the early-morning exercise. To the amusement of the crew, and Sarah's own surprise, she had found she could happily eat a huge bacon roll for breakfast and a three-course lunch, only forgoing something if she felt her corset becoming tight. However, she made sure to finish the roll before she strolled across the lawn. Cress and Jenny were viragos where food and costumes were concerned.

The crew greeted her cheerfully. 'Ready to get your stays bent?' teased Alex as she approached. This was the first love scene to be shot.

'Passion at this time in the morning,' she laughed. 'It's all too much!'

'It's never too early for James,' put in Lenny Clements, the lighting cameraman.

'Just don't tear the frock, James,' Joanna begged, already pulling twigs from the hem. James leant back against the tree trunk, laughingly taking Sarah into his arms and kissing her.

'Take your time, guys, we'll just get some practice in!' They were working under a huge cedar tree and the lighting was complex.

'You can concentrate and rehearse instead of messing about!' Nick snapped. 'We haven't got all day, thanks to the TV people!'

'What's the betting he has the hots for her?' Ronnie murmured to Jenny. 'I have a feeling James is really winding him up.' They both sneaked a look at Nick's furious scowl as James and Sarah giggled together, their arms around each other with the easy familiarity of the friends they were.

69

'And this is only a kiss!' laughed Jenny. 'If that is the case, wait till next week!'

Nick knew he was being irrational, and for once he curbed his temper. He knew it wasn't fair to them, just because James held Sarah so confidently and she was so obviously comfortable with him in a way she certainly wasn't with *him*. It even irked him that she happily allowed Charles to kiss her cheek when she greeted him, yet he knew, deep down, that Sarah had an easy rapport with everyone on the crew, and had done almost from day one. She was openly affectionate with them all. Her reserve was only for him.

On Wednesday no mention was made of Nick's birthday. Even Sarah began to question the wisdom of what she had planned, when he was as picky as ever over her performance, but Karen had made a superb job of the cake so she felt honour-bound to carry it through.

'You're on your own in this one,' the crew had insisted, but, unknown to her, they had chipped in for champagne, waiting till she was halfway across the room to an astonished Nick before they struck up with a loud chorus and produced it.

'My God! How did you find that out?' he demanded in amazement.

'Unit gossip. Happy birthday, Nick!'

To their surprise he was clearly touched by the gesture. Laughing, he obliged by blowing the candles out.

'I hope you made a wish,' Cress told him, as she handed him a glass of champagne.

'Certainly, but I think I may have a long wait for it to come true.'

Cress gave him a quizzical look. 'I've never known you wait for anything,' she smiled.

'Not one of my better traits, I admit.' She leant over and kissed his cheek. 'I could get used to this.' He smiled back.

'So could we. Just ease up on that poor kid for the rest of the afternoon. Do her a favour. She went through hell wondering if you would break her neck for planning this!'

'I'll try,' he promised.

Cress thought suddenly that she had never seen him look so tired.

He did make an effort, even managing to wrap on time, for once, and, making a decision as he did so, he walked over to Sarah as she left the set. Wishes never came true unless you did something about them, he thought ruefully.

'Sarah, wait,' he said quietly. 'Thank you for your surprise. I did appreciate it.' She smiled, the slow, wide smile he was beginning to know so well. 'Look, Charles and I are going out to dinner this evening. Would you like to join us? You might cheer two lonely old men up!'

Sarah considered. 'Well, yes, as long as Charles isn't on one of his long-distance kicks again?'

'No,' he smiled. 'The Priory, it's about half an hour's drive away. Wear your best frock, and I'll pick you up about eight.'

She went down to the wardrobe area in a panic. 'Oh, Ronnie,' she wailed. 'What can I do with my hair?'

'I did warn you.' He brushed out the lacquer. 'Wash it with this when you get back to the hotel, and I'll run over with my tongs. You can't let sir down.' He handed her a treatment shampoo.

He was as good as his word, full of wicked instructions and whirling the curling tongs through her hair like a dervish until he was satisfied with the results. 'There, you'll knock him dead!'

'Them,' Sarah corrected. 'Oh, dear, I think I'd rather go to the disco.'

'Rubbish! Go and butter the old sod up. Might do him good.'

'Old? He's younger than you!'

71

'Only just! Now move! You look quite yummy!'

She hugged him and ran down to the bar, Catherine's jade-green dress swirling around her, and she felt agonizingly shy as she approached the group sitting there.

'Wow!' exclaimed Alex, as Nick rose immediately to greet her, seeming even taller in a beautifully cut dark grey suit. 'I can see you aren't discoing tonight.'

'No, she's playing with the grown-ups tonight,' Nick told him, and took her arm quickly. 'Shall we go?' He led her out before any more of the crew arrived. 'I don't want them to think I'm taking advantage of you,' he laughed. 'Though in that dress it's very tempting to try! That's a Catherine Jayson, isn't it?' Sarah nodded in surprise. 'My wife goes to her,' he said in explanation. He touched her cheek gently as he opened the car door for her, a suddenly intimate gesture that made her shiver. 'I'm glad you came. And I know Charlie will be delighted.'

Sarah leant back in her seat, breathing in the luxury of the expensive car. He was driving one of Charles's Jaguars instead of his Porsche, with firm, assured hands on the wheel. In a formal suit and tie he seemed older somehow, the lines around his tired eyes seemed deeper. Cress was right, she thought, he did work too hard.

In the confined space of the car she was painfully aware that his closeness frightened her, and she was suddenly afraid of being alone with him. It was not the same as swimming in the pool, even though they both had far more clothes on, and she was not at all sure of what to say. 'I'm surprised you're not out with your wife tonight,' she ventured at last. 'Charles and I must come a very poor second.'

'Diana and I don't have that kind of marriage, I'm afraid. And she's very busy at the moment.' He shrugged. 'We're having a dinner party at the weekend, I think. But, please, don't call yourself a poor second. You should have more confidence in yourself. That's half your problem, Sarah. Let's get one thing straight. I'm taking you out to dinner because I *want* to.'

She was astonished. 'What makes you think I have a problem with confidence?' she demanded quickly.

He laughed. 'Sweetheart, it shows every time you walk into a room or onto the set. You breathe in and set your shoulders as you've obviously been trained to do, but your eyes give you away every time. It's as if you're afraid of people looking at you. You're a beautiful girl, Sarah, yet you seem to be terrified to let anyone see it – the way you persist in covering yourself in those baggy great jumpers and that terrible baseball cap. I must admit, there have been times I've wanted to rip that off just to prove you *had* hair! You have a body most women would die for, and you always want to hide it! Do you know, I think this is only the second time I've seen you wear a dress, apart from on set, and it's a vast improvement!'

Sarah considered, in astonishment, the fact that he should even notice. 'The dresses were Cressida's idea,' she admitted. 'I don't really think about clothes much, as long as I'm comfortable.'

'That's obvious! You should listen to Cress *more*. She's very good at her job. Remember, Sarah, you are no longer hiding in children's TV. What you look like *matters* – not just to me, but to the rest of the business as well. You're frightened of your own shadow most of the time! It's good for *me*, in that I can see my bullying paying off, but if you look good you'll have far more confidence to deal with everything else, I assure you.'

'You mean you bully me on purpose?'

'Of course I do! I get results quicker that way, I'm afraid.' He smiled disarmingly. How much younger he looked when he did that, she thought. 'It's been easy so far, though. After this week we have much more difficult stuff to do. I've led you in gently, but those two-handers for you and James will be hard going emotionally – especially for you.'

She knew he meant some of the scenes she dreaded. James's character was meant to be shell-shocked from the War, and she had long, impassioned speeches to an unresponsive figure in a wheelchair. They were planned for most of the next week, with their first love scene on the Friday. Nick had carefully watched her bruises fade, and scheduled accordingly.

'Nick, I'm more afraid of doing that love scene than any of the two-handers,' she admitted, biting her lip in case he was annoyed with her.

Nick was pulling into the restaurant car park. He switched off the engine before he turned to look at her. 'I did ask you about doing those scenes,' he reminded her.

'Yes, and I *said* I would do them.' She was firm on that point. 'It doesn't mean I'll find it easy, or pleasant. Oscar insisted I was to do it. He *made* me agree.'

'Wise old Oscar,' he commented. 'Look, stop fretting. I know it won't be easy. It's *not* something I would like to do myself, I admit, but I promised I would try and help and I will. It'll be a minimum crew, and you can pick who you want of your own personnel.'

Even with a slimmed-down crew it would mean at least eight people, and for a moment he wished he had cut the scene – but as it put the couple's feelings into perspective it had to stay. At least, he thought ruefully, he could be quite sure she was not sleeping regularly with James. If she were, there would be no reticence on her part about the love scenes. She was certainly keeping Charles at arm's length, that he was sure about – much to Charles's annoyance and Nick's private amusement.

'Look, forget about it for now,' he advised her then, and went round the car to help her out. 'Let's see if Charles is on time for once. He isn't usually.'

He wasn't. Nick was delighted to have her to himself for another twenty minutes before Charles finally arrived. Sarah sipped at the Veuve Cliquot he'd ordered and listened carefully as he discussed the complex character

74

she was playing. Now she had worked on Abigail for three weeks or so, she understood a great deal more of what was expected of her. It certainly surprised her that Nick had such a firm grasp of a woman's feelings – he could probe deep into her soul, it seemed.

'The book *Home Leave* is based on is in Charlie's library,' he said, when she voiced her surprise. 'I'll dig it out for you. We're changed a lot of it, but the basics are the same.'

Charles joined them with an exclamation of pleasure. 'This certainly beats dining *à deux* with Nicholas, birthday or not!' he beamed, settling into a chair. 'I thought the waiters' eyes were twinkling a bit tonight!'

They were both courteous and attentive, with the inborn good manners that came naturally to men of their background, but it was Nick to whom she was drawn more and more as the evening progressed. They found shared preferences for rare steak, and she found they shared the same sharp sense of humour as Nick relaxed and the stress disappeared from his tired eyes. Charles, she merrily flattered and flirted with, as the champagne eased her nerves, but it was Nick who held her attention. Why wasn't he always like this? she wondered sadly.

She listened, with growing awareness of the depth of his intelligence, as he and Charles discussed some of the books Nick had obviously been reading from the Hastings Court library. Sarah, who never read anything more taxing than the latest Jilly Cooper or Dick Francis, was enthralled by the way he dissected and critically analyzed books she would have dismissed as boring, bringing out areas of them that she would never have noticed. But she admitted to him that she didn't read much – she had decided long ago never to tell Nick anything less than the truth.

'He's totally boring about literary subjects,' Charles told her sympathetically. 'Comes of having an English degree, I suppose. I prefer *Horse and Hounds* and *Sporting*

Life personally!' Even if he that were true, he understood Nick, she thought wistfully, her eyes clouding.

'Best racing tipster we had at Oxford,' Nick quipped. 'Even in the nursery he read form books.'

'To Nanny's disgust!' Charles laughed.

'Nanny was disgusted by most things,' Nick rejoined. 'When I first came to Hastings, Sarah, I was three, and I spoke better Malay than English because I had been looked after by an ayah. Nanny was absolutely horrified! The times she slapped me for not speaking in English!'

'I can still feel her wet hands on my bare legs!' Charles shuddered. 'She's eighty-seven now, and she still tells me off when I go to see her.'

'She still tells me my hair needs cutting,' sighed Nick.

'Which it does!' Charles grinned.

'We had au-pairs,' Sarah said. 'George used to chase them like mad. They were always leaving in floods of tears. Daddy used to really yell at him!'

'I can't imagine George Campbell doing that,' Charles commented, 'from what I know of him. I've met him a few times recently,' he explained to Nick.

'No, well, Maggie is far too strict with him – but then he's old now. Oh, sh . . .!' She put her hand to her mouth in horror. George was a year younger than either of them, and Charles knew it.

'Well that puts *us* in our place!' He laughed at her discomfort. 'Would you two like a liqueur?' Since Charles was driving back, Nick ordered his favourite malt. Sarah declined, so Charles ordered more champagne for her. She smiled to herself. So much champagne in a few weeks. Life *was* changing. Even *she* was changing, and beginning to feel very differently about Nicholas Grey.

'Penny for them?' Nick broke in on her thoughts and she blushed hotly.

Charles had gone to speak to some friends and they were

alone. Sarah recovered her composure and gave him a wicked grin. 'Maybe one day I'll tell you, but not now!'

'From that one grin, I think I can guess,' he told her.

Sarah fervently hoped he couldn't! She wondered if he was flirting with her, but, shrugging, she put it down to the wine. She wondered again, however, when he elected to sit in the back seat of the car with her. She'd got in the back automatically, assuming he would sit at the front with Charles. But a few minutes later she was laughing.

'You'll never believe this,' she said to Charles in amusement. 'Nick is fast asleep!'

'I would,' Charles told her. 'He did a night shoot in town last night, because someone was ill. I don't think he went to bed at all.'

Nick's head was thrown back awkwardly. Instinctively Sarah reached over to ease him into a more comfortable position, and to her surprise he moved, settling himself against her, his arm going across her waist, though he was obviously fast asleep.

'So much for my sex appeal,' she commented drily. 'I seem to be better as a pillow!'

Charles had watched the almost maternal gesture through the driving mirror, feeling helpless to intervene. Even asleep, Nick managed to hold her full attention. 'I think your sex appeal is working perfectly,' he assured her. 'But even *you* couldn't compete against total exhaustion!'

Sarah leant back against the seat with Nick nestled into her shoulder, his dark hair soft against her cheek and lemony scented from the shampoo he used, his thick lashes dark smudges on his face. She looked down at him. He had shed both jacket and tie as they had left the restaurant, so she was suddenly all too aware of the taut muscle pattern of his body as he relaxed against her, his breathing slow and even. And as she held him steady she realized just how good it made her feel. She shivered to herself as she remembered how his gentle kiss after the cast dinner had affected her for hours afterwards, and the same warmth flooded through her now.

Oh, God! she thought with panic – Was this what falling in love felt like? But surely not with Nick, of all people! Too old – too married – even if he did have a strange married life! And yet she was relishing the sweetness of holding him, the spice of danger that his waking would bring, and she found herself longing for the drive to go on for ever.

But after twenty minutes or so Charles was pulling up at her hotel, and she was forced to disengage herself from Nick. He only stirred briefly, before settling back again. 'He'll kick himself for missing out!' Charles said cheerfully, covering his chagrin, as he escorted her to the door.

'Heavens! Don't tell him!' Sarah was horrified, and then saw he was laughing. 'I hope you can wake him up when you get home.'

'If not, he can sleep in the car! Goodnight, Sarah.' He kissed her mouth gently, the first time he had done so. She smiled at the embarrassed way he drew back, and laughingly returned his kiss. It meant about as much as kissing James on set to her, but it meant victory to Charles, who drove back to Hastings Court in triumph.

Sarah desperately wanted to talk to Cress about her evening, and had got used to gossiping with her late into the night. But as she paused outside her door before she knocked she became aware of James's voice over Cress's laughter, and she drew back, half-jealous, half-relieved that the two had finally got together.

The next morning she had thrashed her way through a dozen lengths before Nick appeared. He dived in beside her and they raced to the deep end without a word. 'I owe you an apology,' he said at last. 'Charlie tells me I fell asleep on you last night. I'm very embarrassed – I'm sorry!'

'That's OK.' She smiled. 'You didn't snore! But he also

told me why, so I wasn't surprised. You work too hard, Nick.'

'I'm well aware of that.' His voice was sharp, and she drew back instinctively. 'There are reasons for it, Sarah, believe me.'

'I expect there are. Nobody works themselves to death without a reason,' she commented quietly. 'Come on – best of five, then I must go.' She launched off from the edge, determined to beat him, but tired as he was he still managed to be half a length in front of her. 'One day I'll beat you!' she threatened, laughing, and splashing him as she reached him.

Nick laughed and cheerfully splashed her back as she dived underwater. They surfaced, gasping for breath, laughing and teasing. He had a hand on her shoulder and for a split second she thought he was going to kiss her. She found herself wanting him to – then he seemed to shake himself away from her. 'Go on, you minx, go and see Ronnie. I'm paying for his overtime after all,' he told her. 'You're doing an old man no good at all!'

'Less of the old,' she retorted as she swam for the side. 'My father was your age when I was born!'

'God forbid! Now move!'

She had rattled him considerably. He had been sixteen himself when Sarah was born, married to Diana before she had started junior school, and yet he had to admit to himself that he was very drawn to her, even if he was not totally sure why. Probably more to do with Charles's absolute devotion to her, he thought shamefacedly as he went upstairs to change. And yet, the more he learnt of Sarah, the more sure he was that she would be hopelessly wrong for Charles. He would never hold her bright young spirit.

Under his easygoing exterior, Charles Hastings was a coldly determined man, with very strict ideas about what he expected from his partner. It would be his first marriage all over again, and Nick shuddered when he remembered what Charles had done to Natasha in his determination to make her conform to the pattern of the wife he felt his position required. Natasha was the one thing he had never forgiven Charles about, and he never would.

CHAPTER 7

As if to prove something to himself, Nick was exceptionally hard on Sarah for the rest of the week *He* knew he was fighting the attraction he felt for her, but the crew were furious at his attitude, and by Friday they *all* hated him for her sake.

They had a difficult scene that afternoon, and Nick knew he had to finish it or call all the artistes back on Monday – which was impossible and expensive. None of them was getting it right for him. John was far too much of a gentleman to throw Sarah as he was meant to, in a vicious argument, and even Ben, a normally competent actor, was having trouble with his lines. One of the arc lamps was playing up too, and they had to wait while another was brought up from the lighting store. It was a night scene, with a real fire in the grate, and the room just got hotter and hotter.

By five o'clock he was seething. They were on take fourteen, when he normally considered six a maximum, and they still had a shot to do. 'Whoops!' muttered Ronnie to Cress, as Nick swung across the room to John and Sarah. 'Get the fire extinguishers, he's about to blow!'

'For Christ's sake, John, get it right!' Nick roared, beside himself with frustration. 'She's your daughter and she's disobeying you. You're fighting for a fortune, not asking her for something trivial! Throw her, for God's sake – don't just push her! Look, like this!' He seized

Sarah by her shoulders and literally hurled her to the floor. 'And *you* – scream at him – don't just whine!'

Sarah picked herself up painfully. 'You bastard!' she yelled at him with a furious glare, as she rubbed at the shoulder he had just bruised.

'That's more like it!' snapped Nick, and strode behind the camera. 'We'll end-board it. Action!'

Whether it was Nick's insults or just luck, they got it right that time. John threw Sarah almost as hard as Nick had done, and Sarah burst into floods of tears as she shouted her lines back at him from a crumpled heap on the floor, throwing John completely.

Nick didn't let up for a second. 'Stay there,' he ordered Sarah, while they moved the camera forward.

She could hardly believe this was happening. Dazed, she lifted her tearstained face to the camera, now only inches from her face. 'Rehearse on film,' Nick instructed. Patti had glycerine ready but Sarah didn't need it, tears fell without check as she said the lines required. There was an agonized pause as she finished, then Nick said quietly, 'Cut. Print the last two.' Both Alex and Ben moved as he said it, but Nick was faster. He swept the still sobbing girl up, totally ignoring the startled and furious crew. 'I'm sorry,' he said, for the second time that week. 'I didn't mean to hurt you.'

'No, you just had one of your stupid paddies to wind me up!' she spat at him. 'You're a complete swine, Nicholas!'

'I suppose I deserve that,' he sighed. 'I *am* sorry, Sarah. I'll make it up to you, I promise.'

'Oh, just get lost, and give us all a break!' She was suddenly aware of all the people around them, and embarrassed at the intimate way he was holding her.

'Gate clear,' the camera operator interrupted.

Alex glanced at Nick for a nod. 'It's a wrap. Eight o'clock Monday in the pavilion,' he announced.

Sarah jerked away from Nick's grasp. 'Have a nice weekend, Mr Grey,' she said sarcastically, and ran from the room, desperate to get away from him. To think, a few days before she had decided she might be in love with this man!

Even Cress couldn't pacify her. She refused point-blank to let anyone look at her hurt shoulder, and went straight to her dressing room, calling impatiently for Joanna. 'I just want to get out of here,' she said, when Cress remonstrated. 'How dare he treat me like that? And don't tell me it's just his way. He ought to bloody well know better!'

She scrubbed her make-up off and thrust her legs into her jeans. Joanna produced sweatshirt and trainers without a word, for her to yank on, and not bothering to do more than throw a brush through her hair she swept out, her car leaving deep tyre-marks as she gunned down to the gates.

'Well!' said Cress as Joanna picked up the clothes Sarah had thrown to the floor. 'I think Nick may have met his match there. But if she treats her clothes like that again, it'll be my tongue she'll get the worst of. I didn't think she had it in her; she's normally so easygoing.'

'Be fair, Cress.' Joanna put the dress on its hanger. 'He's been a pig to her all week.'

'Well, they can fight their battles in their own time,' Cress grumbled, finding torn lace on the shoulder, as she had expected. 'This damn thing will have to be repaired before Monday, sod it!'

'I'll take it home with me,' Joanna offered. 'Calm down, Cress, go on, take the weekend off for once. Are you doing something nice?'

Cress cheered up and thought of James, waiting for her at the hotel with their bags already in his car. 'Yes,' she said. 'As a matter of fact, I am.'

Sarah was joining Peter, and their friends Suky and Johnny, for the weekend, on the boat Peter's father kept at Lymington. She was almost *in* Lymington before she could truly say she had calmed down. At least, she thought, there was little chance of Nick finding her for forty-eight hours.

'Right!' she announced as she swung herself and her bag down into the main cabin of the boat. 'Tonight I am going to get absolutely smashed, I warn you!'

'Bad day, was it?' Peter enquired, raising a lazy eyebrow.

Sarah threw herself at him. 'Oh, just don't tell me I wanted to be a film star,' she moaned. 'I've had it!'

'A few jars will put it right,' counselled Johnny. 'Let's go to the pub.'

It was a gloriously hot weekend, with just enough breeze to move the boat along once they were out of the harbour on Saturday morning. Peter and Johnny were both skilled sailors, and all the girls had to do was provide food and drink at regular intervals. Luckily Suky had done the shopping in a blitz on Marks and Spencer, so there was very little to do except sunbathe.

Sarah made the most of it. They got very little sleep and just let rip, creating chaos in two pubs simply by appearing in the bar. On Sunday night she ignored the fact that she should have returned to Hastings Court and carried on partying, figuring that if she left early enough she could be back before her hair call. Johnny lifted the step that led down to the cabin and produced more bottles of champagne, which sent them all into a new bout of hysterics. Laughing and teasing, they drank several, and Sarah, unusually, fell asleep in a surprised Peter's arms, albeit fully clothed, soothed to sleep by the boat's gentle rocking.

At the crack of dawn, it seemed, Suky quite calmly dragged her up, despite her protests, poured coffee into her, and almost threw her into her car. 'For God's sake, don't get stopped,' she begged.

Sarah kissed Peter through the car window, and waved miserably as she drove off. She had one heck of a headache, and it got worse as she approached Hastings Court. She could barely remember the code as she pressed into the control pad. It took two attempts before she got it right. Cressida and Ronnie ran out to meet her as she parked her car behind their headquarters.

'Where the hell have you been?' demanded Cress, hauling her out of the car. 'You should've been back last night and Nick's been doing his nut!'

'Screw him,' said Sarah, as coolly as she could manage, and ran straight into him as she walked into Make-up.

'At this moment I don't think you'd be capable of it!' Nick thundered, grabbing her by the arm. 'Leave this to me, Cress.' He dragged Sarah unceremoniously into her dressing room and, slamming the door on Cress's anxious protest, threw her on the bed. 'How dare you come back here in this state?' he yelled at her. 'How on earth *can* you be drunk at this time of the morning?'

'I'm not drunk!' Sarah protested weakly, though she was still having problems focusing. 'I've got a bit of a headache, that's all.' Her head was spinning and she drew back as Nick leant over her, beside himself with anger, his eyes blazing.

'I warned you what would happen if you messed me around again,' he told her ominously. 'And I meant it!'

He was past being rational by that time. Furiously, he dragged her off the bed and shook her hard, so hard that it jarred her teeth. Stunned for a second, she stared at him in disbelief as he dropped her again. Tears of humiliation began, pouring down her face, uncontrolled.

'And don't try that one!' he warned. 'I've just about had it with you. I won't tolerate it, Sarah – not from *anyone* on this unit and certainly not from a child like you. Now get dressed! We've wasted enough time and money this morning as it is.' With that, he slammed out into the wardrobe room.

'Get her dressed!' he ordered Cress icily. 'And don't sympathize with her. She doesn't deserve it, frankly. Pour some black coffee into her and get her on the floor in half an hour, or she's really for it!' Ronnie and Cress exchanged horrified glances and Cress ran in to Sarah to find her sobbing on the bed.

'He hurt me, Cress,' she wept. 'He shouted at me just because I was late. I'll sue the bastard, I swear I will!'

'The hell you will! You were late and you are drunk,' Cress hauled her to her feet. 'Grow up, Sarah, you deserved it! What the hell do you expect? Especially after Harriet's accident – and you know *you* drive like a madwoman sometimes. He was frantic about you. We all were. This film rests on you. Remember that!'

Shaken, and horribly embarrassed, Sarah managed to pull herself together, and somehow Cress, Ronnie and Patti succeeded in getting her onto the set in the pavilion, dressed and made-up in the time Nick had allowed them. He was icily sarcastic, and the atmosphere was strained all morning.

No-one on the crew dared to intercede on Sarah's behalf, and she struggled not to burst into tears again every time he turned his sarcasm on her, knowing, shamefacedly, that she deserved every rebuke he threw at her. Only James, irrepressible as ever, dared to challenge him, folding her into his arms when they broke for coffee, ignoring Nick's furious glare.

'We all get the treatment sooner or later,' he soothed. 'He'll get over it, sweetheart.'

'I should live so long!' Sarah moaned into his chest, grateful for his sympathy.

'Don't let the bastard get to you.' James grinned. 'You take it all far too seriously!' His solicitude helped enormously, and by lunchtime her headache had eased. But, unable to face food, or the sympathy of the crew, she sought the sanctuary of the Winnebago they were using as a dressing room down by the pavilion. Wearily, she shut herself in the bedroom and lay down on the bed, her eyes closed against the light, longing for just half an hour's peace.

Five minutes later she opened them to find Nick leaning over her. 'Oh, God, no!' she moaned, rolling away from him, shielding her head. 'No more rows, Nick. I can't take much more.'

'I haven't come to row,' he assured her. 'I came to see if you were OK.' Her instinctive recoil made him feel *really* guilty – doubly so after the angry row he had just had with Cress over the treatment he'd handed out to her. She had ended by literally ordering him to sort it out, and, well as she knew him, Cress rarely dared to lose her temper with Nick.

'I would be if I was left alone for five minutes,' Sarah snapped. 'Oh, I'm sorry, Nick. I didn't mean to be late, I honestly didn't. Things just got on top of me. I really can't cope any more.'

Nick sat on the bed beside her and pulled her towards him, holding her in a grip that left no room for manoeuvre. But in her low state she had no energy left to fight him anyway. The relief that he wasn't shouting was enough. She leant her head on his shoulder in a gesture of defeat, and as he felt her relax against him he instinctively stroked her hair, gently, as he would a child.

'I'm sorry too,' he admitted. 'I should never have lost my temper like that this morning. It was a stupid thing to do. I should have known better.'

'You did warn me,' Sarah reminded him shamefacedly.

'That's no excuse. Oh, hell, Sarah, this has got to stop. It's doing the film no good at all. What on earth got into you to be so silly this morning?'

'I'm trying so hard,' she whispered. 'But even when I think I've got it right you moan at me as if you hate me, and everything I do. I just ran away this weekend to try and forget it all.'

'You *are* getting it right, I promise. The rushes are marvellous. I wanted to tell you on Friday how good you are and you wouldn't let me. I phoned you all weekend. Where on earth were you?'

'Sailing a boat and worrying about sunburn marks!' she admitted ruefully.

Laughing with relief, Nick tilted her chin up. 'As every good actress should! I do like you, Sarah. I probably like you too much for my own peace of mind.' And to her complete surprise, he kissed her, gently at first, with lightly teasing lips brushing over hers as his hands held her face captive. And then the kiss deepened into something harder – closer to passion she realized, startled. It felt astonishingly good to be held so confidently, and suddenly she desperately wanted him to go on. But he let her go just as quickly as he had started, as if he regretted it.

Standing up, he pulled her to her feet and led her into the main area of the caravan. 'I brought you a sandwich,' he said, matter-of-factly, as if the last few minutes had never occurred. 'You must eat something, even with a hangover.' He poured coffee for them and settled casually opposite her at the table, stirring sugar into his.

'You do have a weakness, then?' Sarah couldn't resist teasing as she watched him.

He laughed. 'I have many weaknesses – too many, according to my wife! How about you?'

Despite herself, Sarah smiled back. 'You know my weaknesses, Nick, you trade on them.'

'Maybe.' He looked serious for a moment. 'But it was more than my bullying that upset you over the weekend, wasn't it? It's this Friday that's getting to you, isn't it?'

'Partly . . .' She hesitated. 'Well, yes, mostly, I suppose.'

'Look, Sarah, it has to be done eventually.' Nick put a hand gently over hers. 'Has your cycle gone awry or something? If so, I can postpone it for a week or so, if it will help.'

'No, no, it's nothing like that. I . . . I've been on the pill for a year or so.' Sarah averted her eyes, embarrassed at his

88

candour and surprised at her own ability to discuss something so personal. She was on the pill simply to avoid any such problem in her working life. 'I just find it difficult to take my clothes off in front of other people – even for sunbathing. I know it sounds odd, especially for a dancer, but it's just something I've never done. I had terrible problems getting dancing work, because they always wanted topless girls and I wasn't prepared to do it. I know I have to do the scene, I know we've talked about it over and over again, but the nearer it gets the worse it feels.'

'Oh, hell! Sarah, is that all? Why, for God's sake?'

'What do you mean *is that all?*' Sarah was furious. 'This is my *body* we're talking about, and I hate it!'

'Yes, and there's nothing wrong with it!' Nick leant across the table and jerked her up again, dragging her into the dressing area. His hands were swift and savage as he wrenched her robe undone and ripped open the buttons of the camisole she was wearing, exposing her breasts to the long mirror in front of them.

With her arms pinioned by the sleeves he forced her to face the mirror, to look at herself and her naked breasts. 'I see you in that skimpy bikini almost every morning,' he said firmly. 'That doesn't bother you, so why should this? Shall I go on?' His hand went to the petticoat fastening.

'No!' Sarah bit her lip and faced him through the mirror, wanting to cry with embarrassment, but Nick held her firmly, refusing to let go.

'Look at yourself,' he demanded. 'Tell me what you think is wrong with you? Look hard, Sarah. You *are* truly beautiful. Accept it. Be proud of it. Of *course* it'll be difficult – for a few minutes anyway. But the crew are well aware of that. We've all done this before.' He relented then, and let her go, pulling the robe together as he did so.

'I haven't, though, Nick,' she said. 'And I've only done it once in real life! Not that even that was exactly willing . . . Oh, technically it wasn't rape . . . but it felt like it!'

89

'What happened? Am I allowed to know?' Nick's arm tightened on her waist, and to her surprise she found it incredibly soothing.

'Gerard – my boss – in a club I worked in – he took a fancy to me.' She shuddered. 'He called me into his office one day, and, well, to cut a long story short, I gave in. It was better than getting hurt! Daddy came the next day and fetched me – I never went back. I got into RADA and gave up dancing for ages until I got into *Cats*.'

'Oh, Sarah!' Nick was horrified. 'No wonder you're so frightened! I'm really sorry to have landed you with this. You should have told me.'

'What good would it have done?' she demanded. 'Would you really have changed the script just for that? I'll get by, Nick, never fear. I don't go back on my word any more than you do. Even if I have to get drunk again to do it!'

'I think we can forget that idea!' He was still holding her by the waist, and as he smiled down at her Sarah began to laugh.

'Maybe I should insist that everyone else strips off as well, then,' she suggested wickedly.

Nick shook with laughter. 'Not if you want to keep a straight face.' He shuddered. 'Have you really looked at the lighting grips?'

Sarah cast her mind to Stan and Denis, with their enormous beer guts, and leant against Nick, her laughter bubbling out.

'That's better,' he approved. He could hear the voices of the crew as they returned from lunch, and he paused briefly to brush his mouth temptingly over hers again before he let her go. 'Stay at Hastings tonight?' he suggested. 'I think we should clear the air a bit, and I can make sure you get a decent night's sleep for a change.'

After the morning's exchanges she did not have the nerve to argue, and accepted his invitation politely. 'One thing, though, Nick,' she added slyly. Nick paused, puzzled. 'Would you tell Jenny that *you* ripped all the buttons off my camisole?'

It was Nick's turn to look embarrassed. 'I will if she gives you a hard time,' he promised shamefacedly. 'Try and get dressed before she sees it, there's a good girl. She's even fiercer than Cress!'

'You look a bit more cheerful,' James greeted her, when she went back onto the set.

'I feel it,' she assured him. 'Though I must admit this morning I felt like you look now.' Patti had done a superb job of making James look ill and hollow-eyed.

'Frightened Cress to death!' James quipped. 'But I could get used to this kind of acting.' He lay back on the sofa while the prop-man folded blankets around him. 'I just wish it wasn't so hot!'

'You can't have everything!'

Sarah was laughing again, and they were all relieved to see it.

Even with the agony of being on her knees all afternoon, she turned in a beautiful performance. It was a long, difficult speech, with no visible reaction to it until right at the end, when all James had to do was smile and lift his hand to her face. To a man the crew burst into spontaneous applause as they achieved their final take, while James pulled her down on to the sofa with him and kissed her.

'Race you back to the house!' he challenged, rolling her back onto the floor. 'I need the exercise!'

'I've got carpet burn on my knees!' Sarah rejoined in excuse, but she obediently swung up her skirts and sprinted after him up the slope to the house.

Cress had dashed up to London after her set-to with Nick, and she arrived back just as the two were changing. She went straight to Sarah and hugged her, her own harsh words forgotten, and was relieved that Nick had obviously listened to her. She had even remembered to collect the things Sarah wanted from her flat.

'I'm staying here tonight,' Sarah admitted, when everyone was talking about dinner plans.

'Oh, yes? He making up for beating you?' James teased, and laughed at her sudden red face. 'You can't hide that, Sarah. I'm afraid it's going to be a legend you two will have to live with. Cheer up! Just pray it doesn't hit the gossip columns.'

'And that Maxie doesn't get hold of it,' put in Ronnie. 'Imagine what he'd do with it, especially the way he hates Nick!'

'Stop it, you two,' said Cress crisply. 'Don't take any notice of them, Sarah, they're just trying to provoke you.'

Sarah was still worrying about it as she walked through to the main house, meeting the housekeeper in the hall. 'I put your things in the room you had before,' the efficient Mrs Johnson told her. 'Nick asked for dinner at seven-thirty, as Sir Charles will be late back and he thought you might be too hungry to wait.' Sarah wondered idly if Nick had known Charles would be late, and she went upstairs, smiling.

Bathed, with the sea-water washed out of her hair, she pulled on the voile summer dress she had taken with her to Lymington and not worn. Not bothering to plait her still damp hair, she slipped her feet into the soft pink suede shoes that matched her dress, and went back downstairs with it cascading down her back.

'I hesitate to offer you a drink,' Nick said, smiling as she walked into the drawing room.

'As long as it's not champagne,' she told him solemnly, 'I think I could manage one.'

He had been a model of patience all afternoon, and was now being a perfect host in Charles's absence. The row with Cress had shaken him to the core. She had forced him to look realistically at his attraction for Sarah. Now it was as if a huge weight had been lifted, and he felt able to relax with her at last.

After dinner they walked down to the lake, with Charles's labrador, Hoover in tow. Sarah took bread to feed the geese, as she often did at lunchtimes, but Hoover was a total hazard, chasing the bread into the water and sending geese and ducks rushing for cover.

Nick threw a large stick for him to chase, but he preferred the water – and shaking himself all over them when he came out. 'Bloody stupid animal!' he cursed. 'He's worse than our dog. He'll be here as well this week. Diana's going off to Portugal with her parents, and Boots drives the kennels crazy so I've been lumbered with him.'

'Why is this dog called Hoover?' Sarah brushed the water off her wet dress. 'After President Hoover?' That would be typical of Charles, somehow.

'No.' Nick laughed. 'After the vacuum cleaner! You should see him eat! And he has hot air between his ears too!' He looked at his watch. 'I think I should do my heavy act and send you to bed early. You've been yawning all evening.'

Sarah was exhausted, but she hated to admit he was right. He certainly didn't miss much.

Back in the house, he took her into the library and found her the book that the film was based on. Sarah drifted around the oak-panelled walls, exclaiming with pleasure at the paintings and the beauty of the room. 'That's a Stubbs, isn't it? Oh, and a Romney?' Then she paused in front of a modern portrait of a beautiful dark-haired girl in a white evening dress. 'How lovely – who is she?'

'Natasha Hastings,' Nick said briefly. 'Charles's wife. She died.'

'How? She must have been very young.' Sarah was shocked.

'A car accident. She was twenty-six. It's rarely talked about now.'

Sarah longed to ask more but his attitude did not

encourage it. She wisely left it alone and took the book from him. Hesitating, she lifted up her face, uncertain eyes meeting his.

'Oh, Christ!' Nick exclaimed, and took her into his arms. 'I'm about to make the biggest mistake of my life!'

For the second time that day he kissed her. Not the momentary brush of the lips of earlier, but the searching kiss of a man who desperately wanted to kiss her, and he stunned her with his urgency. Almost in shock at his reaction, her lips parted with the pressure of his mouth. Intense, expert, his tongue coiled around hers as his hands came up to cup her face, his thumbs caressing the corners of her mouth as he did so.

Her trembling legs were hardly holding her up as Nick fell back into a huge leather armchair, taking her with him, breathing soft kisses along the line of her throat, and she shivered when he gently pushed aside the straps of her dress to release her breasts to his exploring mouth.

She gave a gasp of surprise at the new sensation of his tongue circling the swiftly aroused nipples, automatically arching towards him as he planted delicate kisses in a line from one swollen breast to the other, knowing from the hard line of his body against hers that he was as aroused as she was.

'I did myself no good at all this lunchtime,' he confessed huskily as he finally paused in his passionate assault on her.

'Why?'

Nick laughed softly and slid an exploring hand along her bared thigh to caress the curve of her hip with his fingertips under the lace that covered it. 'I undressed you to prove something to you,' he said, 'and I ended up wanting you all afternoon. This is wrong. I should stop. I promised myself I wouldn't do it.'

'But you want to?' And she knew he did from the look of pain that crossed his face.

'More than anything,' he sighed, 'I'd like to take you to

bed, Sarah, and make love to you all night. But I can't. At least, not tonight. Charlie will be back in a minute and I can't hurt his feelings to that extent. He *is* my best friend, and we both know how he feels about you.'

Sarah wound her arms around his neck, pulling him closer. 'To hell with Charles. This is between us, and strangely enough – I want it too. I can't quite believe I do, especially after today, but . . .'

'I think I was so angry because I was so worried about you,' he admitted. 'Maybe tomorrow, then. Maybe at the weekend. I'll think of something. I want you very badly, Sarah.'

It hardly seemed to matter that she was wearing a dress, the delicate fabric appeared to melt under his hands. Oblivious to their far from private situation, she lay across his lap, absorbed by the way his sensual hands roamed over her body, until the noisy whir of Charles's helicopter sweeping low over the house drew them reluctantly apart.

Slowly Nick lifted her to her feet. 'Go to bed,' he said. 'You need sleep more than you need me.' He touched her cheek in the gentle gesture she had come to know and guided her out into the hall, only loosening his arm at the foot of the staircase. 'I'm so glad we made it up,' he said as he kissed her fervently. 'I'll see you in the pool.'

'As long as you don't try to prove a point again,' she teased.

Nick smiled, a little sadly, she thought.

'Sarah! Go to bed before I change my mind!'

'I'll see you in the morning,' she promised. 'Unless you want to come up and kiss me goodnight?'

He laughed wickedly, his vivid blue eyes suddenly alight with mischief. 'I might just do that! Now go!'

Sarah ran up to her room in a state of shock as Nick went out to meet Charles. Her skin tingled; her eyes were sparkling at her in the bathroom mirror. She touched the faint redness his beard growth had left on her face and neck, and wondered what on earth she had awakened in him and whether she could cope with it. Her body still remembered the few minutes she had spent in his arms, and trembled at the thought of Nick making love to her. She doubted that he would come to her while Charles was in the house – he had been quite clear that they must put Charles's feelings first – but . . . She shrugged. One never knew! She put on the delicate silk nightdress Cress had brought from the flat by mistake amongst her things, before she went to pick up the book and curl up on the sofa with it.

When Nick came up half an hour later, he found her fast asleep on the sofa, the book hardly started. Probably just as well, he thought ruefully. Carefully, he lifted her up and carried her to the bed to put her into it, and she only stirred as he put her down. Her body was warm through the thin silk, and he was only too aware of it as she moved. With gentle hands he covered her, feeling the desperate urge for her building up inside him as he leant over her.

The dilemma over his feelings still churned as he went downstairs to join Charles, who poured him a drink and held it out silently. Nick carried it over to the window, staring out into the evening, battling with the new and frightening emotions he was feeling. For a man always in charge of his life, it was a disturbing experience.

'You know you're in love with that girl, don't you?' Charles said, sharply.

'What makes you think that?' Nick asked warily, startled by his perception.

'Just watching you, it's obvious. But typical, I suppose. And the other night when you were asleep in the car she was only concerned with *you*. I might just as well have been invisible.'

'What the hell am I going to do about it, Charlie?' Nick asked despondently, leaning his forehead against the cold glass.

'You need to ask me?' Charles was incredulous. 'I expect you'll do what you usually do – bed her and then use Diana as an excuse. You're a fool, Nick. She won't forgive you so easily either. One more dalliance and old man Mackenzie will take you apart!'

'Sod him! That stupid thing with Stephanie was three years ago! It meant nothing much either to Steph or me – and, frankly, Diana damn well drove me to it! She's about as warm as the South Pole in winter when it comes to sex!' Nick muttered irritably. 'My private life is nothing whatever to do with Diana's father anyway. Frankly, I'm sick of the sanctimonious old idiot! He's not so pure himself. I know he's been knocking off his secretary for years.'

'Maybe.' Charles looked grim as he watched Nick swallow the whisky uncharacteristically fast. 'But you are married to his daughter, and he'll protect *her* with his last breath, however unpleasant that makes your life. For heaven's sake, Nick, the guy lent us the money to start the company. Oh, I know he could afford it then, and he got it back with a huge profit, but morally you still owe that family a great deal! A bit of consideration for his daughter is the *least* he can expect. It's time you learnt you can't take everything you want without hurting someone. One thing *is* for sure; you hurt Sarah in any way and I'll kill you – I mean it, Nick.'

'From your description, I'll probably be the one to get hurt,' Nick said bitterly. 'Alistair Mackenzie's a pig, but he's my problem, not yours. I'm the one who's married to his daughter after all.'

'Yes, and may I remind you that he is also chairman of the company that owns the lease at Wardour Street?'

'About the only thing that bankrupt bloody company *does* own these days!' Nick grumbled. Mackenzies had been hit badly by the downturn in the property market, but the Wardour Street property stayed in their portfolio, somehow – mostly to spite Nick, – he was sure.

'Nick, why on earth don't we try and find new premises?' Charles said. 'At least then we'd be completely free of him. It's not as if we can't afford to move, after all.'

'Forget it, Charlie! The hassle would be enormous! Anyway, I've just spent half a million on the small studio, and the lighting console in A is held together with gaffer tape. We'll need a huge injection of cash for that soon. Where the hell would we move to, anyway?'

'Maybe we should just get smaller offices and use other people's studios for a change?' Charles suggested mildly. 'It would certainly be cheaper.'

'No! You're even beginning to *sound* like an accountant!' Nick slammed his fist onto the windowsill. 'I've spent ten bloody hard years building that company up and we've always had our own studios. That was my first priority. I wouldn't even consider going to a four-waller situation.'

'You do for features.'

'That's different and you know it! We couldn't shoot that many commercials at Pinewood or Shepperton – the clients would never wear it – and that is where I'd shoot a studio feature. We are *keeping* Wardour Street! The lease is safe for several more years and Alistair can't touch us, Charlie. I won't let him.'

'Then you'd better keep your hands off Sarah Campbell,' Charles told him, with a gleam of satisfaction. 'Or all your hard work will be for nothing, Nick. Because, secure as our lease is, old man Mackenzie would get to you somehow. For God's sake! You know how I feel about Sarah, and you still can't resist having a go for her, can you?'

'Sarah's not for you, Charles. You must know that deep down, just as you knew Natasha wasn't.'

'We had the same argument over Natasha,' Charles remembered sadly.

'Yes, and look what it did to her!' Nick went to pour another drink. 'It bloody well killed her.'

'That was just as much your fault as mine!'

'It damn well wasn't, and you know it! Don't you dare bring that up again!'

'Natasha was on her way to see *you* when she crashed the car!'

'After I told her not to be so stupid! You were the one who drove her into drugs, Charles! As you probably would Sarah. I *won't* let you ruin *her*, I promise you.'

'Sarah is *not* Natasha,' Charles snapped at him.

'No, by the time Tasha was Sarah's age she'd dabbled with every drug known to man out of boredom! She was a free spirit, Charlie, and you trapped her. Just as you'd trap Sarah.'

'Tasha chose *me*.' Charles slumped back on the sofa. 'You never forgave her for that – or me, come to think of it.'

'Tasha almost broke me, mentally and financially,' Nick pointed out. 'As you know perfectly well. I was well rid of her, frankly. Oh, I loved her at first, I admit that, but God, was she destructive! She almost killed *you*, with that heart attack you had. I think you had a lucky escape, if you must know!'

'Don't be so snide! You'd have married her like a shot if she'd wanted it.'

'Oh, no! That was one mistake I refused to make!'

Nick laughed suddenly, but there was no joy in it, and, if he was completely honest, there was not much truth in his statement. He had been head-over-heels in love with Natasha Verney, in a way he had never been since with anyone, including Diana. But the secret was something that lived deep in his heart along with the devastating pain she had caused him.

'I slept with her for a year – but marry her? I had more sense, old son, as you should over Sarah. You can't turn her into the lady of the manor and deny her the chance of stardom that she's got. It would be an appalling waste. She'd end up hating you, as Natasha did.'

'So I can't marry her because you want her to be a star? You selfish sod, Nick!'

'No, Charlie, it's what *Sarah* wants, and that's what counts. If she wants me then you'll have to accept that, as I accepted that Tasha wanted to marry you. But I'll make you one promise – if you did, by any chance, – persuade Sarah to marry you then I would certainly leave her alone. I *never* want to be in the same situation we had with Tasha.'

'I'll *never* let you take Sarah – *never* Somehow I intend to marry her, have no fear of that! I've got all the advantages where she is concerned, and I won't hesitate to use them. I'll fight you every inch of the way.'

Nick gave a start of shock, before he pulled himself together. The old arguments were suddenly very much alive, long after he had considered them buried, and there was a new edge of hysteria in Charles's voice that was completely at odds with his calm exterior. 'Don't be so bloody naïve,' he retorted. 'She's nearly twenty-five, and I can assure you she has a mind of her own. You won't persuade her to do anything she doesn't want to do, believe me!'

'I suppose that means you've tried already?' Charles was bitter, and Nick shuddered at the venom in his voice.

'No, as a matter of fact I haven't touched her – yet. But I will, I can assure you of that! Leave her alone, Charles!'

Charles hurled a cushion at him in exasperation. 'Is that a challenge, then?'

'Certainly! Don't worry, Charlie,' Nick added as he moved to the door, glad to get out of the chilling atmosphere of Charles's fury. 'You won't get a chance to get near her!'

Taking his drink, he went to the gun room to sit for long minutes staring at the photographs of Sarah that he still had in his briefcase. He slumped over the desk, the shooting script forgotten in his dilemma over the girl he had held so briefly. He knew he was going to break every rule he had made for himself, and the promise he'd made to Diana after the last time. It was going to create a rift between himself and the man he considered his best friend, and yet still he couldn't stop.

Sarah was an ache, a need that wouldn't go away. Despite Diana, and Charles, Nick knew he couldn't stop now. Just the memory of her smooth young body in his arms made him twist with desire.

He drank far more that evening than he normally did, in a futile effort to sleep, but he still lay awake half the night tossing restlessly. He cursed his own weakness, telling himself it was wrong, knowing the damage he could do to Sarah herself. Just once, he told himself, I'll take her just once, then the need, and the pain, will go away.

CHAPTER 8

Sarah was awake early, and lay stretching luxuriously into wakefulness as she listened to Charles's helicopter take off and turn low over the house in the direction of London. Despite his professed poverty over his Lloyds losses, he still lived differently from anything she had ever dreamt of, she realized as she watched it swirl away in the early-morning mist.

Somehow it never occurred to her to close the curtains at Hastings Court. The heavy damask drapes looked as if they had been hanging in those folds for years, though she knew her room had only recently been redecorated. Charles had taken her on a tour of the house not long after she had arrived that first week, and lovingly detailed the work he had done on it in the last few years, as his time and money had permitted. For a business-orientated man, she acknowledged, he had very good taste, having accomplished the design work single-handed.

It intrigued her why he had never remarried after his wife's death so many years ago. He was, after all, titled, as well as being an obviously charming man. Her brother had spoken highly of Charles when Sarah had asked George about him, and there must be dozens of girls around, she thought, who would be far more suitable and anxious to marry Charles Hastings than she was.

She was aware of Charles's admiration for her, and dismissed it. Though he and Nick were a similar age, they were light years apart in outlook. Nick seemed years younger than Charles, not just physically, or in the clothes he wore, but in his attitude to life in general. Nick lived in the modern world, albeit an expensive version, whereas Charles was rooted in the aristocratic style of life his parents had dictated, and he found no real reason to change it.

With Nick suddenly in her mind, she pulled a very businesslike swimsuit from her weekend bag and slipped into it. Let him try getting this off, she grinned to herself, and made her way down to the pool with a towelling robe from her bathroom over it. She had no intention of any of the crew seeing her in a compromising position with Nick if she could help it – that was if he had *meant* what he had said the night before. Though Nick rarely said things he didn't mean.

The pool was empty, and she paused by the windows at the end looking out dreamily over the acres of green lawns and the curve of the stone bridge over the lake. It was a peaceful moment at Hastings that she always enjoyed before the film crew shattered it with their noisy banter and revving car engines.

Nick made her jump as he joined her, on silent bare feet, sliding his arms around her waist from behind. 'Too busy dreaming to swim?' he enquired. 'Or were you waiting for me?' He *had* meant it, she realized, suddenly embarrassed, and wriggled away from him, throwing off her robe.

'It's not much fun racing myself,' she grinned at him, as he took in the swimsuit with a challenging smile.

'Business as usual?' He raised an eyebrow.

'Something like that. Ten lengths?'

'That's gone up!'

'You're getting into practice,' she challenged, poised to dive. 'But I'll let you kiss me if *I* win!'

'That's the most underhand bribe I've ever heard, young woman!'

'Take it or leave it!' Sarah dived, neatly and cleanly, a

103

good ten feet in front of him. To her fury Nick still beat her, laughing as he did so.

'No way are you bribing me. Come here!' He grabbed her purposefully and hauled her out of the water, her wet hair streaming. He laid her on one of the loungers and proceeded to kiss her until she was breathless, leaving her in no doubt that he really had meant every word he had said the night before.

'You're insane!' she protested, when at last he allowed her some respite.

'Maybe it's the effect you have on me,' he allowed. 'Have dinner with me tonight?'

'With or without champagne?'

'Wait and see! I think I'll keep you in suspense all day.' He ducked her swinging fists with a surprising agility for a big man, and then lifted her to her feet. 'I'll do my best to be patient today, I promise, if you can manage to keep your hands to yourself!'

'You can talk!' Sarah was still laughing as she ran upstairs to get dry and throw on some clothes, before she went through to Ronnie.

'So, have we kissed and made up?' James enquired with a grin when she waltzed in.

'I guess so. But mind your own business, James,' she rebuked cheerfully.

James couldn't believe it that morning. Sarah forgot her lines, missed her marks and seemed totally disorientated, yet Nick forgave everything and let her get away with it.

'How the hell have you managed not to have him break your neck?' he demanded at lunchtime. 'You must have wasted miles of stock this morning.'

'I'm sorry, James.' Sarah giggled. 'I'm just a bit off this morning.'

'A bit! I'll strangle you if he doesn't!' James grinned. 'Get yourself together, woman. What *are* you doing to keep him sweet – screwing him?'

Sarah almost choked over her salad as she hastily denied it. 'I'll be all right this afternoon,' she added.

'You'd better be,' he threatened, laughing, 'or I'll take a leaf out of his book and beat you – but it'll be on the set, in front of the crew!'

Somehow, with that in mind, Sarah pulled herself together, and they were back on schedule by the time they wrapped and Nick strode over to her. 'Come through to the drawing room when you've changed,' he said, quietly. 'We can have a drink in peace and we'll go out later.'

'My, aren't we civilized?' Sarah couldn't resist teasing him as he turned to go. Then she saw the swift rise of his dark brows and it made her shiver suddenly.

Half-inclined to dawdle, she went to the pool area to shower and wash her hair – to be ready for dinner, she told herself – letting Ronnie dry it and put it up for her, after slipping into the fresh jeans and halter-necked white body that Cress had brought over for her.

'Another evening with Nick?' Ronnie teased as he pushed in a final grip. 'We are getting cosy!'

'Purely business,' Sarah assured him airily. 'It beats fighting!'

'Oh, I don't know. A little rough stuff seems to have worked wonders with you, madam!'

'Leave it, Ronnie.' Sarah stood up, her tone sharp, but she regretted it as his face fell. 'I am more than capable of dealing with Nick, and I do have a perfectly adequate boyfriend – remember?' She blew him a kiss in apology, and, pushing her feet into sandals walked slowly across the yard to the house.

It was true, she did have a boyfriend. She remembered their pranks and games on the boat, but suddenly Peter seemed like a childhood memory she had left behind. Now the reality was Nick, and the new effect he was having on her previously reluctant body. She knew there was a great deal more to lovemaking than Gerard's vicious assault, but very little about how to react.

To her surprise, Nick was sitting at the grand piano that was set across the corner of the room between the windows, playing it softly. Liszt or Chopin, she wasn't sure, – but he was totally involved in the music until she crossed the room to stand at the end of the piano. Smiling up at her, he paused, then reached over to hand her a glass of champagne.

'I didn't realize you played so well,' she complimented him. 'Don't stop.' She smiled back at him with recognition at this signal as she drifted around the room, sipping at the wine. Nick rippled his hands over the keys as he watched her. In her slim, figure-hugging clothes she seemed taller than usual, her graceful body unconsciously stretching to the music.

'I'm very rusty now,' he admitted, 'but I wanted to be a concert pianist long ago, before I discovered what hard work it could be – and discovered women! I love music, though, that certainly hasn't changed, and I always like directing anything with a musical content. One of the first things I ever directed was a children's serial for television – a thing called *Happy Feet*.'

'Oh, Nick! I remember that so well!' Sarah began to laugh. 'I was about ten. It was on just before I went away to school. It was about a dance school, wasn't it? I so wanted to be like those girls in the show.'

'Oh, God!' Nick looked aghast. 'That makes me feel like Methuselah!'

'No, just the man who inspired my career!' She grinned at his discomfort. 'Before that I wanted to be Lucinda Green, because *all* the other girls at Pony Club wanted to be three-day eventers. But then Daddy took me to see *Sleeping Beauty*, and then there was *Happy Feet*, and I was hooked.'

His fingers automatically strayed into the *Sleeping Beauty* waltz and he watched her move easily to the music, stretching into an arabesque, her back leg reaching high above her head in a straight line with an astonishing ease.

'I'm impressed!' he told her. 'I'd forgotten you danced until you mentioned troupe-dancing the other day.'

'I would've loved to do classical ballet,' she sighed, 'but I got too tall. That nearly broke my heart.'

'Their loss was theatre's gain,' he comforted. 'I bet you made a gorgeous cat.'

'All claws!' Sarah reached over, as she had been longing to do, and ran her nails gently over the dark mist of hair in the open front of his shirt. Nick, too, had changed – and shaved, she noticed. His loose white Lauren shirt, though tucked into his jeans, had only the bottom two buttons fastened. Immediately he stopped playing and caught her hand in his, lifting it to his lips, kissing her fingertips one by one.

Sarah stopped teasing then, as his other hand went to her hair, tangling in it, pulling her closer. They forgot that the piano was in full view of two windows as he kissed her, with deep, exploring kisses that brought her arms up around his neck, as she clung to him, taking everything his lips gave in those few minutes. As delicately as he had played the piano, Nick stroked her breasts with his fingertips through the thin jersey fabric. She was bra-less under the tight halter, and he was quickly aware of her throbbing arousal. 'I think we'd be a lot more comfortable upstairs,' he suggested softly. 'Does that meet with your approval?'

'Not on the piano? I would have thought that might appeal to you, Nick?'

'On a Bechstein?' He sounded horrified. 'Maybe in movies, but I have far too much respect for a good piano – and Mrs J's feelings if she caught us! Come on.'

Laughing at their conspiracy they ran up the stairs together, anxious not to be seen by the staff, not relaxing until they had gained Nick's room and he had locked the door behind them.

Suddenly, Sarah was hesitant, knowing what he was intending to do and unsure whether she wanted the same now. The room was flooded with the early evening sun, lighting the soft chintz of the four poster bed as Nick drew her towards it and threw back the covers. There would be no darkness in which to hide from him, she realized as she trembled in his grasp, and her heart sank.

'Don't be nervous, Sarah,' he said, gently, mindful of her confession. 'I'd never do anything you didn't like, I promise. Nothing need even happen if you don't want it to. I'm happy just to kiss you.'

Slowly, Sarah put her hands on his chest inside his shirt, feeling the hard muscles and the strong beat of his heart, taking reassurance from him. His heart was pounding almost as much as hers was. 'I want it, Nick,' she said. 'I'm just frightened you'll be disappointed in me.'

'That's hardly likely!' He sounded relieved, and his kiss, when it came was long and penetrating, growing in intensity as he laid her back on the bed, his hands on the fastening of her jeans. They were tight, and he eased them off with some difficulty, chuckling at the discovery of the garment under them. 'You don't believe in making things easy for me, do you?' he chided as he searched for the poppers he knew held the body together.

'It's only one thing – far easier than underwear,' she pointed out, with a tremor in her voice, as he pulled the offending garment upwards, dislodging her carefully pinned up hair.

'True!' He knelt on the bed beside her for a moment, stripping off his shirt, his eyes never leaving her face when he stood, then, to impatiently shrug off his own jeans. She had seen him in brief swimming trunks almost every day, but completely naked Nick's broad build was awe-inspiring. She felt every muscle under his tanned skin as he joined her on the bed. There was no way, despite her confident boast to Ronnie, that she could fight him off – even if she'd wanted to. And now she didn't – not on her life!

Against all his baser instincts, Nick forced himself to relax and take it slowly. He moved carefully at first, touching and exploring with his fingertips, learning the shape of her body, following with his mouth, once he heard her gasp with pleasure at his gentle touch. As his lips found her breasts she remembered the sensations of the previous evening and arched expectantly towards him, her hands in his hair, moaning with delight at the new sensation as he sucked on the tips of her nipples, making them almost vibrate with pleasure.

It was as if her whole body was on fire for him. She was feeling sensations in nerve endings she'd never known she had as his hand slipped between her thighs. Helpless with longing, she gave a low scream then, as his fingers slid into her, never still, probing for and quickly finding the delicate pressure point inside her.

He gave her no respite, bringing her again and again to the point of hysteria as she writhed and twisted under his tortuous hands. Only when she was trembling all over did he give in and roll onto her, slipping easily between her wide-spread thighs to thrust deeply into her. For a few minutes he battled with his control, then gave up completely when she instinctively ground her hips against him, wrapping her legs around him as he drove into her. Despite his resolve, Nick took her more fiercely than he had ever taken any woman, but his dominance was gone as they both strove to take the maximum pleasure from each other's bodies, their breathing harsh and laboured in the last frantic seconds of climax.

Collapsing together, they lay still for long minutes, their arms around each other, their bodies still joined. Sarah had always assumed her hot body would be distasteful to a man, but Nick seemed to take pleasure from holding her close, his weight transferred to his arms in a considerate gesture, but still holding her tightly.

'One thing is certain,' he said eventually as their breathing eased, and he pressed his lips to the damp valley between her breasts in sheer, sensual pleasure. 'I could never find you disappointing! I didn't hurt you, did I?'

'No, of course not! That was wonderful, Nick, just wonderful!' Sarah realized then that she had experienced the real thing. The orgasm the books raved about – and they had not exaggerated the effect one bit. She was only too eager to try again!

His mouth was warm on hers; he still needed to kiss and touch her, with a feeling of pure tenderness that was completely new to him. And she had quite forgotten her fear of being naked as she began to return his caresses with a new confidence, her nails gliding gently over his smooth back then firmly tracing his spine with her thumb.

'Much more of that,' he commented huskily, after enduring minutes of it, 'and I'll be obliged to show you what it does to me!'

Sarah looked down, and smiled with anticipation. 'I see what you mean!' she commented. 'I thought it would take much longer than that!' Gleefully she stepped up the pressure, and was immediately rewarded by the speed with which he moved over her again.

'Every single time!' he told her, laughing, catching her wrists and pinning her down to the bed as he thrust into her, teasing and playful for a while, now he was sure of her – until his passion took over.

Was this the arrogant, cold Nick she had come to know? she wondered afterwards in amazement, when they were laughing together in mutual satisfaction? Sprawled naked across his bed, she hadn't a care in the world while he was touching her. 'You're so different,' she murmured into his shoulder. 'I like this Nick Grey.'

'Give me a break! I can't be tough all the time, my darling.' Gently he tugged at the tangled honey-gold hair spread across the pillow, and slid her onto her back so he could look at her. 'If you think Friday will be hard on *you*, just think what it will do to me now. I shall have to be very tough with myself then. And James, the rat, will be doing his best to wind me up! He can sense weakness quicker than anyone I know.'

'Hmm.' Sarah was thoughtful. 'So this was not meant as a warm-up exercise, then?'

'For heaven's sake!' he expostulated. 'What do you think I am, Sarah?' He shook her hard, his fingers gripping her bare shoulders. 'I should *really* spank you for that nasty little jibe. *This* is tempting me, miss!' His hand came down, curving over her bottom caressingly, and Sarah jumped in alarm.

'Don't you dare! OK I take it back! Anyway, the marks will show!'

'Luckily for you,' he laughed, then looked closer at her stretched out body. 'Talking of marks, how come there are no sunbathing lines on you if you don't sunbathe nude?'

'James's idea,' she confessed. 'We both hated the thought of body make-up, so we've been using the hotel sunbed – separately, of course!'

'You mean James doesn't want Patti making him up, he's so terrified of her!' He lifted her to a sitting position. 'Let's take a quick shower – I think we need one – then I'll take you out and feed you.'

'Thank goodness! This has really made me hungry. I'm starving! Can I wear my jeans? My bag's in the car, and neither of us can fetch it like this!'

'There's a good little restaurant in Aldbourne; we'll go there. It's not far, and they won't mind jeans.' He moved casually around the room naked, collecting up their scattered clothes, and Sarah marvelled again at the muscular strength of his body. 'Now move, darling, before Charlie comes home and finds I've had my wicked way with you.'

Even then, he could barely keep his hands from her as they stood under the shower together, not at all in a hurry, it seemed, as they dressed, and then struggled to brush the tangles out of her hair. 'Leave it loose,' he suggested in the end. 'I like it like that anyway. Heaven knows what happened to the grips that were in it.'

'The maid will find them in your bed.' Sarah looked worried.

'So?' Nick shrugged, then laughed. 'Don't worry, angel, they'll probably stick into me first, during the night!'

'Well, at least you'll think of me,' she responded, laughing back.

'I'll do that anyway.' Nick curved an arm around her shoulders as they walked downstairs. 'Sarah, I couldn't think of a nicer thing to do tonight than sleep with you, but I can't – not till the weekend anyway. Charles will be away then, apparently, and we can have the place to ourselves. If not, I'll take you away somewhere, perhaps?'

'You care a lot for Charles's feelings, don't you?'

'He *is* my best friend, Sarah. We've known each other since we were toddlers. I wouldn't deliberately hurt him if I could help it. I wanted to make love to you, but I just prefer not to flaunt it, I know how he feels about you. Hopefully he'll get over it.'

'But I don't feel anything for Charles,' Sarah complained. 'He's nice, but that's all.'

'I'm glad to hear it! I think I could be very selfish where you are concerned, given half the chance.'

It was the nearest he had come to any declaration in the two hours or so they had been making love. Sitting beside him in the Porsche, she wondered about it as she watched him handle the car with his easy skill.

'Doesn't your wife mind about you doing this?' she asked, surprised at her own boldness. Nick's face suddenly hardened.

'My wife has nothing to do with this. I live my own life; she lives hers.'

'Meaning don't ask?'

'Something like that, I mean it, Sarah. It may sound odd to you, especially after this evening, but even though we live apart Diana is still my wife, and I prefer not to hurt her feelings.'

'Then why the hell do you feel the need to screw me? Stop the car, Nick, I want to get out!' Sarah was deliberately crude, wanting a response, and she got it.

112

With an exclamation of fury he almost threw the car at the verge and jammed on the brake, throwing her hard against her seat belt. Before she could open the door he grabbed her, his mouth hard and demanding as he kissed her.

'Calm down, you idiot,' he rasped at her, 'and leave things alone that aren't your concern. Can you do that or not?'

Trembling, she stared at him, shaken by his reaction. 'Yes, Nick,' she said at last. 'I guess I can.'

'Try, Sarah,' he urged. 'You're a very special lady, but I can't and won't hurt my family, especially my daughter. If you want to get involved with me, we must get that clear first.'

'Cut and dried. Just like that?'

'It's the only rule I make.'

Sarah wanted him too badly to argue. 'I'm a big girl, Nick, I accept your terms. Don't let's talk about it again. I *don't* want to break up your marriage, I assure you.'

'I'm only trying to protect you – you know that, don't you? Oh, hell, Sarah, I shouldn't have touched you. I should have known better! It was pure lust to start with, I admit that, but now I want you so much that it's painful. It's crazy. I'm going to *hurt you*. I know I am!'

Reaching over, she touched his hair as he slumped dejectedly over the steering wheel, furious with himself. Nick was ruthless at times, but he was a deeply sensitive man under his hard exterior, and always had been. 'I wanted you just as much,' she whispered. 'At least you've been honest with me. I knew about you and Diana from the start, and I respect that. Come on, let's go eat.'

With a rueful smile of relief, Nick put the car into gear and changed the subject as he drove the last few miles to Aldbourne. He made a concerted effort to entertain her and even managed to contain his irritation when a couple of teenagers recognized her as they crossed from the car to the restaurant, and, eyeing him with suspicion, asked if he was her father. Sarah giggled with delight at his embarrassment, and murmured that she hoped not – for his ears only.

'Perhaps it *is* a substitute father you are looking for?' he suggested wickedly as they sat down. 'To take you to the ballet and things.'

'Don't be so disgusting, Nicholas Grey!' Sarah kicked him under the table sharply. 'I don't appreciate jokes like that! Anyway, Peter is hardly a father figure, is he? We have a great time socially, and we do crazy things all the time – like kids, really.'

'But the rest of your relationship with him isn't so hot, is it? The fact that you couldn't overcome your problems enough to go to bed with him proves that.'

'Nick!'

'Angel, I'm sorry.' Nick reached for her hand across the table. 'But it's pretty unusual to be so untouched at your age, you must admit!'

'Is it *that* unusual for someone my age to be so inexperienced?'

'To me it is,' he admitted. 'But a refreshing change for once!' He looked around quickly, checking that the waiter was out of earshot. 'However, I rather got the impression that quite a few of the things we did tonight were very pleasing to you – am I right?' She nodded reluctantly, and he smiled. 'I shall enjoy teaching you more, Sarah.'

'What a chauvinistic remark, Nick!' she retorted. 'Our feminist make-up lady would take you apart for a statement like that.'

Nick shuddered. 'Patti's a great make-up artist, but I share James's view of her as a female! She's definitely a ball-breaker! Don't let *her* influence you, for heaven's sake. She'll glare all the way through Friday. She doesn't approve of nude love scenes as she thinks they degrade women.'

'Couldn't we just have Cress on set with us?' Sarah

wheedled. 'I know James would prefer it, and I certainly would.'

'Cress may not,' Nick pointed out wryly. 'But maybe it would keep James in line if she's around. I'll talk to her. Just her? Not Ronnie? Or James might like to have Adam?'

'He certainly doesn't want Ronnie! He feels very uncomfortable with him! I think he's teased him a bit too much.' Sarah giggled. 'I don't know about Adam, he's *James's* dresser. I don't mind him personally, but I think just Cress would suit us fine.'

'I'll have the union down on me if we're not careful, but we'll try.'

Two sound men, three camera boys, including Lenny, a prop man, the continuity girl and Alex – the list still seemed endless to Sarah, yet she knew Nick had done as he'd promised by cutting the crew to the bare essentials, and that he had banned any mention of the scene's content to the ever-lurking press-men. She realized that he really was doing his best for her. Shrugging, she decided to put it behind her, and concentrated on dinner.

She really was starving, and ate her way through the menu, much to Nick's amusement. Any adherence to her diet had certainly gone out of the window on this shoot!

'You are going to prove expensive, angel!' he joked as he drove her back to the hotel.

'Oh, goodness, do you mind?'

'Not at all! I'll happily feed you – after I've made you hungry,' he teased her. Reluctantly, he pulled up outside the hotel and turned off the engine. 'I won't come in. It will only start more gossip,' he said, and drew her into his arms again. 'I want to keep this from the crew as long as we can.'

'Is that so important?'

'At this stage, yes. Sweet dreams, darling. I'll get Alex to drive you over in the morning. Would you like to go out tomorrow evening?'

Sarah bit her lip in embarrassment. 'I did rather promise I'd go out with James and Cress,' she confessed reluctantly. 'Unless you'd like to come too?'

'Why not? I'll mention it when I talk to Cress. Maybe we'll give Charlie's tennis courts some usage for once.'

CHAPTER 9

Cress argued, but the combined pressure of the other three finally persuaded her to give in and be on set for the love scene. Ronnie and Patti were delighted to get the afternoon off, particularly as it was a Friday and they would be able to get an early start to the weekend. 'Though I'll spend Thursday evening on your hair,' Ronnie warned Sarah, twirling a long curl disdainfully in his fingers. 'There's far too much chlorine in this for it fall properly in that sexy unveiling shot.'

'Agreed.' Sarah knew Nick was going home to collect the dog on Thursday – to Cress's disgust.

'Do we really have to suffer that appalling mutt?' she asked teasingly, as they walked back to the house after playing tennis on Wednesday. 'He's dreadfully badly behaved.'

'Cress! He's a pedigree!' Nick protested, hurt at her insinuation, like any dog-owner.

'He's a delinquent,' she laughed. 'Wait and see, Sarah. He pees on everything!'

'Well, nearly everything,' James corrected her. 'He chews up the rest.'

'Better keep him off the set on Friday, then,' Sarah put in. 'You won't have much defence, James!' And she smiled up at Nick as he squeezed her hand.

'That's more like it,' he congratulated her.

* * *

117

By the time Ronnie had finished with her hair, it was like silk. 'There won't be a dry eye in the house when he lets this down,' he prophesied, running his hands through it as he finished drying it.

'I told you he was good,' Cress said, having sent James for a drink with Alex so that she could join Sarah. 'Have another drink, Ronnie?'

Ronnie shook his head as he packed up his gear. 'I've got this nice little waiter coming off duty soon,' he twinkled. 'Mustn't get too pissed – you never know. Bye-bye girls!'

'God, he's so outrageous! No wonder James doesn't want him seeing him without any clothes on!' Cress said.

'Serves him right for teasing him. Poor Ronnie!' Sarah rejoined as the two girls settled down to watch a TV movie, comfortable together. She stretched out her legs and then looked at them critically. 'Hell!' she exclaimed. 'Do you think I should shave my legs?'

'For heaven's sake, Sarah, stop panicking,' Cress chided. 'They look fine. Just slap some cream on them.'

But at that moment James burst in on them, bringing some wine and quite obviously several drinks ahead of them. 'Alex had to retire to bed,' he announced, grinning. 'He was fool enough to say he could murder a pint of *crème de menthe*!'

'You didn't buy him one?' Sarah was horrified

'Lenny and I did just that! You should have seen his face, but he managed most of it. Mind you, I think he might spend most of tomorrow in the loo! It will teach him to make sarky remarks about my bum!' James laughed gaily, totally unconcerned. 'Here, let me do that – I love massaging ladies' legs'

'And the rest!' Cress put in, giggling.

'I'm only getting some rehearsal in! Keep still, Sarah.' He was just offering to do her back, and she was quite cheerfully fighting him off, when the telephone rang.

'Oh, hi, Nick,' she cried in surprise, pushing James towards Cress. 'Where are you?'

'Halfway between Oxford and Hungerford,' he replied. 'What on earth are you up to there?'

Sarah was a little embarrassed that he had caught her giggling like a teenager. 'Oh it's just James and Cress,' she excused. 'We're having a drink.'

'James into threesomes now, is he?' Nick sounded amused, then he cursed, as another driver tried to cut him up.

'No, massage,' Sarah teased. 'Is everything OK?'

'Everything's fine,' he assured her, 'except for dog hair all over my car! I simply wanted to talk to you, and to remind you to bring some clothes with you tomorrow. We'll go somewhere nice on Saturday evening.'

Sarah felt her insides melt suddenly. 'It's still on, then?' she tried to ask coolly, but her hand was shaking as she held the phone.

'I certainly hope so. I'm looking forward to it! Goodnight, angel.'

'What was that all about?' Cress demanded. 'Checking up on you again?'

'Something like that.' Sarah was evasive, but almost hugging herself with renewed excitement. Just the sound of his soft, caressing drawl was enough to make her want him.

Once James and Cress had gone she spent a frantic half-hour trying to decide what to take with her, what sort of clothes Nick would like to see her wear. Or not wear, she reminded herself, and spread the lotion over the rest of her body.

With the luxury of an eight o'clock call, James and Sarah had breakfast together at the hotel before leaving for Hastings Court. Although she managed to eat, it was an effort, and she was practically forcing each mouthful, which was unusual for Sarah.

'We *should* eat now,' James told her. 'I don't suppose either of us will feel like eating at lunchtime.'

'Don't tell me you're nervous!' exclaimed Sarah in surprise.

'I know, I'm supposed to be the one who doesn't worry about anything.' James's velvety brown eyes twinkled. 'If it's any consolation, Sarah, I'm probably as nervous as you are. I've spent about an hour in the bath this morning, and I shaved twice because I forgot I'd just done it!'

Sarah laughed with relief to find she was not alone. 'And I'll have to buy some more body lotion. I've put so much on I'll probably slide off the bed!'

'The worst thing is I've let Cress take the Merc this morning. I wouldn't have done that if I hadn't been worrying about today.' The Mercedes sports car was James's pride and joy, and Sarah lifted her eyebrows in astonishment.

'You must be serious about Cress to even consider it.'

James waved to the waitress for more coffee. 'Yes, I suppose I must be,' he said slowly. 'Funny, isn't it? With two bust up marriages I ought to know better. Still, third time lucky, perhaps. I've always liked Cress. She's different from all the bimbos I *have* been seeing – excluding you, of course!'

'Of course excluding me! She already bosses you around like a wife!'

'Cress bosses everyone – even Nick sometimes! You should have heard her, when she went for him over bullying you! I thought she'd take him apart. Even *he* quailed!'

Sarah smiled at the thought of Cress being the instrument of her new friendship with Nick. 'I *wondered* why he suddenly apologized,' she mused. 'Cress is tougher than I thought!'

'I think it comes with the job,' James said thoughtfully. 'Whatever it is, I think I rather like it.'

'Well, miracles do happen occasionally! Come on, we'd better go, if you really are serious about me driving you to work.'

She drove over to Hastings with the roof off the car in her usual brisk style. 'If I am shit-scared,' he announced as she pulled into the yard, 'it's because of your driving! Have you never heard of brakes, woman?'

'Only in an emergency!' Sarah retorted, waltzing into Make-up.

Patti began teasing about body make-up the minute they appeared, and the laughing and joking that went on relaxed them both. By the time Nick came in, they were fully made up and Ronnie was putting Sarah's hair up.

'OK, plan of campaign!' he said firmly. He was wearing his glasses to go through the script with them, and it made him seem more remote, somehow. 'This morning we'll do the first three shots, to the point where your clothes come off, then we'll rehearse the rest and shoot that this afternoon. So we're going to have to motor a bit.'

He smiled at Sarah. 'You can wear something to rehearse in, as long as it's skin-coloured and doesn't leave marks.' Cress had already organized that, Sarah realized with relief. 'Jenny, go and get Sarah into that camisole and petticoat so I can see it, please.'

Cress had thoughtfully stitched another layer of chiffon under the petticoat and put more lace on the bodice, but as Sarah put it on she began to shiver with fear. In the dressing room mirror it looked opaque, but she knew enough of film lighting to know it would look transparent on camera, and there was a full crew for the morning shots.

Jenny had gone to get Sarah's dress when Nick came into her dressing room. Laughing with mischief, Sarah fell into his arms, hugging him, and Nick couldn't resist a long, deep kiss. 'I missed you last night,' he confessed as they drew apart. 'We'll make up for it later, I promise!' He turned her around, gently. 'That *is* lovely. Cress was right,' he added as Jenny came back with her dress and he slipped back into being the impersonal director. 'Bare feet,' he instructed. 'And your pants show through – sorry, Sarah.'

She laughed. 'I knew you'd spot that.'

'I don't miss much,' he reminded her as she stepped carefully into the delicate voile dress. 'Did you alter those buttonholes, Jenny?'

'Every bloody one!' Jenny said, with feeling. She had spent hours adding elastic to the button loops, after Cress had discovered they were too tight for James to unfasten them easily.

'I'll take your word for it, then.' Nick remembered the camisole buttons he'd ripped off. '*I* won't try them!'

'It does feel wicked,' Sarah told James as they walked down to the pavilion, 'to walk around without any knickers on. My mother would have had a fit about all this!'

'Mine gets embarrassed in the Co-op every time I do a scene like this,' James admitted.

'Have you really done that many?'

'A few. I did one with Tam once. We had a real row halfway through!' Sarah was giggling with amusement at his wicked description of that as they walked into the set.

The main room of the pavilion had been turned into the doctor's bedroom by the set designer, because a double height ceiling meant they could use a tower, and shoot from above. Heavy velvet drapes were closed over the windows, and a fire blazing in the hearth already made it warm. With a smoke machine misting the dimly lit atmosphere, it seemed oppressive to both of them.

'Bloody hard bed,' said James, testing it. 'One of us is going to get bruises on her backside from that!'

Even in the warm room Sarah began to shiver and, when Nick touched her as he was positioning them her hands were icy. He ached to comfort her, but knew he couldn't in front of the crew. Wistfully, he retreated to the high stool he used behind the camera to watch the monitor. They had three shots; the two running into the room, as if from downstairs, some dialogue, and then James unfastening her dress and letting her hair down before kissing her. The first two they did in a couple of takes, although Sarah wanted them to go on for ever.

Strangely, the audible gasp of admiration from the crew as the dress fell and she turned into James's arms wearing the thin chiffon comforted her more than words ever could. Holding position, as Lenny moved some lamps and changed filters to light Sarah's cascading hair, James hugged her to him. 'They're all lusting after you,' he said, and grinned. 'Does that make you feel better?'

'A bit – but I still wish it was all over.'

She only began to laugh again when Nick asked James to lift her up and slide her down his body. After a couple of attempts he turned to Nick in exasperation.

'I'm going to do myself a mischief,' he complained. 'Have you any idea how heavy she is?'

'Yes, I have, and you're just not doing it properly.' To the amusement of the crew, he demonstrated exactly what he wanted, with an easy skill that had Sarah laughing in seconds.

'So he's Superman.' James grinned and tried again, more successfully.

'Yes, but I wish he'd taken that pen out of his pocket!'

By the time they had done the shot to Nick's satisfaction, and then repeated it for the reverse, her hair had been repinned a dozen times and her head ached from the constant pulling and pinning.

'Your head aches from too much coffee first thing,' Jenny admonished, proffering tea and aspirin as they changed in the Winnebago while the camera was moved and the lighting changed for the afternoon shots.

'Or the wine last night,' James reminded her.

'I'm just tense as hell,' Sarah grumbled as Ronnie brushed out her hair.

'Soon fix that,' James swung her hair over one shoulder and began massaging her neck and shoulders. 'Told you I was good at this, didn't I?'

'Oh, that's wonderful,' she breathed. 'I think I might marry you after all, James.'

'Well, we'd have a very public honeymoon first, if you did!'

As James had forecast, neither of them wanted the lunch that Joanna brought them. Even the wine Nick sent went mainly untouched. Alone together in the Winnebago, James smoked moodily and Sarah sat hunched up on the banquette, hugging her knees, her face hidden by the curtain of hair falling over it.

'It must be bad if you can't even drink champagne,' he teased at last, perturbed by her silence.

Sarah raised stricken eyes to his. 'James, I can't do it! I had no idea he would ask us to do all that – I'm not surprised he made himself scarce just now. He daren't face me, the bastard! None of that was in the script! He was making it up as he went along, I swear it!'

'Don't be silly, sweetheart.' James put a comforting arm around her. 'I told him to leave us alone. I thought you'd prefer it. Look, Sarah, he really has tried – I promise you. The last time I did a love scene for Nick, the actress and I were stark naked for two whole days! He's cut this right down to one afternoon for your benefit, I'm sure. We can do it – you know we can – we just need to get into the mood.'

'And how do you propose we do that?' she demanded. 'I'm going to throw up in a minute, I'm sure I am!'

'Rubbish!' James had a gleam in his eye that she suddenly didn't like. 'We have two options. Plan A, I could take you into the bedroom here and prove you can do it . . .'

'*No!*' Her cry of protest was so immediate and sharp that he had to laugh.

'OK, then,' he relented. 'Plan B. Put your shoes on, we'll go for a walk and I'll wear you out instead!'

'Like this?' Sarah looked down doubtfully at the towelling robes which were all they were wearing so that they wouldn't have clothes marks on their skin.

'No one will see us – except perhaps the crew, and they won't worry. Come on, we won't go far. The fresh air will do us good.'

They walked up into the woods that stretched from behind the pavilion way up into the far distance. It was cooler under the trees, and totally peaceful, with the only noise coming from the odd bird above them and the rustling of the dead leaves under their feet. Sarah began to relax, as she always did in the open air, breathing in the scent of the wild garlic and laughing as a squirrel burrowed around in the undergrowth.

James held out a hand to her as they walked, and she let hers creep into it. 'Better?' he smiled. 'Not feeling sick now?' Smiling back, she shook her head.

James perched himself comfortably on a fallen log. 'Has Nick got you into bed yet?' he asked casually. 'He is fussing about you enough to make me think so, and he's fancied you ever since that audition.'

'Mind your own business,' she retorted, far too quickly, and James frowned.

'Be careful with Nick, sweetheart,' he warned her quietly. 'He can be a ruthless bastard, and I'd hate to see you get hurt. I'm very fond of you, you know.'

'Just because I look young it doesn't mean I can't look after myself,' she retaliated. 'Anyway, Nick is worried about it himself – he's not as ruthless as you think.'

'He's proved he is more than once, my love,' James said. 'You may think I screw around, and occasionally I do, but I didn't when I was married – at least only once, and I suffered for that!'

'I heard about that one!' She grinned. 'It's a very small world in this business!'

'Yes, and as far as Nick is concerned, don't you forget it.'

'Don't worry, I won't!'

Surer of herself now, she kissed him, then was astonished to find him kissing her back with a surprisingly passionate sensuality.

'You're pushing your luck,' he told her. 'Especially when that dressing gown is falling off like that!'

'Wasn't that the general idea? I feel much better now, James.'

'Come on, then, let's go and face them before we lose our courage!'

Cress, back from shopping, greeted them cheerfully, alternately encouraging Sarah and threatening James. 'I'm going to stay out here,' she told them. 'I'll pop in from time to time, and Alex will call me if you need me. Nick won't mind, and I have phone calls to make.' Anything she thought, rather than watch James make love to Sarah, even if they *were* acting.

'Are you OK?' Nick asked as Sarah sat on the bed to brush out her hair and check her make-up. She resisted the temptation to giggle, and put on a sober face. Aware of the crew, he bent and kissed her cheek lightly. 'It will soon be over, angel,' he comforted. 'Then we can really relax.'

'I still think we should make the crew all strip off as well.' She tried to joke as they took off their dressing gowns and tossed them to Cress, before settling themselves into position on the bed.

James began to laugh. 'Tam did that once. She got the entire crew down to their underpants, *including* the director, before she gave in. It wasn't a pretty sight, I assure you. Watch it though, guys, she might mean it!'

He was turning it into a joke, thought Sarah gratefully, laughing with him as Lenny made last-minute adjustments to the camera, high above them on the tower. She was suddenly aware that the crew were all tactfully busying themselves with their equipment.

'I expect they have a bet on as to whether you're a natural blonde or not!' James whispered in her ear as he twisted a strand of her hair in his fingers. 'You're *gorgeous*,

Sarah. Come on, relax – we'll show them. You could really make Nick squirm if you wanted to. Wind him up, sweetheart – he deserves it!'

She began to shiver as he stroked her face gently. Nick was way above them on the tower, seemingly concentrating on his script, his glasses perched on the end of his nose. He didn't seem to care at all, she thought miserably.

'Tip your head back, Sarah,' he instructed, suddenly breaking into her thoughts, 'James, move your shoulder, you're blocking Sarah's key light.' And then they were both aware of the unusual gentleness in his voice.

It was easy while the camera and the operator were far above them. It was agony when they brought it down to floor-level, and it seemed to be only inches from them as James was poised over her. In terror, Sarah shut her eyes when she heard the familiar 'Speed', 'Mark it' and Nick's soft, 'Action' and she wanted to cry with embarrassment as James slid down her body, kissing her breasts, then her stomach, as Nick had instructed in rehearsal.

'Oh, come on, you two,' Nick pleaded. 'You can do better than that. She won't break, James!'

'Yes, I will!' murmured Sarah into James's ear and he quietly waved Nick away. 'Oh, God! Help me, James.'

So concerned with Sarah was he, that James forgot to be nervous himself. Gently, he concentrated his energies on coaxing her to relax, and Nick made the crew wait until she seemed almost to unfold, stretching out against James.

Watching them, Nick thought bitterly how well their beautiful young bodies matched. He knew he was pushing them to the limits all the time, despite shortening the scene, and hated what he was putting them through. Never in his long career had Nick ever found himself in the position he was in now, helplessly watching Sarah naked in James's arms, physically feeling desperate enough to want to wrench her away from him, and knowing that he couldn't.

As the afternoon wore on, however, he began to be both

amused at the sweat on Lenny's brow and then unaccountably irritable as Sarah began to respond to James's expertly caressing hands. It became a kind of game between them – how far they could go before Nick blew up – and Sarah began to almost enjoy what James was doing, being drawn into the game despite herself.

Only when it got to the last close-up shot did they complain. They were hot and tired, their backs and legs ached, and they had both run the full gamut of cramp and pins and needles in their arms and legs. It was almost seven o'clock, and they'd both had it.

'I've never felt less like an orgasm in my life!' James groaned when Nick told them what he wanted. 'No disrespect, sweetheart.'

'Just do your best,' Nick cajoled. 'You'll feel a lot more like it here than trying to dub it on over the long shot in a sound studio!'

Sarah reached for the glass of water that Alex held out for her and swallowed some gratefully. Laughingly, she dipped her fingers into it and smoothed them over James's forehead in an intimate gesture that made Nick furious, but it seemed to wake James up.

'He should've done this earlier,' he complained as they settled down again, waiting for Alex to rearrange the covers around them.

'Golly, I'd forgotten how heavy you are!' she exclaimed. The last couple of shots had been side by side.

James hugged her tighter. 'So soon,' he whispered back, 'I'll show you!'

'In your own time.' Nick sighed, watching them giggling together, ignoring him. The camera was almost on James's shoulder, tight on their faces, and Nick turned away to concentrate on the monitor behind it, signalling to Lenny to start the camera to hide his discomfort.

James pulled himself together, and Sarah struggled to bring Nick's lovemaking to the front of her mind for inspiration. As she twisted against James she could almost feel him, and James's body, astonishingly after such an exhausting afternoon, hardened against hers. She was so strung out, it seemed only a few seconds before she frightened them all – and herself – by giving a shuddering scream of pleasure, clutching James's head down to her, her fingers grasping into his hair. To his credit, though she had yanked incredibly hard on his hair, James just about managed to keep control and produce a creditable conclusion.

'OK, we got it,' Nick announced with a sigh of relief. 'Check the gate!'

He watched with an aching jealousy as, locked together, James and Sarah fell back, their eyes closed as the crew tactfully melted away round them. Then he too turned away, and walked out of the room without a word.

They lay exhausted in each other's arms for long minutes, until James eased himself from her and slowly lifted her up as he realized they were alone. Almost loath to let go of him, Sarah let him wrap her in her dressing gown before he put his own on.

'It's all right,' he said. 'It's all over, sweetheart, and it's going to look great, I'm sure.' He sat down again on the bed and curved a hand around her neck, pulling her towards him. 'I really *wanted* you just now. If you knew how much control I had to exercise to keep from actually screwing you, I'd get a special Oscar for it! Apart from the fact that you pulled half my hair out, of course!'

Sarah leant her hot face against him. 'I really didn't mean that to happen. I just . . . well . . . sort of got carried away.'

'*Really*? Well, never mind, I enjoyed most of it! Thank goodness we had the blanket! It's the first time I've had a hard-on during a take!'

'I *am* sorry, James,' she said shamefacedly, suddenly thinking of Cress. 'I think we'd better forget it happened, don't you? Let's go and finish the champagne.'

They walked slowly across to the Winnebago, breathing

129

in the luxury of the fresh air after the hot smoky room. Cress had made tea for them and they sat on the steps drinking it while she went to retrieve their costumes from the set.

'You shower first,' Sarah suggested. 'I just want to sit here and recover for a while.'

'There won't be a scrap of hot water left,' Cress warned as she came back. 'I've never known anyone who can stay in the shower as long as he can!' She sat on the grass in front of Sarah, smiling warmly at her. 'Are you feeling better now?'

'I'm fine, Cress, just glad it's over.' Sarah sighed. 'You and Nick were right. James was a great help.'

'I just wish I knew where I stood with him.' Cress looked unhappily across to the shower room door. 'I love him so much, Sarah.'

'I'm *sure* he feels the same about you,' Sarah comforted her.

'I wish I was as convinced! Oh, Nick said he would be back in a minute. He went to get the dogs, so you'd better try and get James out of the shower.'

'I'm out,' James announced. 'Stop maligning me, woman! We should have shared it, Sarah!'

'Don't push your luck, Willoughby.' Sarah winked at Cress and disappeared into the shower.

'Come and help me get dressed?' James suggested to Cress, when the door was safely shut.

'Dressed or undressed? In your dreams, buddy boy! I'm hungry. Get a move on.'

Despite the fact that they had been naked on a bed all afternoon, Sarah felt quite shy with James, and went into the dressing room to dress and make up, reappearing only as Nick came back with the two dogs at his heels. Even though Cress and James were watching, and teasing, he swept Sarah into his arms without any hesitation. 'You were just sensational!' he told her. 'Poor old Lenny had a hard-on all afternoon – and he's a veteran!'

'He wasn't the only one!' James rejoined with a grin. 'Sorry, Cress, but it was the most frustrating afternoon I've ever had.'

'I'm delighted to hear it.' Nick looked down at Sarah. 'If you tell me you're starving, I'll strangle you!'

'What?' Cress queried, staring at Nick's obvious pleasure in the girl he was holding.

'Private joke!' he assured her. 'How about a steak at the pub? Mary tells me she has some half-decent claret in the cellar, and no one does a steak *au poivre* like she does.'

'Great!' James hunted around for his shoes. 'I definitely *will* admit to being hungry, and Cress certainly is. We'll drive down – if she brought my car back in one piece!'

'Oh, it's fine,' she assured him. 'I only got one parking ticket!'

'*We* are going.' Nick laughed cheerfully at James's howl of protest. 'The walk will do us good.'

They cut through the woods and Nick threw sticks for the dogs as they walked. 'How the hell *did* you achieve that last shot?' he asked curiously, as he lifted her over a fallen branch, reluctant to let her go.

Sarah paused, then reached up to touch his mouth with her fingertip. 'I thought of you, making love to me the other night. It just happened then.'

'Oh, Sarah!' Nick ached for her as he held her. 'I think this is going to be the fastest meal on record. It's indecent the way I want you all the time.' Her dress, a short, slim denim, chosen for him, had buttons down the front, and he unfastened the top ones, sliding a palm under her left breast, lifting it free of the lacy bra to touch it with his lips. 'I wanted to *kill* James at times this afternoon,' he admitted, his voice heavy with desire.

'As you keep telling me, Nick, it was just a job,' Sarah reminded him sweetly. 'And thank God at last it's over!'

Reluctantly Nick refastened the buttons. 'If I hadn't had that damn dog with me, I would've stopped off at the hotel last night,' he said reflectively.

131

'After all you said about keeping this quiet?' she chided, then laughed as she saw Boots lift his leg against a tree. 'I see what Cress and James meant about your dog, he just can't pass a tree!'

'Boots sees every tree as a personal challenge.' Nick grinned. 'Wait till we walk back, after he's had a pint of beer.'

'Beer? You're joking!'

'Not about that! He's renowned for it in our local at home. Don't look at me – he's Diana's dog and she's spoilt him since the day she got him. He's supposed to be a hunting dog, but all he hunts are my shoes and the contents of the larder!'

'Surely he'll grow out of it?'

'He's five now, and he just gets worse. He and Hoover make a good pair – as daft as each other.' He caught Sarah's arm as he pointed out a rabbit the dogs had completely missed, crouched terrified and motionless in the bushes a few feet away from them. 'That shows how stupid they are!'

With the thought of Nick making love to her again Sarah had hoped that the meal *would* be a swift one. Somehow, though, it didn't turn out like that. James was in good form, as happy as Sarah that the afternoon was over, and Nick relaxed in his company, though he rarely took his eyes from Sarah during the entire meal.

He *is* in love with her, Cress realized, watching, and seeing Sarah's rapt expression as Nick and James discussed a film they had worked on together. Her heart went out to Sarah, knowing just what havoc Nick could wreak if he really got to her.

They both refused brandy when James offered it; Nick was clearly ready to go. 'I must go and see Alex and Dave for a minute,' Sarah cried gaily as Nick insisted on paying for the meal, and left them to run over to the bar where the two men were drinking.

'She's a real cracker!' exclaimed James with a wicked smile at Nick. 'Are you going to walk her back to her car, or shall we take her?'

'I'll do it.' Nick said firmly. 'And stop looking so po-faced, Cressida it's far too late for that! You worry about James behaving instead.' He went to retrieve the dogs from the pub yard, and was frowning slightly when he met them at the door. 'Did you see the guy talking to Dave and Alex as you came through the bar by any chance?' he asked James, puzzled.

James looked back to check. 'Didn't particularly, but now you mention it he does look familiar.'

'My thoughts exactly, but I can't place him.'

'It'll come to you – at the wrong moment,' James laughed, and opened the car door for Cress. 'Bye, now. Sweet dreams!'

With the dogs firmly on leads, Nick and Sarah walked along the village street towards the back gate of the house. Quite by chance, Nick looked back as he unlocked it and spotted the man from the pub standing in the road by his car, watching them. Even as he paused to let the frantic dogs loose the car drove slowly past the gate, and the realization hit him. 'That guy! He's a reporter on the *Unicorn*!' he exclaimed furiously. 'He's obviously digging for something nefarious or he would have gone through the press office.'

'Probably heard we were shooting a nude scene,' Sarah said, worried. 'That's the sort of thing the *Unicorn* love. They couldn't have got any photographs though, could they?'

'No chance.' Nick was quite sure of that. 'The rushes went to London with our own courier and they'll be watched all the way through processing. The only other photographs are the ones I took, and they're quite safe.'

'Well, there's nothing else to report on.' Sarah shrugged. 'Unless they're chasing James and Cress.'

'It's possible, I suppose, but it could've been *you* and

James they're after. I just get jumpy about anyone from the *Unicorn.*'

'Ronnie told me you'd had trouble with Maxie.'

'Is there anything Ronnie doesn't know?' He laughed, then his face changed. 'Never talk to Maxie, Sarah. He is always bad news.'

'It's a pity we went to the pub, then,' she suggested. 'I hope that man didn't overhear any of our conversation.' Nick laughed, then paused to kiss her deeply, and at length.

'I can't really sneak about with you, can I? I did consider taking you away for the weekend, but finding somewhere discreet enough at such short notice would be almost impossible! Luckily Charlie is away till Sunday, so Hastings is the safest place to be.'

'The curse of *Do or Dare,*' she told him. 'The papers think I've never grown up.'

'I had no idea children's programmes created so much interest, or that the presenters were so sexy!'

Reminded of Peter, Sarah was silent as they walked, throwing sticks for the dogs, only breaking the silence when they met the road leading to the house, and the house itself came into view. 'Oh, I never tire of the sight of that house!' she breathed. 'Charles is so lucky to own all that!'

'Marry him,' suggested Nick casually, remembering his conversation with Charles, and knowing now that he was safe. 'It would all be yours.'

'How on earth could you suggest that?' she demanded, hurt. 'You're planning to sleep with me, aren't you?'

Nick stopped and took her by the shoulders. 'I'm teasing,' he reassured her. 'Though I'm not really good news for you, Sarah. You realize that, don't you?'

'Stop lecturing me, Nick!' she said sharply. 'I've thought about everything you said but at the moment I don't think it matters very much.' It will, she thought I'm sure it will, but not now – please, not now. 'And, unlike you, Charles is quite old-fashioned – not my type at all.'

'At least he's single!' Nick said, and kept his arm possessively around her as they walked the short distance to the house. 'We'll go in through the kitchen, then I can shut these two up.' He seemed to have keys for the whole estate, she thought, watching him unlock the doors.

'Basket, hounds!' he commanded, and the two dogs scampered for their baskets without protest. Sarah hugged them both as Nick drew a bottle of champagne from the huge fridge. 'Boots can open most doors.' He smiled as he shut the kitchen door firmly. 'I don't really want him leaping on us.'

'What about Mrs Johnson?' Sarah asked nervously.

'She'll have gone to her own flat by now,' he assured her. 'We have the place to ourselves, I promise.' He led her to the drawing room, opened the champagne and poured it for them. 'Just one more thing – give me your car keys. I'll go and put your car away just in case anyone is prowling around.'

Sarah fished her keys out of her handbag. 'My bag's in the boot, if you think I need it!'

'Well, you might need a toothbrush!' He touched her cheek briefly with his lips and went out to move the car.

Standing at the window, Sarah watched the floodlights suddenly switch on as the evening light became night-time. The lake was bathed with a golden glow as the stone bridge rose over it magestically in the light, the white geese like a mass of white flowers scattered on the surface.

'"*Sweet, goodnight. This bud of love, by summer's ripening breath May prove a beauteous flower when next we meet*"' She spoke the words aloud, remembered from her RADA days. '"*Goodnight, goodnight! as sweet repose and rest Come to thy heart as that within my breast*"'

'"*Oh! wilt thou leave me so unsatisfied?*"' quoted Nick softly from behind her. Startled she turned to him.

'"*What satisfaction canst thou have tonight?*"' she returned, laughing, as the lines came back to her.

'Quite a lot, I hope!' He took her into his arms. 'I directed *Romeo and Juliet* at Oxford,' he remembered. 'You would have been about three at the time!'

'I'd love to play Juliet,' she said wistfully. 'But then I suppose most actresses would.'

'Not many have your advantages,' he told her, unbuttoning her dress to reveal one of them. He was unhurried as he touched her, his tongue lazily exploring her mouth. His whole aim was to relax her and break down any barriers that still remained from her experience at Gerard's hands. 'Let's go for a swim,' he suggested then.

'What? *Now?*' Sarah thought regretfully of her hair.

'Why not? Indulge me? I've longed to see you swim naked,' he confessed, smiling down at her. 'How about it?'

'If you let me wash my hair afterwards,' she challenged. 'Since Ronnie has only just sorted it out.'

'I promise.' He lifted her up and carried her effortlessly along the corridor to the pool, laughing as she clung round his neck, her dress half undone.

He only switched on the underwater lights. 'That's quite enough,' he said, and pulled towels from the cupboard before turning back to her. Sarah let her dress drop to the floor, then hesitated as he came to kiss her. 'Too many clothes,' he teased her, stripping off the rest of them.

Her hands went to his shirt, pulling at the buttons. 'You've been looking at me naked all afternoon,' she said softly. 'It's my turn to look at you.'

Nick laughed, kicked off his shoes and then shrugged out of his shirt and jeans. 'Is that better?' he asked as he scooped her up and carried her into the water.

It was warm, and as he let her go she floated gently on the surface before she began to swim lazily across the pool. After a few minutes she began to enjoy the sensual feeling of the water on her naked body, and started to tease and provoke him as she moved through the water. Nick swam alongside her, his tanned body pale under the lights, the dark hair of his chest and legs looking even darker. He

seemed almost menacing, with his height and the width of
his shoulders, and she turned to him, reaching out for him
to hold her.

Swimming with her in his arms to the shallow end, he
laid her on the steps, cradling her against the hard surface
as he plunged into her.

'Put your legs around me,' he ordered her, and she
obeyed him instinctively, clinging round his neck, her hair
floating around them in the water. They slid down into it
as he climaxed, and surfaced, laughing and spluttering,
gasping for breath.

'Nothing like trying to drown me!' she told him,
giggling. 'And you haven't even got me into bed yet!'
Nick lifted her up, as he had asked James to do, and kissed
her body as he slid her down.

'It's only a matter of time,' he said. 'Let's rinse your hair
quickly. I'm not very patient.'

Sarah had never washed her hair so fast, as she did then,
tilting her head back to let the shampoo rinse out as Nick
sluiced the water through it, and she revelled in the
sensual feel of his hands on her hair and body before he
wrapped a towel round her.

'You have five minutes to dry it,' he said. 'Go upstairs,
I'll have to turn the alarms on. Penalty of country house
living, I'm afraid.'

He had taken her bag up to his room, and she quickly
found her dryer and ran it through her hair on the hottest
setting, brushing it out frantically. By the time he appeared, bringing the champagne they had abandoned, it
was almost dry.

'That'll do,' he said, running his hands through it and
pulling the towel away from her.

Sarah felt no alarm now at standing naked in front of
him. She knew that since the afternoon those days had
gone for ever. She leant back against the dressing table,
meeting his eyes steadily as he reached out to slide his
palms slowly up from her waist, exploring, using the heel

of his hand to lift and knead the fullness of her breasts. Slowly, tantalizingly slowly, he grazed the nipples with his thumbs, bringing them to new life as he did so. He heard the swift catch of her breath as he lowered his head to them, but she made no move as his lips closed over the now taut nipple and she felt the steady pull of his mouth.

Bracing herself against the edge of the dressing table behind her, she felt the lift of his loins under the towel he had thrown around his hips, and then felt his hardness pressing against her stomach, and still she stayed motionless, her breath coming in soft gasps as the pressure of his mouth increased. Nick was a master with his tongue, and she was almost passing out with the sensations he was inducing. Gradually the feeling grew, to the point where she *had* to touch, had to touch him as he was touching her, and she reached out to pull at the towel.

'No,' he said softly. 'Not yet.' But he did lift her and carry her to the bed. 'We have all night to make love,' he told her, 'and there are many ways to do it. I'm going to find out exactly what you like, and then I'm going to teach you how to please me.' He felt her shudder with anticipation as he said it.

'Last weekend, I hated you,' she said reflectively.

'And I was worried you'd run away. I'm so glad you didn't.'

Sarah closed her eyes and dreamily gave herself up to his hands and mouth, to the searching, probing tongue that so quickly reduced her to a state of quivering submission. No longer afraid of him, or her body, she made her own demands then. Not with words, but in her movements, her wild cries of pleasure and her hands gripped in his hair, pressing his mouth even closer as he tasted the moist warmth between her thighs.

He paused a moment to let her drink the champagne he had brought, but teasingly drew a finger, wetted by the liquid, around her throbbing nipples. 'Can you die of pleasure?' she gasped as he played with her.

'Not yet, please,' he laughed. 'We've hardly started! Your turn now.' He moved then, gently persuading her to make love to him.

Hesitantly at first, she tried, and then with more confidence as she heard him groan at the touch of her tongue, wrapping lengths of her hair around his hands as he encouraged her onto him. She could taste him still as he lifted her so that she was astride him, and he could reach up and touch her when she leant back, the length of him deep inside her as he thrust up into her. Quickly she learnt to lift away from him, drawing back only to bring herself down again, hard onto him, until he could bear it no longer and threw her onto her back, thrusting without any thought of anything but his own need and satisfaction. Her shuddering scream of climax triggered his own and they finally collapsed, breathless, in a tangle of limbs and Sarah's hair, unable to move from sheer exhaustion.

Less than a week after screaming abuse at him and about him, Sarah lay in Nick's arms, her sweat mingling with his, unable to deny him anything he asked of her, scarcely able to believe such a complete capitulation was possible. Or that she could still want him again. But she knew then that she did, over and over again.

'No regrets?' he asked her softly, when they were finally still and on the brink of sleep.

'None at all.' Her voice was heavy with fatigue.

He smiled in the darkness and hugged her tightly against him, and the disturbing thought of Diana came to him as he too drifted on the verge of sleep. An affair on location didn't count – they all told themselves that. He tried to convince himself that the last few hours had meant nothing to him, but they did and he knew it.

Sarah woke finally to find herself alone in the huge four-poster bed. Nick had first woken her with gentle kisses long before dawn, and they had delighted in the sleepy coupling that had come without any preliminaries – just an

139

instinctive need for each other – before they had drifted back to sleep again, still wrapped together in the tangle of blankets.

Stretching and yawning, she woke slowly in the luxurious knowledge that she had the day off and that she was sharing it with Nick. There was time now to appreciate the beauty of the room. The softly understated chintzes gave it the air of having been like that for centuries, yet with its thick carpets and generous draperies it had a feeling of modern luxury about it too. A wonderful room to be seduced in, she thought gleefully, by a man who was, indeed, even in her limited experience, sensational in bed.

Testing her aching limbs carefully, she climbed out of bed, and, wrapping herself in Nick's discarded dressing gown, wandered to the window, drawn by the sound of the dogs barking. Nick was out on the lawn in front of the house, throwing tennis balls for them to chase, laughing and teasing them, holding the balls high so that they had to jump for them. He looked so relaxed and happy that she smiled, willing him to look up to the window and waving when he did.

Five minutes later, as she was running a bath, he appeared in the bedroom carrying a glass of orange juice for her. 'Good morning, my angel,' he greeted her, and kissed her with a surprising energy for one who had been kissing her half the night.

Holding her breath, Sarah slid her aching body into the bath, wincing as she hit the water. Laughing, Nick lounged into the armchair. 'Maybe I'd better not suggest going riding this morning!'

'You're a total sadist!' Sarah replied, chucking a water-filled sponge at him and shrieking as he calmly hurled it straight back at her.

'Hush, sweetheart, you'll frighten the staff,' he warned. 'Now, what would you like to do today? Walk, ride, swim, play tennis, or any other of the revoltingly strenuous activities you're so fond of?'

'Don't you usually work on Saturdays?' she asked curiously.

'Yes, but I promised we'd have this weekend, so I denied myself your company early this morning to get my paperwork done. We can now have the day to ourselves.'

'In that case let's go for a walk,' Sarah suggested. 'It's about all I have the energy for at the moment.'

'I'll tell Mrs Johnson we're ready for breakfast, then. I take it you're starving, as usual?'

'Does she know I'm here?'

'Yes, I confessed,' he laughed. 'But I ruffled the bed in the Lady Edward room as an alibi! The staff all go off at lunchtime today, as Charlie's not here, and I said I didn't need anything. Don't be long. Or do you want a hand out of the bath?'

Sarah picked up the sponge again. 'Don't push your luck!' she retorted as he retreated, still laughing.

Mindful of the staff, she collected up the clothes Nick had brought up from the pool and tossed them in her bag at the bottom of his wardrobe, her hands lingering on the neatly ordered rows of jackets, trousers and jeans hanging there.

There were only a couple of suits, she noticed, and a dress suit, the rest were casual clothes, all with the soft, smooth feel of expensive cloth that she had come to associate with Nick over the last few days. She loved the way he wore a tweed jacket with jeans. With his athletic build and long legs he made it look like a Savile Row suit, she thought, smiling, and then closed the door quickly as she started to feel guilty at being so inquisitive.

In jeans and T-shirt, without any make-up, she looked no older than Charlotte as she joined him in the morning room. 'My God!' he exclaimed in amusement. 'I feel as if I could be done for child abuse!'

'I don't feel like a child!' she admitted, 'but I'm very hungry.' She was starving, and happily demolished a huge

141

plate of scrambled egg and bacon. 'Your loving is definitely no good for my waistline,' she told him. 'You use up all my energy and I have to eat all the time to refuel.'

'I intend to use up a lot more of your energy,' he promised her. 'Before tomorrow is over.'

It was a heavenly morning, warm and sunny. They walked for miles, the dogs at their heels, talking all the time, laughing and kissing. Nick felt her youthful glow take hold of him, making him carefree in the sunshine. For once, walking was a pleasure, with a girl who could match his stride and his strength. Diana had always hated walking, and avoided it whenever possible.

Hungry again by lunchtime, they foraged in the fridge. Mrs Johnson had left a game pie for them and Sarah made a salad and a French dressing without messing it up. She had a sinking feeling that Nick would be quite fussy about things like that, but he dipped his finger in it and pronounced it fine, to her obvious relief. Carefully, she carried the tray outside to the terrace while he opened wine for them.

'I really can't cook,' she confessed as they sat in the sunshine and peace of the garden. 'George is always telling me off about it.'

'Well, I don't think you'll have much time to learn in the near future,' he told her. 'Not if I have anything to do with your career.'

'Do you really think so?' She sounded anxious.

'I know so. With the right scripts and contacts you'll be sensational. I work with Seth Waterston a lot, don't forget, and you can't get much higher than him.'

'What a lovely thought,' she sighed, and threw their leftover bread to the birds. 'But are all film directors as difficult as you?'

'Some are a lot worse, I can assure you!'

He hadn't felt so good in a long time. Spending a weekend doing absolutely nothing was almost unheard of for Nick, and he realized just how much he needed it.

Going back to Oxfordshire at weekends was rarely very restful. There were always friends to see, things around the house and grounds to organize, and if Charlotte was home it was a constant ferrying operation since they lived in a village. The most taxing thing he had to do that day was decide where to take Sarah to eat in the evening.

Watching her playing with the dogs, pony-tail flying as she ran with them, he felt the urge for her growing, and strode across the lawn to sweep her up. 'I need a siesta after such a sleepless night,' he suggested with a wicked smile. 'How about you?'

'I could be persuaded,' she said, her stomach lurching with anticipation as he walked her back to the house.

'Not sore any longer, then?' he asked, grinning.

'No, that went with the bath. I'm fine now.' Sarah had never felt so happy in her life, all she could think of was Nick, and wanting him.

The phone ringing as they reached the house seemed an intrusion on their relaxed mood, but Nick only grimaced as he gestured for her to go upstairs.

'Go up – I'd better answer it.'

'Nick,' said James, when he picked it up. 'Is Sarah with you, by any chance?'

'Yes, as it happens she is,' he answered cautiously. 'Is there a problem?'

'Only bloody reporters! That guy you recognized *is* from the *Unicorn*. They've been pestering us like mad about yesterday's scene – among other things. Cress is going mad!'

'You haven't told them anything?'

'Leave it out!' James was indignant. 'I told them that Sarah is nothing to do with me, and that as far as I was concerned she was away for the weekend. But they do know about your little argument from somewhere, I'm afraid, and I don't suppose Cress and I will get much peace from now on. Still, it might take the heat away from you two if we let them follow us around. I don't want

Sarah to go through this. She's not used to this kind of harassment; I am.'

'I'll get the press office to sort it out,' Nick said. 'I don't want Sarah upset either. I think I got some reasonable stills – that should keep them quiet. Thanks, James. If you *can* keep them off our backs, I'll owe you one.' He rang his PR girl at home immediately, and then rang the estate manager to alert him to possible intruders, before going up to Sarah.

Sitting in the huge bed, with the sheet drawn up around her breasts, she looked very vulnerable and anxious. 'I thought you'd abandoned me!' She smiled with relief, holding her arms out to him as he threw off jeans and shirt.

'No, just a little business.' He pulled the sheet away from her. 'Now, where were we?'

Without the urgency of the night before, his lovemaking was far more tender and gentle. He kept her guessing at every encounter, she thought, and they fell asleep with the sun streaming across the bed.

He surprised her again when they were dressing to go out to dinner. Sarah had retrieved her black chiffon dress from her car and left it on the bed while they showered. Nick smiled with pleasure at the sight of it.

'I think seeing you in that was the first time I really wanted you,' he said reflectively, then picked up the tights and pants she had put beside it. 'Do something for me?' he added as she dried herself. 'Don't wear these. Just wear the dress?'

'What?' She was horrified, and aware he was testing her again.

'I just love the idea of it,' he grinned. 'Don't if you don't want to.'

But to please him, she acquiesed. Sated with his love-making, she would have done anything to please him.

After James's phone call, Nick had opted for the safety of the Priory, since he knew the discreet waiters would protect their privacy. What he hadn't allowed for was the car that dropped in behind them as he drove out of Hastings Court's gates.

'I don't believe this,' he cursed, after several miles and numerous turns. 'We're being followed.'

'That's stupid! Who would follow us?' Sarah demanded, turning to look at the Cavalier behind them.

'Either my wife has a detective on my trail, or it's the press guys who have been plaguing James and Cress all morning!' Nick said grimly. 'James rang me. Hold on for a while.' They were not far from the M4, and Nick swung the car towards the slip road. Sure enough, the other car followed. But it was no match for the Porsche, or its driver.

Ducking and weaving, Nick drove along the motorway and then doubled back at the next intersection. He was off and on the way back long before the other car reached the intersection and roared straight on. 'I hope the editor turns down their petrol expenses!' he laughed as he turned off again at the Hungerford turning.

With Rene the head waiter's co-operation, their evening was undisturbed and relaxed. They drank champagne and held hands across the table, with eyes only for each other. Nick knew he was being reckless, but he cared very little at that moment for the consequences.

Returning to Hastings, though, he became more cautious, driving through a rarely used gate and up a fairly rough road to the back of the house. 'Good job this car is tough,' he grumbled. 'Bloody press men!'

The breeze was ruffling Sarah's skirt as she got out of the car, and laughing, she sidestepped as he reached out for her. She was like an eel, slipping out of his reach and running away across the lawn until her high heels caught in the grass and she fell. Scooping her up, Nick threw her on the garden seat, her skirt above her waist.

In the bushes, only ten feet away from them, the sweating reporter from the *Unicorn* watched in envious amazement. Having driven miles along the M4 before he realized he had been conned, he had doubled back and phoned every restaurant in the area listed in the *Good Food Guide* to no avail, before deciding to stake out the Hastings Court estate.

He cursed as he realized he had hit the jackpot. They had come out to cover the *Do or Dare* girl and James Willoughby, but he had an even better story happening right in front of him and he knew he couldn't even print it.

'The lovely Miss Campbell,' he told his envious colleague later, 'was being screwed by the man Maxie has been after for months, and, screaming deliriously, Miss Campbell was obviously loving every minute of it.'

He only gave up his vigil when Nick carried her into the house while she clung around his neck. 'Lucky, lucky bastard!' he muttered viciously to himself as he started the long walk back to his car, cursing the fact that he couldn't even substantiate his information with a photograph. Maxie would be furious.

CHAPTER 10

It was ten o'clock when Charles walked into the kitchen at Hastings and got the shock of his life. He realized he had been thoroughly out flanked as far as Sarah was concerned.

Nick and Sarah were locked in each other's arms, so absorbed in each other that they were completely unaware of his presence. Sarah, wearing Nick's dressing gown was perched on the edge of the table, her bare legs wrapped around him as he held her, his mouth pressed to her throat. He wore just a pair of faded Levis that served only to emphasize, to a furious Charles, the narrowness of his hips and the power of his shoulders against his own lesser build as he bent over her. Embarrassed and angry, he turned to leave, and only then did they become aware of him.

As casually as he could manage, Nick loosened his arms and lowered Sarah to the floor. For once in his life he was at a loss as to what to do. Sarah felt his unease and took the lead, going quickly to Charles and reaching up to press a kiss on his cheek before she took a cup and saucer from the dresser and poured him some coffee. Her skin smelled of Trumpers 'Curzon', a cologne that Nick had used for years, and he felt his fury compounded, instead of feeling the pleasure that her kisses usually gave him, however brief.

'Go and get dressed, Sarah,' Nick suggested, in a voice

147

that brooked no argument, and reached to pull a sweatshirt over his head. 'I wasn't expecting you back until much later,' he confessed to Charles as Sarah left them.

'Obviously!' Charles snapped. 'You forgot, I suppose, that you and I are supposed to be lunching with the Saunderses?'

Nick threw a hand to his head in dismay. 'Oh, hell, Charlie, yes, I did. I'm sorry!'

'Too busy with other things,' Charles shrugged, his tone bitter. 'Never mind, we'll take Sarah with us. Liz won't mind, and Rupert will be delighted, I'm sure.' He opened his ever-present briefcase. 'I brought the rushes. They were delivered to the office yesterday.'

'I'm not sure I should show you these,' Nick said as he picked up the can of film.

'I'd rather see her acting with James than wrapped around you,' Charles replied. 'Go on, go and tell her we're going out. If I can't see her one way, I'll see her another. I'm not giving up, Nick.'

Possession, though, thought Nick triumphantly as he went upstairs, was everything.

Sarah had made the bed and was sitting on it, half into her jeans, gazing disconsolately into space. 'Are you going to be working now Charles is back?' she asked sadly. 'Is he very upset?'

'He'll be all right. But I'd forgotten we're going to some friends for lunch. It's OK,' he added as her face fell. 'You're coming with us. You'll like Rupert and Liz, though if Rupert makes a pass at you I shall probably thump him! I tend to get a little possessive about the people I love.'

'Do you?' The hazel eyes had widened into pools and he was definitely drowning.

'Love you?' He paused, finally facing the inevitable. 'Yes, Sarah, I think I probably do. Not . . .' he hesitated, searching for the right words '. . . not in the same way as my family, I admit, but I love you enough to want this to go on.'

148

Sarah threw herself into his arms. 'Oh, I wanted you to say that. I couldn't bear not to see you again.'

'You will see me, I promise. Just as often as we can manage without hurting Charlie.'

'Poor Charles. Was he very angry with you?' she asked, remembering his anguished face.

Nick shrugged. 'He'll get over it – I hope. Now he knows, there's not a lot we can do about it. Still, we've been fighting over ladies since we were five! I seem to remember blacking his eye over Liz Saunders at one point. We were all of nine, I think!'

That made her giggle with delight. 'It's a good job he didn't come back last night when we were in the garden,' she commented. 'He really would have had a shock! Now, what do I wear?'

'Typical female! Leave your jeans on. Rupert breeds racehorses; he'll doubtless have you on one before the afternoon is over.' He kissed her slowly, and then released her so that she could finish dressing, approving her silk shirt, but fastening an extra button. 'Some things I want to keep to myself,' he said firmly. 'Rupert is enough of a lech as it is!'

Suddenly Sarah noticed the film can. 'Are those Friday's rushes?' she asked, and he nodded.

'Do you want to watch them? We have time.'

'I'm not sure *I want to* . . .' She hesitated. Sarah had always hated watching herself on screen.

'Try it,' he suggested. 'You might even like them.'

She doubted that very much, but she followed him down to the basement room Charles had turned into a cinema years before videos became popular. He still preferred to run a movie than watch a video, so the equipment was expensive and up to date. Consequently Nick used it every day to view his rushes.

Charles, his composure back together, joined Sarah as Nick disappeared to thread up the projector.

The first few shots were straightforward; she only

149

tensed when the third shot appeared. Nick had printed four of the twelve takes, and she was only too aware of Charles's intake of breath as the first one came up. She had to admit the lighting and soft, smoky atmosphere made it look good.

'That's beautiful!' he breathed as Sarah realized that on the second take the rearranged lighting had indeed made her clothes transparent. With a sinking heart she slumped further down in her chair and watched the afternoon's shoot float in front of her.

Charles was engrossed, Nick seemed to be coolly making notes, and she wriggled with embarrassment, watching herself and James making love with seemingly total abandon. Nick only seemed to react when he heard her scream in the last take, since it was a cry he had provoked often enough in the last couple of days, and he finally realized how close to real it had been that afternoon. Sarah felt the bile rising in her throat and she fled the room in panic. She only just made it to the cloakroom before she threw up.

Weak from the effort, she slumped over the basin, coughing and choking, wiping her streaming eyes, until she managed to go up to Nick's room and tidy herself up. It was there that Nick found her, hunched on the floor in his bathroom, her face hidden in the chair seat, after he and Charles had searched everywhere downstairs and all around the garden.

Anxiously, he gathered her up in his arms, cradling her against his shoulder as in vain he tried to convince her that the scene would look much better after editing. But Sarah was not to be persuaded.

'It makes me look like a total whore!' she protested. 'How could you do this to me, Nick? How could you? It's like *nothing* is left out!'

'Sarah, some of those shots are the most beautiful I've ever seen in a love scene. I'm not taking them out. They're far too good.'

'Even though I'm begging you?'

Nick hated seeing the distraught face raised to his, and he kissed her eyelids over eyes bright with tears that this time he knew were genuine. 'I love you, Sarah, very much,' he said. 'But the way I edit has nothing to do with that. You'll have to trust me as a professional director; it's that simple really,' he told her finally.

It was not simple at all in her book, but she had to be content with it. Nick was not going to be manipulated or charmed into changing the scene, and she was too much in love with him to quarrel with him any more.

The Saunderses did indeed seem delighted to meet her. They were jolly and welcoming, and Sarah felt she had known them for years in a few minutes. Both Charles and Nick had known them since childhood, and all three men were a similiar age, with Liz just a year or two younger.

Broad-hipped and rosy-cheeked, her dark hair held back in an Alice band, she had a booming laugh that rang out frequently, and a wicked tongue when she let fly. Rupert, almost as tall as Nick, had the chunky build and healthy outdoor glow of the farmer he was. His main occupation now was breeding horses, at which he was very successful, and naturally he and Charles soon fell into a horse-orientated conversation over pre-lunch drinks.

Their ten-year-old son Jonty sat gazing at Sarah with eyes full of hero-worship while they talked – until she noticed him. And then Nick watched with pleasure as she drew him out until he was chattering furiously, dragging her off to see his new puppies. There were always new animals to see in the Saunderses' house.

They all laughed when Jonty brought Sarah back and announced, 'I'm going to marry Sarah when I grow up!'

'Join the queue!' said the three men in unison.

'Nick is outrageous!' declared Liz as Charles's Range Rover disappeared down the drive some hours later. 'He could barely keep his hands off that child for five minutes.

I don't know why Diana lets him get away with it.'

'If Diana punts off with Mummy and Daddy for two months at a time she only has herself to blame,' said Rupert. 'You know as well as I do that Diana only wants Nick around for his money these days. And you can't blame Nick for fancying Sarah Campbell! I'd have a crack at her myself given half a chance!'

'If you did you would have nothing left to fancy her with,' Liz responded quickly. 'Charlie didn't like it either. She must be something to have both of them panting after her.'

Rupert sighed. 'Sounds like the Natasha saga all over again.'

'I certainly hope not,' Liz said grimly. 'I wouldn't want to live through that again. Charlie had a heart attack over that woman. Another one would really finish him!'

'Natasha was unstable and delicate, not to mention being a total bitch!' Rupert pointed out. 'And Sarah Campbell is certainly none of those. She rides like a dream as well. I'm afraid I only remember the rows those two had over Natasha.'

'Do you remember how she set fire to her dress at the Hunt Ball once, when she'd had a row with Nick?'

'Yep, and the callous bastard threw her in the lily pond and told Charles to get her out,' Rupert reminded her.

'I suppose Nick was a bit of a swine in those days,' Liz sighed.

'He still is at times,' Rupert said. 'But I must admit he was a damn sight more relaxed today than I've known him be in a long time.'

'I wonder how long it will take Diana to catch on to this one?'

'If he's as indiscreet everywhere else as he was here, not long.' Rupert grinned. 'And there are enough people around that he's been foul to over the years to make sure she does find out.'

* * *

152

But Nick Grey was a seasoned veteran at the secrecy game. In the past his few indiscretions had mostly gone undiscovered, and, relaxed as he had been with the Saunderses, he was determined to protect Sarah from gossip and the Press.

At work, he was his usual self, critical and arrogant as ever, pushing her to the limit in the ever more difficult scenes they were doing. Occasionally she yelled back at him, when he really tried her patience, but most of the time she shrugged it off. Rarely during the day did he touch her, or spend more than a few minutes in conversation with her in front of the crew, though she soon realized that he hated to see her joking and larking about with them and the other actors.

She was quickly getting used to long drives in the Porsche, and the luxury of his expensive way of life. Nick's lifestyle was totally different from hers and he lived well – to the limit of his income most of the time. Sarah was soon rushing out to buy new clothes to keep up with it all, finally enjoying the pleasures of clothes-buying, and always trying to find new ways of doing her hair to disguise her appearance when they were out in public.

Her whole life had changed. It revolved completely around Nick and his demands on her time and energies.

Once away from the set, and the eyes of the unit, Nick was relaxed and loving, wanting to show his feelings in a way that was totally new to him. Though previously inexperienced where sex was concerned, Sarah had quickly blossomed, now as eager to make love as he was, and ready to learn and experiment, confident of her ability to please him. Drawing her out was a complete pleasure to Nick. He found himself longing for the weekends, when she would belong to him and not be shared with her devoted crew.

But it was the crew who rose to her defence when the *Unicorn* printed a piece of sly innuendo after a week or so of skirmishing with their reporters.

The *Unicorn* had finally been given the photographs Nick had taken on set in the morning scenes of James and Sarah, carefully chosen to reveal very little, but Max Moreton had made the most of it in almost a full-page piece, hinting at Sarah's lust for her co-star, despite his new girlfriend, and the commenting on the reality of their love scenes. Sarah and James laughed at that, but it was the last paragraph that really shook Sarah.

For once discretion got the better of her, and she flew to Nick almost in hysterics.

'Look at that! They can't print that, can they?'

Nick read with growing fury.

Rumours of ill feeling and arguments abound on the set of Home Leave however, between Nick Grey and his new young protegee. They apparently spend much of their time fighting furiously, and it has been whispered that the beautiful Miss Campbell incensed him so much at one point that he played macho-man and put her across his knee and gave her a sound spanking! Further developments are awaited eagerly!

'The whole thing makes me sound so awful,' wailed Sarah. 'And it's not even true. Okay, Nick shouted at me and I was upset, but as for putting me over his knee . . . what *can* we do?'

Alex was appalled. 'Leave it to us!' he declared firmly, and within an hour a letter signed by the entire crew, supporting and defending Sarah, was faxed to the *Unicorn*. The gesture touched Sarah deeply, especially as she hadn't spent so much time with them lately, so wrapped up had she been in Nick.

'I just hope they don't go too far the other way now,' Nick said in trepidation, when the *Unicorn* printed the letter in full. 'We'll have to be bloody careful in Chagford.' They had spent several weekends in a cottage owned by a friend of his on Dartmoor.

'We never get out of bed in Devon,' Sarah pointed out, laughing. 'But maybe we'd better not go out to eat.'

'I said be careful, not starve to death!' Eating out was a pleasure to Nick, even after many years of doing so and he still delighted in finding new restaurants. Chagford was particularly well served by several of his favourites.

Sarah loved the tiny cottage, though they were both in permanent danger of cracking their heads on the low doorways.

The Friday night drive to Dartmoor quickly became an integral part of her life, even if she and Nick did differ violently in the choice of cassettes in the car stereo. Rare steak in the pub was a weekly ritual on their arrival, before they retired to the huge brass bed in the tiny dormer-windowed bedroom. On Saturday mornings Sarah was trusted enough to take the Porsche into Chagford to shop while Nick worked on a new script.

'Definitely a measure of my love,' he'd joked, the first time he'd let her take it. 'But just try denting it, and our last row will be a conversation in comparison! A spanking will be nothing!'

'That would really give the *Unicorn* something to print!' Sarah giggled. She had bought a tapestry to occupy herself while Nick worked, but somehow very little of it got done. By the time they had eaten lunch they were always both ready to return to their bed for the afternoon, only rising to go out and eat.

It was precious time. Lying in each other's arms, making love when the mood took them, they talked for hours, probing deep into each other's memories and thoughts. Nick smiled at the revelations of the little Guildford schoolgirl, secure with her ponies and ballet classes, and Sarah learnt a great deal about Nick's lonely childhood, about the solitary Army child travelling between school and the bases all over the world where his father had commanded during his career.

Nick found he was telling her things he had never

spoken of before, much to his own surprise, and bringing to light the close relationship between him and Charles.

The only person he never talked about was the mysterious Natasha. Sarah was wild with curiosity about the beautiful girl in the portrait, but however often she tried to bring the subject up, Nick skilfully avoided it.

It was her turn to surprise *him* one Sunday morning, when she announced that she was going to early-morning communion. 'It's the anniversary of my parents' death,' she told him. 'I make a point of going then.'

Nick took one look at her unhappy face and elected to go with her. Being married to a Catholic, he rarely went to an Anglican service nowadays.

She was astonished to find he knew the words of the service by heart. He hadn't seemed to her to be a church-going person.

'You forget – Canterbury Cathedral was my school chapel,' he reminded her as they walked back to the cottage afterwards. 'I'd forgotten how nice it is to go to church.'

'I felt a little guilty kneeling at the altar with you,' she confessed.

Nick laughed. 'Adultery being blessed!'

'I certainly hope the vicar didn't know who you were,' Sarah commented.

'Does it bother you very much? My being married?' He sounded worried suddenly.

'Not as much as it should,' Sarah admitted. 'But my mother would have been furious with me and Daddy would have taken *you* apart!'

'I'd better keep away from your big brother, then,' he smiled. 'In case he feels the same way.'

'I think George would like you nearly as much as I do. At least I hope he would.'

Nick suddenly realized that it mattered to her that her brother approved; he knew how much Sarah relied on the only father figure she had left.

'For the moment, my darling, I think it's better that your brother doesn't know about us.'

'Rather like your wife?'

'Especially like my wife!' Nick decided the time had come to tell Sarah his news. 'Look, I've asked Diana to bring Charlotte over to France for the first two weeks we're out there while you have two weeks off. It seemed the safest option. I actually prefer that you two don't meet again.'

Sarah thought of the cool, dark-haired lady she had met briefly. '*I'd* prefer not to meet her again too,' she said slowly. 'Though I loved Charlotte.'

'Charlotte thinks you're snaring James away from her.' Nick grinned. 'She'll think he's really fickle when she finds out about Cress.'

'He's certainly not fickle about Cress, that's for sure.'

'I'm glad,' Nick said softly. 'Cress deserves to be happy. She's had a bad time with men, generally.'

'Like you, for instance?'

'How on earth did you find that out? Not from Cress, I'll bet!'

'No, Ronnie – who else?'

'I might have known! Embroidered like crazy as well, if I know Ronnie!' Nick raised his eyes to heaven. 'I've never slept with Cress, Sarah, I can assure you, but I've always been very fond of her. Do you mind?'

'Good gracious no – why should I? Anyway, I suppose I'll be an ex sooner or later, when Diana finds out.'

'If we're careful, not for a long time, I hope.' His face was serious. 'You *will* get tired of me eventually, Sarah. I'm far too old for you.'

'Not now, Nick. I don't want to think about it!' They had reached the cottage and she threw her arms around him, hugging him tightly to her. 'I don't want to talk about your wife or your age.'

'As long as you know I'm not going to leave her,' Nick said slowly, painfully aware that by stating the fact he could lose Sarah there and then. But Sarah clung round his neck, her face buried in his shoulder.

'I know, I know,' she murmured. 'It doesn't make it any easier, but I'll accept anything to stay with you.'

She found it incredibly hard to understand how he could be so loyal to his wife that he wouldn't leave her, and yet still profess to love *her* at the same time, but it was not a question she dared put to him. She simply had to believe that he could. Her other problem was how to break it to Peter that it was all between them over. He was due back from Queensland that week, and she dreaded it.

'Don't tell him for a while,' Nick suggested when she voiced her fears. 'You have enough excuses to be too busy to see him for a bit.'

'No, that's not kind,' she reasoned. 'I have to tell him, it's only fair.'

'Well, don't tell him it's over because of me,' he said. 'Tell him that, and the Press will soon know.'

'Peter's not like that.'

'It depends on how much he loves you,' Nick said wisely.

'I'll wait until I'm back in London,' she decided. 'Then I'll *have* to tell him. Unlike you, Nick Grey, I find one lover quite enough to cope with!'

CHAPTER 11

'Are we keeping you up Sarah?' James enquired on the last day of shooting at Hastings. 'You'll never make it through the party at this rate.' She looked and felt shattered. 'What *does* Nick have that I haven't?'

'Shut up, James,' she snapped. 'I'm tired, that's all!'

'Sorry, sweetheart. Look, I've got something to tell you – or rather Cress has.'

'Don't tell me she's pregnant!' Sarah said, winding him up.

'Not yet!' he laughed. 'But she's moving in with me as soon as we get back from France.'

Laughing with delight, Sarah hugged him. 'I'm so pleased for you both. Nick said Cress deserved to be happy. You'd better look after her.'

'Don't worry, I will. I mean it this time. Cress is the best thing that's happened to me in a long time.'

Nick interrupted them. 'I know we have an easy day but we do have to work at some point,' he said, and hauled them onto the set.

At lunchtime Sarah intrigued Nick by disappearing with Sir John and then coming back giggling with Cress and John like conspirators. John was old enough to know better, he thought, annoyed. Sarah smiled her secret smile at his frown, making him ache for her all over again, even after making love to her most of the night and early that morning – swimming had been forgotten.

Charles arrived back to watch the last few shots of the afternoon, joining in the laughter and inevitable practical jokes that went on, then taking Sarah aside as she finished the last scene. 'Would you do something for me, Sarah?' he asked.

She looked nervously at him. She and Nick had heard him leave that morning, holding their breath in case he saw them. But it was something quite different.

'Would you consider visiting a child at the local hospital when you've changed? Apparently it's quite urgent – she's not very well.' He searched her face for reaction. 'Her mother is a friend of mine and Naomi has been a fan of yours for a long time.'

'Of course I will, Charles.' She smiled with relief. 'Just make sure Nick doesn't need me any more, and I'll get changed.'

'That's OK, I checked. Thank you, Sarah, I'll pick you up at the hotel in . . . half an hour?'

The child, it turned out, was dying of leukaemia. She was seven years old, sweet-faced and serene. Fighting her tears, Sarah spent half an hour telling her about the programme, and Peter, before walking round the rest of the ward full of children – some just as sick as Naomi, others cheerful and full of chatter. Despite the gratitude of the nursing staff, she was drained by the time they got back to Charles's car.

'We'll stop off for a drink,' Charles suggested, patting her shoulder awkwardly, worried by her stricken face. 'I'm sorry, Sarah, I didn't realize quite how ill she was.'

Sarah was doing her best not to cry. 'I felt so helpless, Charlie. She's so little.'

'You did what you could, and that's the important thing,' he comforted.

'I just wish I could do a little more to help,' she replied sadly.

'You probably did more than any treatment could.

160

Being a famous face can be a problem, Sarah, I know, especially in your situation. But your time with someone like Naomi is a gift you can give. It's so important to her, and it probably stops you getting too wrapped up in your own importance.'

'Oh, Charlie, do you think I am?' She was horrified.

'No, not yet.' Charles pulled into the pub yard. 'But you could be if you get too insulated from real life, which is very easy to do in this business, once the work takes over.'

Sarah thought about it, and was shocked to realize he was right. It was months since she had had to think for herself. Her life had become ruled by Oscar and George, and now Nick. Apart from a few swift shopping trips, she had hardly mixed with people outside the crew since the middle of May.

Charles brought her brandy out to the garden. The late afternoon sun was still hot, and she relaxed, lifting her face to it. 'I feel as if I'm playing hookey.' She smiled. 'Aren't you drinking, Charles?'

'I don't really,' he admitted, playing with the glass of tonic water. 'I'm driving anyway, but I had a heart attack years ago, and was told I should stop drinking so I did. I don't really miss it, I must admit, though Nick and I used to really drink ourselves stupid at college.'

'I can't imagine not drinking at all,' Sarah confessed.

'You'd be surprised how easy it is to give up if your life depends on it,' he commented drily.

'Does it still?'

'No, not now. I've had the all-clear for years – I'm even allowed to fly the helicopter – but I'm still careful.'

'I guess you would be if you'd had a heart attack,' she said, and smiled. 'What caused it?'

Charles laughed. 'I think you could call it a very unsuitable marriage.'

'To Natasha?' she queried, suddenly realizing that here was her chance.

'Yes,' he said, surprised. 'Have you seen her portrait in

161

the library?' She nodded. 'She was so beautiful,' he added sadly, 'and so very sick.'

Sarah took the plunge. She was so curious. 'What was wrong with her?'

'She was a drug addict, Sarah, long before I married her, and I didn't know till I had. I think Nick did, but I certainly didn't.'

'What did Nick have to do with her, then?' She wasn't sure she wanted to know, but it was the one thing Nick wouldn't tell her.

'Nick was in love with her,' Charles said bitterly. 'All the way through Oxford they were crazy about each other, but, unfortunately for Nick, Tasha changed her mind when I inherited my title and the estate at a time when Nick had very little money. And I married her before she changed her mind.'

'So she married you for your money? That doesn't seem very fair,' she commented.

'It wasn't,' he admitted. 'And we both suffered for it. Nick hated me for it for ages, and I had a wife I couldn't cope with. He married Diana a few months afterwards. I'm not sure he can cope with her either. She's so much brighter than he is.'

'That, if you don't mind me saying so, sounds quite bitchy, Charles.'

'No, it's quite true. Diana is a genius in her field, and her IQ is in the stratosphere somewhere,' Charles insisted. 'Nick has an Oxford degree, certainly, but he was lucky to scrape a second, he spent so much time there directing plays or with Tasha. But Diana's in a different category altogether. She has a superb brain and is very involved in her job, even if she is only part-time.'

'But she doesn't need to work, does she?' Sarah protested. 'Nick is enormously wealthy.'

'True – far more than me – but she's far too bright to stay at home and pander to Nick. I don't particularly like Diana, but I do sympathize with her on that score. She'd go crazy. It was just a shame that Nick got himself tangled up with her, frankly. We all warned him against it, but he took no notice. He was simply on the rebound from Tasha.'

Suddenly Sarah felt quite sad for Nick, but she felt pleased at Charles's confidences. It gave her some reason for Nick's devotion to *her* – at least she was very different from Diana.

Charles hated the conversation turning to Nick, particularly when he'd ended up defending him, best friend or not. 'She has a lot to put up with, though, where Nick is concerned, Sarah, don't ever forget that. And she does still care for him.'

'I know, Charles, don't worry. Nick has made that perfectly clear,' Sarah snapped at him, swallowing the brandy that she didn't really want.

'I'm sorry. I don't want to pick on Nick. I know how you feel about him,' Charles said placatingly, surprised at Nick's honesty with her.

'I can't help it. I do love him, even if you don't approve.'

'No, I don't. I think Nick is behaving very badly over you. But then I'm old-fashioned enough to believe you should be able to offer a lady something before you approach her.'

'Nick offered me something I couldn't refuse at the end of the day,' Sarah said firmly. 'And I wanted it. I'm not a child, Charles, I'm sorry.'

'A child is the last thing I would accuse you of being.' Charles sighed, smiling at her. 'Look, what are you doing on your two weeks off?'

Sarah shrugged, and sensed his discomfort. 'Not a lot. Some *Story-Times* for Paddy, a couple of game shows and an audition for Nick for a perfume commercial. Why?'

'How would you like to come to New York for a couple of days, week after next?' She thought for a few seconds, working out her timetable. 'It's OK,' he added, 'I have a suite at the Plaza, so you can have a room of your own. I'm

163

not that keen on upsetting Nick. I just need an escort for a very grand party.'

'It sounds nice,' she confessed. 'If Nick doesn't mind, and I can find a dress for this very grand party.'

'No problem. Just go and order one from your friend Catherine and send the bill to my office,' he said. 'I'd love to take you, Sarah.'

'I'll pay for my own dress, Charles Hastings,' she told him proudly.

'No. If I want to pay for it, it's my privilege, and you'll need one for the première anyway.' Charles was firm. 'Do I take it you'll come?' He knew she wanted to ask Nick first. 'Just remember, Sarah, you are free to do whatever you want to do. It's Nick who's trapped.'

'OK, Charles, I'll come. I may need to get away from London for a few days!' Her thoughts had suddenly turned to Peter. If he turned difficult – and Sarah was aware that he might – his temper could be quite frightening sometimes. New York was about as far away from him as she could get.

'That's great!' He leant across the table and kissed her cheek. 'I'll enjoy showing you off, Sarah,' he said, with an air of triumph. 'Would you like another drink?'

She shook her head. 'I'm not used to drinking brandy. Perhaps we should go? I need to get ready for the party.'

Reluctantly he drove her back to the hotel. 'I'll see you later. Save a dance for me?'

'Oh, more than one,' she promised, and smiled as he kissed the palms of her hands. It seemed now, a totally sensuous gesture. Maybe New York would be fun, she thought, as she went upstairs. She could do some shopping if nothing else.

With a wicked grin, she chose a dress from her wardrobe that Nick hadn't seen. If he was as determined as he had said to stay away from her all evening for form's sake, she knew this dress would break his resolve.

Bathed, and fragrant with Chanel, she slid into the

short, slim, white strapless dress just as Ronnie popped his head round the door to do her hair. 'Well, well! And who are we out to snare tonight, then?' he asked as he set to work.

'Wait and see,' Sarah teased. 'Just make it look good, please, Ronnie.' He did. She twirled in front of the mirror, knowing she looked sensational.

'You'll kill 'em,' Ronnie grinned. 'As you always do. Wait till the French get an eyeful of you!'

'I'm not interested in the French,' Sarah told him. 'Come on, Ronnie, escort me. Let your principles go hang!'

'*Madame*, I'd be proud to!'

'Shouldn't that be *mademoiselle*?'

'I thought that only applied to virgins!'

They were late down into the room at the hotel that Nick, Charles and Chris had hired for the end of shoot party. Most of the cast and crew and their assorted wives and partners were already there. It was quite amusing for Ronnie and Sarah to match newly arrived wives with their husbands – Ronnie with incredibly bitchy remarks about them all, as usual.

James and Cress bore down on them, giggling with their pleasure in each other. It didn't stop James from kissing Sarah, though, skimming his fingers over her cleavage. 'I'm allowed,' he told her, grinning. 'I've been in there before – and that is some dress, lady!'

'I'm going to kill him!' Cress threatened, laughing.

'Oh, don't, Cress!' Sarah said, 'he's not grown up enough for me.'

'In that case, dance with me, Sarah.' Sir John took her arm and led her to the dance floor. 'My lady wife is allowing me some practice before our cabaret.'

Arriving a few minutes later with Charles, Nick watched her dancing with John and cursed. He knew the sleek white dress was to wind him up. Resolutely turning his back on the dance floor, he concentrated on

165

doing the rounds of his crew, greeting the wives, remembering names, ordering drinks, being the host. Until he saw Sarah dancing with Ben, laughing, writhing to the music in front of him, teasing and moving as only a trained dancer could.

Excusing himself, he crossed the floor to them as the music came to a pause and caught Sarah as she spun to a halt. 'Pardon me, Ben, I'd like to dance with Sarah.' He was almost curt as he took Sarah from Ben's grasp.

Sarah laughed, and settled easily into his arms as the band changed to a slower number. 'I knew you wouldn't last long!' she challenged, her eyes sparkling. She knew she had won this round. To the astonishment of everyone around them, Nick kissed her. They were oblivious of everyone else for a moment, and in that split second the whole unit knew the gossip was true. No one had been really sure until that moment, so careful had he been, and now he had blown it, with one incautious gesture.

'To hell with it!' he exclaimed when he realized what he'd done. 'I suppose it's safe enough amongst this lot. They were bound to find out sooner or later.'

'I'll dance with Charlie in a minute,' she promised, 'that'll fix them. Charlie won't know what's hit him!'

'Don't overdo it,' he warned, frowning. 'Especially now he's taking you to New York.'

'Do you mind about that?' she asked sweetly. 'Because I won't go if you don't want me to.'

'No, you go. Charlie knows I'd throttle him if he tried to lure you away from me,' Nick assured her, with more confidence than he felt. 'You can always do some interviews while you're there.'

'Don't you ever stop thinking about work?'

'Long enough to tire you out, you little baggage! Go on, then, go and flirt with Charles for a few minutes!'

He left the unit in no doubt as to his feelings as the evening progressed. He was in such a relaxed mood that he laughed heartily at James's wicked take-off of his directorial style, and at the end of the song and dance act that Sarah and Sir John put on, he acquiesced when the crew shouted for her to do the cartwheels she was well known for on the TV programme. Amused that she looked to him for permission, he gave a nod of agreement before she sprang around the floor with a series of perfect cartwheels, finishing with the back-flip that she had always been good at.

'Christ!' said James quietly to Nick. 'If she does that every night I'm surprised you're still standing!'

'And you're very lucky to be!' Nick retorted. 'I think I must be mellowing with age or something.'

'More likely something wearing you out!' James told him, grinning. 'You look like a cat that has the cream every time she comes near you!'

Sarah's hair had tumbled out of its swept up style, and it fell loose as he loved to see it. His face had indeed softened as she approached them, smiling at him.

'Well done, sweetheart.' With his arms full of Sarah, he turned back to James. 'I hear some sort of congratulations are in order?'

'Some sort,' James agreed.

'In that case, if you're not busy, come out with us tomorrow evening? I'll get some tickets for the National.'

'On a Saturday?' James was impressed.

'I have my sources, and anyway, I want Sarah to meet Barry Harper.'

'Goodness, if that's the result of sleeping with you, when is it my turn?' James ducked Nick's good-natured thump. 'We'd love to come. I'll go and tell her ladyship.'

Sarah smiled at his departing back. 'Why do I need to meet Barry Harper?'

'Because he's doing *Romeo and Juliet* next season. I had a drink with him when I went up to town last week. I told you all you needed were contacts.'

'Oh, Nick! He really is the best at the National!'

'You have to impress him first!' he reminded her, and

hugged her. 'Which I'm sure you will. Now, as I went to the expense of booking a room here tonight, shall we creep out soon?'

'What a waste of money,' she pointed out.

'I *was* protecting your reputation – until you tempted me into blowing it! Go and say your farewells, my darling, because I need you very badly.'

Carefully Sarah went round to say goodbye to the actors who were finishing. Only she, James and Tony were going to France with the crew. The rest of the cast would be new, supplemented by French extras. She was sad to see the end of the shoot. After all her worries at the start, the crew and cast were like old friends now. France would be like starting again.

'No tears?' Nick asked, surprised, as they went upstairs.

'No, not tonight, I'll see them again at the première.' She was philosophical, and all she really wanted at that moment was Nick and his arms around her.

CHAPTER 12

In some ways it was a relief to be home. Out of breath from lugging two suitcases from the car, Sarah opened the door to the flat to find it immaculate and smelling of polish. George and Maggie had obviously been to the theatre lately. They often used her spare room to save driving back to Guildford late at night, and Maggie in return tidied up from time to time, and filled her freezer.

Sarah pushed a load of washing into the machine, and opened a mountain of mail. George had taken the bills to pay them, as he usually did.

When Nick rang to confirm their theatre booking, she decided everyone should have an early supper at the flat, since they were all tired and as Maggie had left a large lasagne in the fridge – though she had to dash out shopping for everything else.

It was after four when she got back to the flat, in a mad panic to make a salad and one of the few desserts she could produce without resorting to the phone for advice from Maggie. Table laid and food ready, she leapt into the bath. When the doorbell rang at six o'clock, she swore. They were early – too early. Her hair was very damp, and she was still fastening her denim dress as she went to answer it. She stepped back in horror.

It was Peter. Bronzed and cheerful, delighted to see her – and she had quite forgotten to call him. She was reluctant even to kiss him.

'What's the matter?' he asked, walking in. 'You look as if you've seen a ghost – aren't you pleased to see me? It's been almost two months.' Then he took in the table, the chic dress and tumbling hair, which was a style new to him, and he looked at her enquiringly.

There was no easy way to do it. Sarah knew the others would be there any minute, so she took the plunge, blurting out that it was all over between them, surprising herself by realizing just how little he had meant to her, and hoping he would go.

For a moment Peter stared at her, uncomprehending, then in a blaze of anger he slapped her hard across her face, taking her totally unawares. 'You disgusting little whore!' he roared at her, and slapped her again. 'You spent half your time with me trying not to go to bed with me because you didn't like it, yet the minute my back is turned you ditch me for someone else and suddenly it's wonderful! How could you, Sarah? Did I mean so little to you?'

Sarah threw herself into a ball on the sofa, warding off the blow's he was raining on her with her arms protecting her face.

'Who is he?' Peter demanded, shaking her in a blind fury. She had never seen him in such a state, and she was petrified. How on earth could he have read so much into so little? she thought in desperation.

'I'm not telling you,' she sobbed. 'Leave me alone, Peter, for God's sake!'

'Leave you alone! He hasn't, has he?' Peter ripped at her dress. 'Christ! You haven't even got a bra on! Perhaps now you won't be so prudish with me.'

She fought him off with all her strength, until he grabbed her hair, forcing her head back, making her scream with pain. 'Come on, Sarah, show me how much you've learnt from this wonderful lover of yours.'

His mouth was brutally hard on hers as his hands pulled at the fastening of her dress again, wrenching it off her as he pushed her to the floor. Struggling and twisting, she sobbed with panic as his assault grew more frightening. She was terrified now that he really would kill her, as his blows rained ceaselessly down on her.

Her screams were audible when Nick and James reached the door at the same moment. 'Oh, my God!' James threw himself at the door, which yielded not one iota.

'I've got a key,' Cress cried, and scrabbled in her bag to hand it to Nick. 'Oh, quickly, Nick!'

Nick unlocked the door and hurled himself across the living room, his fist making contact with the side of Peter's head with a satisfying thud. He wrenched him away from Sarah's body, his language ripe as he then threw him across the room. It was only too apparent who the new man in Sarah's life was. 'Nick, oh, Nick!' was all she could manage, hysterical by that point.

'It's OK, darling, I'm here. You're safe, I promise.' He was cradling her in his arms as James dragged Peter away from them, and the realization dawned on Peter as he watched Nick and Sarah.

'Call the police!' Cress demanded as Nick bent over Sarah.

'No!' James said. 'No, we can't. It'll create all kinds of problems!' Peter was by now white-faced and shaking with remorse, and James grabbed at him again and pushed him towards the door. 'Get out!' he ordered. 'While you still have the means to walk! And don't come near Sarah again, or we *will* call the police.'

Peter stared at Nick for a moment as James hustled him to the door.

'I might have known it was him!' he said dully, and then in his panic at what he had done he shouted. 'You can't screw your way to the top, Sarah, and *he's* old enough to be your father!'

'Get out!' Nick's voice had an icy quality that said he was having great difficulty in controlling his temper. He knew that if he didn't, Peter would not still be standing there. 'Now!'

'You're welcome to her,' Peter snapped. 'You obviously had more luck with the frigid little bitch than I had!' he added as James marched him out of the door.

'I'll make sure he leaves,' James said, and shut the door behind them. Frantic, Nick lifted the sobbing, almost naked girl up, horrified at the red marks and bruises Peter had left on her skin.

'Get some ice, Cress,' he ordered. 'Quickly, or she'll really bruise. It's all right, darling, it's going to be all right,' he soothed, and Cress wrapped the ice that Sarah had put out for drinks in a napkin and handed it to Nick, who touched carefully to her bruised face. He knelt on the floor, his hands gentle, his voice soft as he soothed her, checking all the time for damage to her body. 'You don't appear to have broken anything,' he said, relieved. 'It's just bruising as far as I can tell. Oh, darling, I wish I'd got here earlier.'

'It's not your fault,' Sarah whispered. 'And don't worry, he won't come back.'

'Nevertheless you can't stay here alone next week,' he said, worried, as he lifted her onto the sofa.

Sarah clung to him as Cress went to pour her a drink. 'I'll be fine. I'll get someone to come and stay with me if I get nervous. Or I'll go down and stay with George. But I'm glad you're here now, Nick.' Carefully Nick held the glass of whisky for her and made her drink some, oblivious of Cress for a moment as he kissed her very gently.

'I'll do anything to make sure you're safe,' he assured her, and Cress drew back, feeling as if she was intruding.

'I'll see to supper,' she said, and backed away into the kitchen, embarrassed but reassured, somehow, that Nick really did care for Sarah – enough to show his feelings publicly, in a way she had never seen him do before.

Practical as ever, Cress took over serving the meal as Nick helped Sarah to change clothes into a pair of trousers

172

and a long-sleeved shirt, then redid her make-up to cover the worst of the marks. The ice pack seemed to have worked, and Sarah insisted they still went to the theatre. 'I'd rather be out,' she said firmly.

Despite everything, they enjoyed the evening, merrily picking the production to pieces from three different angles before they went off to the bar at the end to meet Barry Harper. If Sarah was a little more subdued than normal, it only showed to Nick, who never took his eyes from her for a second, or his hand from hers.

When James dropped them off at her flat she was patently nervous about going in, even with Nick's protective arm around her, and once they were in bed she gave way to shaking sobs. For the first time they slept without making love, since her body was aching and sore.

Nick found some painkillers for her and held her gently, reassuring her as best he could, knowing that if Peter went public on them, life would be very difficult. He was not happy about Charles taking her to New York, but in the circumstances he knew it had to be the best solution.

After being together every day, being apart from Nick was agony. Sarah suffered dreadfully from withdrawal symptoms during her few days in New York with Charles. Even if the City itself enthralled her, the nights were lonely and empty.

It was a huge relief to be able to phone him when Oscar called her in New York to tell her she had the commercial Nick had sent her to be auditioned for. At least it was a valid excuse to call him, and to her relief he seemed delighted to speak to her. The agency had acquiesced to his demands, and they often didn't.

'We'll get a few days in Portugal out of it anyway,' he told her. 'Even if half the agency come with us, and I've booked us a few days after we finish here. There's a lovely hotel near Monte Carlo. We'll go straight down there after the shoot finishes. You'll love it, and I can introduce you to Seth Waterston – he'll be at his villa in Cap Ferrat.'

'You mean you can't let Charlie get away with taking me to New York!' she teased, thrilled at the idea of a holiday alone with him.

'Something like that!' He laughed. 'This could prove ruinous for us both!' Then his tone changed. Diana had obviously come in, for he became almost brusque.

For once, Nick found life with Diana really difficult. Normally, after three months away, he would have been happy to see her, but it took days to adjust to her again as it never had before. Though they were far from close, they were friends, and they understood each other incredibly well, but their first night together was disastrous, and they ended up at the far sides of the bed, not speaking.

Diana found him cold and preoccupied, even more than was usual at the end of a long shoot. She tried to make allowances, but the more patient she was, the more annoyed with her he became. Finally they had a cataclysmic row about nothing in particular, until Nick's conscience got the better of him and he made an enormous and finally successful effort to repair the damage. He could never bear to hear Diana cry, and, knowing it, she employed her tears to great effect.

Late into the night he tossed around the bed and struggled wildly with his chaotic feelings. Oh, God! he thought to himself in despair, as dawn finally began to filter through the room. What on earth am I going to do?

CHAPTER 13

Sarah and Charles got back into London from New York at around seven in the evening, leaving Sarah with very little time to repack her suitcases for France, and to respond to her mail. A note from Peter was thrown in the bin after a quick scan. That was well and truly over, she told herself, still, at least he was apologizing, which was something. A note from Oscar quickly had her on the phone to him in excitement.

'Great news!' Oscar exclaimed. 'I've got several offers for you, and that perfume commercial is going to be real big bucks with the repeats. I'll bike over some scripts to you, but I must have some answers quickly. You're in demand Miss Campbell! I think you'll be working every day till Christmas!'

'I'll read them in the car tomorrow on the way to Cambrai and ring you then,' she promised.

'The other thing is,' Oscar added, 'I had a call from the National. Barry Harper is asking about you.'

'So quickly! He's doing *Romeo and Juliet*. I met him a couple of weeks ago.'

'So I hear. Well, he's interested – though I'm not so sure it's a good idea to commit yourself to that just now.'

'Oscar, whatever else I do, I want to do Juliet. Don't you dare turn it down!' Sarah stormed at him. 'I don't care if the whole of Hollywood rings!'

175

'Lousy money,' he moaned. 'And what's with this ordering me around suddenly?'

'To hell with your commission. I'd do it for nothing and don't you forget it!'

'I'll never get my swimming pool paid for at this rate,' complained Oscar, laughing. 'OK Miss Actress, culture will win.'

'Cheer up, Oscar, Nick's taking me to see Seth Waterston in a couple of week's time.'

'Well, bully for Nicholas. He does a lot of work with Seth.'

'I promise to charm the pants off him, then. Goodnight, Oscar.' She had hoped that Nick would ring her, but instead Cress rang from London.

'Nick is babysitting James,' she laughed. 'I came over to get some extra costumes, and I'm coming back with you in the morning.' So much for reading scripts in the car, thought Sarah happily, and, finally finding a letter from Nick in the pile, she went off to bed hugging it to her.

She was thrilled to see Cress again, and fell back into the gossip of the film as the Mercedes sped towards Dover and the hoverport. 'Nick's been really dreadful!' Cress confided. 'But you should hear him, Sarah. He yells in three languages: English to us, French to the extras and German to the new operator – and he swears in all of them. I'd forgotten how good his languages were.'

'What happened to Derek?'

'He fell off the crane the second day out and broke his leg.' Cress grinned. 'He'd got very pissed the night before. Lenny got someone in Paris to fill in and he turned out to speak French and German but very little English.'

'How was Diana?' Sarah asked, curiously.

'Hardly saw her,' Cress admitted. 'They were in a different hotel to us. Nick moved over to stay at ours on Thursday, after she went back. We're scattered all over the place, but there's only you and Nick and James and I at the Château Honoré, and it's lovely!'

With her usual forethought and efficiency, Cress had provided a picnic meal so that they didn't need to stop at a restaurant to eat. 'Takes too long to lunch in France,' she declared. 'And I, for one, am anxious to get back.'

'I wonder why?' Sarah teased, but she too was anxious to get to Cambrai. 'I think that means get your foot down, Bill,' she added to their driver.

He took them at their word and certainly moved faster after lunch. By four o'clock they were a few minutes from the hotel, and Cress phoned ahead to let them know, learning into the back to wake Sarah as she did so. Jet-lag had caught up with her. She was sound sleep with the scripts unread in her lap, knocked out by the heat.

Laughing and stretching, the two girls climbed out of the car as Nick, wearing shorts, came down the steps to great them. With a shriek of joy, Sarah threw herself at him, and Nick swooped her up with a kiss that, as Cress commented afterwards to James, made her almost need oxygen by the end of it. Their pleasure at being reunited was obvious, even to the cynical Bill, who was privy to a great many of Nick's secrets.

'I'll take these, Bill.' Nick picked up Sarah's bags. 'You look after Cressida.'

'Where's James?' Cress demanded as they went into the stone-floored hallway.

'Topping up his tan by the pool, I think.' Nick grinned. 'And being chatted up, no doubt!'

'What changes?' Cress sighed.

'I'll have you know, madam, that even with extreme provocation he stayed firmly on the straight and narrow last night – away from some very pretty ladies. Both Alex and I will back him on that! We all had hangovers to prove it this morning!'

'Well, I'd better go and give praise where it's due, then.' Cress hugged them. 'I'll see you both for supper, hopefully.'

'We'll try!' Nick led Sarah up to her room, having already collected her key.

It was a really pretty room. Sarah ran round it exploring, exclaiming at the sloping ceilings and antique furniture before turning back into Nick's arms to be kissed.

'I've missed you so much,' he confessed. 'Even more than I thought I would.'

Laughing as she hugged him, she tried to stop him unfastening her dress. 'Can't I have a shower first?' she asked. 'I'm really hot and sticky!'

'No! You'll be even hotter and stickier in a minute!' he told her, and tumbled her back onto the bed. 'I certainly can't wait for you to shower.'

The memory of her own frustration during the last two weeks came back to her, and she undressed herself, displaying her body eagerly, wrapping herself round him in her need to be close to him.

He took her with a force that astonished her, holding her wrists above her head – then apologized afterwards. 'That was sheer lust, I'm afraid. I'm sorry,' he said softly, untangling her hair. 'I promise next time will be better.' She didn't care. It proved to her that he wanted her, and her own desperation was almost as strong.

They showered together eventually, and went down to meet James and Cress in the bar, their glowing faces betraying them completely. James teased Sarah as usual, but casually included Nick in the banter now. Both he and Cress accepted Nick's open affection for Sarah, and they all forgot his true status in the newly relaxed atmosphere.

The weather was scorching – well into the nineties every day and half the night. The crew worked clad only in shorts, and even Nick gave up wearing a shirt, and his skin turned an enviable mahogany as the days went by. Sarah suffered dreadfully in her heavy nurse's uniform, cursing Cress for insisting that she wore all the correct number of petticoats under it, and a corset. James too suffered, in his Army doctor's khaki, even though he looked unbelievably handsome in it. All the girls playing nurses were crazy about him, provoking endless jokes at their expense from his wicked tongue.

En masse they hated Sarah – for her often steamy scenes with him, and the now well gossiped about affair with their director. There was little privacy for some of the love scenes now, as James and Sarah were for the most part fully clothed, and no one saw any need to ban others from the set. They were well in tune with each other, and, despite the camera seeming always to be in tight close-up, they found the scenes relatively easy while they were working on them. It was the vicious remarks afterwards from the other actresses that were harder to bear from Sarah's point of view.

Bewildered, and unused to such treatment, she retreated more and more during the breaks to the Winnebago. The much enlarged crew were too scattered around the massive château masquerading as a hospital to be much help to her, and Cress and Patti also had bigger teams to control, and were worked off their feet most of the time. Patti had two cheerful special effects make-up artists to churn out endless disgusting-looking damaged limbs, and several other personnel. Joanna and Adam had been supplemented by a dozen or so other dressers – some English, some French. Cress battled, as Jenny did, in the two languages; they were both envious of Nick's fluency.

The old crew were scathing about his wife's visit, and delighted to have Sarah back with them. 'At least he's bearable when you're around!' Lenny told her a few days after she arrived.

'He's too knackered to yell much now,' Alex laughed. 'Keep him at it, Sarah!'

'You keep your grubby minds to yourselves!' retorted Sarah cheerfully. 'Anyway, he has a hell of a lot to cope with here – he's entitled to yell a bit.'

'Let's hope he stays calm when you and James are rolling around in that stable tonight, though,' Lenny rejoined wickedly. 'What a way to earn overtime!'

'We don't get overtime,' Sarah reminded him. 'And you should be paying us, you dirty old man!'

Nick had decided to shoot their final short love scene at night, because of the heat, and he and Lenny were going to shoot it themselves and dispense with the rest of the crew except for a sound man, since the stable set was so small, and even the dim lighting would make it unbearably hot. Sarah was surprisingly easygoing about it, shrugging it off without a murmur.

'It won't take very long,' Nick had assured her. 'I shan't even bother to rehearse much. We'll just shoot as the script and cut it afterwards. I'm sure you two can turn up something convincing.'

James was amazed at the difference in Sarah that evening. She went willingly into the scene, and, since Cress stayed out of the set, she was totally uninhibited in her actions. This time it was Sarah who was gaily winding James up, and making Lenny sweat even more. 'Beats wearing that costume,' she giggled, pulling straw out of James's hair as they paused for a few minutes. 'Where are we eating tonight, Nick?' she asked. 'I'm starving.' The other three couldn't understand why Nick roared with laughter. 'Honestly, I'm just hungry!' she said wickedly.

'Then you'd better get your act together, James,' Nick told him.

'Talk about screw to order!' James grumbled, rolling Sarah over and making her squeal as her bare back hit the scratchy straw instead of the rug they were lying on.

Nick knew they were working well together, and so confident was he of his hold on Sarah that he found he didn't mind at all this time. He included Lenny and Dave in the invitation to dinner afterwards, and it was a fairly lively evening in a noisy restaurant. Inevitably the conversation turned to their next projects, since they had less than a week to go, and the next job was always foremost in any of their freelance lives.

James was going straight to Pinewood for a month, on a new spy thriller, and then into another costume drama. 'So I'll be able to keep milady in style for a bit – until the Inland Revenue catch up with me!' he commented, smiling at Cress.

She laughed. 'With all your expenses, I think I'll be safer working!' she retorted. 'Even if Tamzin *is* supposed to be getting married again!' Tamzin had been a drain on James's resources for some time, as Sarah had suspected.

'And I'm going to play a Barbara Bentley heroine!' grinned Sarah. 'Imagine, I get to keep all my clothes on!'

'And one chaste kiss at the end?' joked James. 'I bet Nick chose that script!'

Lenny was booked for their Portuguese perfume commercial shoot, as was Ronnie. Nick always tried to use the same people, and rarely worked with new technicians if he could help it. NGA helped in that department, since he could always offer work in between films to his favourite staff. He would be editing and tied up with this film for weeks ahead, but his next project was well on in development too, hence the trip to Monte Carlo to see Seth Waterston.

With weeks ahead of being back with Nick, Sarah was content with life; only the animosity on the set spoiled things for her as the days passed. The other girls' taunts grew worse as the time passed, and she began to dread going to work. Protected in the past by the nature of her work, she was not used to that kind of treatment, and she took it to heart far more than others might have in her situation. James tried to protect her, but if anything he made it worse. Cress was furious, and took Sarah to task over it.

'Stick up for yourself,' she told her firmly. 'Give Helena a taste of her own medicine, or tell Nick.'

'Shut up, Cressida. It's nothing to do with him. Helena is sniping at me over James as much as Nick.'

'Then *I* will sort out Miss Stafford, never fear!' Cress retorted. 'But if you're too scared of Nick to tell him I'm surprised at you!'

'I'm *not* scared. I'm just not telling him.' Sarah was determined, and she stuck it out to the bitter end.

Her relief was obvious as Nick drove away from Cambrai, on their way south. Only then did she tell him.

He didn't seem at all surprised.

'It's a very thin line you're treading by sleeping with me,' he told her. 'You'll just have to get used to it, I'm afraid. I can help you, and I will, because I believe you're worth it, but there will always be those who'll hate you for it.'

Privately, he knew that Helena would suffer in the cutting room, but he didn't tell Sarah that. He wanted to put the film behind them. They were both exhausted, and desperate for the five days ahead of them with nothing to do except please themselves. He had schemed very hard to get them.

'Have you been to this hotel before?' Sarah asked tentatively as they drove into Beaulieu the next day.

'La Reserve? Not with Diana, if that's what you mean.' He laughed. 'I came once, with my mother after my father died, and I sometimes come on my own after a film, or to work, so you're quite safe from my memories!'

Beaulieu was a small, pretty town clustered around its harbour filled with expensive boats, their lines clacking against the metal masts in the breeze. The hotel, long and low above its rocky beach, was beautiful in the afternoon sun, with its flowers, and balconied towers overlooking a sea as blue as the cloudless sky.

She didn't notice how Nick had signed the register until the receptionist called her Madame Grey and she laughed with amusement – and not a little regret – as they followed the porter up to their room. Nick too was amused. 'But I

hope the *Unicorn* are not camped out in the next room!'
Sarah told him.

'At these prices!' Nick raised his eyebrows. 'Why do you
think I chose this place?'

Where the château had been crumbly and quaint, La
Reserve was elegant and luxurious. Their balcony over-
looked the sea, and the marble-floored room was beautifully furnished. Sarah was glad she had bought new
clothes recently; even if Nick preferred her without
them, she would need them here.

After two weeks together, night and day, they were very
comfortable with each other, and to onlookers the attractive couple seemed obviously very much in love – even if
they rarely spoke of it between themselves.

There was only one moment of dissent, when Sarah
began putting on some emerald earrings Charles had given
her in New York when they were dressing to go up to Cap
Ferrat to visit Seth Waterston. At the time she had argued
furiously with him, but had been obliged in the end to take
them for the sake of peace.

'Those are pretty,' Nick commented idly. He was used
to her wearing her mother's good jewellery, but this time
he picked up one glittering piece and whistled in surprise.
'These aren't your mother's, are they? And they certainly
aren't paste!'

'No,' Sarah shrugged and tried to sound casual.
'Charles gave them to me for my birthday.'

'That's not till next month.'

'It was an early present.' She took the earring from him
and put it on. She could see he was annoyed and rather
wished she had left them in her jewel case.

'You realize Charlie is trying to lure you into his bed?'
he snapped. 'Are you *sure* he didn't try anything in New
York?'

'No, he damn well didn't! And I would've said no if he
had! Stop being silly, Nick. I'll take them off if they upset
you so much.'

'No, leave them,' he relented. 'They do go beautifully with that dress.' He had to admit, reluctantly, that Charles had very good taste, even though he resented it. 'It's important that you look your best for Seth,' he added placatingly.

'Between you and Charles I feel like a dressed up doll!' she complained. 'All you ever want to do is show me off!'

Nick seized her by her shoulders and shook her. 'I want you to meet Seth, amongst others, looking as beautiful as you do now.'

'I'm sorry, Nick.' She leant against him. 'I'm used to doing my own thing, I'm not used to all this dressing up and social stuff.'

'Well, you had better *get* used to it! This is going to be your life from now on.' He kissed her gently. 'I love you, Sarah. I want the best for you.'

Sarah felt trapped. Painted and unreal. But her body stirred at his touch, then, and her qualms were put aside. 'I won't let you down, darling, I promise,' she said contritely. She finished her hair as Nick tied his bow tie and slipped into his dinner jacket.

'In that dress,' he commented as she stood up, 'I think you'd better be careful how you *sit* down!'

The white silk dress was only held together at the sides with thin lacing. They had bought it that afternoon in Monte Carlo. On anyone else it could have looked tacky; on Sarah's beautiful body it was sensational. Nick was jealously aware of all the men's eyes on her as they had a drink in the bar. It made him want her all the more, and he drove up to Cap Ferrat with his hand on her thigh most of the time, feeling like schoolboy with his first date.

Seth's villa was the grand, electronic-gates type, with security guards prowling the grounds with very fierce dogs. Nick casually announced his identity, with the ease of a frequent visitor, and zoomed through the gates. Their host seemed delighted to see him, and studied Sarah carefully as he greeted her. 'You're very welcome, honey,' he replied to her greeting. 'Now come and meet everyone.'

'Everyone' included a world-famous Hollywood star and his wife, who lived next door, an archduke and duchess and a Parisian dress-designer with his boyfriend. The designer eyed Sarah's dress and smiled. 'You have very good taste, *mademoiselle*. That's from my new range!'

'And you are very clever, *monsieur*.' Sarah smiled back at him and, despite his glaring boyfriend, he was hers for the night.

With a casual confidence Nick left her to it, and she charmed them all. It was Charles's New York party all over again – except this time she had Nick to turn to, and his smiling eyes on her when she needed reassurance, where Charles had calmly left her to cope while he talked endless business.

They dined on the terrace overlooking the sea, shaded by the tall cypress trees. The banks of candles flattered the women's faces as music from a string quartet floated over the still, warm summer evening. It was *so* over the top that Sarah, from the safe haven of her youth, wanted to laugh. But she concentrated on not letting Nick down and on flattering Seth, knowing, as she did so, that the men's eyes were on her body all evening. Nick was putting her on display, she knew, and though she hated it she knew it had to be done if her ambitions were to be realized.

'Come and join us on the yacht tomorrow,' Seth invited as they made their farewells. 'Eleven at the quay in Monte?'

'Love to,' said Nick, his hand flexing in Sarah's, warning her.

'Damn!' he said as he drove back to Beaulieu. 'Last thing I wanted!'

'Hush – remember it's be nice to Seth week,' Sarah laughed. 'I'll wear my new bikini!'

185

'I want you to myself, not displayed to that randy lot for a second occasion,' he grumbled.

'You have me every night. Make the most of it!' she told him. 'I intend to.'

This time she didn't suffer the frustrations she'd had in New York. Nick was with her, loving her, fulfilling every last craving her body had for him.

He lay beside her later, watching her sleep, arms thrown above her head, her hair spread on the pillow a warm gleam in the moonlight, and wondered again what the hell he was doing. Their legs were still entangled after their lovemaking, and he was loath to move, though it made sleep impossible for him. When he touched her, she moved towards him, and he responded just as quickly to her. Even asleep, she was able to rouse him. Her power over him was beginning to frighten him, yet he knew there was little now that would persuade him to give her up.

Sarah was as good as her word next day, taking with her the new swimsuits she had bought in New York. 'With my own money!' she pointed out firmly to Nick, and delighted Seth and his friends, when they anchored the yacht in a quiet bay, by diving off the side into the sea.

Seth was worried about his potential investment. 'Is she safe?' he asked as Sarah waved to them.

'With the training she's had, I'd trust her with *my* life in the water,' Nick assured him. 'Come on, Seth, don't let her show you up!'

Seth, only ten years older than Nick, was into the Californian healthy body regime, but even so climbed down the ladder into the water. Nick laughed, and dived after Sarah.

Of the party on board the yacht only the American actor and four pretty girls stayed on the boat. He preferred to keep his toupee dry, and the girls were definitely not swimmers. Sarah found herself playing water polo with a darkly handsome Italian film idol and three executives from Seth's LA office. Vito almost put Nick's looks in the shade, she thought fleetingly, before Vito manhandled her away from the ball with exploring hands. Quite calmly, she ducked him, and left him spluttering with fury. She was a far better swimmer and evaded him with ease after that.

Seth roared with laughter. 'I see what you mean, Nick!' he commented, cheerfully. Luckily, Vito was an old friend of Nick's.

'I need a few minutes on my hair,' Sarah confided to Nick as they went back on board. 'Especially with those girls around. They're so pretty.'

Nick looked at the four girls sunbathing on the deck and shrugged dismissively. 'Don't worry about them, they're nothing – dessert, more than likely!' He turned to Seth. 'We'll be a few minutes, Seth,' he called, and led Sarah along the passageway to the cabin they had changed in.

She gave a shriek of amazement as he opened a door in it. 'It's got a real bathroom!' she cried staring at the marble-faced shower and its gold fittings. On Peter's boat there was one basin, and a loo which needed pumping.

'This *is* a billionaire's pad,' Nick reminded her, pushing her under the shower. 'You should see the main stateroom – it's all mirrors and concealed cameras! I'll get Seth or Miriam to show it to you.'

'Is Miriam his wife?'

'Good God, no! Well, not yet, but she's working on it!' Nick laughed. 'He calls her his secretary. You'll see her at lunch. He divorced his third wife some time ago.'

Suzan dried her hair, and Nick made her leave it loose, as she had worn it up the previous evening and when they had arrived. With hardly any make-up, and a vivid sarong tied round her hips, she was a startling contrast to the other girls. Nick was quite aware that the crotch of Vito's shorts was bulging as he stared at her with unconcealed lust.

'Reminds me of Grace,' Seth said reflectively to Nick as Sarah took a drink.

'Grace who?' asked Sarah, interested.

'There was only ever one Grace in this area, honey!' Seth told her. 'And don't you ever cut that hair!'

It blew gently in the breeze, looking good, but irritating Sarah. To everyone's amusement, she tied it back with a serviette in desperation, until they had finished eating. Lobster, she decided, could become her favourite meal.

Nick and Seth talked business all through the meal, and got up to continue in the saloon afterwards.

'Come and join *us*, Sarah?' Vito invited, indicating the loungers laid out under the awning where the girls were already spread out. But Nick moved swiftly. He knew what Vito had in mind. Not so long ago he would have happily joined him in taking the girls to a cabin for a pleasant afternoon, now the thought revolted him.

'I don't share, Vito – not any more – and neither does Sarah.' He took her arm. 'Come into the cool darling. Give Seth something to distract him while I argue money with him.' So Sarah lay on the sofa in the opulent saloon, reading fashion magazines while they talked, grateful that Nick had noticed.

By the time they had finished, and they went back on deck for tea, everyone except Miriam and Rex, the American actor, had disappeared. 'Siesta!' Miriam said smiling at Seth, who laughed knowingly.

'Saved from a fate worse than death.' He winked at Sarah.

'Oh, I'd have made one too many,' Sarah told him innocently.

'That's never worried Vito!' Nick remarked. 'Not since I've known him! I think two at a time is his speciality!'

Sarah stared at him for a moment, then wisely left it alone. It was all beyond her. Even Nick seemed different, and rather frightening in this élite company. They were amongst the top people in their field, and all of them respected him for his expertise – even Seth bowed to his demands, she had discovered during their conversation. Nick was as comfortable with them all as he was in Charles's aristocratic world, but she was still curious about his remarks concerning Vito.

'How do you know Vito likes two at a time?' she finally had to ask as he drove back to the hotel.

Nick laughed. 'Your nosy questions will get you into real trouble one of these days! Because I've helped him try it, miss, that's why!'

'I bet Diana wasn't there!' Sarah was shocked rigid and trying to cover it up.

'I don't ask for trouble, and it *was* a few years ago.' He smiled at her effort to appear cool. 'Don't worry, I told you, and Vito. I don't share, not now. You belong to *me*, and me alone.'

'Oh, yeah?'

'Quite definitely! Now, what would you like to do this evening? Gamble at the casino, or go up to that inn in the hills to eat?'

'The inn – I'm starving! I can wear jeans and eat snails in garlic butter.'

'I give up! OK, then, I suppose as it's a holiday we might as well both reek of garlic as it's the only time we can!'

Arriving back at Heathrow on Wednesday afternoon, Sarah walked into a barrage of pressmen, screaming questions at her. Bewildered, she looked frantically around for Bill, and smiled with relief as he battled towards her.

Big and burly, he elbowed the photographers away and took her bags, hustling her out of the terminal. He'd left his car on a yellow line deliberately, so that he could whisk her away quickly.

'What the hell was all that about?' she demanded, panic-

189

stricken, as he swung into the chaotic traffic of the airport one-way system.

'Have you not read the papers for a few days?' he asked, and passed her a couple. 'Try the *Unicorn*. The boss is going to love it!'

Sarah opened the paper and stared in horror. 'SEXY SARAH STEPS OUT!' screamed the banner headline on the inside page, above pictures of her with Charles coming back from New York, and, more worryingly, with Nick. The large picture had been taken on set, presumably during a hot lunch-break, when she had discarded her dress, and they were laughing together as he bent close to her. It looked exactly what it had been, an intimate moment in a fraught day, and she wondered how they had achieved it when Nick had been so adamant that the Press were not to be allowed anywhere near them.

To crown it all they had added in a still of her lying naked in the hay kissing James. Luckily it was a close-up, which must have been taken from the film stock, as it had been processed after the scene in the stable. There followed a great deal of lurid prose, insinuating that she had ditched her boyfriend in favour of a variety of older men. Someone on the unit had been at work.

Helena! And she had been good friends with Peter at one time. She knew then that they *had* to be the source, and her fury boiled to the surface. 'I'll kill him this time!' she swore as Bill finally reached her flat, to find the doorway swarming with reporters. 'Haven't you bastards got anything better to do?' she yelled at them as Bill escorted her inside and the doorman closed the door on them.

To her total relief, George was in her flat waiting for her. With a thankful sigh, Sarah fell into his arms and Bill left her a little more cheerfully.

'We'll go straight home,' he announced. 'For a day or

two anyway. You can't stay here. I've packed a bag for you. Leave those.'

'I'll just make a couple of phone calls,' Sarah said quickly, and went into the bedroom to call Oscar.

'Don't worry,' he told her blithely. 'They'll be after someone else tomorrow. Just stay out of sight for a day or two and learn that *Secret Agent* script. Rehearsals start on Monday. There's no time to worry about the *Unicorn*.'

He clearly didn't know the rumours about her and Nick were true, and she didn't enlighten him. Nick's car phone was unavailable, and as he was driving back to England he was totally out of touch any other way. Unhappily, she followed George out of the back entrance of the flats to his car.

'So what *have* you been up to?' he demanded. 'And where have you been? Filming finished a week ago.'

Sarah didn't lie to George, at least not completely. 'I went to Monte Carlo with Nick, to meet a producer for a new film, and the rest of it is my business, George!'

Gaily she changed the subject as she told him about Seth's dinner party guests and the day on the yacht, which amused him nearly all the way to Guildford. That gossip helped with Maggie too, since she was a very straight lady, and none too thrilled at having her sister-in-law spread in a naked embrace across a newspaper.

'Wait till you see the film, Maggie,' sighed Sarah. 'There'll be a damn sight more of me than that on display!'

She produced the pretty dresses she had bought for their daughter Becky in New York and Monte Carlo, which appeased Maggie slightly, then settled down to an evening of playing with Becky and keeping the peace.

Nick went straight to his office from Dover and got in just after Jane arrived. Having driven overnight, with just a couple of hours' snatched sleep, he was not in the best of moods, and Jane wisely kept quiet and made coffee while he changed and shaved.

'Diana's not going to like this,' she warned him then, as she put the coffee in front of him along with the newspaper cuttings. 'And neither are you!'

She was right.

His language was fairly ripe when he had read them. They were getting at him through Sarah, he could see that, and he was furious.

'If we'd known where you were, it would have helped.' Jane rebuked. 'David and Julia did their best, but we couldn't find you or Sarah – or James come to that. They wanted shots of the nude scenes, but obviously we said no.'

'That's the last thing those beggars are getting!' Nick roared, and picked up the phone. 'Sandy, get me Max Moreton!'

'Nicholas, dear, how nice to hear from you,' Max oozed down the phone. 'We've been looking for you for days. Where were you?'

Nick ignored the false pleasantries. 'What the hell are you trying to do to Sarah Campbell?'

'Your little girlfriend?'

'Max, let's get one thing straight – she is *not* my girlfriend. When that photograph was taken we were on the set surrounded by dozens of people, which you conveniently don't show.'

'Oh, just a little journalistic licence old boy,' Max said, and laughed. 'You should know that by now! It was unfortunate, though, that we didn't get pictures in the garden at Hastings Court that night.'

Nick went white. 'What the hell are you talking about?'

'A couple of months ago? Surely you remember, Nick?' Max chuckled. 'One of my lads watched you . . . how can I put it delicately? . . . getting your leg over the lovely Miss Campbell? Dear me, Nicholas, what would all those little boys and girls think about their heroine then?'

'Print that, and I'll sue you for every penny!' Nick

gasped furiously. It was two against one and he knew it. If they'd had any proof they would have published weeks ago.

'I won't print anything – yet,' Max said. 'But I'll get you in the end, Grey,' he warned. 'This is just for starters. It's only a pity that pretty little girl will have to go down with you!'

To come from the bliss of France into this was about all Nick needed, and his promised weekend at home with Charlotte was going to be hell! He sat for long frantic minutes as his predicament sank in, and then he wearily reached for the phone again, to find Sarah.

Finally he located her in Guildford, and practically ordered her to stay where she was. He decided not to tell her about his conversation with Max. 'Oscar's right,' he comforted. 'Something else will distract them in a day or two, but it's a pity you can't tell them about the beating Peter gave you.'

'Why can't I?' she demanded.

'Because it will stir up a slanging match, and we can't afford that,' he sighed. 'They were right about one thing, though.' He was on his private line and there was no chance of being overheard. 'You're definitely one hell of a sexy lady!'

'Not frigid, then?'

'Certainly not frigid!' he laughed. 'And I'm going to hang onto you, never fear. Just keep your head down for a few days and refer any reporters to Jane or Julia in the office. I'm going to Oxford tonight, for the weekend, but I'll see you on Monday, I promise. Can you bear to eat in for a night or two?'

The reminder that he was going home to Diana only added to her feeling of being let down with a bump, but she knew he was desperate to see Charlotte. Everything had been so perfect in France, and now suddenly reality was catching up with her.

For a day or so the reporters besieged George's home,

and her, until she was on the point of hysteria as they dogged her footsteps everywhere she went. Then, as Oscar had predicted, a new scandal broke, and they all high-tailed it back to London.

CHAPTER 14

It was not easy going into rehearsals on Monday morning. At least the rehearsal block was in North Acton, and as *Do or Dare* did not rehearse Sarah was spared from bumping into Peter. Her problem became Patrick Lythgoe, the star of *Secret Agent* and a popular, somewhat conceited actor, whom she knew from way back at RADA. He greeted her with a leering 'Hi, sexy!' and it deteriorated from there.

Sarah could have tolerated him normally, but he was very jealous of her publicity, and lost no opportunity to let her know it.

They had a few days' rehearsal and a week's filming, followed by two days in the television studios. By the end of the first day's rehearsal Sarah wanted out. But she was an actress, and she prided herself on being professional, so she knew she had to grit her teeth and get on with it.

'We picked a real bum one in this job,' she sighed to Nick when he came to her flat on Monday evening for supper.

'It's a top series,' he encouraged. 'It got all the awards at BAFTA this year, and Patrick's a good actor.'

'He's the pits!' Sarah declared. 'The thought of doing a love scene with him is turning my stomach.'

'You were spoilt having James as a leading man,' he teased.

'I know I was!' Sarah shuddered. 'Patrick just doesn't seem to know about soap. His feet and armpits stink!'

'Maybe it was a bad day for him too,' he suggested. 'We all have those, and weekends too!'

'How was Diana?'

Nick shuddered. 'Not fun!' He smiled. 'Thank goodness the politicians took over your publicity.'

'For how long, I wonder?'

He pulled her onto his lap. 'We'll just have to be very careful, and stay out of sight for a bit – even if I have to cook!'

'Is my cooking really that bad?' She sounded hurt.

'No, the steak was surprisingly good, after what you said about your cooking. It depends on what else is in your repertoire.'

'Not a lot,' she admitted ruefully. 'Damn Peter!'

'Best therapy I can think of,' he smiled, as they went to bed later. 'Roll on Portugal!'

'Three whole weeks to wait,' she sighed, but knowing she could come home to Nick in the evenings made up for her days with the smelly Patrick.

Nick went off to recce his locations in Portugal for a few days, and Charles took the opportunity to invite her to his box at Covent Garden for a new production of *Swan Lake*, with a raved about French dancer Sarah was anxious to see. Lonely without Nick, she was delighted to see Charles, and appearing in public with him would be a great deal safer at the moment than appearing with Nick, she thought, so she accepted, and went happily.

Charles had also invited George and Maggie, to her surprise, having bumped into George at a City Livery dinner a few days before, and Liz and Rupert Saunders also joined the party. Sarah practically gave two fingers to those members of the audience who recognized her, and positively crowed when a few of the gossip columns mentioned the occasion in the papers a day or two later, much to Patrick's fury.

The high spot of the week was going to audition for

Barry Harper at the National. Nick had found time to coach her on the scenes she had to prepare, and Barry was delighted, she knew. He auditioned her on the stage of the Lyttleton, since it was not being used that day, and even the empty theatre inspired her as she performed to the half-dozen or so production staff.

The morning she was due to fly to Portugal Oscar rang to say she had got the part, so she and Nick celebrated with their inevitable champagne on the plane. Champagne and flying first class was becoming a way of life for her, she thought gleefully, and decided there and then that it was going to continue if she could possibly manage it.

Nick had arranged for them to fly out a day earlier than the rest of the crew after an initial panic when Diana had thought that perhaps she would come as well, since her parents' villa was so close by. Nick had struggled to talk her out of it on the grounds that he would be too busy, but he only breathed easily when she was asked to take over a colleague's class for a few days.

At least he could travel openly with Sarah, since they were working together, and he didn't give a damn what the agency thought about their sleeping arrangements. The agency producer was an old friend anyway, which was the reason Nick was doing the shoot, and he knew he was quite safe with Gareth. He had tolerated Gareth's illicit girl-friend on a shoot more than once. Overseas commercials were always a great opportunity for the agencies to have a good time, away from wives and regular partners.

On his first recce with Gareth they had booked a small villa complex for their use rather than a hotel. They usually ate out in the evenings on a job like this any-way, and only needed a maid to do the cleaning up and serve breakfast, so it suited their purpose admirably.

Flying out early meant that he and Sarah had two nights and a day before the others arrived – officially for Nick to recheck the locations, but spent, in fact, lying by the pool in the still warm sun or in bed.

Sarah knew that was where she was at her best for him and she never tired of his demands. He always seemed to find new ways to surprise her, and he only had to touch her for her to be ready for him, so desperate was she not to lose him.

Ronnie was amazed to find they were still heavily involved. 'I would've thought that pretty young boy-friend was much more your scene,' he told her as he did her hair the first morning of the shoot. 'I'm surprised you ditched him.'

'I'm afraid I have a taste for vintage wine these days,' Sarah teased. 'Even if there is a great deal of aggravation and awful publicity attached to it.'

'Keeps the spice going,' Ronnie advised wickedly. 'Just be careful; he might decide to marry you, then all the fun would be gone!'

'I don't think there's much chance of that,' she sighed. 'Anyway, I've only known him for five months.'

'Time enough for some – look at James and Cress! How's Sir Charles, by the way? You certainly live the high life these days!'

'He's fine, I think.' She was non-committal. 'I'm going riding at Hastings Court with him when I get back.'

'That should get the Press going again! You really like living dangerously, miss!'

'Oh, sod the Press! I don't think I care any more!' Sarah shrugged, but she did, and she knew it.

In the next few days she felt like saying sod the agency and the client, as they all interfered with every shot and constantly discussed her hair and wardrobe, driving Nick to distraction.

It was all teasing, lingering shots of two beautiful people. Nick on a commercial was an inventive director with a creative eye, and used every possible opportunity his locations gave him.

With her hair and make-up attended to between every

shot, Sarah had never looked better, and her riding skills were being tested to the full. Wearing a long, fairytale dress on horseback, and riding on every surface from beaches to clifftops and pine forests, she needed her wits about her, and she was grateful that her leading man was also an expert rider.

Commercials were the one time Nick had to bow to the opinions of others, but to her surprise he was amazingly patient with actors and clients alike. He was so different from how he was in his film work that Sarah hardly knew him.

'That's why NGA is so successful,' Ronnie said when she voiced her opinion. 'And why the clients want Nick every time. He's also the best pack-shot director in the UK, and as that's the most significant part of the shoot it's quite important.'

Sarah was rarely in the studio when the close-up shots of the product were done – they always liked to get rid of the artistes before they started on them – so she was intrigued. It had seemed to her a strange thing to be thought good at doing, until she watched Nick at work.

She had the afternoon off while they did it, on the afternoon of her birthday, when Nick deemed the weather to be perfect for it. He and the crew spent the entire time almost waist-deep in the sea, with the perfume bottle on a rock, struggling to catch exactly the right wave around it. Time and time again Nick shouted, 'Cut,' and they began again, until Sarah could bear it no longer and went off to ride with her Spanish leading man.

Luis was a charmer, and she adored him. He spoke very little English – just enough to tell her she was beautiful, which didn't go down too well with Nick, and just enough to tell *Nick* that he would take care of her while they were exercising the horses that afternoon, which annoyed him even more.

'Stop being so possessive!' she told him with a grin that evening as she lay on their bed posing for him while he finished off a roll of film. She was trying to provoke him into making love to her, but he was still annoyed with her.

'I have every right to be jealous,' he told her firmly. 'Remember, I speak Spanish. I've heard exactly what Luis would like to do to you!'

'Well, like Charles, he won't get the chance,' she retorted, and rolled over, holding out her arms to him. 'Come here, Nick,' she demanded. 'And put that camera down for a while. What if Diana sees these pictures?'

'She won't, don't worry. These will live in my office safe! The rest will go to the agency.' However, he did as she asked and put the camera down, gathering her up against him. 'I hadn't forgotten it was your birthday, you know, if that's what you thought when you were trying to make me jealous – and succeeding, I might add.'

'I thought the flowers and stuff this morning were my birthday present.'

'Only from the boys.' He fished in his briefcase. 'Twenty-five is a special age; it deserves a special gift!' He was competing with Charles, though he tried to deny it to himself, but Sarah gave a shriek of delight at the Cartier watch she unwrapped. She had ruined her previous watch, diving off the boat in France.

'You are clever, Nick. I can think of you every time I look at it!'

'That *was* the general idea, only don't go deep-sea diving in it this time! The Rolex like mine that you covet so much will come when you get your Oscar, I promise!'

Sarah wound her arms round his neck. 'I won't. Now, have I time to thank you properly before we go out?'

'No,' he said sadly. 'You'll have to wait, for once. We can't keep everyone else waiting – much as I'd like to!'

In the run-up to the première of the film Sarah thought she would go mad. Her life was a nightmare of work: the Barbara Bentley play, interviews, photographic sessions and the game shows she had always done – and was even more in demand for now that she was more of a celebrity. Trying to dovetail it all in with Nick's busy life was proving to be impossible half the time.

They snatched lunches in the daytime, or quiet dinners and occasionally the theatre, or he would come to her at midnight some nights, exhausted after a hard day, and just fall asleep in her arms. The more she knew of the pressure he worked under, the more aquiescent she became – trying to be there when he wanted her, spending long hours alone waiting for him, learning first-hand what it was like to be the girlfriend of a married man when he went home for the occasional weekend with his daughter. Finally she gave Nick a key to her flat, and it gradually became their habit to use her home rather than his. Sarah always felt uncomfortable at Regent's Park, knowing that Diana could turn up or phone at any time.

He was soon keeping spare clothes in her wardrobe, and his toothbrush and shaving equipment lived in her bathroom. Used to looking after himself, he was quite at ease shopping for food on his way to Oakley Street if they felt like eating in, and, to her astonishment, was not even averse to cooking if Sarah was later than he was. For all the exalted position of his working life he was a surprisingly practical man, she found, quite able to repair broken items and fix things that had been irritating her for months.

There were even rare, relaxed evenings when she felt almost married, as Nick sprawled comfortably on the sofa with a book or a script and she sat working on her tapestry while they played some of her father's precious collection of records and tapes of old musicals. She was well aware that she saw more of Nick than his wife did, yet she always knew that Diana had first claim on him, and she frequently had to bite back her frustration on that score. But Nick had been honest from the start about Diana, and though Sarah had the option to break it off, as he also did, she knew that nothing would make her do that.

Cress worried about her, knowing that Sarah would

accept very little sympathy. 'She'll get tired of it eventually,' James counselled after they had dropped her off one evening. 'Or Nick will get bored.'

'I'm not so sure about that,' Cress said. 'They both seem very determined to carry on somehow. Nick really is unfair to mess her around like this; she has no real life of her own.'

'Well, at least she's started to spend time with Charlie instead of moping around all weekend.' James shrugged. 'Maybe something will come of that. Charlie dotes on her.'

'Maybe, but she doesn't think of him that way,' Cress asserted. 'Mind you, after those earrings he gave her, I think *I* would!'

'He and Nick will bankrupt themselves fighting over that girl,' James said wryly. 'I'm very glad you don't expect that of me!'

'There's only one thing I want from you,' Cress laughed.

They were so happy together. Cressida often had to pinch herself to remind herself it was real. Their erratic lifestyles had dovetailed together with amazing ease, and James, to his surprise, had quickly adapted to domesticity in the house he had owned and maintained for several years in a state of chaos, which had been swiftly transformed by Cress into a comfortable home.

Fortified by her cooking skills, and now able to find a clean shirt by opening a drawer instead of going out and buying a new one, he had begun to look forward to going home in the evenings, instead of heading for the nearest pub for company. All they had to worry about was his ex-wife actually marrying the man she had announced her engagement to. Cress resented furiously the hassle she put James through over money, judging, quite accurately, that he was too easygoing to argue with her.

A couple of days before the première they felt confident

enough to invite Nick and Sarah around for dinner to watch the television review programme which was previewing the film.

'This is wonderful!' Sarah enthused, looking round. 'You've worked miracles, Cress!' She had heard stories of the house, when James had lived alone, and had been appalled.

'She even wanted *me* to do some decorating!' James sounded mortified.

'Did you?' Nick raised his eyebrows in surprise.

'The hell I did! I got a man in for her instead,' he replied, grinning. 'Wish I hadn't, though. It's costing a fortune!'

'About time!' Cress put in, pouring wine at the kitchen table. 'I think it must've been wartime when this place was last painted.'

'I have to admit, life has improved,' James admitted. 'I open drawers and find socks in pairs.'

'I'm still *finding* odd socks and shirts!' Cress laughed. 'I can't believe the shirts he's got.'

'And she keeps taking things to the cleaners,' James added, teasing.

'I employ a lady to do that,' Nick grinned. 'It's cheaper in the long run.'

'You also have a wife to organize things,' Sarah said quietly.

Nick felt relaxed enough to kiss her in front of them. 'We're not talking wives tonight,' he told her. 'Don't frighten James completely.'

Cress had made a *boeuf bourgignon* – 'After I spent a week cleaning the oven!' – and its quality was matched by Nick's careful choice of wine. Sarah felt slightly uncomfortable faced by Cress's cooking prowess when her hostess then produced a perfect pavlova for dessert, as she knew Cress had been working all day.

'It's an easy recipe,' Cress assured her. 'I'll show you'

'Sarah's not as bad a cook as she makes out,' Nick

defended, his hand on hers. 'I haven't starved yet in her flat, and her chilli is great!' They were easy with James and Cress, the only friends they trusted.

James produced an Islay malt for Nick, knowing his tastes, and Cress turned on the TV in the living room for the show. 'Let's see what sort of an idiot Nick made of himself in this interview,' she teased, knowing Nick's hatred of appearing in front of a camera.

'Lets see what sort of review they give us,' Nick rejoined, pulling Sarah back against him on the sofa. The programme was renowned for its acerbic comment on films.

Laughing, they watched the inevitable clips of James and Sarah making love, before the interview Nick and Sarah had recorded with the presenter in Nick's office the week before came on.

'Were you drunk?' Cress demanded, in hysterics as she listened to Nick's evasive answers in reply to the interviewer's questions on the reported problems between him and Sarah.

'We had our moments,' Nick had said finally. 'There were times I wanted to strangle her, I admit, but we are the best of friends now.'

That had all of them in hysterics, not just Cress.

The important thing, however, was the programme's opinion of the film.

'Sarah Campbell,' the reviewer pronounced at last, 'is sensational. Totally believable as Abigail. Unusually for screen lovers, she and wonderful co-star James Willoughby have a compatibility you can believe in. From their first meeting to the incredibly realistic love scenes. Definitely one to see, folks.'

'Wowee!' cried Cress. 'That is some credit – especially from him! I'm not so sure about the realistic bit, though! James . . . Sarah . . .!'

Sarah avoided James's eyes quickly.

'Only acting of the highest calibre!' James shielded the

lower half of his body from Cress's assault as they rolled around on their sofa.

'I told you!' Nick hugged Sarah. 'We're on a roll! BAFTA, here we come!'

Sarah only shivered, still not wanting to believe stardom could come from displaying her body so freely.

She hated the lovemaking shots. They were all the TV shows and newspapers were using. Maggie was giving her hell about it, and George, as she'd told Nick, had laughed. 'You've certainly grown since I had to bath you!' he had teased, though he was taking some stick about it in the City and threatening to raffle her off in his office. She still had not seen the film in its entirety, managing to avoid, so far, any showing of it. Nick had given her a video, but she hadn't even managed to watch it in the privacy of her own living room.

CHAPTER 15

Charles was taking her to the royal première of *Home Leave*. Once she accepted that Diana was going with Nick, it was inevitable.

On the night, with Charles's hand on her arm, Sarah sat in the car staring with fascination at the sight of her name above the film title on the poster emblazoned across the cinema. The central motif of the film was a drawing of James kissing her in the chiffon slip, with her hair flowing across the poster. Seeing the crowds, she braced herself. She was wearing the blue-green dress from her New York trip, with a close-fitting jacket added by Catherine to combat the November chill. With her hair loose, she swept through the onlookers at the cinema, aware of Nick and Diana's eyes on her as she played the star. Hugging James in the doorway, she knew the flashbulbs were popping. Her whole being was concentrated, then, on showing Diana how special she was.

But watching the film, knowing the Princess was watching too, knowing the entire audience was watching her on screen made her feel sick again. Clutching Charles's hand so tightly that her nails were biting into his flesh, she crawled with embarrassment. The love scenes dominated the film, whether she liked it or not. They *were* beautiful to look at and afterwards when she was presented to the Princess this view was confirmed, but Sarah wanted the floor to open up and swallow her.

To add to her misery, Nick hardly came near her – at the cinema or at the party afterwards. Diana seemed to demand his whole attention.

Briefly he danced with her, seemingly afraid to be seen touching her in front of Diana, and Sarah, already paranoid, freaked. 'Take me home, Charles,' she demanded, after half an hour at the party. She knew she was behaving like a spoilt child, and for once she didn't care, but Charles was furious with her.

'Don't be silly, Sarah,' he remonstrated. 'The party is for you as much as anyone. You have people to meet, for heaven's sake! Behave yourself!'

'I want to go, Charles, *Now!*' She was on the edge of hysteria, and Charles took a careful look at her face and gave in, albeit reluctantly.

'OK. Get your jacket. I'll get the car. Don't you want to say goodbye?'

'No, let's just go.'

In the blue-green froth of dress she was so beautiful and looked so unhappy that his heart went out to her as he drove her home.

'Come in with me, Charlie,' she begged as he pulled up at her apartment block. 'Please?'

Worried, he parked the car and took her up to the flat. She was frenzied – making coffee, pouring it, talking about the film – completely disjointed as if she was drunk, yet he knew she hadn't had a chance to drink much. Puzzled, he took her by the shoulders, shaking her. 'Sarah, stop this! What the hell's the matter?'

Sarah fell into his arms, and Charles felt her warmth and her softness against him. It would be so easy. He could take her now and Nick would be beaten. He kissed her slowly, gently, wanting her so badly.

Yet he pushed her away. It took every scrap of determination he had, but he said no to her. 'I want you, Sarah,' he said softly, 'but on my terms, not yours. I'm not going to be your revenge on Nick for tonight.'

She was crying. Long, hard sobs that tore at his very soul.

'Stay with me, Charlie. Please don't leave me,' she begged him finally.

'I'll stay until you're asleep,' he promised. 'I'm not sure my will-power will last much longer. Go and get ready for bed.'

While she did so, he picked up the tray and took it into the kitchen, and turned off the lights, being practical for once, before he went to Sarah. She had simply dropped her dress on the floor and done the sketchiest clean off of her make-up before she had climbed naked into bed.

Charles sat on the edge of the bed and unfastened the bracelet from her wrist, aware of how much she was provoking him. He held her hand against his cheek, stroking her hair, and she fell asleep finally, with tears still staining her face. Only then did he leave her, regret- fully, but knowing he was right. Sarah would come to him soon enough, he told himself. He only had to wait.

Sarah had not been the only person in the audience who was unhappy that evening. All the way through the film Diana Grey had fumed silently, seeing the beautiful girl dominate the screen whenever she appeared, hearing the murmurs of the audience around her, watching the glori- ous golden body writhing around James in their first love scene and feeling Nick tense in the seat beside her. Instinctively, then, she had known this girl was doing the same thing with her husband.

He had given no sign of it during the inevitable con- gratulatory chat afterwards, or at the party. She had watched jealously every time his eyes slid to Sarah, even resentfully as he had danced briefly with her before returning to her side, and then suddenly Charles and Sarah had gone, within half an hour of arriving.

Nick had obviously been furious at Sarah's disappear- ing act, having to explain it to various press people and make placating noises to them. He hated apologizing to anyone.

Because Bill was driving them, there was no way they could talk in the car, and the atmosphere only crackled into fury as Nick unlocked the front door of their house. Diana threw her wrap and purse onto the living room sofa and turned on him furiously. 'You're sleeping with Sarah Campbell, aren't you?' she accused bitterly, unable to hold it in any longer.

'And why, suddenly, does it matter to you if I am?' he demanded angrily. 'Since you've made it quite clear on many occasions that sleeping with me is something *you'd* rather not do?'

'As you are rarely in the same country, let alone the same bed as me, it *is* rather difficult, Nick.'

'So tonight, if I asked you, you'd come willingly to bed with me, just because you think I'm seeing someone else? That's what you normally do, isn't it?'

'Not just because of that, no! How could you think that, Nick? I'm your *wife*!'

'Only when it suits you!' Nick strode across the room and reached for the decanter of malt whisky. 'Take tonight, for example. It's the first time I've seen you in weeks. And it's only because *you* want to be in the limelight – the director's wife!'

'So you would rather have paraded that little slut on your arm, would you? She's a mere child, Nick, only ten years older than your own daughter! You're disgusting!'

'Stop it, Diana! Just stop right there! I've spent the last six months working with Sarah, of *course* I see her.' He slammed down the glass in his hand so hard that it broke, and whisky splattered unheeded down his trousers. 'What I do in my business life has nothing to do with you; you've made that quite clear too.'

'Maybe, but this isn't all business, is it? Screw around if you must, husband dear, but never, *ever*, humiliate me like you did tonight, or one of these days you'll go too far! You couldn't keep your eyes off her, and everyone could see what you were doing.'

'So you'll divorce me for it, I suppose?' he asked sarcastically.

'Oh, no, Nick, I'll never do that. You can be quite certain on that score! You married me and you're going to stay married to me! And since you asked so charmingly, yes, tonight I *will* go to bed with you! Maybe I should find out what Miss bloody Campbell sees in you! Because I sure as hell can't remember!'

'Well, unfortunately, *wife dear*, there could be a problem with your very generous offer,' Nick said. 'I'm afraid it takes two to tango, and I *certainly* don't feel the urge to make love to you right now. I think I'd be more inclined to throttle you, frankly.'

'Sure! Violence is your thing, isn't it? Just like the last time we made love? So what does your whore think of that kind of behaviour, then?'

'How dare you talk about her like that? Leave Sarah out of this!' Nick had finally been pushed too far, and he reached out to grab Diana by her shoulders in a fury, hurling her to the sofa. 'Don't ever refer to her like that again!' he roared at her. 'Sarah is a sweet, decent girl and I will *not* listen to that about her! It isn't true, and you know it!'

Frightened now, Diana began to cry. 'Nick! Please, I'm sorry! I know I've no right to be jealous, but I am! Please, I'd rather you admitted to sleeping with anyone but *her*!'

'I'm admitting to *nothing*. We've led separate lives for getting on for five years now. At your request, remember? I don't consider that what I do, or who I see, has *anything* to do with you any more.' Nick turned on his heel, unmoved by tears that would normally have melted him in a moment, knowing that this time they were a deliberate ploy. 'I'm going to shower and then I'm going to bed! Where *you* sleep is a matter of complete indifference to me, but I prefer that it's not in my bed!'

He went to bed, but sleep was impossible. He realized he had been unnecessarily cruel to Diana, and he felt wretched about it once he had calmed down. They rarely quarrelled as they just had, and he hated himself for it, but knowing that Charles had taken Sarah home did nothing for his peace of mind either. He desperately wanted to phone her and check if Charles was still there with her, but eventually he managed to put the temptation out of his mind. Sarah would accuse him of behaving like an idiot, and she would be right, he told himself ruefully. He was behaving like a complete fool and he cursed himself for his stupidity.

At four in the morning, when it was still dark, he finally gave up on the futile exercise, and let himself out of the flat to run several miles around the deserted park in a final attempt to push his body into exhaustion. He crept back indoors and simply threw himself into his bed to pull the duvet tightly over his head and shut out all the bitter doubts and accusations. Only then did he manage to sleep.

CHAPTER 16

Being plunged into the unremitting round of a family Christmas, after months of pleasing himself, was, Nick decided a few weeks later, the nearest thing to hell that earth could provide.

Diana, on the other hand, seemed to thrive on the chaos of having three demanding parents, two dogs and Charlotte constantly underfoot. She was determined to be efficient and incredibly well-organized, but with no domestic help over the holidays she was heavily occupied most of the time. Nick was expected to entertain his despised in-laws and his own mother, much to his chagrin, since Diana had invited them all without his knowledge.

Intending to get most of a new script written and typed, he retreated more and more frequently to the office he had created in the old staff flat above the garage, and often Charlotte crept out to join him. Consequently the two of them played endless games on the computer instead of Nick working, and he got more and more behind on the script.

'If Granny Grey tells one more story about when you were a naughty boy to your ayah, I think I'll scream!' Charlotte complained bitterly on Christmas Eve, erupting into the office to find Nick sighing with frustration after yet another battle with his computer. 'Oh, Daddy! Come on! Let me do that!'

'I wish Jane was here. I hate using this damn thing!' Nick thumped the desk in annoyance, and glared at the machine on it. 'It never does what I want it to do! The picture's gone really small, and I can't get it back.'

'That's only because you've hit the wrong key somehow,' Charlotte said sensibly. 'With computers, there's always a reason for them going wrong.' Infuriatingly, within seconds she had sorted out the problem and Nick was back on course again. 'If you hate it so much, why don't you ask Madeleine Miller to help you out?' Charlotte added. 'Uncle Paul says she's bored stiff at home with nothing to do, and she *is* a secretary, remember?'

'*Uncle* Paul?' Nick looked surprised. 'Since when has Paul got so friendly with you?'

'Oh, he's always here,' Charlotte said innocently. 'He and Mummy are working on a book or something. Madeleine will be at the party tonight, why don't you ask her?'

'I might just do that! What a good idea of yours, moppet.' He reached to hug his daughter and Charlotte slid easily onto his knee to hug him back as she always did. It was a comfortable relationship and he relaxed in it for a few moments – until Diana appeared in the doorway, an irritated expression on her face as she viewed the evidence of a warmth that had been denied to her certainly since the row after the première, and, if she was really honest, that she had not wanted for years. Now, faced with their obvious camaraderie, she saw red.

'Charlotte! For heaven's sake!' she commented acidly. 'Aren't you a little old for sitting on Daddy's knee? Get off!'

'Don't be ridiculous, Diana,' Nick chided. 'What harm is she doing? Apart from straining my back with her weight?'

'It's hardly decent at her age! What would my mother think? Or yours?' Diana pointed out.

'To hell with them! Sanctimonious old biddies! Did you

213

want me for something?' Nick deliberately hugged Charlotte to reassure her as Diana glared.

'Yes, I did. Would you come and make up a four? The parents want to play bridge, and I have to finish the stuff for tonight. I simply haven't the time.'

Nick groaned. 'Only as long as I don't have to partner your mother! She's really hopeless. Let Alistair keep her in line; he's used to it.' Nick had learnt to play bridge at his own mother's knee, and was an expert player, as she was, when he put his mind to it.

'Promise! Thanks, Nick.' Diana reached over and, surprisingly, dropped a kiss on his cheek. 'I'll make it up to you.'

'You'd better!' he threatened.

'That's more like it!' Charlotte commented. 'It's about time you two did something rather than yell. You've been bitching at each other for weeks now! Even the grannies are beginning to gossip about it!'

Nick and Diana looked at each other guiltily over Charlotte's head, and finally Nick smiled. 'I suppose she's right,' he acquiesced, and held out a hand. 'Pax?'

'I guess so.' Diana looked relieved.

'Happy now, Lotts?' Nick ruffled his daughter's curls. Charlotte pressed her own noisy kiss on his cheek. 'Don't call me Lotts!' she protested. 'It's so babyish!'

'Oh, yes? So what's this, then?' He tipped her off his knee.

'That's different, that's a hug, and I like that anyway.'

'And this?' With a sudden change of direction he scooped Charlotte high up in the air and ran down the stairs with her, amid shrieks of delight from her, ignoring dire warnings from Diana, who followed at a more sedate pace behind them, relieved that the atmosphere had lightened at last.

He managed to keep up his good humour, even after a taut session of bridge, and it lasted all through dinner, but it was with a great sense of release that he set off to deliver

Charlotte to a party in nearby Woodstock later that evening, knowing he could ring Sarah from the car in privacy.

She was so pleased to hear him, and his stress melted as he talked to her – for so long that he started to feel chilled in the stationary car. After he rang off, he started the engine, but sat staring out into the already frosted countryside, mulling over the conflicting emotions inside him.

He suddenly realized he had been sitting there for nearly an hour, dreaming in the darkness, and he slammed the car into gear frantically, in a panic to get back, remembering they had guests coming.

'Sorry, darling,' he lied as he rushed in. 'I stopped to help someone.' He realized just how many lies he was telling these days.

Later, circulating amongst the friends and neighbours Diana had invited, he was aware he was operating on autopilot – until he drew the delectable Madeleine aside. Really, he thought, she was far too young and sparky for dull old Paul Miller.

'Why, I'd love to work for you, Nick!' she cried. 'I'm desperate for something to do. Do you want me to come up to London?'

'Possibly,' he said cautiously, thinking how Madeleine would brighten up the office. 'But for the moment it's just this one script – if you can sort out the mess I've made. I'm afraid I'm not exactly gifted with computers!'

'Give me your notes and I'll transfer your stuff onto a disk so that I can take it with me, if you like, then I can do it on my own PC,' she offered.

Relieved to find someone who understood his problems, he sat talking to her for ages, until Diana's mother pointedly suggested he was neglecting his guests. 'Diana can't cope alone all night,' she chided. Nick sighed, but he was anxious to keep the peace, and went back to his duties as host.

* * *

215

Despite her misgivings, Sarah found she was enjoying her holidays. It was always comfortable staying with George and Maggie, and she adored little Becky, the grandchild her mother had not lived to see. Nick phoned her as often as he could, usually from his car or from his portable phone when he was walking the dog, so she had very little chance to miss him.

Sarah loved her sister-in-law, but she sometimes found her snobbishness a little hard to take. However, over the holiday she played her part happily enough, knowing what Maggie expected of her. This year she was more of a celebrity than usual to the Campbell friends and neighbours, but was aware that it was the men who were admiring her now, and not just the children.

The relaxing part of it was driving over with Becky to visit Cress and James on Boxing Day at Cress's parent's home just outside Winchester. Cress came from the same kind of middle class home that Sarah did – a large, friendly crowd who had accepted James into their midst without question and took equally to Sarah when she appeared with Becky.

Flying down the steps of the house to meet her, Cress waved her hand to Sarah in excitement. 'Look, Sarah,' she cried. 'Just look!' Delighted, but with a twinge of envy, Sarah took in the aquamarine and diamond ring Cress wore on her engagement finger. 'He asked me on Christmas Eve, on one knee and everything. Oh, I'm so happy, Sarah!'

Sarah put aside her feelings of jealousy, and hugged her friend. 'I'm really pleased for you. I'm glad he got his act together at last!'

'It was the novelty of being looked after that did it,' Cress laughed. 'Come on in.'

She stayed far later than she had intended, and when James carried a flaked-out Becky to her car, it was eight o'clock. Watching him gently tucking a blanket round her made her smile wistfully. James smiled back at her. 'Kids are great when they're asleep,' he quipped. 'I think I'll only love mine that way!'

'Thinking about them already?' she enquired, eyebrows raised.

'Cress is . . . about four so far!'

'That'll certainly ruin your image!'

'Well, as long as it doesn't ruin my figure,' he laughed. 'I think I'm going to love it!'

She drove carefully, aware of the sleeping child on the back seat, her head full of her friends' happy plans, and suddenly she began to feel very lonely. It was ridiculous, she told herself firmly. She was going to be a star, with the world opening up at her feet, so why on earth was she crying, and envying two people who wanted to stay at home and have babies?

CHAPTER 17

The only time everyone female agreed on a TV programme over Christmas in the Grey household it was on the Barbara Bentley drama the day after Boxing Day – apart from Diana, who wanted to opt out when she discovered Sarah was in it.

Seeing her in the delicate, clinging Regency costumes, with constant close-ups of her wide, trembling mouth speaking lines that they had laughed over in bed together several times in France, only made Nick feel his usual incredible lust for her, and he wriggled constantly.

Charlotte, tactless as ever, didn't help. 'Isn't she gorgeous, Granddad? You should see her in Daddy's new film, though, without her clothes on! She's got fantastic boobs, hasn't she, Daddy?'

'I'm going to strangle her!' Nick hissed at Diana, who, despite herself, began to laugh, as her mother looked askance at both of them.

'Actually, the hero's a bit like you, Daddy,' Charlotte added. 'All black hair and frowning, like you are now.'

'That's it! Fancy a cigar, Alistair?' Nick got up. 'I'm going to have one . . . in the study,' he added, as *both* mothers glared.

'Don't mind if I do.' Alistair Mackenzie joined him with alacrity.

Nick passed the cigars to him, and poured large malts for both of them. It was one of the few things they agreed on. 'Damn pretty girl, that Sarah Campbell.' Alistair drew luxuriantly on his cigar. 'I hear you've been seeing a lot of her recently.'

'No more than the star of any film I've made,' Nick said carefully. 'The papers have gone to town on her a bit, since she came from a children's programme that was very popular.' He was ever wary of Alistair's protective attitude over Diana.

'Saw your new film the other day,' Alistair admitted then, shocking Nick to the core. Alistair never normally took any notice of his work, and the Mackenzies never replied to invitations to showings. 'Popped along one afternoon. Wouldn't say so in front of Dorothy, but young Lotte is right! I must admit, *I* wouldn't mind a night of her company!'

The thought of Sarah in Alistair's arms made Nick want to throw up, but he managed to smile. 'I think she would prove your undoing, Alistair! Poor old Charlie Hastings is finding her a handful, and he's got thirty-odd years on you!'

'Seeing Charlie, is she? I'm glad to hear it – especially after some of the hints in the papers.'

'Never believe gossip in newspapers,' Nick assured him, thankful for Charles's devotion to Sarah. 'Diana and I agree on that score.'

'Time you and Diana got your acts together,' Alistair said, quietly. 'Living like you two do isn't exactly an ideal marriage.'

'My business is in London,' Nick pointed out, 'and Diana's is here. She doesn't have to work. It *is* her choice. The arrangement suits us, Alistair.'

'It suits *you* more to the point.'

'I *have* to work,' Nick told him. It was the same old argument. 'I asked Diana to come back to London five years ago, but she prefers it here. I don't think you'll find her complaining.'

'Unlike her mother.' He gave Nick a conspiratorial

wink. 'Who never stops where you are concerned, young man.'

'I haven't been a young man for some years now,' Nick reminded him drily. 'And you may assure Dorothy that Diana and I are fine, thank you.'

We *are* fine, he thought, ruefully, as fine as we'll ever be. But he still wanted Sarah, wanted her even more after seeing the TV play. Cautiously he glanced at his watch. The play would be over soon. Somehow he sat through another half-hour of Alistair's company, then he rose, saying he would walk the dogs. Poor Boots was getting blisters with so much exercise.

Throwing on his Barbour and whistling to Boots and the Mackenzies' retriever, he strode out into the night. The frosty air cleared the cigar smoke from his lungs as he walked down the lane, well away from the house, before he pulled his portable phone from his pocket. Thank goodness for modern technology, he thought as he dialled.

Sarah herself answered the call.

'I lusted after you far too much to watch a great deal of the play. I was giving myself away,' he admitted. 'Do you mind?'

'Not at all. It was total tripe,' she replied cheerfully. 'I hate watching myself anyway, but at least Maggie approved of it! I do miss you, Nick. Seeing the play reminded me of France.'

'It did me. And I miss you too,' he said softly. 'Look, could you get up to town tomorrow? I have to drive my mother home. I could meet you at your flat for a few hours?'

'What sort of time?'

'About one?'

'I'll be there – somehow. Maggie will go mad if I disappear, but I'll manage,' she promised, feeling the sudden glow of expectation rushing through her. What should have been a fortnight's separation had turned into a week.

Feeling better, Nick turned back to the house after a few more minutes, and went back in to play the host and reassure his parents-in-law that everything between him and Diana was going beautifully.

The flat was cold when Sarah got in, just before twelve. Shivering, she ran round turning up the heating, even switching on the electric blanket. Since she had raced around that morning helping a harassed Maggie with her dinner party preparations before she went out, she decided to have a bath to get rid of the cooking smells. Maggie had been furious, since she had expected Sarah to look after Becky for the afternoon. She'd been in a bigger state than usual, since she had invited Charles to dinner – to Sarah's fury. Thankfully, George had stepped in. 'I'll take Becky out,' he offered. 'It must be important for Sarah to need to go up to town today.'

Not bothering to dress, she dried her hair quickly, and was just spraying herself with Chanel when she heard Nick's key in the door. With a cry of joy she ran to him, throwing her arms around his neck as he lifted her up.

'God! How I've wanted you,' he sighed, and carried her into the bedroom as her hands went to his jacket buttons.

Nick took her cue, and threw off the rest of his clothes, taking her eagerly into his arms and sinking back, only to cry out in astonishment. 'This bloody bed is *hot!*'

'Oh, hell! I put the blanket on!' Sarah giggled. Holding her against him, Nick began to laugh too. She kissed him, playing her own fingers against his chest as his fingers explored her before he gently made love to her. 'We really should try and do other things,' she sighed then. 'It seems all we want to do is make love.'

'Not so,' he corrected. 'I seem to remember trekking all around the Louvre when we were in Paris a while back – not to mention Versailles – *and* being made to ride all day on Dartmoor not so long ago!' They had managed a few precious days at the Devon cottage just a week or so before Christmas.

'Yes, and I had to spend all night massaging your back!'

'That was because I hadn't ridden for a long time!' he defended. '*That* bit *was* fun! What's brought this mood on suddenly? Come on, tell me. Something's bothering you.'

'How would you know?' she slid against his shoulder so that he couldn't see her face, buried as it was by her hair.

'Because over the last seven months or so I've learnt all your moods.' He smiled. 'I *know* when you're unhappy, I *know* when you're covering things up – I even know when your period's due. You can't hide anything from me, darling.'

'How do you know *that*?' She was astonished.

He laughed. 'Because the day before it starts you're as scratchy as hell! Now what *is* the matter?'

Trying to be casual, she told him about Cress and James. Nick knew at once how much it had hurt her, and he cuddled her gently. 'Cress is a lot older than you,' he pointed out. 'By the time you get to thirty-two, you'll probably be married to some wonderful man and thinking of babies of your own.'

'Oh, are you thinking of making me pregnant, then?' she enquired cheekily.

'God forbid! It's the last thing I want.' Nick shuddered, and Sarah stared in surprise at the vehemence in his tone. 'I don't ever want any more children.'

'Never?'

'No! I'd never knowingly put any woman through the purgatory Diana went through having Charlotte.'

'Maybe she was just unlucky,' Sarah suggested, horrified.

'Maybe, but I still wouldn't do it. Don't even think about it, my darling!'

'Well, not for a while anyway!' She sighed, since there was only one man she really wanted to have a child with.

Nick, she decided, would simply have to be talked into it once the time was more appropriate. She certainly refused to take him seriously – every man on earth wanted a son, didn't they? 'I shall just have to settle for being rich and famous instead.'

'Is that so bad?'

'At the moment, I'm not sure. I'm afraid of what's happening to me. It's all so sudden.'

'You've been fighting off fans for almost two years,' he said. 'It's not *quite* so sudden.'

'Not like this,' she said. 'I'm beginning to feel hunted every time I go anywhere, and some of the mail I get is frightening. The children never wrote things like that!'

'Throw it away and forget it!' Nick advised, remembering Alistair Mackenzie's comment. 'I must admit, though, even my awful father-in-law fancies spending the night with you!'

'I bet that gave you a fright!'

'It certainly didn't make me feel too comfortable,' he confessed. 'Forget it, darling. Shall I make some tea? I shall have to go soon.'

'My! You have got into the domestic routine suddenly!' she laughed. 'But you may. I even remembered to bring some milk – and some of Maggie's cake.'

Nick was as good as his word and made tea. Then, even though he knew he should be leaving, he reached for her again, finding he couldn't bear to leave her so soon. It was six o'clock before they reluctantly drew apart, knowing they had to leave, and dressed hurriedly. Kissing her fervently as they reached their two cars in the garage, he still held her.

'If Charlie tries to propose under the mistletoe what will you tell him?' he asked her sadly, his face buried in her hair.

'That I'm totally and absolutely satisfied, for the fore-seeable future,' she replied firmly.

'I hope so!' He kissed her again, and bundled her into

her car. 'Go on, before I take you again on the back seat,' he ordered her, laughing.

'After this afternoon I doubt that even *you* could manage that,' she challenged, her eyes bright with tears. 'I love you, Nick. I really love you.'

He couldn't trust himself to speak then, just touched her cheek gently and blew her a kiss as she drove out of the garage then swung into his own car to follow her up the ramp out into the deserted streets, his eyes too, surprisingly, also blurred by tears.

Later that week, Charles and Nick had yet another a sharp exchange on the subject of – in Charles's opinion – Nick's cavalier treatment of Sarah. But to Charles's intense annoyance, Nick laughed at him. 'I've never heard Sarah complain about the way I treat her,' he told Charles firmly. 'And until she does, I suggest *you* mind your own business! I told you months ago she wasn't right for you, and I mean it even more now I know her better.'

Frustrated, Charles had to swallow his worries, biding his time until Nick went off to America in January for several weeks and he could safely invite Sarah down to Hastings.

He knew she loved to come at weekends, to ride for hours with him in all weathers. She had earned the respect of his more down-to-earth friends for her resilience in the often appalling conditions that winter, and amid the noisy group of riders gathered in the pub, or the Hastings Court kitchen after riding, Sarah was relaxed. Her being an actress mattered little to them, the way she took a fence or sat her horse meant far more. No one watched much TV in that crowd, and they certainly didn't go to the cinema.

Nick, Sarah knew, hated her going to Hastings, especially since the atmosphere between him and Charles had cooled, but Sarah shrugged off his sarcasm. In fact she was terribly lonely, and Charles filled a large gap. Over the months he had carefully and unobtrusively become a fixture in her life, as indispensable in his way as Nick was, but for completely different reasons. Otherwise, apart from work, she spent her free time alone in her flat, working on her tapestry, or with George and Maggie in Guildford. Cressida, apart from being totally wrapped up in her love for James, was busy on her new film and could only manage the odd hurried lunch.

Away in Los Angeles, Nick longed for her, phoning her whenever he could, worrying as Sarah grew more and more involved with Charles and her visits to Hastings. Yet when he returned, towards the end of February, going straight to her before he went home to Diana, she was ecstatic to see him and he was reassured within minutes of arriving.

She was a bundle of nerves over her impending first night. Even the announcement of the BAFTA nominations soon after Nick got back from Los Angeles failed to cheer her very much. Being nominated for best actress meant very little when she was having trouble remembering her lines, as she was then. Nick, however, was delighted with their five nominations; best film, director, actor, actress and editor. All it did for Sarah was increase her interview-load.

In vain, Nick tried to buoy up her spirits, but as the dress rehearsal approached she grew more and more depressed.

'I haven't done stage work since *Cats*,' she wailed one evening. 'I'm out of practice. I want to quit.'

'Don't be ridiculous,' he chided. 'You always want out when the going gets rough. You know perfectly well you can do it.'

But the dress rehearsal did, indeed, turn out to be a nightmare for her. In a totally black mood of despair she drove home, refusing a drink with the other actors, nice as they were. The sight of Nick's Porsche, parked in the garage, lifted her spirits enormously, since he had been back in Los Angeles again for several days. Parking her own car haphazardly, she raced up the stairs to her flat, throwing herself at him as he opened the door to the sound of her flying feet.

'Oh, Nick, it was awful!' she cried, her head burrowing into his shoulder. 'I forgot all my lines, and my nightdress fell off, and Tim slipped on the balcony . . .'

'It sounds like a typical dress rehearsal to me,' Nick said drily. 'I've just spoken to Barry – he says everything is fine. Come on. I ran a bath for you and I made supper.'

Despite his own fatigue, he fussed over her, bringing her a drink in the bath, making her eat, listening to her pouring out the problems of the rehearsal. Sarah ended up on his lap, laughing, and ready for bed.

Overwhelmed by jet-lag, however, having worked a full day since landing that morning, Nick was asleep as soon as his head touched the pillow. Sarah curled herself around him, happy just to have him there. He could be so gentle and thoughtful when he chose to be. She wished he could be like that more often, but – she smiled in the darkness – it would not be Nick if he was, and she was now used to his mercurial moods. Carefully she slid her hands down his relaxed, sleeping body, and her stroking fingers quickly produced a reaction.

'Stop molesting me, woman,' Nick said softly in her ear suddenly, surprising her.

'I thought you were asleep,' she told him.

Nick laughed. 'I am!'

'Shall I stop?' She paused, but his arms went firmly round her as he arched against her.

'No! I guess I'm awake now,' he chuckled. 'And, since I'm stuck with bringing Lotte with me tomorrow, I'd better make the most of tonight! Do your worst – but I warn you, I may fall asleep again unless you work really hard!'

* * *

226

As Sarah wasn't due at the theatre until four, they stayed in bed half the morning. Nick, being careful to keep her occupied, then took her to San Lorenzo for lunch.

'This is taking a bit of a chance isn't it?' Sarah remarked, rather smugly looking round as people stared at them and whispered.

'Not at all,' he assured her. 'We are celebrating your BAFTA nomination if anyone asks.' He nodded to some agency people he knew, and ordered a bottle of Chablis.

'Do you think I should drink today?' she asked, doubtfully.

'Why ever not? I'm not going to get you drunk, Barry would never forgive me.'

He got her to the theatre in good time and in fairly high spirits. Leaning into the back of the car, he produced a bulky parcel. 'Open that when you get inside,' he instructed. 'Not now!' he added as she tried to open it.

Sarah laughed with pleasure and leaned over to kiss him. 'I'll see you after the show,' she said. 'If I survive it.'

'You'll be wonderful, I'm sure,' he replied, crossing his fingers. 'Just remember I'll have Charlotte with me. We'll be in the bar on the top level.'

'I'll follow James's groupies,' she teased, and climbed out of the car, then stood waving rather forlornly as he drove away. She was thrilled to have such a large crowd of people coming, but still panic-stricken at the thought that she might let them down. It had been quite a surprise that Nick was bringing Charlotte with him, but it was half-term, and with Diana away he was loath to let her go to her grandparents for the night. She understood only too well how much Nick valued time with Charlotte, though her slightly more wicked half wondered if Diana knew where he was taking her for the evening!

Her dressing room was full of flowers, everything from the white roses Nick invariably sent her, to a basket of lilies-of-the-valley from Peter. She pushed those to the back to open Nick's parcel and laughed with delight. It contained a huge woolly lamb with a pink ribbon round its neck holding a card saying, 'Hug me if you need one!' written in Nick's sprawling black handwriting.

With cast notes and last minute walk-throughs it seemed no time at all before the ASM was calling the half-hour, then the ten minutes. Sarah did not appear for several scenes, but, dressed and ready, she stood waiting in the wings, watching the first rowdy fight scene.

The actresses playing Lady Capulet and the Nurse, paused to give her words of comfort as they took their positions to go on. Her dresser checked her dress and rebrushed her hair as she waited, setting her velvet cap more firmly, then giving her a little push as the Nurse gave her her cue. *'What, Juliet!'*

'How now! who calls?' she replied, and she ran on stage.

It went so smoothly she was quickly at ease, her lines flowing easily. Tim Farmer, playing Romeo, was tall and athletic with dark hair and deep dark eyes, a perfect foil for her golden beauty. Their first kiss in scene five followed by their tenderly erotic balcony scene had the audience raving in the interval.

'Oh, Daddy,' sighed Charlotte as they rose. 'Isn't Sarah wonderful? She's so beautiful! I think I want to be an actress, just like her!'

Nick laughed with relief at the obvious fervour in her voice. 'Last month you were going to be a vet,' he reminded her, thinking to himself just how good Charlotte's delicate bone structure would look on screen.

'Well, I've changed my mind! I can't wait to meet Sarah again!'

'I wonder if that has anything to do with her sexy co-star?' James teased her as he caught the end of their conversation.

'As if it would – I'm devoted to *you*, James,' Charlotte assured him. 'But of course, if you must desert me for

Auntie Cress, I suppose I have to learn to understand about older women.'

'*Older* women – *Auntie* Cress?' James hooted with laughter. 'Don't let *her* catch you calling her either of those!'

Nick found himself next to a male, blonder version of Sarah in the bar. 'You have to be George,' he guessed, holding out his hand. 'I'm Nicholas Grey.'

George Campbell was as attractive as Sarah, with the same thickly lashed hazel eyes, and slow, wide smile, which showed as he recognized the voice on the telephone over Christmas. He wanted to be angry with Nick, but Nick turned out to be as charming as Sarah had led him to believe, and reluctantly he soon found himself liking him.

Maggie seemed overwhelmed to find herself surrounded by such glamorous and exciting people. James was attracting his usual crowd of admirers, and Charles and Nick, though cool with each other, were equally friendly to her. She was *so* pleased that she had been to the hairdresser's and bought a new dress for the occasion.

The fact that the entire audience were praising Sarah made Nick ache with pride for her. He watched the love scene after the interval with a wistful smile at the two young lovers' passionate exchanges as they played the scene, half on the crimson-draped bed, half on the floor. Sarah's experience at his hands had certainly prepared her well for this, he thought wryly, and his mind went back to Natasha playing Juliet for him at Oxford all those years ago. He wondered if Charles remembered it too.

How different she had been; slender, almost waif-like, with a cloud of dark hair, waxy pale compared with Sarah's healthy glow. He had fallen in love with Natasha then, and been sucked into her terrifying, black, moody world, and he shuddered now, remembering the despair and rage she had inspired in him. Yet he *had* truly loved her, and at that moment he realized that Sarah was the only girl he had loved since with the same intensity. Since Natasha, Nick had been determined not to let a woman get to him, and he had stuck to his resolve over the years. He knew exactly why he had married Diana Mackenzie, and he didn't always like what he'd done. But it *had* been done, and he was stuck with that.

He knew that part of the reason he was 'stuck with it' was his never-ending guilt over Diana's suffering during her pregnancy with Charlotte and then the baby's birth. Never would he forget the agonies Diana had endured to give him his perfect daughter. And, however empty his marriage was, and always had been, he couldn't in all conscience just abandon his wife.

The realization of his feelings for Sarah hit him hard, and for a moment he shut his eyes, reeling with the shock, and then wondered what on earth he was going to do about it. Could he really risk leaving Diana for a girl of twenty-five? Abandon his wife, and lose his daughter into the bargain – for Diana would never allow Charlotte to forgive him, he was sure, much as Charlotte admired Sarah.

The idea of leaving Diana was certainly very tempting, however, when he remembered the sensual hours he and Sarah had shared the previous night. Then he thought of the company, and the people who were dependent on him for their livelihood – with regret. He would lose control, and without him the company would certainly struggle. There was no way he could work for NGA with someone else in charge. Although, theoretically, other people could run it, it was due to Nick's talent alone that the company thrived as it did.

Alistair had always threatened he would demand a huge financial compensation for Diana's share of it if anything happened between Nick and Diana, and Nick *knew* he meant it. Buying her out, and possibly Charles as well, would certainly bankrupt him. For all their success, that kind of sudden cash demand would be impossible to meet and there would be no way he could start NGA again – particularly without the valuable financial knowhow of Charles Hastings. No way would *he* help Nick in a new life with Sarah.

He slid lower in his seat, struggling to push the thoughts to the back of his mind, to concentrate on the stage, and prayed that for a while Diana would not find out exactly how he felt about Sarah . . . that maybe, just maybe, there was a solution if only he could think of it – a way to save his employees and marry Sarah. But he knew sadly that it was the last thing he could discuss with her.

Cress caught his eye and smiled fleetingly, thinking it was Tim being just a little too sincere for Nick's comfort that had made him look so sad.

The applause for Sarah's curtain call was tremendous, and as she was pushed forwards by Tim to stand alone, slim and trembling in her white and gold brocade dress, Nick thought for a moment how vulnerable she looked, and how terribly young. Then she turned and took Tim's hand, so that they could take the applause together, and her smile broke through.

Being a film and TV personality, Sarah found the applause a heady new experience, but she still approached her friends in the bar with caution, waiting anxiously for Nick's approval. Despite Charlotte's presence, he laughingly swept her up first, and shocked Maggie to the core in the process.

Barry Harper appeared, and gradually most of the cast, all ready to congratulate her. Charlotte was as enthusiastic as everyone else, demanding that Sarah sign her programme and then persuading her to introduce her to the rest of the cast – particularly Tim Farmer.

'I think you may have just lost yourself an admirer, James!' Nick teased him as they watched Charlotte hanging on to every word Tim uttered.

'Such a fickle lady!' James grinned. 'She was swearing her undying loyalty in the interval, too.'

'Thank goodness for Tim, then!' Cress grinned. 'I must say, though, it was brave of you to bring her, Nick.'

'Not much choice,' he admitted ruefully. 'Still, a little culture won't hurt her, I suppose.'

'And at least having met Sarah on her own ground she'll perhaps learn to see her as the charming girl she is,' Cress said. 'Because you can bet your sweet life she hasn't heard much good of her at home!'

'I hope you're right,' Nick sighed. 'God, Cress, what *am* I doing?'

'Getting yourself into one great big jam, Nicholas! That's what you're doing!' Cress said tartly. 'And not just at home. Charlie looks about ready to commit murder too!'

'Charlie has got to learn to live with it!' Nick snapped. 'As I did over Natasha. And the sooner he does, the better!'

'Easier said than done, Nick. Charles is besotted with her.'

'Then more fool him,' Nick returned. 'God, Cress! I'm a total idiot. I'll wreck Sarah's life as well as my own at this rate.'

'Then give her up, Nick.' Cress squeezed his arm in sympathy. 'You know it's the wisest thing to do.'

'It may be the wisest,' Nick said. 'But it's not what I want to do.'

'You may have to, darling. Or sit down and do some very hard thinking.'

CHAPTER 18

Nick did that many times in the next few weeks. With hours to spend flying between Heathrow and Los Angeles, he had plenty of time to think about Sarah and the predicament he was in. Ironically, Diana seemed to be making a huge effort to make their marriage work: coming up to London frequently, often letting her own work suffer to do so. Since the night of the film première Nick had continued to sleep separately from her, but lately he was becoming more and more aware of her desire for him to move back into their joint bedroom, a move he was very reluctant to agree to as the temptation to ask for a divorce became stronger.

Fully committed with her National appearances and preparations for a new film, Sarah had very little time to worry about Nick, or the coming BAFTA awards. Until Nick announced that, unusually, Diana had decided not to attend, so he was free to escort Sarah. Then she panicked and raced Cress all over London looking for another new dress. The green one, beautiful as it was, had been relegated to the back of her wardrobe. After the débâcle of the film première she had decided she would never wear it again.

Nick, on collecting her on the night of the awards, approved of the slim column of grey silk, much to her relief, and she laughed as she held him off when he wanted to do more than kiss her.

'Bill's waiting downstairs,' she protested, 'and you'll crease it, Nick, please!' She realized very quickly that he had been drinking, and she was careful not to antagonize him, tonight of all nights.

'All right!' He gave in gracefully enough, sensing that for once she meant no. 'But wait till we get home!'

'You'll never make it if you carry on drinking as you obviously have been!' Sarah rebuked. 'Have you had a row with Diana, by any chance?'

'Mind your own business!' he almost snapped at her, then he laughed. 'Come on, you were the one who didn't want to keep Bill waiting – though it wouldn't be the first time!'

'I bet it wouldn't!' She took his cue, and forgot her question, following him obediently downstairs and greeting Bill cheerfully. He often drove them now, and he was very fond of Sarah, though he heartily disapproved of Nick's affair with her.

Nick had been a member of BAFTA for many years, and had served on the Council for several. Busy as he was, he had found the time to chair one of the juries for the awards, as he normally did. Like a lot of other members, he found the awards ceremony long-winded and often immensely boring – unless it involved his own work, of course!

This year he felt a little more kindly towards attending, especially as Diana wasn't. She had cited the sycophantic table-hopping procedure before and after the awards as her reason for staying away. But they both knew it was because she would have to sit at the same table as Sarah for several hours.

Sarah herself was happy, sweeping into the hotel with Nick, feeling as if she belonged. As nominees, they were fêted, and she had learnt to like it. Nick, more laid-back about it, calmly ordered extra bottles of wine for their table. 'It's a long night,' he explained to Sarah, when she protested.

234

She shuddered at the thought of him drinking malt all night. He rarely drank to excess, but when he did she had learnt to be very wary. Sitting down at their table, she prayed he would win his awards, or he would be impossible.

As it was, he disappeared with Seth for quite some time during the early part of the evening, leaving Sarah alone. Relaxed, then, with James, Charles and Cress for company Sarah ignored his absence, knowing that his business with Seth was likely to involve both her and James. Seth was setting up a film in Ireland for later that year and she knew he and his director wanted both of them for it. Her thoughts were diverted by Cress, trying to persuade her to be a bridesmaid at their autumn wedding.

'How the hell can James be married in church?' Sarah demanded. 'He's been divorced twice!'

'I have a sympathetic minister,' Cress grinned. 'And my father's a church warden!'

'I'm far too tall to be a bridesmaid for you,' Sarah complained.

'My sister is nearly as tall as you,' Cress said, brooking no argument. 'And almost as blonde – though *she's* had some help!'

'Well, if you insist.' Sarah gave in reluctantly. 'And if I'm not stuck on location somewhere.' Their happiness suddenly seemed to cast a shadow on her cheerful mood. She would have given everything she had to be discussing weddings with Nick, as James and Cress were.

'Only wedding around,' said James quietly to her, 'where the bridegroom has publicly made love to the bridesmaid!'

Sarah cheered up and hit him, just as Nick returned.

'Stop fighting, children, I've just sorted out a very nice job for you.' he said, sliding into his seat next to Sarah and pouring himself a drink.

'Stop it, Nick,' Sarah chided quickly. 'You'll be legless at this rate!' His eyes were glittering dangerously already.

Nick touched her hand to his lips and ignored her comment. Charles flashed a warning glance at him, guessing rightly, that he had had a row with Diana, but Nick took no notice whatsoever. Rows with Diana usually had that effect on him.

They were all ignoring the awards going on round them – film people were never interested in the TV people – and then Nick seemed to sober up as he glanced at his programme. 'Tidy up your make-up, sweetheart,' he said to Sarah. 'Just in case.'

Obediently she did so, and started to pay attention. The actor announcing the nominations for best actress was one whose name she knew from her childhood. She stared, fascinated, as the film clips appeared, and for once they were showing her long, impassioned speech to James and not their love scene. Nick reached for her hand as the actor unfastened the envelope.

'And the award goes, for her very first film, to . . . Sarah Campbell!'

Sarah heard the applause around her, and even with the camera on them Nick swept her up to kiss her before pushing her towards the stage. In a daze she struggled through the tables to the stage to collect the gold mask from the actor before being guided to the microphone. 'I'd just like to thank,' she murmured, conscious of having to be brief, 'the cast and crew of *Home Leave* for being so kind to a newcomer, and especially Nick Grey, my director, for being so patient with me!' That brought the knowing house down, and she escaped back to her seat during the laughter and applause.

James, much to their chagrin, lost out to an American, but Nick swept the board with best director and best film, which Chris collected. He ordered champagne all round to add to Nick's whisky, and they toasted each other merrily, until the Press dragged them away, anxious to catch their late editions.

'Come on, Nick, give her a kiss,' they cajoled, after

several photographs. He kissed her cheek. 'No! Come on, a real one!' they persuaded him.

Several drinks the wrong side of sober, Nick lifted Sarah up in his arms and kissed her thoroughly, to the delight of the Press and the amusement of the film people around them. Most of them were well aware of the situation between the couple.

Worried, Sarah then accompanied him on his rounds of the tables, being congratulated and fêted all around. But she hadn't missed the triumph on Max Moreton's face. 'You're going to regret that, Nick,' she said, when he paused.

'Stop worrying,' Nick assured her casually. 'We'll go in a minute. I have an incredible urge to make love to you.'

Sarah's heart sank, Nick being aggressive was not the way she wanted a triumphant evening to end, and she could read his mood just from the grip of his hand on her arm. But she fetched her wrap when he asked her to, and Nick went to call Bill.

He took her back to Regent's Park despite Sarah's protests, and dismissed Bill with a hefty tip. 'Will you be OK, miss?' Bill asked her quietly. 'He's a bit tiddly. I don't mind waiting for you.'

'I'll be fine.' Sarah tried to sound confident. 'He'll be asleep in a minute,' she added, crossing her fingers.

'Don't bank on it,' he warned, knowing Nick as he did. 'If you need to, ring me. I'll come back for you.'

'Cheer up. Bill.' Sarah could see Nick getting impatient. 'I'll get a taxi if all else fails.'

'What was that about?' Nick demanded as he guided her upstairs to the flat.

'Nothing. Just Bill worrying that you were drunk. Shall I make some coffee?'

'No, I don't want coffee.' He reached for her, pulling her towards him, and Sarah pulled away. He smelled of whisky and her disgust was obvious.

'Nick, go to bed,' she demanded. 'I've changed my mind. I'm going home!'

'Oh, no, you're not!' He seized her by the arms, yanking at the zip of her dress, forcing her to the marble floor of the hall. She fought him with all her strength, kicking and scratching as he struggled to hold her. No way, she decided, was he going to treat her like this, and she twisted frantically until she finally managed to drag herself away from him and pull her dress back on.

The telephone began to ring as she pulled at the zip, and, cursing, Nick got up to answer it. He could never leave an unanswered phone. Seth was on the other end, so there was no way he could slam it down then.

Frantic, Sarah grabbed her bag, and, flinging open the door, she raced down the stairs, struggling with the heavy street door before racing out into the night. Then she realized what a crazy thing she had done. Bill had taken her at her word and gone home.

It was raining, a steady downpour that left her soaked in minutes. She thought, regretfully, of her expensive dress as she struggled to get her bearings, knowing she would have to walk to Baker Street to have any chance of getting a taxi at that time of night. Then she realized that in her rush to get out of the flat she had forgotten to put her shoes back on. At least, she knew she had enough money in her bag, but she certainly didn't have Bill's phone number.

Terrified, she suddenly heard footsteps behind her in the empty park, and she froze, aware then of just how vulnerable she was. The next second Nick had caught up with her.

'What the hell are you playing at?' he shouted at her. He had raced after her within seconds of her leaving the flat, and was only wearing shirt and trousers, already soaked.

'I'm going home,' she retorted, trying to push him away again with no effect. He had her firmly by the arm, as she beat at his chest.

'Do you want to get us both arrested, you idiot?' he demanded as she struggled and the strap of her dress tore from its stitches. He ignored her protests and carried her back up to the flat, seemingly sobered up by the cold rain and fresh air.

Dropping her on the bed, he stripped off the dress, properly this time, and eyed it with regret. 'Go and have a shower,' he ordered her. 'You're frozen,' he added and threw the sodden dress on a chair. 'I think *that* has had it!'

Sarah went, wanting to lock the door on him but not daring to provoke him. When she came back into the bedroom he was wearing a bathrobe and towelling his wet hair. Aware of her earlier distaste, he had cleaned his teeth and now seemed amazingly sober.

Smiling sweetly at her surprised face, he pulled the covers back on the bed. 'Get in,' he said. 'You didn't really think I was going to risk my licence driving you home, did you? You're just going to have to put up with me!'

He was making no apology for his earlier behaviour, as he had so often done before. This was Nick at his worst, and though she hated it she knew she had no option. Mutinous, she rolled as far away from him as possible, but Nick pulled her back, kissing her set, angry mouth as she twisted her head from side to side, still determined to resist. She lay rigid under him, but it soon became a game as their two strong wills fought for supremacy.

He laughed with triumph as he felt her respond to his persuasive hands, hearing her moan with pleasure as she finally gave in, her body weak with longing as, at last, he moved gently into her. 'Oh, why do I always give in to you?' she sighed as he did so.

'Because you love me,' he told her. 'And I don't give up!'

In the morning, however, she had the upper hand when he woke up with a hangover. 'Serves you right!' she taunted. 'I take it you won't want any breakfast?'

Nick hit her with a pillow and pulled the covers over his head. He really did look rough. Sarah relented, and fetched him some Alka Seltzer, collecting the papers and her shoes from the hall as she did so. 'Good job you didn't ruin those as well,' Nick commented, seeing the Emma Hope label in them as she dropped them to the floor.

'The dress will clean, I'm sure,' she said hopefully. 'But I shall have to borrow something of yours to go home in.'

'I'll find you some clothes in a minute,' he promised. 'Right now, I'm going to stand under the shower and hope for the best,' he added, wincing as he stood up.

Laughing heartlessly at his discomfort, Sarah sat on the bed, sipping orange juice and flipping through the pile of newspapers. Their success was popular with the Press and their photographs were well used in most of them. She was pleased until she got to the *Unicorn*. The photos were on the inside page, as usual, but she stared at the prose with growing panic. This time there were no holds barred, and the whole had Max Moreton's by-line.

Director Nick Grey kisses his lover Sarah Campbell after they both won BAFTA awards in London last night. The couple, whose affair has been the talk of the film industry for months, came out in the open at the prestigious awards ceremony – a close friend confirmed to our reporter that the couple are crazy about each other, and that the long-time married director is on the point of leaving his heiress wife for the beautiful young star!

If only, thought Sarah miserably, knowing that this could well be the end of everything. For the first time their relationship had been openly described.

'"Heiress wife"! That'll be the day! Old man Mackenzie is on the verge of bankruptcy most of the time; he'll never leave Diana a penny!' commented Nick, looking over her shoulder. 'Damn! That bastard swore he'd get me, and I think he just has!'

'What on earth are we going to do?' Sarah asked, panic-stricken. 'Can we sue them?'

Nick gathered her into his arms, cradling her head

against his damp chest. 'We can't sue them for telling the truth, darling, and they know it's true. I've never told you this, but I had a conversation with Max after the last salvo. One of their reporters watched us making love at Hastings, in the garden that time. If we protest too much he'll use it somehow, I'm sure of it. There's sod all we can do about it, except deny we're getting married.'

'Oh, God, Nick, how can they do this to us?' Sarah raised tear-filled eyes to his.

'Vengeance can do very nasty things to people,' he admitted. 'It's me he wants, not you. I think you'll be safe enough. It's Diana I have to worry about. We had a steaming row about you yesterday, which was one of the reasons I got so drunk, I guess. It's not going to be an easy ride, darling.'

'Would it be so ridiculous? Do we have to deny it?' she asked hesitantly.

'Getting married?' Nick shook his head in defeat, though the thought had occupied him for weeks. He had to sound casual and even uncaring until he had worked out the best way to save the company. 'Sarah, I have told you before, I *am* married – to a devout Catholic – and apart from that I know I'm far too old for you, long-term. Look, don't worry. I'll think of something. Get dressed – I'd better get you out of here before the Press find out you are in my bed or Diana comes storming in. Though I don't suppose she's even up yet!'

Sarah knew he had a hangover, but she found it difficult to understand his swift dismissal of her question. Lots of people had affairs and got married, she thought angrily as she pulled on one of his sweaters and a pair of tracksuit trousers, why not them? Because – she remembered Ronnie's words – Nick always went back to that stuck-up little wife of his.

Smouldering with resentment, she sat beside Nick in the car as he drove her back to Chelsea, cursing his headache as he did so. It was rush hour and she slumped

low in her seat, watching his frowning profile terrified of
being recognized. His face only softened as he leant over to
kiss her goodbye.

'I'm going to the office,' he told her. 'If you have any
problems with the Press, ring me there.' He knew she had
a performance that night, so she couldn't go off to
Guildford as she had done before, and *she* was aware
that now he definitely had to go to Oxford that evening. He dropped her at the garage entrance to her flat so
that she could slip in the back way, even the soft clunk of
the car door jarring his throbbing head.

He walked into chaos at NGA, with reporters all over
the foyer. Sandy was frantically trying to deal with them
single-handed. With a few choice epithets Nick strode
through them. 'Call the police, Sandy, if they're not out of
here in ten seconds!' he ordered, and swept into his office.

Jane was trying to answer two phones at once and
looked close to tears. Swiftly Nick put both phones back
onto the hook. 'Never mind those,' he said. 'Just get me a
coffee, please, Jane, and some aspirin or something.'

'Hangover?' She was more sympathetic than Sarah had
been, but then he hadn't treated her as badly as he
remembered treating Sarah.

'You could say that!' he groaned, and picked up a phone.
'Don't put any calls through, Sandy, until I tell you.'

'Diana rang,' Jane told him, as she put the coffee down.
'She said to tell you Max had rung her.' Nick put his head
in his hands.

'This isn't going to be my day!' he said thickly.

Too right it isn't, Jane thought grimly. She had been
fielding Press calls since eight o'clock that morning. But
she adored Nick, and she hated seeing him in such a state.

'It's my own fault,' he told her, seeing her sympathetic
face. 'I don't often get drunk, but I certainly did last night,
and I handed it to Moreton on a plate. Now be a good girl
and give me five minutes to speak to Diana.'

His hand was shaking as he pressed the button on his

phone for the Oxford house, using the private line since he was sure Diana would have switched the main phone onto the answering machine. 'Hi, it's me,' he said, as calmly as possible, and then held the phone away as his normally calm wife screamed abuse at him. 'It's only Maxie being vicious,' he reasoned hopefully, but knowing Max had surely told Diana about Hastings he knew that he was well and truly caught in his nasty little plot. 'I'll be home this evening,' he promised. 'We'll discuss it then.'

He was *too* calm. Diana threw the phone down in disgust and paced the room in a frenzy. 'Little bitch!' she muttered angrily. 'I'll sort her!' And she raked through her desk, searching for Nick's copy of the unit list for the film. Sarah's number was listed on it, and she dialled with trembling fingers.

Sarah answered the phone quickly, hoping it was Nick, and recoiled as if the receiver was hot when her worst fears were realized. Suddenly it all came home to her as she heard the obvious anguish in Diana's voice. Nick's wife was no longer a distant being; she was there at the end of the phone, and she was hurting – probably more than Sarah was herself at that moment.

Regret and real remorse filled her mind as it swept through every suddenly illegal detail of her life with Nick while she listened to his unhappy wife. Her parents would have been horrified, and she realized then just what she had done. She had let them down and made a dreadful mistake. Nick was Diana's husband. He would never be hers. But oh, God, she wanted him still.

'There's no point in denying it, Sarah,' Diana said at last, coldly. 'I know all about you and Nick. Max Moreton told me a great deal this morning.'

'I wouldn't dream of denying it.' Sarah hesitated, then said tentatively, 'What do you want, Diana?'

'I want you to stop seeing my husband right now, you little slut!' Diana's voice was suddenly cool and level, as if she had gathered herself together. 'I'm not going to divorce him; I can promise you that. And if he leaves me I assure you he'll lose NGA. He knows that and he certainly won't run that risk, however much *you* think he loves you!'

'It's very sad that you can only hold onto your husband with threats,' Sarah retaliated, though she was shaking as she listened. 'But I think that's up to Nick, don't you? I don't think we should discuss it. I'm sorry, Diana, I didn't want things to turn out like this, but they have, and it's his decision over what happens now.'

Nick was as much to blame as she was – surely? Or had she led him on? Provoked him? It had, after all, been she who had offered herself that first evening at Hastings, hadn't it?

She hung up before she let herself down by bursting into tears. The phone rang again immediately and she answered it, trembling. 'Oh, Charles, thank goodness!'

He insisted on taking her to lunch, despite her protests. 'Hold your head up, Sarah,' he told her firmly. 'You have nothing to be ashamed of! We'll go to Antons. I'll pick you up at twelve-thirty.'

He arrived on the dot, guiding her through the knot of reporters outside the flat, ignoring their questions as he helped her into the car. Sarah was rigid with fear, for as they walked into the restaurant, expensive though it was, the clientele all seemed to look at her and be discussing her as Charles guided her to their table.

'Many congratulations, Miss Campbell.' The proprietor smiled as he bustled to attend to them. Sarah stared at him in surprise for a moment, then realized it was the award he was talking about. In her misery over Nick she had forgotten about it.

'Why, thank you, Anton.' She smiled back gratefully at him, and decided she was hungry after all. 'I'd love lobster, Charles, if that's OK?'

'That sounds more like you!' He laughed back, and

244

Sarah shook herself, and gave him her full attention from then on.

'I'll send Bernard to take you to the theatre,' he promised. 'And to take you home afterwards.'

'That's not necessary, Charles.'

'Yes, it is!' There was to be no argument, she found. 'The Press can be horrific and I'm taking no chances with you. If Nick can't protect you, I can.'

'Nick has to see Diana,' she pointed out.

'You do realize he won't come back, don't you?' Charles asked casually. 'Diana has a terrible hold over him.'

'She's already phoned me,' Sarah admitted, and told him about Diana's call.

'The bitch!' he exclaimed furiously. 'What *are* you going to do?'

'Whatever Nick decides,' she sighed. 'Don't let's spoil lunch, Charles, please.'

Diana had hung up the phone in a storm of tears. Only the day before she had asked Nick about Sarah Campbell and he had fiercely denied any involvement with her, outside business. Now Max Moreton was openly speaking of their affair. Not sure whether it was his lies she hated most, or the humiliation of the press coverage, she sobbed for an hour or more, totally unable to stop, ignoring the constantly ringing phone. Every time she tried to stop, the tide of misery swept over her again.

Finally, a banging on the door brought her to her senses and she ran downstairs to it when she recognized Paul's car. Everyone should have a Paul, she thought as he dried her tears, patting her shoulder awkwardly, and then made her some coffee.

'Lets face it, Diana,' he said as they sat each side of the kitchen table. 'It's not the first time he's done this, is it? And it probably won't be the last, living as you two do.'

'He lied to me about Sarah Campbell,' she sobbed anew. 'I can't bear that!'

'There may be nothing in it,' Paul reasoned. 'You said yourself, that reporter has it in for Nick. He may well have used the photographs and a bit of gossip to make something of it.'

'No, Paul, this time it's all true. The reporter actually *saw* them making love. The bastard couldn't even do *that* behind closed doors! I've known for months deep down; I just turned my back on it, hoping it would all go away like it did over Stephanie. But it hasn't; it's just got worse.'

She hated Nick for what he was putting her through, but under her fury was the infuriating knowledge that she still wanted him under her control. The row that would come was a small price to pay for keeping him, and she knew she would do that, whatever happened when he got home. There were still a lot more she wanted from Nicholas Grey.

Paul took her out to lunch in a quiet pub a few miles away, comforting her and calming her down, relieved in a way that Nick had been having an affair with Sarah Campbell as he had begun to suspect Madeleine. She had become rather too friendly with Nick of late, since she had been working for him up in London, and he had been furious when, despite his objections, Madeleine had insisted on continuing to work for him.

Everything came far too easily to Nick, Paul had decided, years ago, and he hated him for what he perceived as his careless treatment of a beautiful wife. Though loving Diana as he did made it far easier to comfort her and understand her distress, he told himself ruefully.

When Nick pulled his car into the drive around five o'clock Diana was ready for him, dressed and made-up, her hair smooth and sleek, showing no sign of the storms of the morning. Playing for time, he seemed to take for ever getting his bag and briefcase out of the car, before he opened the front door, calling to her where she waited in the drawing room, watching him from the window.

Very slowly, she went towards him across the hall, conscious of the roses he had sent that afternoon still lying on the hall chair. Nick ignored them and bent to kiss her unsmiling mouth. Without a word, Diana turned back into the drawing room, picking up the flowers as she did so. 'I'll get a vase for these,' she said, quietly as he put his briefcase down on the coffee-table, giving him a chance to relax slightly as he watched her arrange them.

It was too early for a drink, he thought, and then poured one. Diana shook her head when he offered one to her. The atmosphere was electric.

'Well?' she asked at last. 'What are you going to do? I've had Daddy on the phone half the afternoon.'

'I bet you have,' Nick said drily. 'He's given me a hard time too. I'm not going to do anything, Diana. It's up to you. I suggested a divorce months ago, remember?'

Blast him, Diana thought bitterly, ready to hit him with frustration. 'No divorce, Nick! I told you that and I meant it! I'll see you in hell first – which is where I've been all day after listening to Max and all his rancid little tales! Have you any idea what that's like?'

'I'm sorry, Diana.' Nick stared down into the glass in his hand, unable to look at her suddenly. 'I really didn't think Max would stoop so low as to tell you all that.'

'Well, he did! He didn't leave much out either. You disgust me, Nick! You're forty, not a teenager, surely to God you have some control over your urges? Making love on a garden bench – at your age! It's revolting!'

She made what had appeared to him as a wonderful interlude suddenly seem so sordid somehow, and Nick winced. 'I have the normal instincts of any man,' he defended. 'Just because they don't correspond with yours doesn't mean they're wrong! Face it, Diana, we just aren't compatible!'

'We were. Once.'

'No, Diana. Don't kid yourself! We have a friendship, I admit, and surprisingly it's one I'd prefer to continue. But I don't think you've ever liked me to touch you – you don't even approve of Lotte hugging me, for heaven's sake! I make no excuses over Sarah, and I refuse to let you denigrate her in your sanctimonious fashion.'

'She's nothing but a slut, Nick! A cheap little tart! Can't you see all she wants is your influence to help her to make it in the business? It's all those ignorant little bitches ever want! And you're too stupid to see how you're being used!'

'Oh, no! That's where you are completely wrong! Possibly Stephanie did, but not Sarah! This is different – very different! This time I want out, Diana. Out of this marriage, out of your life altogether!'

'Yes?' Diana turned bitter eyes on him. 'Fine, Nick. You do that and you'll never see Charlotte again. I'll see to that! She's still young enough to come under the ruling of the courts, and no judge would even grant you joint custody, not after the things I could tell them. I'd make sure you never got near her again. And once Daddy has finished with the financial side of things, you won't have your precious company either. I can claim a third of it, and I will – believe me, I will. In cash too! Where will you and your sweet little girlfriend be then, eh, Nick? With no money? She'll soon desert you. For Charlie, probably. He's been panting after her long enough.'

'Sarah's not like that!' he said sharply, knowing that on that score he was completely right. But the harsh reality of Diana's threats confirmed everything Nick had feared. He bent down, burying his face in Boots's fur as he bounded up to him, and Diana got up to leave the room, knowing triumphantly that she had hit home.

'You have to give her up, Nicholas, and that's all there is to it! It's her, or Charlotte and the company. Think about it,' she commanded quietly, and walked out.

For the first time since Natasha's death, Nick gave way to grief, tears stinging his eyes as he crumpled, hugging the patient dog. All day, as he had battled first with reporters and then with Alistair Mackenzie, he had known deep down that it would come to this. Half of him wanted to walk out on the marriage right this minute, but then he thought of the hold Diana had on both his precious daughter and the business, and the other half of him told him it was impossible.

Later that morning, after his raging head had subsided, he had walked through the building being greeted and congratulated by the staff, who were as proud of his awards as if they had won them personally. They admired him, they relied on him for their livelihood and they needed him, and without him it would all fold. He wondered bitterly if Max had known of Diana's share of the company – with that man's connections, it was *more* than likely – and Max knew *exactly* how to twist the knife. Ironically, he had made Diana a full partner to give her an income of her own; now his generosity had thoroughly backfired on him.

Sarah had sounded so cheerful too, when he had spoken to her as he drove out to Oxford. Charles had taken her to his Dolphin Square flat when they discovered even more reporters outside hers. She had spent most of the after-noon asleep, as she normally did before a performance, and had done her best to reassure him that everything would be fine.

He had to find a way to keep her; he would go mad without her. Slowly, he dragged himself to his feet and went into the study, pulling the list of calls he had to make from his briefcase. Deliberately he left the door open so that Diana would know he was simply making business calls. It was ironic that most of the calls he had received during the day had been congratulatory ones. He worked conscientiously until Diana came to say that supper was ready. He was shooting a commercial the next day so in fact he had plenty to do, and he had done very little during the day, so distracted had he been.

It was a stilted, difficult meal, with neither of them seeming to know what to say to each other. Nick finally pushed his hardly touched plate away. 'I'm sorry, I'm really not hungry,' he admitted.

Diana shrugged. The meal had not been up to her usual standards. 'Nick, what are you going to do?'

'I don't know.' He leant back wearily. 'For now I'm going to take Boots out. I need to think.' Thankfully, she didn't offer to go with him, so Nick whistled the dog and went for a long walk through the nearby woods in contemplative mood.

He hated himself for being so spineless and so utterly unable to make a clear decision. And, he thought, suddenly he was feeling old. He knew the lines around his eyes were deeper, and, though thankfully his hair was still thick and showed no sign of receding, there was definitely grey over his ears now. How could he seriously even *think* of marrying Sarah, he wondered bitterly, tying her down to an old man? She was too young and vibrant, too full of life.

Yet they shared so much. Like him, she could place any song in a musical – thanks to her father – and they had a shared passion for music and theatre that both rejoiced in. He remembered the absorption on her face as she had listened to Verdi in St Paul's with him, and her determination to sit in the upper circle rather than miss it when even *he* hadn't been able to get her favourite dress circle seats for a show they desperately wanted to see. Diana would have thrown up her hands in horror.

Sarah loved the open air, competed happily in most of the sports he challenged her with, and cheerfully tramped galleries with him when time permitted, offering pithy and frequently accurate opinions of paintings he thought of buying.

Though he admitted to treating her like a child to be spoilt, there was still far more to Sarah than a pretty exterior. Moreover, she loved him desperately, and he was going to devastate her if he broke things off. He couldn't do it, he decided, wanting to howl out his frustration to the dark, silent trees around him. He slammed his fist against the unforgiving trunk of an oak, almost rejoicing in the pain the blow produced, and decided then, to go back to London that night. Away from the suffocating atmosphere of Diana's influence. Back to Sarah. This time to stay.

Marching back into the house with his new resolve, he was horrified to find several reporters hammering on the front door and Diana in tears in the kitchen. 'Nick, oh, thank goodness! Get rid of them, please?' she begged him, all animosity gone.

Angrily, Nick forcibly ejected the four men with threats of legal action for trespass that he knew quite well he had no way of fulfilling. But it was enough to shift them to the sanctuary of the gate, out of view of the house. He returned then to pick up his overnight bag, and Diana suddenly realized he was leaving.

'Nick! Please don't go!' she begged him, tears still obvious on her cheeks. 'Don't leave me alone in the house – not tonight, – please. They'll come back. I know they will!'

Very slowly he looked at her, and knew he couldn't leave her on her own. His sense of decency was being tested to the limit, and in the face of her distress he simply couldn't do it. 'It makes no difference, you know,' he said, firmly. 'I can't go on like this, Diana. But I will stay tonight.'

'In my bed?' Diana stopped crying in an instant.

'No, in my own bed,' Nick decided. 'Take it or leave it, but that's the one condition I am going to stick to. It's never worried you before.'

'Well, it does now.' Diana was equally firm. 'Nick, I know what we decided after Charlotte was born, but have you ever thought that we should have another baby? It could be the one thing that would give some purpose to what's left of our marriage.'

Nick stared at her in complete horror as her words sank in. 'Are you out of your mind?' he demanded. 'You damn well almost died having Lotte, and you want to risk another child – after all the doctors told you?'

'For you I would.'

'The *hell* it's for me!' Nick turned angrily away from her. 'It's just another way to trap me and make me feel guilty! No way would I allow any woman to go through the hell you went through and you know it! For goodness' sake, Diana, you talk about my age, but *you* are acting like a stupid child. To have a baby at thirty-nine is no joke, even if it was straightforward, and you know damn well it wouldn't be! It would be suicidal and I refuse to even consider it!'

'It's the duty of every married couple to have children,' she protested.

'Not if it risks life itself,' he retaliated. 'Nothing is worth that risk. I won't have that on my conscience!'

'Well, at least it proves something.'

'Oh, and what's that?'

'You do have some feeling for me, Nick.'

'Yes,' he said slowly, almost reluctantly. 'I do, I respect you – I always have. You're far more than I deserve most of the time, but I need more, Diana. I can't live like a monk for the rest of my life. You may think I'm too old to need – well – sex, if you want to put it bluntly, but I do. Not the cold mechanics of it, but love – real love. I want someone who feels like I do, who actually doesn't *care* if I want to make love on a garden bench. For years I thought I could live as you wanted me to, and I did try. But it's different now. Sarah changed all that.'

'Nick, you could have that with anyone else, but not Sarah Campbell. I can't cope with her! I know *I* can't change that much, and I know that you'd want someone else occasionally, but not her.'

'How can you even contemplate a life like that?' he demanded curiously. 'Living here, alone, knowing I was with another woman. Surely it would be far better to end it, start again with someone else?'

'No, Nick. I could never do that! Oh, don't think the offers aren't there, they are – several, in fact. But I chose to marry you, and the sanctity of my marriage vows is very important to me.'

Wearily Nick turned away. 'Then I hope you don't live to regret that decision,' he said sadly. 'There's not much more to say, is there? I'm going to bed. I have a long day's shoot tomorrow.'

'Will you come back home tomorrow evening?' Diana tried to be casual.

'I'm not sure.' He was quite honest. 'I think it would be better if I didn't, don't you?'

'I want you here,' she admitted.

'And you'll threaten me with turning Lotte against me if I don't come home? Forget it, Diana. I may give in over asking for a divorce – for the time being – but I will *not* be threatened over Lotte. Is that understood?'

Time – it was all he needed. Time to get the company under his financial control, even to start a new one if he needed to. Nick left her alone in the kitchen and took himself off to bed. But, like many other nights recently, sleep eluded him. Miserably he tossed around, again endlessly searching for a solution to his problems. Diana – or Sarah? One of them or both? Tears pricked once more at his eyelids as he realized the futility of it all. Rolling over, he cried silently into the pillow as his despair took over. Whatever he did, one or other would be hurt, and he hated himself for what he had done.

Diana lay in her own bed and listened to him, appalled that he could be so unhappy over another woman, but totally unable to bring herself to feel sorry for him. This was his battle, and as far as she was concerned he was going to have to fight it – alone.

* * *

Nick had two frantic days of shooting before he could get away to see Sarah. Two days of being foul to his hard-pressed crew *and* having to go back to Oxford after long days on location in Sussex did nothing for his temper. Still, beseiged by reporters as Diana was, he couldn't leave her alone to cope with them, and she refused point-blank to go to her parents' home for refuge.

He spoke to Sarah on the phone several times a day, though she was busy too, in rehearsal for a television drama she had somehow fitted into her busy schedule. Yet he was still unable to come to any decision. No one who knew him would have believed the turmoil going on inside him as he drove into the garage of Sarah's flats early Thursday evening.

She was smiling as she met him at the door. 'Guess what! I've just had a call from Patrick Lythgoe. He wants me to sing with him in a charity gala next weekend!' She had done another *Secret Agent* since that first one, and she and Patrick had become better friends, though they would never be good ones.

'Are you going to do it?' he asked, surprised.

'Why not? It should be fun, even with Patrick.' Cheered by her smile, Nick gathered her into his arms and held her in a grip so tight she could hardly breathe as he kissed her. 'Was it that bad?' she asked as he finally released her and led her to the sofa.

'Yes, I'm afraid it was,' he admitted. 'And my crew must hate me. I've been awful to live with.'

'Poor darling.' She curled up against him. 'What are we going to do?'

'I want to hold you in my arms,' he said, laughing for the first time in three days. 'But I may not be able to for a while.'

'I don't think I like the sound of that.' She sat up, turning his face towards her. 'What is it, Nick, tell me?'

'Later – we'll discuss it later,' he promised. He was

passionate and loving as he kissed her over and over again, bringing her to the brink of tears as she realized his distress was as great as hers.

'It sounds as if I'm going to need this,' she commented, seating herself on the floor at his feet and sipping at the drink she had poured for them. Nick played with her tumbled mass of hair and told her of the trauma of the last few days.

'For the moment I can't get a divorce, Sarah,' he finished quietly. 'I want one, and I've asked Diana for one, believe me. But I have no grounds and she refuses to even consider it. Oh, I can carry on as before – she can do nothing about that – but I can offer you nothing else at the moment, and I just don't feel that's fair to you. I want to give you so much more than that. It *could* easily take years. To be honest, I've been wondering if maybe you and I *should* have a breathing space.

'I've treated you both very badly. I never meant for things to go this far, – believe me, but now they have and I have to find a solution. I love you very much, Sarah, but I must save the company – or I could end up hating you because I'd lost it, or got it into such a financial mess that I might just as well have done. Maybe living together would work, maybe it wouldn't – I don't know. But you have to think about it carefully before we do anything. I refuse to rush you into something you might very much regret later.'

'So you won't simply move in with me now?'

'No, darling. Not because I don't want to, I do – very much. But I can't – not yet, don't you see? The Press would ruin you, and it matters at this stage of your career, take it from me.'

'The hell I will!' Sarah jumped up. 'I've had time to think too, Nick. While reporters have hammered at my door and I couldn't even go out shopping because of them! You *won't* make a commitment to me, will you? That's your problem. Well, this time I've had enough! I've dreamt about us getting married – just like Cress and James are. Yes, I know, orange blossom and confetti – all that! I want it too, Why shouldn't I?'

'I can't give it to you, darling.' Nick sighed. 'Not yet anyway. I simply can't make that promise at the moment. We need to think.'

'Stalling! That's all you're doing, Nick Grey! Well, I've had it! I've had it with you – I don't need it any more! I won't be your 'bit on the side' any longer. I'll . . . I'll marry Charlie instead.'

'Then more fool you! Sarah, be sensible,' he pleaded. 'Just give it a little time. I'll work something out with Diana eventually.'

'No, it's now or nothing, Nick! I want commitment. A ring, even – a real life together. I don't mind about the company. If you really loved me it wouldn't matter to you either. You'd let it go!'

'I can't! Sarah, don't you realize? I have thirty-five employees at Wardour Street, not to mention all the freelancers we employ. If I let the company fold, they'd all be out of work, and they have families – mortgages and things. Could you really live with knowing that I'd deliberately let them all down? Because, frankly, I couldn't. I may be fairly ruthless but I'm not cruel, and I can't do it. If Diana got wind of any plans I had with you she and her damned father would immediately demand all her share of the business – in cash. She has that right and she'd do it, out of sheer spite. I have to find a way to avoid that – and I can, given a little time.'

Sarah was beyond being reasoned with. 'There *is* no time,' she said stubbornly. 'I won't play second fiddle to a load of accountants! It's over, Nicholas. You were right; you're far too old for me, I want fun, discos, parties, kids of my own age, and to wear clothes that I want to wear, not what you consider suitable!'

'*The hell you do!* I have *never* said no to anything you wanted to do or go to, and you know it!' he protested. 'The only thing I've *ever* objected to is that wretched baseball cap!' But the realization had hit him that she meant what she was saying. All his anguish over the last few days was for nothing, and she was making the last decision he had expected.

'I mean it, Nicholas.' She faced him squarely and tried not to cry. Ironically, it was the one time she held onto her tears. If she had wept at that point Nick would have given way, but for some unknown reason she stayed calmly dry-eyed.

'In that case, there's nothing much to say, is there?' Nick rose, his height making him suddenly tower above her, and her resolve crumbled a little. 'I'm glad you made a decision before too many people got hurt. Make no mistake, Sarah, I fell in love with you the moment I saw you. I tried not to, believe me, I tried very hard. But I'll go on loving you.' He hung onto his self-control – just – and bent to kiss her rigid cheek before turning to go.

Stony-faced she watched him leave, refusing his offer to return her key and stood like a statue in the middle of her living room as her misery slowly gave way to anger. Deep down, the sensible, decent part of her knew she had done the right thing. From now on, she would go it alone, without him. Let his wife have him!

She would show the bastard – who needed him? she thought bitterly. Staring at herself in the bedroom mirror, she knew she was beautiful, well, now that she was notorious too she could have any man she chose! *Any*, she told herself, and the tears began to roll down her face again. The problem was that she didn't want another man. Nick had spoilt her for anyone else. But she had to start again, somehow she had to put him behind her. She would show Diana Grey that she wasn't beaten. There had to be someone around who could make her forget Nick, Someone better than Nick, someone, somewhere . . .

Eventually, slowly, she reached for the phone and

dialled Tim Farmer's number. She would start close to home. 'Hi, Tim!' She put on her most cheerful voice. 'Is that party still on for tonight? Because if it is, I'd like to change my mind and come.'

CHAPTER 19

In the next few months it seemed that Sarah Campbell's scandalous name was never out of the newspapers or magazines as she worked flat out on as many productions as she could fit in. She turned nothing down, taking parts that she would previously not have looked at, and stripped off without compunction as the directors asked her, fitting a social life around her work which would have floored most people. Personal appearances alone netted her a fortune that summer as she filled up empty spaces in her weekend diary, almost afraid to have any spare time, it seemed.

Her appearance with Patrick at the gala had opened up yet another avenue for both of them when they were invited to record the song they'd sung together. Gleefully, they went on *Top of the Pops* and plugged the song on all the chat shows – leading to bitter comments from Marie Louise, Patrick's girlfriend, which were automatically picked up and exaggerated by all the newspapers.

Bruce Webster, the record company boss, soon became another escort, provoking more comment about Sarah's preferences for older men. Sarah didn't give a damn, and plunged into the wealthy, extravagant world that he lived in with a cheerful abandon, working all day and partying all night. Bruce was forty-five and in the middle of a divorce, and whatever reputation Sarah still had soon plunged to an all-time low, to the distress of both Charles and a despairing Nick, who carefully kept an eye on her from a distance.

In vain, Oscar and Charles begged her to slow down. 'You'll burn yourself out,' Charles said worried, looking at her tired face one day at one of their infrequent lunches. 'And since when have you started smoking?'

She had done her best to avoid him, ashamed of her party life, knowing his main ambition was to keep her from it, but Charles had persisted and was still very much around. With a clatter she dropped her fork and faced him.

'One more lecture, Charles Hastings, and I'll walk out on you,' she warned. 'You are *not* my father!'

'If I were, you would've been across my knee by now!' He frowned. 'Sarah, you don't look well. I'm worried about you.'

'We were shooting a commercial all night.' She tried to make it sound easy. 'I haven't had any sleep. I'll be fine tomorrow.'

'Then you should've stayed in bed today!' He was horrified. 'Why on earth did you say you'd come out?'

'Because I knew it was hopeless trying to sleep. The flat's too noisy during the day, and my doctor won't give me any more pills.'

'Have you been taking sleeping pills?' he demanded, regretting not keeping a better eye on her – at least via George if nothing else. He was sure that George knew nothing of pills, and he immediately blamed Bruce, whom he knew and distrusted.

'I need them, Charlie,' she said sadly. 'I don't sleep well, and I need to if I'm going to keep working. There's nothing else to do.'

Charles looked at her hard. She had lost a lot of weight, he realized, and her eyes, usually so sparklingly hazel, looked as if someone had drawn a veil over them. He signalled to the waiter to take their plates and bring Sarah some coffee. 'I'm going to make a phone call,' he said firmly. 'Just stay there.'

With a sinking heart Sarah watched him go to the phone, fearing the worst. All she wanted to do was lie down and shut her sore eyes, not have the confrontation with George that she feared Charles was arranging.

'Right,' he said when he returned. 'Come with me. It's time I took you in hand. I should've done this weeks ago. You're going to see my doctor *now*. Luckily he has time to see you.'

'Charles! This is ridiculous,' she protested. 'I have a perfectly good doctor, if I need one, and I don't!'

'You're going to do as you're told,' he replied. 'Even Oscar is worried about you at the moment.' He was well aware of her angry eyes glaring at him but he ignored them, marching her firmly into the Harley Street surgery of his London GP.

Sarah was furious, but too tired to argue. Stripping off for a doctor was not her idea of a peaceful afternoon but Dr Archibald was very pleasant, middle-aged, and incredibly thorough. By the time he had finished with her she felt as if there was nothing he didn't know about her, or an inch of her he hadn't examined. Finally, smiling, he patted her arm and told her she could get dressed.

'Nothing much wrong, Miss Campbell. I think you'll live!'

'I could've told you that,' Sarah grumbled. 'And saved Charles all this money!'

'A check-up is never wasted money, my dear.'

While she was dressing, he called Charles into his office. 'You were right, Charles,' he said quietly. 'Sleeping pills and too many cigarettes. And I don't like the amount she admits to drinking. It usually means double. However, basically she is healthy enough, though a bit underweight for her height, and her blood pressure is a bit high, but nothing a good rest wouldn't put right. Take her away for a week or too, make her eat and sleep, and get her off the cigarettes if you can. They'll affect her voice sooner or later.'

'Thanks, Richard, I'll see what I can do.' Charles rose to go.

'I should be thanking you.' Richard Archibald smiled. 'Most of my patients are very dull compared to Miss Campbell. I'll give you one piece of advice, though . . .'

Charles looked back enquiringly.

'If you have marriage in mind, Charles, she has good child-bearing hips! Time you thought of getting married again; she could be just what you need!'

I've been working on that for months!' Charles grinned. 'But I'll have to talk her into a holiday first!'

'That was three times worse than any film medical,' Sarah grumbled as they got back into the car.

'Rubbish!' Charles said crisply. 'You needed it!'

'I beg your pardon, Charles, I did *not*! Have you ever seen a speculum?'

He laughed. 'So you had a smear test; it's not the end of the world. And no more of these.' He reached over and took her cigarette from her fingers. 'No cigarettes and no more pills. I'm going to sort you out.'

'I think the doctor did that!'

'That's what I intended. Now give me your diary. I've let you cut loose for far too long and now you're going to do as I say.' Carefully he went over her next few weeks' workload as Bernard drove to Chelsea. She had several more days on her current film, and then it appeared, went straight into a fortnight of press interviews and TV game-shows before starting an episode of Paddy's new series in Crete. At least, he thought, horrified, she had finished at the National. 'You can cancel all those interviews next week,' he told her. 'None of them are important.'

'I can't do that! Oscar would be furious.'

'*Oscar* can cancel them. You are going to plead illness and come away with me, and I shall tell him why.' Back at her flat, he got on the phone to Oscar, and then his own office. 'I was going to the Caribbean next week anyway,'

262

he said, 'to visit a hotel I've been working on. I'll extend the trip and take you with me. Oscar agrees with me, and so will George when I tell him!'

'It's my permission you need, not George and Oscar's.'

'We *all* care about you,' he told her. 'Sarah, since you and Nick split up you have been working yourself into the ground. How long is it? Four, five months of lousy publicity and questionable dates. You can't go on like this!'

'If you mean Bruce Webster, Charlie, you can forget it – he's a friend. I have *not* been sleeping with him, if that's what's worrying you! I haven't slept with anyone since Nick. I don't even take the pill any more.'

'I don't want to know, quite honestly,' he assured her. 'That's your business.' But he was quite obviously relieved.

Sarah smiled suddenly, that slow, bright smile he hadn't seen for months. 'I *will* come with you, Charles. You're right, as usual. I need a holiday.'

She needed a break from the press coverage, from the snide articles about infidelity that seemed to be in every paper suddenly, the hints and insinuations about younger women coming between happily married couples, "How does a wife cope when her husband is sleeping around?" being a common *Unicorn* theme, sometimes naming her, always blaming her. And photographers dogged her footsteps on every date these days. What on earth had happened to the innocent young girl of a year ago? she wondered bitterly and frequently whenever she read the more lurid of the articles. Was she completely lost now?

Going away with Charles wouldn't silence them, but at least he was single and totally above reproach. Despite herself, Charles had become the one she'd relied on as she'd struggled to come to terms with what she increasingly saw as Nick's betrayal of her, even if she had been the one to finally break things off.

Losing him didn't get any easier to bear. She still

hugged the white lamb at night, and she still cried if she heard Dire Straits on the radio, which was a tape Nick had played incessantly in the car and they had always argued over.

The lamb even came to Antigua, much to Charles amusement, but he was wise enough not to question her about it when he saw it on her bed. He had a special suite at the hotel, kept exclusively for him – a long, low bungalow almost on the beach. Private enough for Sarah to sunbathe naked, if she wanted to, by the pool. But it was hot, almost too hot to sunbathe for long, and in her exhausted state she soon found herself sleeping during the afternoon when Charles was working.

With the freedom of his beautiful hotel – built up from a wreck he had bought eighteen months before – Sarah began to feel human again. She quickly made friends with the water sports facility, and spent most mornings water-skiing, or updating her scuba diving techniques ready for Paddy's filming. Often she lunched with the assorted instructors. Because they didn't smoke or drink, she found she wasn't doing so either, and on going back to the bungalow in the early afternoon she found she could sleep more soundly than she had done in ages.

Usually Charles came back in time for dinner, sometimes taking her into St John's to a restaurant or another hotel, sometimes ordering dinner in which they ate alone on the veranda of the bungalow. But always he cosseted her, persuading her to eat the right things, being careful over what she drank and forbidding her to smoke. This was hardest of all, going from the many cigarettes a day she had built up to during the last few months back down to nothing was like purgatory, but to please him she tried.

It was still the nights that were the hardest. The warm, tropical nights when her body craved Nick's brand of satisfaction and she lay alone. Then she cried, as he had done months before, silently into the pillow till it was wet

264

with tears and she had to turn it over, only to soak it all over again.

Listening to her for the third night he'd been aware of it, Charles agonized over what to do, and then finally got up and went in to her. Sarah was lying on the bed clutching the lamb, sobbing quietly into its fur – still wearing her dressing gown, he was surprised to see. He sat beside her without a word and took her very carefully into his arms until she was crying into his shoulder. Patiently he stroked her hair until the sobs gave way to shuddering sighs, then he lifted her back into bed.

'Don't go, Charles,' she said softly as he moved to leave her. 'Just stay and hold me, if you can bear to. It will help. It did before.' Once before he had rejected her, but this time he slipped into the bed beside her, and she crept into his arms, seemingly content to be held, challenging his will power every inch of the way, but in minutes she was asleep.

When she woke in the morning he had gone for the day, but he came back early that afternoon when Sarah was sitting, half in, half out of the pool to cool off. Her bikini top was on the chair behind her and she immediately reached over for it, he noticed, amused.

'I'm going to swim myself.' He smiled. 'Shall we go down to the beach?' He was a surprisingly strong swimmer, and they kept pace with each other easily as they swam out into the bay and around the little promontory before heading back to the beach. Laughing, they ran back to the bungalow, Sarah winding her hair into a twist to rid it of some of the sea water as she ran. Flopping out on one the loungers on the veranda, Charles reached out and took her hand. She let it lie there, content with the physical contact but wondering how long it would be before he worked up the courage to approach her.

Strangely, he left her to sleep alone for several nights. It was only on he night before they were due to leave that he made any sign of wanting to continue where they had left off. They had dined with the hotel manager and his wife and lingered over coffee afterwards, so it was later than usual when Charles and Sarah walked back to their bungalow.

After ten days in the sun, Sarah had never felt better. She had put on a little weight, her skin had a golden tan and she glowed with health. Only her hair had suffered slightly, from the salt water and sun, but she confidently expected Molton Brown to sort that out when she got back to London. Charles's pride in her was easy to see and she went easily into his arms that evening. After two weeks of very little alcohol, the wine at dinner had gone to her head more than a little.

Slowly, shyly, he kissed her, feeling her response for the first time, and when he led her to his bedroom she went willingly. As far as Sarah was concerned, sleeping with Charles was another step on her road to recovery from Nick. She lifted her dress over her head and, kicking off her sandals, she stretched out on his bed, holding out her arms to him.

Whether it was her willingness that had frightened him or something else he wasn't sure, but even after long minutes of kissing her he realized with horror that he was totally incapable of doing anything 'I think I'm very out of practice,' he apologize at last somewhat, ruefully. 'It doesn't matter Charlie,' she lied, to comfort him. 'Actually, it's nice just lying together like this.' He was rather like a cuddly bear holding her, and very comfortable somehow, his body so much softer than Nick's hard, muscular one. But she fell asleep realizing that she had almost made a big mistake, and she knew then that she could never feel the same depth of sensual pleasure with anyone that she had always felt with Nick.

'I saw the pics of you and Charlie coming back from Antigua,' Cress teased as she supervised the last fitting

266

for Sarah's bridesmaid dress. 'Has he popped the question yet?'

'Will you stop matchmaking, Cressida!' Sarah ordered, turning in front of the mirror. Her dress was white and set off her tan beautifully as Catherine set a wreath of flowers in her hair to see the effect.

'They'll be real on the day,' Cress explained.

'It's lovely, Cress,' Sarah smiled.

'Wasted on a bridesmaid,' Cress sighed. 'You'd make a lovely bride, Sarah.'

'I'm afraid I have to find the bridegroom first,' Sarah teased. 'And at the moment he's not free.'

'Are you still carrying a torch for Nick?' Cress demanded. 'I thought you'd be over him by now. It's been almost six months!'

'Would you be?' Sarah taunted, and sank miserably down into a chair. 'No I'm not, and I'm not getting involved with Charlie until I am – although I admit I like him very much, and I know he would marry me tomorrow if I encouraged him. Have you seen Nick?' It was the first time she had asked Cress.

'Yes,' Cress said slowly. 'We had lunch when he was in London a few weeks ago. He's still rushing round the world on that spy film.'

'Is he all right?'

Cress looked uncomfortable. Nick had tried very hard to look confident and cheerful, but Cress had known him long enough to see straight through the façade. 'He's fine,' she lied to Sarah. 'I think he and Diana are trying very hard to get things together. She's out in LA with him at the moment. Forget him, Sarah, he's not worth the hassle. Stick to Charles or Bruce Webster – at least they're single.'

The thought of Diana being with Nick made Sarah feel even more bitter, but Diana had every right to be there, she had to remind herself, wondering if Nick had ever really loved *her*. Somehow she doubted it. 'I take it he's not coming to the wedding?' she asked.

'No, he won't be back in time,' Cress comforted her. 'You'll be quite safe.'

'I'm looking forward to it!' Sarah assured her.

'Oh, so am I!' Cress breathed. 'And I'm determined I'm going to get pregnant on my wedding night!'

'I hope James is up to it!' Sarah teased. 'Look, I have to see this doctor, can we meet for lunch?'

'Doctor? What on earth for? You look so healthy!'

'I am – it's just some test results. Charlie made me go through this horrendous medical check before we went away. I'm sure he's a sadist under that sweet exterior!'

Richard Archibald was delighted to see her again. He retested her blood pressure, declaring it normal again, and asked a lot more questions. 'As we expected, all the tests came back normal,' he said smiling. 'Come back to me, though, Sarah, if you have a problem – however small,' he added. Sarah put his card in her bag. He was so much nicer than her own harassed GP.

Crete was great fun. Paddy had found her a part in the second part of his series, and she had three weeks of action-packed location work in another warm climate. Although they worked hard, she was so fit and well rested that she never felt tired.

She was, however, very grateful for the diving practice she had had in Antigua. Paddy had hired her partly for her skills in that area, and she had been fairly rusty. The diving sequences were difficult, and floored her leading man completely. In sequences where it was impossible to use a double she had to help him several times, much to his fury.

After eating out in a taverna every night she began to wonder if she would ever get into her bridesmaid's dress on her return, but it didn't stop her eating. 'I see nothing

has changed your location habits!' Paddy laughed one day;
when she was the only one to order dessert.

'Oh, but they have,' Sarah rejoined. 'See – no cigarettes – not for weeks now!' And it was true. She hadn't
smoked since Charles had taken her cigarette from her
more than a month before. She had hoped Charles would
be at the wedding too, she needed the support of his
comforting presence, but he was due in Japan that
particular weekend.

'He's given us a wonderful wedding present, though,'
James told her as he drove her down to Winchester the day
before the wedding. 'Cress doesn't know, so don't let on,
but we have his helicopter to take us to Gatwick and the
use of his suite in Antigua for two weeks.'

Sarah laughed. 'I know, he told me. You'll love it,
James, it's absolutely perfect, I promise.'

'Tested the bed, have we?'

'Both of them! Just in case Cress gets fed up with you.'
She looked serious for a moment. 'She won't though, will
she?'

'Not a chance! Mind you, I can't quite believe I'm
actually getting married again – neither can my parents.
You'll meet them tonight at dinner, God help us!'

'What's the problem? I bet they're as nice as you
are!'

'I hope you think that later! You should hear my mother
about you!' He launched into his natural Yorkshire accent.
'Never been so ashamed in my life, our James. Took Mrs
Burton from over the road to see that film, and what do we
see but you rolling around with all your private bits
showing – and as for that brazen little hussy you was
doing it with! Well! She was no better than those girls
down Whiteley Street, and she's in all the papers chasing
some married man!'

Sarah shrieked with laughter. 'I can guess what Whiteley Street is!' she giggled. 'I'd better wear something
respectable tonight, then.'

'Don't worry! It's my last night of freedom. Flash your boobs – my Dad will love it – and I might as well have some fun, even if I have to look and not touch!'

'That'll make a change!'

'I've got more respect for my private bits! Cress would chop them off! You'll be quite safe with me in Ireland.'

'That'll be fun, I think.'

'Not bad, is it? Running off with the bridesmaid three weeks after the wedding!'

'I expect the weather will finish us off. I went there a couple of months ago and it was freezing. How did your gun-training go?'

'Not bad – they were quite impressed. I might even take it up as a hobby.'

They were playing undercover agents in a modern comedy thriller, and the director, as much a perfectionist as Nick, had asked them to take lessons in using a gun properly. The film was scheduled for American cinemas, and like all Seth's productions had a big budget and a great deal of publicity already. She would have a lot to thank the absent Nick for if this was succesful.

She took James at his word that night, and drifted down to meet him in the bar with Ben and his parents, her tan well displayed in a white silk dress and Charles's emerald earrings in her ears making every pair of eyes in the place pop as she walked in. 'What are you trying to do to me?' James demanded as Ben hugged her. 'That dress is indecent! Christ, I don't dare touch you! You can't possibly have any knickers on!'

'Stop being such a prude, James, I'm surprised at you,' she laughed. 'If you must know, it has knickers built in. Satisfied?'

'You are perfectly evil!' he groaned. 'Come and meet my parents before I disgrace myself!'

With relief, he watched her work her charm on his overawed parents as he drove to the Blakes' home. Within minutes, it seemed, his mother was clucking over her parentless state, and had forgotten her earlier censure of Sarah's morals.

He and Cress had worried for months over Sarah's grief for Nick. Charles's intervention had been a godsend, he thought, watching her sparkle as she turned in the car to talk again to his mother.

'Not quite Whiteley Street, is she, Mum?' he couldn't help teasing, provoking Sarah to peals of laughter and his mother to complete embarrassment.

It was obviously going to be a fun wedding, Sarah thought.

And it was – from the hilarious breakfast at the hotel, with James and Ben in full flow, through to Cress and James's surprisingly nervous exchange of vows in the flower-filled church. But their happiness was infectious, even to Sarah.

The shock came as she took one of the little bridesmaids back to the marquee after taking her to the loo. Standing looking around for Rosie's mother, she froze. There, talking and laughing with Cress, was Nick.

How could Cress do this to her? she thought in total panic. He wasn't coming; she had said so. There was no way out. Nick had seen her, standing, trembling, clutching the child's hand. 'There's Mummy,' Sarah whispered in relief. 'Go on, darling.'

She gave Nick no help. She was unable to move, her legs turned to jelly, her eyes fixed to the floor as he made his way to her across the marquee. Reaching her, he said nothing, simply drew her into his arms and held her while her heartbeat steadied back to normal.

'You weren't coming,' she accused finally, her eyes at last meeting his. He looked thinner, and the stress lines were etched deeper round his eyes than ever.

'I changed my mind. I got in at four o'clock this afternoon,' he told her. 'Sarah, I wanted to see you again so badly, I took a chance you'd want to see me.'

'How can you be so unfair to me?' she demanded. 'How am I ever going to get myself together if you keep changing the rules?'

Nick looked around, taking in the people watching them with frank curiosity. Cress's family obviously read the *Unicorn*, he thought wryly, and he quickly led Sarah onto the dance floor. Luckily the music was slow, and he could hold her. Sarah knew quite well she would fall down if he didn't.

'That's the one, isn't it?' James's mother hissed at him in complete awe – just wait till she could tell Dottie Burton all this – 'The one there was all the fuss about in the papers?'

'Yes, Mum,' James snapped, unusually for him. 'Just leave them alone, for God's sake! They won't thank you for barging in on them.'

'As if I would!' She was indignant. 'He's really handsome, I must say! That poor little thing. She looked so sad early on, now look at her!'

James watched Sarah's face change as she danced from chalk-white panic to glowing joy. He wasn't at all surprised Nick wanted her back, and in that swirling white dress, bare-shouldered and tight-waisted, she looked enchanting that evening. 'I hope we've done the right thing persuading him to come?' he whispered to Cress.

'I don't know, but it's too late now. It's up to them,' Cress said as James led her onto the dance floor.

'One more dance, my darling, and we will have to leave them to it,' he told her. Dancing, they drew level with Nick and Sarah. Completely oblivious to everyone, they could have been alone on the floor. 'They'll be fine,' he assured his wife confidently, and soon guided her to the edge. 'I think it's about time we disappeared to start making a few babies, don't you?' he suggested. 'Come on, let's get changed. I can't cope with this collar much longer – it reminds me of work!'

Giggling, they ran into the house and James helped her out of the froth of silk and lace. 'Beautiful as that is, I still prefer you without,' he laughed. 'But can we take your veil with us?'

'*Now* I find out you're kinky!'

'Too late!' he rejoined, pulling his sweater over his head. 'Let's go, sweetheart, I think our transport is here. I bet Ben won't be able to decorate *this* wedding car!'

Cress watched in amazement as the helicopter dropped down on the lawn behind the marquee. 'Special present from Charlie,' explained James. 'Only the best for my wife – don't forget your bouquet. I think there's someone who really needs it to be thrown at them!'

Nick and Sarah stood with their arms around each other, watching the newly married couple make their cheerful farewells until Cress whirled over to them, kissing them both. Sarah hugged her back. 'Thank you, Cress,' she said softly as James caught her hand.

'See you in Ireland, Sarah.' He waved to her, and Cress was laughing as they ran to the helicopter.

'Catch, Sarah!' she cried, and threw her bouquet high in the air to land in Sarah's arms.

Almost in tears, she held the bouquet in one hand as the machine rose above them, blowing her hair against Nick's face as she clutched her wreath of flowers with the other. They began to laugh as they disentangled themselves, and Sarah pulled a white rose from the bouquet to put in his buttonhole. 'I think we can safely leave now,' he said. 'I'm sure no one will mind.'

'I'll go and change,' she suggested, but Nick shook his head.

'Don't,' he said. 'You look so gorgeous in that and I think it'll fit in my car.'

Sarah ran upstairs to get her day clothes, bundling them into her bag frantically, and went back to say her own farewells as quickly and gracefully as she could. She was especially charming to James's parents, introducing Nick to them with an almost transparent pride.

He folded her skirts around her in the passenger seat, then swung into the car himself. Only then did he have the chance to kiss her, and he took his time, his soft, warm lips exploring hers. Sarah leant back in the circle of his arms and opened her mouth to him, giving little sighs of pleasure as she did so. 'Lucky I booked into the same hotel,' he told her. 'Your room or mine?'

'What makes you think I'm going to leap straight back into bed with you, Nicholas Grey?' she asked him as he sped down the narrow lane towards the main road. 'I think you're taking a lot for granted.'

'Maybe, but from the way you kissed me just now, I *could* get the impression that I could talk you into it,' he suggested, his eyes twinkling. 'I came a long way to be turned down.'

'How long are you here?'

'About a week – it depends. Then I go away for two. After that I'll be back for good. Jane and Chris have run NGA long enough, and we have new plans, thanks to you.'

She was curious, but he was giving nothing away.

At the hotel, he collected their keys and ordered champagne to be sent up to Sarah's room. 'I need to catch up with you,' he said, and smiled.

'I've hardly had a chance to drink anything,' she confessed. 'I still seem to be a magnet for every child in the place!'

'I prefer that to their fathers!' Nick teased as he shrugged off his jacket and loosened his tie.

Sarah threw her bag on the floor and flopped onto the wide window seat. 'I'm whacked!' she sighed. 'Weddings are hard work!' She filled him in on the ceremony that he had missed, repeating the better jokes of the speeches, in which both James and Ben had been on top form – anything, she knew, to slow things down.

274

When the room service waiter came with the champagne, she escaped into the bathroom. Staring into the mirror at her shining eyes, she took off the now faded wreath and cleaned off her make-up. Running out of things to delay her, she cleaned her teeth before she went back to him. 'I thought you'd climbed out of the window,' he joked, handing her a glass.

'I probably *could* parachute down in this skirt,' she laughed back, but she was shaking.

Nick let her take a sip of the champagne, then he took the glass from her and drew her towards him by the wrists. 'Don't panic, Sarah.' His voice was husky with emotion. 'I just . . . I can't say it . . . I just want you back, darling. Oh, hell! Are you going to make me beg?'

'I thought you'd left me for good!' She was angry then. 'I've spent months trying to get over you, and just as I think I'm getting somewhere you come back and throw me completely. I'm not sure I can take it again, Nick.'

'Is there someone else? Charlie or Bruce?' he demanded, suddenly afraid, but Sarah shook her head. He thought of the agonies of the last few months, of the fruitless rows he had had with Diana, the number of times he had wept bitter tears of frustration over his situation, learning just how much emotion he was capable of once the floodgates were open. 'Please, let's try, angel.'

He was pleading with her, and Sarah stared at him in amazement. The arrogant, all-conquering Nicholas Grey was really begging her, and she knew she was going to give way. Even as he kissed her she knew. Turning, she lifted her hair so that he could unfasten the tiny buttons down the back of her dress.

'Cress and her bloody buttons!' he joked, struggling with them. He let the dress down and the froth of petticoats attached to it dropped with it. Sarah stepped out of it, kicking it away, standing very still in front of him in the lace pants and hold-up stockings which were all she wore under it, hearing his gasp of amazement as she released her hair. She and Cress had joked that afternoon as they had put on stockings, but she had assumed she would be taking hers off alone. Cress had obviously known differently.

Even so, she gave him no help, watching with a soft smile as he struggled with stubborn cufflinks, dragging off his shirt half-buttoned in his impatience. Only then did she take off the lace pants, letting him remove the stockings slowly, teasingly slowly, and shivering at his hands and lips on her legs as he did it.

'I've ached for you so often during the last few months,' he sighed when they were finally both naked, and he laid her on the bed, trailing his fingertips over her, making her tremble and then twist with desire as they quickly became bolder; moving to explore the soft gold tangle of curls at the apex of her thighs, persuading them to part easily, allowing his mouth to take over his devastating exploration.

They had all the time in the world and he took it, marvelling at her body as he remembered and rediscovered it. Her desire for him hadn't dimmed as she had begun to think it had. She measured her length against him, sliding her toes along his bare legs, making him cry out as she touched him, wielding all her old power over him again in seconds. Diana might have been around, she thought triumphantly, but Nick felt to her as if he hadn't seen a woman in months. She was driving him insane.

With a groan of need, he threw himself onto her, all gentleness gone in his desperate need to possess her, to spill himself inside her and make her his again.

'Has there really not been anyone else?' he asked, when he had come for the second time, and Sarah lay in his arms gently running her fingers through the soft hair on his chest.

'No, really, no one.' She smiled. 'Almost once with Charlie, but nothing really happened.'

'Getting it up has always been Charlie's problem,' he commented disparagingly 'Not with Bruce, though? I'm surprised. He's not the type to leave you alone, I know.'

'Bruce is sweet, but he's just a friend, and very mixed up over his ex-wife. I just made him look good to everyone else while he was getting over her.'

'He's one of the most evil men I know!' Nick shuddered. 'He's into coke in a big way, surely you realize that?'

'Yes, but he never made me use it. I wouldn't anyway. You should know that!'

Nick pulled her close. 'I nearly freaked when I saw a picture of him with you in *Variety*. You looked so ill.'

'You thought I was into drugs! Oh, gosh – I bet that's why Charles dragged me to see his doctor! He must've thought the same. For Christ's sake, Nick, I'm not like Natasha! How could you think that of me? I had a bad cold when that picture was taken. I hated it!'

'If Charles took you to see Richard he *must* have been worried,' Nick said. 'I take it everything was OK?'

'Yes, yes,' she assured him, 'and I've stopped smoking too.'

He laughed. 'So how did you manage without me, if you didn't sleep with anyone else? Were you as frustrated as I was?'

'Oh, I managed.' She was evasive.

'How?'

'Oh, you know . . . a little DIY.' She bit her lip in embarrassment. 'It saved a lot of hassle.'

'Show me?' He was intrigued, and very turned on, tired though he was. Sarah was reluctant, but he finally persuaded her, teasing and coaxing until she demonstrated, and then it made him so hard he had to make love to her again, before they settled down under the blankets.

It was only then that Nick began to talk, to tell her about the complications of his business and his life with Diana. And at last, at long last, he talked about Natasha, and Sarah listened with growing horror as he revealed the story of his deep love for her and the torture she had put him through, both mentally and financially, as he had sought to cope with her growing dependency on heroin. By the time Natasha had left him for Charles he had used up every penny of his inheritance from his grandparents and he had been deeply in debt.

'I'd been getting more and more involved with Diana over the worst months and I married her very quickly after that,' he admitted. 'I was fond of her, but I realized quite soon after we got married that I'd made a mistake – too late, I'm afraid.'

'I wish you'd told me all this before,' she said gently. 'I would have understood you better, I'm sure.'

'Maybe I should have done,' he sighed. 'But I've always kept my feelings to myself . . . until you came along. I was so determined you weren't going to get to me. I was going to stay away from you and let you start again with someone else, but I just couldn't. When Cress said you were miserable too, I just took a chance and jumped on a plane. I want you back, Sarah, more than I can tell you . . . if you'll have me?'

'What about Diana?' She sounded doubtful.

'It's going to be difficult, because she won't consider a divorce at the moment. She will, however, discuss money, so I started there. I may well have to wait the full amount of time for a divorce – unless we can find a settlement figure!' he admitted.

'I've spent hours with lawyers and accountants, and I've talked to Chris at some length about the business. He has a really good financial brain, and to my surprise he was very interested in joining me. He's raising new finance and joining us as a full partner, so in fact he can take over the day-to-day running of the business. With Charles, that makes three of us, and with the additional finance we can afford to buy out Diana and move to the only kind of premises I'd find acceptable. Chris knows of some in Covent Garden. At long last, darling, I'll be free of any

278

interference. Diana will ask for a fortune as a settlement, but if I have to I'll sell some of the paintings. Luckily, the bulk of my money is in the States, and out of the reach of her lawyers.'

'As long as you're not trying to con me?' Sarah was still uncertain.

'No, I'd never do that. I promise, Sarah. I just need a little more time to work it all out. By the time you come back from Ireland we'll be in the new offices, and I can concentrate on what to do next. Without the day-to-day management of the company, when Chris takes over, we can spend a great deal of time in America rather than here. My name will still be on the letter-heading to satisfy the clients, so the jobs will be safe. It'll be good for me and a great opportunity for you, living in Hollywood. Seth has plans for a musical next year, and we can both do it – though I admit the only fly in the ointment is that getting Seth to agree to the musical meant I have to do some pig of a job for him in Brazil first!'

'You really have thought about it, haven't you?'

Nick reached over and refilled the glasses they had discarded earlier. 'I've thought about nothing else. I knew there had to be a solution if I looked hard enough, but I really did feel I should do the right thing for once. Diana wanted me to stay so badly and I felt such a heel over the way I'd behaved. Having an affair behind my wife's back never really bothered me much before – probably because the woman involved didn't mean much I suppose. But you did . . . do . . . and I got to feel really awful, frankly, about both of you.

'Thankfully, your ultimatum was the spur I needed. I did what Diana wanted for a while, just to show willing, but it really was hopeless. All I could think of was you! Now I know I can't work it out with her, and I feel I can put the past behind me with a clear conscience. That's if you'll have me back, after all I've done to you.

'I prayed so hard that I wasn't going to be too late. I

dreaded Charles talking you into marriage before I could get it all together. Believe me, darling, I'm really *not* the bastard everyone thinks I am; you have definitely found my weak spot!' he admitted, handing her a glass. 'To us, Sarah. I just hope you know what a tired old man you're taking on!'

CHAPTER 20

They had just over a week while Nick was in England. He moved into Sarah's flat with her, after collecting some clothes from Regent's Park, and swore all the staff at NGA to secrecy as he and Chris worked to organize the complicated move. Sarah was busy with the shopping trips for the Irish film and her shooting lessons, but she spent every precious minute she could with him before he went back to Los Angeles.

Flying off to Dublin almost as soon as Nick got back from LA was almost more than she could bear. To be back together for two nights only to part again nearly finished her, and she boarded the Aer Lingus jet with a heavy heart, but wearing a ring of delicately plaited gold interspersed with diamonds on the third finger of her left hand.

'The nearest we can get for a while,' he'd told her as he put it onto her finger during their last evening together. 'The minute we can make it official I shall buy you the biggest diamond I can find!'

'I don't want that,' Sarah had protested. 'This means far more to me, and it's gorgeous!'

She looked at the beautiful ring a great deal during the flight, twisting it continually; it was becoming a nervous habit already. Perhaps it was her substitute for holding a cigarette, she thought, amused, still wondering how serious Nick was about leaving Diana. It appalled her how much money he would need to divorce her.

281

Nick was the first question on James's lips when she saw him in the foyer of the Shelbourne when she arrived. With a shriek of delight she flew at him as he stood talking to Alex, and hugged them both. 'I didn't know you were on this, Alex,' she cried, kissing him.

'I'm the only English member of the crew!' he replied. 'Apart from you two, everyone else is Irish or American.'

'Back for some more crème de menthe?' Sarah teased. Alex shuddered.

'I still owe our bridegroom for that!' he threatened. 'I'll get him sooner or later!'

'How's Cress?' Sarah asked, then admired James's tan. 'That's nearly as good as mine! Does it go all the way round, or is it just on your back?'

'All the way!' he grinned. 'And I haven't got a white bum either!'

'Shame we haven't got a full nude scene, then!' Alex grinned. 'Maybe I'll persuade our director we need one! Dinner with him at eight?'

James walked Sarah up to her room, anxious to know about Nick, since he knew she wouldn't talk about him in front of Alex. 'We felt a little guilty,' he admitted, 'dumping you two together like that.'

'I think it worked,' she told him cheerfully. 'I *think* he's finally left Diana. He says he's asked her for a divorce. Though I'll only really believe it when I hear the wedding march!'

'Oh, no, if Nick says that, he means it. He can be vicious and cruel – I've seen him be both – but he keeps a promise, that I'll guarantee, and I *know* he adores you.' James ruffled her hair. 'I think somehow, Miss Campbell, you may have brought our tough man to his knees! There will be many a lady out there wondering how you did it when the news gets out!'

'It won't get out yet, I hope.' Sarah looked worried. 'We have to keep it really secret from the Press. Diana just knows he wants a divorce, but not why.'

'Well, the leak won't come from me. My lady wife wouldn't be pleased if I did the dirty on you two!'

'You sound as if you've been married for years, not weeks. You'll be calling her ''er indoors' next!'

'Only when I'm mad! Pick you up in an hour – we can brave Mr O'Hara together. I hear he is one for a bevy or two with the boys – definitely not like Nicholas.'

Their director, a jolly, roly-poly Irish-American, was certainly a total contrast to Nick. Easygoing and full of filthy anti-British jokes, Bob O'Hara believed in enjoying life to the full and Ireland was his spiritual home. Originally he hadn't really wanted two English stars, but Seth had overruled him, and, being the man he was, and after viewing *Home Leave* he'd accepted the status quo and had wisely decided that Seth was right.

Bundled up against the chill wind that blustered relentlessly across St Stephen's Green, they explored a few local bars after dinner, and in the glow left by a great deal of Guinness they all began to get on famously and soon cemented their friendship.

The Americans in the crew could hardly believe how easy their two stars were to work with. Totally without airs and graces, and always cheerful despite the awful weather on the first two weeks of location in the Wicklow mountains, they never complained. Being an American-financed film, there were luxurious caravans for all the stars, but James and Sarah, to the crew's astonishment, preferred to share the same one, playing backgammon when they weren't required to work or the weather closed in on them.

The backgammon competition almost threatened to overtake the poker school as time went on, and more of the unit were drawn to take part. James was winning so handsomely they all began to pray for better weather!

Alex got his own back on James within weeks of starting. They were shooting a scene in a cottage which called for James and Sarah to be handcuffed to a brass bedstead by the enemy they were pursuing. Amid great hilarity, and a lot of doubtful jokes, the scene progressed until lunchtime, and then, as the crew broke for lunch, Alex grinned. 'Have fun kids!' he told them, his eyes twinkling, and walked out of the cottage with the hand-cuffs key in his pocket.

'I don't believe this!' James exclaimed in amazement.

'He said he'd get you!' Sarah began to giggle. 'What on earth shall we do?'

James tried wriggling out of the bracelets. 'Not a lot, is the answer. Damn it, I walked straight into this!'

'Try yelling to get them to come back. Perhaps Alex just forgot,' she suggested, still laughing as she sat on the bed.

'He didn't forget! And I am *not* giving him the satisfaction of yelling for him. That's just what the bastard wants.' James began to smile at their predicament. 'Move over – after all that Murphys last night I need a kip!'

When an apologetic Alex came rushing back to release them, having truly forgotten about them after the initial ten minutes were up, he found them both fast asleep on the bed. It seemed a shame to wake them, he thought, and simply unlocked the handcuffs and left them to it. But naturally enough he couldn't resist taking a Polaroid or two.

'You might have pulled my skirt down!' was Sarah's only complaint, but she laughed as she said it.

'Just back me up if it gets back to Cress,' James begged her.

'Hen-pecked already, James?' Alex teased.

'Just watch your Murphys tonight!' was the furious retort.

The practical jokes were endless after that, James and Sarah smuggled half a sheep's skeleton into Alex's bed one night. James found his gun substituted for a water pistol and soaked one of the stuntmen not best known for his good humour. Alex then found his wardrobe filled with ladies' clothes when his wife opened it on her first visit.

Sarah was having such a good time she almost forgot to miss Nick.

Playing comedy was a new thing to her after all the drama she had been doing, though she had always clowned around with Peter on the TV programme. She learnt a great deal from James over the weeks – he was certainly a master at it, she decided – and the two grew even closer now they were relieved of any sexual element in their relationship. They made convincing and passionate love for the screen, and hugged and kissed in private, but both felt safe with each other.

Bob O'Hara viewed his rushes with growing pleasure, and the enthusiasm was repeated in Seth Waterston's office in London. Nick passed on the enthusiasm in his long phone calls from Los Angeles. He was as good as his word and came over to see her as often as he could in between transatlantic trips, usually coming with Cress. With the help of some of the Irish crew, James and Sarah sussed out a selection of country hotels and the four of them went together, safe in the freedom of the Irish countryside. No one knew or cared who they were. James introduced Nick to the Murphys and Beamish he was getting to know well, and to his surprise Nick enjoyed the experiment more and more.

'Could be the oysters and smoked salmon that make it taste good.' Sarah laughed, still uncertain, herself, of the dark strong brew.

'Certainly tastes different here than it does at home,' Nick commented.

'That's because you're drinking so much more of it,' Cress declared, laughing. 'Oh, just look at those children!'

They were watching some little girls entertaining the bar customers with their Irish dancing. Sarah's feet were already tapping in sympathy. Laughing, the children's leader caught her hand and pulled her into their midst, expecting to make the regulars laugh at the English girl. But Sarah proved her wrong, picking up the rhythms

285

quickly and earning rounds of applause for her flashing feet.

'I've done it before,' she confessed to Nick as she went back to them. 'I did it at school.'

'That was obvious!' James commented wickedly. 'Showing off as usual, woman.'

'Well, they're playing grown-up dances now,' Sarah rejoined. 'Come on, big mouth!' She whirled him onto the floor, leaving Cress and Nick together.

'Should we join them?' Cress asked, watching anxiously as James flirted merrily with the girls he was dancing with.

'I don't suppose we have much option,' Nick replied with a grin. 'I'm beginning to know that one only too well!'

'And loving every minute of it by the look of you,' Cress said. 'She's taken years off you, Nick!'

'Long may it remain so.' He sighed. 'I love her, Cress. I'm crazy to do it but I can't help it, I'm afraid.'

'You had to come unstuck sooner or later,' she said softly, and took his hand. 'Come on, let's join them.'

Nick held her back for a moment. 'You're good at giving me advice,' he said, 'let me give you some, Cress. Don't be so possessive with James. You never take your eyes off him. He's committed to you – he's not going to leave you – not now.'

Cress smiled sadly. 'You're right. Love does strange things to people, doesn't it?'

The next weekend Sarah rented a cottage from a farmer near to where they were filming in Wicklow. She borrowed a unit Range Rover and drove James out to the airport to catch a flight to London and sat in the bar waiting for Nick's plane to arrive, trying to look inconspicuous.

It was bitterly cold and she was bundled up in a new fur-trimmed parka she had bought in Grafton Street in desperation against the climate. Nick hardly recognized her as he came into the bar. Laughing at his bewilderment,

Sarah threw herself at him, shaking the hood down, lifting her face to be kissed.

'There was a group of English people in here so I was trying not to be seen,' she explained. 'I've planned everything,' she added as she led the way to the car. 'I've organized food, and some whisky, and Neil is going to leave a fire for us.'

Nick smiled at her enthusiasm. 'Does that mean you're planning for us to stay in all weekend?'

'It's too cold to do anything else!' She handed him the keys to the car as they reached it.

'Where's my assertive girlfriend, then?' he laughed as he threw his bag in the back. 'Are you frightened of driving me suddenly?'

'No, but it's just a bit rough on those tracks, and slippery – wait and see!'

'This *is* a four-wheel drive car.'

'We'll need it, I assure you.' She leant over to kiss him. 'How are the new offices?'

How comfortable we are, just like an old married couple, she thought, smiling as he drove and told her about the first week in the new studio complex. She chatted easily about the shoot, and the latest practical jokes, almost forgetting to tell him about the turning as she did so.

'The Ritz, it isn't,' she told him as she unlocked the door. 'But it's really cosy.' While Nick carried their bags in she knelt to light the fire laid in the hearth and then ran to the tiny kitchen to heat up the supper she had craftily persuaded the film caterers to provide for her. Priding herself on her efficiency, she brought him a whisky as he got his bearings in the tiny cottage.

'It's lovely,' he enthused, drawing her against him. 'And I've missed you this week.'

He was amused by her efforts and insisted on helping her, bringing in wood after they had eaten and helping her wash the dishes. 'That's enough work,' he told her then, and fetched the quilt from the bed to throw on the floor in front of the fire, 'I need you now. I can't wait until we go to bed. Anyway, this room is warmer.' He was gentle and tender as he made love to her, wrapping the quilt around them afterwards as they drank wine, and made plans for Christmas, two weeks away.

'I have to go home for a few days,' he told her, knowing she would hate it. 'I need to see Charlotte, even if things aren't too comfortable with Diana.'

'Does Charlotte know yet?' Sarah asked.

'No.' He was firm. 'I won't tell her yet. She's in the middle of exams. It will only upset her unnecessarily.'

'I hate all this hiding,' she sighed.

'So do I,' he admitted. 'But don't worry, it'll happen – I promise. Now, how would you like to come out to LA just after Christmas? You have two weeks off, don't you?'

'Oh, Nick, yes,' she breathed. 'Do we dare?'

'Of course we dare! I have my house in Malibu so we will be completely private. You'll love it; it's right on the beach. I've booked two seats the day after Boxing Day.'

'So you're *telling* me, then?' she laughed.

'I guess so.' He smiled. 'I assumed you'd want to come. I'd take you skiing, but Seth would kill me if I let you break something with three weeks' shooting left!'

'I can live with Malibu!' She grinned. 'Can we go to Vegas too?'

'Anywhere you like, my darling. I'll look forward to being a tourist for once.' He reached over and built up the fire to keep them warm in the bedroom, then lifted her up in the quilt and carried her to the bed.

From the cold and damp of Ireland to the comfortable warmth of California was a lovely surprise. Even at LAX airport tanned people were wandering around in shorts and T-shirts, and Sarah quickly shook off her light lethargy as she absorbed the sun. At Nick's instigation she had exchanged her wintry polo neck for a shirt on the plane and she was glad she had as he led her out to the waiting car. In dark glasses, with her hair twisted into a knot, she had avoided being recognized by their fellow passengers – to Nick's relief. He knew they were taking a risk in travelling together, but for ten days alone he had decided the risk was worth it.

He seemed at home the moment the car met the Pacific Coast Highway, eagerly pointing out features and places as they drove into Malibu, only slightly dismayed when indicating Alice's Restaurant – from Arlo Guthrie's song – to find that Sarah was too young to have even heard of it. She was more fascinated with the wildly varying houses that clung to the side of the highway, precariously perched over the beach itself, in every style, it seemed, from mock Tudor to timber shack.

'I used to have one of those,' Nick said. 'Now I've moved up the hill a bit – better view and more privacy.' He leant forward to give the driver a key to the gateway he had pulled into. Sarah had the impression of a lush green garden, thick vegetation, and palm trees surrounding a small, deep blue pool as they stopped outside the front door.

Nick put her bags down in the hall, and for a moment he was busy with the gate control for the driver. Then with a smile he turned to her and swept her into his arms. 'Welcome to my house, darling,' he said softly. 'Our house soon, I hope.'

For the whole of the ten-hour flight he had longed to kiss her, and finally he could, at length and deeply, his tongue finding hers, his palms slowly caressing the point where her breasts curved into fullness. 'I should have carried you over the threshold,' he said regretfully as he eventually lifted his head.

Sarah smiled and looked around. 'Think how that would have shocked your driver!'

'Cosmo? Nothing would surprise him! This is Holly-

289

wood! And before you ask, only Diana has been here before you, and she hates the place.'

'I can't imagine why. Nick, it's lovely,' Sarah protested. He let her go, and moved around the vast cathedral-ceilinged living room opening curtains and then windows to reveal the deep turquoise ocean in front of them.

'She doesn't like America, period,' he said shortly, and disappeared into the kitchen behind the living room to check the cupboards. 'Good, Maria has left enough food to prevent us from starving,' he commented. 'But I'll have to run up to Trancas later for bread and stuff. You'll like that, it has a great deli counter – all your favourite olives!'

He opened a carton of orange juice at Sarah's request and carried the glasses to where she stood on the deck that ran the length of the front of the house. The back was always the front when it overlooked the ocean, he told her. 'I want you to love it as I do,' he confessed. 'It'll be our home together; I promise you.'

Watching a man and his dog running along the beach, Sarah sighed with pleasure. 'It's beautiful, Nick, much nicer than Regent's Park. That seems so formal; this is . . . well, comfortable, somehow.'

Nick looked back at the airy living room with her eyes. He had chosen every piece of fabric and furniture with comfort in mind, and she echoed his feelings exactly. Huge, squashy beige sofas and bleached oak furniture predominated. The occasional black lacquer Chinese-style piece relieved the paleness, as did the cushions and a chair in a modern, splashy deep purple and cream print. The inevitable piano, also in black lacquer, stood across one corner, carefully shielded from the strong sun, and a tall bleached-oak cabinet with two side-wings held hi-fi equipment and the stacks of books and tapes that Nick was always surrounded with, in office or home.

'Well, I love it,' she said firmly. 'Just as it is.'

'And you haven't seen the bedroom yet!' he teased. 'You can even lie in the jacuzzi and look at the ocean.'

'Jacuzzi? Really?'

'Standard fixture!' He lifted her up and carried her into the master suite, then went to run the bath. He was right, she thought, a few minutes later, when she lay in the softly frothing water, her head cradled against his shoulder as he soaped her body, and she gave a sigh of contentment.

'You really could take a swim in this thing,' she marvelled.

'Warmer than the sea too,' he said. 'That's *not* to be recommended at the moment – even the surfers wear wet suits! But the pool is heated, and the garden is private enough for swimming naked. I often do.'

'Oh, Nick, I can't wait to live here.' Sarah turned then, her body slick with soap, and slid her hands over him, making him groan with desire as she did so. Wet and slippery with soap, his body claimed hers as she knelt astride him in the bubbling water, her hands gripping his shoulders to balance herself as he thrust powerfully into her, making her scream with pleasure. Even dulled by the water, a glorious climax overwhelmed them swiftly, leaving Sarah blissfully relaxed in his arms as he held her.

'I've lain here night after night longing for us to do just this,' he confessed huskily as she finally lifted her head to press long kisses on the soft, smooth skin of his neck. 'I love you so much,' he added. 'I want to marry you more than anything I've ever wanted.'

'Even though I've never heard of Arlo Guthrie?' she teased gently.

'I can live with that,' he assured her. 'Can you *really* live with me?'

'We have ten days to find out,' Sarah promised him. 'I don't care if Diana leaves us with just this place. I have a flat in London too, remember? I just wish we were together now.'

'I know,' he sighed. 'But I'm going to be travelling all over the place for the next few months. I *can't* take you with me, much as I'd like to. A South American jungle is no place for romance, believe me! Be patient, angel.' And with that, she had to be content.

They were happy together, and in love, during those warm days of freedom. Rising late and pottering round the house and garden, not bothering to dress, they were completely relaxed and at ease with each other, making love whenever the mood took them – and wherever. It was even a novelty to go shopping together in the supermarket along the road, teasing and laughing over each other's likes and dislikes.

Nick kept a Jaguar XJS in the garage, though he frequently had a studio car if he was working, and she was soon out on the highway in the Jag exploring the local area. Alone, and then with Nick as her guide, she especially loved the Getty Museum he took her to, perched up on the cliff-side, and marvelled at the elegant Roman-style villa and the mind-blowing paintings and artefacts on display.

Confident that they were unrecognized, they took a few days' trip up the coast to San Francisco and then on to Las Vegas as he indulged her expressed wishes. 'I'm only sorry I can't emulate Charlie's helicopter,' he smiled at her as they boarded a United flight at LAX.

'Forget it.' Sarah smiled, her hand in his. 'I'd rather be with you, Nick.'

He took her to stay at the Mark Hopkins, and to see the view from its famous top floor bar; they rode the cable cars for hours and then took a boat to Sausalito to browse around the many craft shops, where he bought her delicate silver jewellery and pretty glass beads that she enthused over. Then they moved on to Caesar's Palace in Las Vegas, where they caught the legendary Broadway star, Mark Winford, in cabaret and Nick taught her to play blackjack in the casino – only to be mortified when she won and he lost.

Back in Los Angeles, they indulged in their joint passion for Ralph Lauren in Rodeo Drive and went to dinner with

Seth Waterston – because Nick said she had to go to at least one Hollywood watering hole and he had to see Seth anyway.

'Well turn you into the biggest star this damn town has ever seen,' Seth promised her, his teeth clamped on his cigar after the meal, while they were drinking coffee.

'I bet you say that to all the girls!' Sarah smiled, completely at ease with Seth now.

'Not many are as talented as you,' Seth assured her. 'Or as beautiful.' He was excited, only too aware of the way the jaded eyes of the other diners had lit up and followed her as Nick had escorted her to his table. '*Emerald Isle* is going to be a great movie for you,' he prophesied. 'And Mark Winford can't wait to work with you on *Chrysalis*. He went ape over *Home Leave* and he doesn't excite easily!'

'He's gorgeous.' Sarah glared at Nick. Even after seeing him in Vegas, she'd had no idea that *he* was the star of the film Seth had promised her. Nick had kept *that* little gem from her! 'As actors go, of course. I can certainly live with him as a co-star, I suppose – until I get a job with Richard Gere or Kevin Costner of course!'

Nick winced, and Seth laughed.

'Sweetheart, they'll soon be begging you to work with them, believe me,' Seth returned. 'And that's a promise I'll happily make to you!'

CHAPTER 21

'You're not going to mope,' James told her firmly, when he found her in her room at the Shelbourne in tears. 'Come on, we'll drown our sorrows together.'

'I don't think I feel like a drink,' Sarah admitted. 'I don't feel very well, frankly.' For weeks she had occasionally felt sick, though she had hidden it from Nick. Deep down she knew exactly what was wrong with her.

'Then get into bed, sweetie,' he said, concerned. 'I'll get us some tea sent up instead. It's probably just jet-lag. There's a good movie on; we'll watch that.' He insisted she got into bed, and sprawled on the bed with her, watching the film and catching up on the gossip until Sarah finally fell asleep.

In some ways, James was as familiar with Sarah as Nick was, and he soon realized there was something wrong with her as the last few weeks of the shoot went on. They were, thankfully, back in the studio at Ardmore when she really began to feel sick one day, completely unable to face the breakfast she normally ate with gusto. Worried, James threw a coat over her shoulders and took her out into the cold fresh air which revived her a little.

'This has been going on for weeks, Sarah,' he accused. 'You must see a doctor.'

'I don't need a doctor,' she insisted. James swung her round to face him. The concern in his brown eyes was obvious.

'You're pregnant, Sarah, aren't you?' he ask, and immediately saw his answer in hers.

'Yes,' she said, hesitantly. 'I think I may well be. I'd only just gone back on the pill when Nick first came back. I obviously hadn't been on it long enough. Oh, James, what am I going to do? He's going to be furious!'

'Well, you had better see a doctor first,' he said sensibly. 'No use panicking till you know for certain. There must be one on the unit list.'

'I suppose you're right,' she sighed, hugging the coat round her as she shivered.

'Leave it to me,' he told her. 'We've got the afternoon off so I'll make an appointment for you.'

'They'll think it's yours!' she laughed.

'I wish!' he said bitterly. 'Cress is beginning to think I can't do it! Nick certainly doesn't seem to have my problem!'

'You've only been married a few months,' she pointed out.

'We've been trying almost from the beginning,' James admitted ruefully. 'How do you think I knew *you* were pregnant? I've had the signs written on my heart for months! Don't worry, Sarah, I'll look after you.'

He was as good as his word. Between them, they found the doctor's surgery, in a sweeping Georgian terrace. 'I'll wait outside if you like,' he offered.

'No, come in. I'll probably be ages,' she said, sighing and she was. The doctor was brisk and polite, but obviously suspicious of the girl sitting in front of him. He asked a lot of questions, and finally nodded at her.

'I think it more than likely that you are pregnant, Miss Campbell, but we'll take a look first, shall we?' Suddenly he smiled at her, and Sarah felt better, he seemed friendlier then. 'Don't worry, I won't hurt you!'

With a feeling of resignation, she went with the nurse and put on the gown she was given. Lying on the examination couch, she concentrated her attention on the flower picture on the wall in front of her as the doctor probed inside her, putting pressure on her stomach until she wanted to scream.

'No mistake about it,' he said at last, discarding the gloves he had used. 'I'd say you were three months pregnant at least, possibly more. I hope it's good news?'

Sarah pulled the robe around her and moved cautiously. 'I think so,' she said slowly. 'A little unexpected, but . . .' She shrugged.

'You're a healthy girl.' He smiled. 'You'll be fine. I'll write a letter to your own doctor while you get dressed.' Shaking with shock, Sarah struggled into her clothes, her fingers trembling on her jeans zip, but she had regained her composure by the time she went back into his office. 'The young man with you, is he the father?' the doctor asked casually as he waited for the letter to be typed.

Sarah laughed at last. 'Good heavens, no! His wife is my best friend. They have the opposite problem to me.'

'Well, I hope it all works out for you,' he said. 'And don't stop making films, Miss Campbell.'

'I can't afford to stop,' she assured him. 'Thank you, Dr Clare.'

James was looking anxious as she appeared. 'Just let's go!' she said urgently, and caught his arm, almost dragging him out.

'Well?' he enquired as they reached the car. Sarah slid into her seat without waiting for him to help her. 'You are – aren't you?'

'Yes.' She nodded miserably. Her distress saddened James – he knew just how much Cress would have given to be in the same position – but he was generous enough to see it from Sarah's point of view. He knew Nick's attitude to babies.

'You could have a termination,' he suggested as he sought to comfort her. Sarah looked up at him in horror.

'No, never!' she cried. 'Don't even talk about it, James! This is my baby and I want to keep it.' Sarah was mutinous. 'I just don't know how on earth I'm going to tell Nick. He has always said he doesn't want any more children, not after what happened with Diana. For heaven's sake, James, don't mention this to anyone – not even Cress.'

'Especially not Cress,' James said grimly. 'I wouldn't dream of it. We've only got another week left here. Are you going to be OK?'

'Of course I will. Most of the difficult stuff is done. Oh, come on, I need a drink. Let's go to O'Malleys.'

'It'd better be orange juice, then,' he laughed. 'No more booze.'

'Rubbish!' she said crisply. 'I'm going to have to give up enough as it is!'

'I can see this child arriving with hiccups and alcoholic poisoning,' he teased. 'Well, at least you've already given up the fags!'

Somehow James had always had the power to cheer her up, she thought gratefully as they made their way to O'Malleys Bar.

Once he knew that she was serious about keeping the baby he was in fact a tower of strength during the last week of filming, and when she slipped in the mud on a mountain track one day he was full of concern.

'Give over, James!' Alex chided, brushing Sarah down. 'She's not a bit of china!'

'How would you know?' James snapped, and Sarah had to calm them both down.

Cress met them at Heathrow when they arrived back from Dublin. Sarah knew Nick was casting in Los Angeles, and she was quite happy to go back with Cress and James for supper when Cress suggested it. 'You don't mind, do you darling?' she asked James apologetically. James hugged her.

'Of course I don't,' he said. 'Sarah needs us at the moment, more than you know.'

'What's the matter?' Cress was immediately wary.

'I'll tell you later – just look after her.' Sarah tried to eat, but it was obviously an effort, and she drank only mineral water, to Cressida's astonishment.

'OK, you two!' she said at last. 'What's going on?'

James looked at Sarah. 'It's no good, Sarah, you'll have to tell her. She's got a bloodhound instinct built in!'

Cress was looking bewildered, and getting angry.

'It's OK, Cress,' Sarah said. 'It's nothing to do with James, I promise!'

She broke the news and typically Cress was more concerned for Sarah than jealous of her pregnancy. 'You're right,' she exclaimed. Nick is *not* going to be amused. He's really going to blow his top!'

'Don't I know it!'

Cress sprang from her chair and threw her arms around Sarah. 'Stay here with us tonight,' she suggested. 'You can't go home to an empty flat.' She felt Sarah shudder as she held her. 'He'll calm down eventually,' she comforted. 'I'm sure he will. He loves you very much, Sarah.'

'You have more faith in him than I have,' Sarah said flatly, but she went to bed feeling slightly better.

It didn't stop her tossing around half the night, however, and she looked dreadful when James took her home in the morning when she insisted. 'I'm going to see Richard Archibald,' she announced. 'I've already made an appointment. I'll be fine on my own.'

'He's not going to tell you anything different from the guy in Dublin,' James argued.

'Perhaps not,' she agreed. 'But I'd rather have his opinion.' She trusted Richard Archibald, and he did indeed confirm the Dublin doctor's opinion. He was at least gentle, making jokes as he examined her, and Sarah put her faith in him.

He was matter-of-fact and practical, and Sarah began to discover just how complicated it appeared to be to have a baby. She left his surgery in a daze, hardly knowing how she drove back to the flat. She was past crying about it by then, just battling with herself to get things into perspective. Deep down she had guessed about the pregnancy weeks ago, but had hoped all the time that it was her new pills that were making her body play up.

Sitting on the sofa, hugging her already precious secret, she knew she couldn't ever bring herself to terminate a pregnancy. To Sarah the baby was alive already and she wanted it without question. How she was going to cope with Nick's reaction was another matter entirely.

Yet when he arrived, late one Saturday evening, astonishingly she was completely unable to relax with him and tell him. To her horror she found herself barely able to talk to him at all without starting to cry.

'What the hell's the matter, darling?' he demanded, bewildered – this was so unlike her. But Sarah wouldn't answer, she simply crept into his arms, desperate for comfort.

'Nothing, I promise. I just want you to hold me, Nick, please,' she begged.

'If I've done something to upset you, Sarah, you only have to say,' he soothed her gently. 'I'd never deliberately hurt you.'

'I know, I know. Let's go to bed. I'm tired and I'm sure you are.'

Shrugging, Nick put her strange mood down to depression at the film ending; she was often like that for a few days after shooting finished. 'Ireland did you good, though,' he commented later as he watched her brush her hair, something she knew he loved to see her do. 'All that location catering. I'm sure you've put on weight! You certainly haven't been pining for me!'

Sarah felt the shock of his comment and struggled not to show it. 'I certainly hope I haven't,' she said quickly. 'I'm working on Monday and they wouldn't appreciate it if the frocks didn't fit. Polka Dot are as mean as NGA when it comes to clothes.'

'Working for the opposition, are we?' he teased. 'Do you ever stop working?'

'It's only a two-day job. I like working for Rob; he's gentle and he doesn't yell like you do.'

Nick came up behind her, curving his palms caressingly over her naked breasts, making her ache with pleasure. 'Yelling at you *and* being violent!' he commented softly. 'Is this a time for pointing out my faults?'

'Could be. It may be important.'

'As important as this?' He swept aside the swathe of her hair and slowly kissed the curve of her neck. 'God, Sarah, I've missed you these last few weeks! Why don't you forget all the work here and come out to LA now? I really don't want to live without you any longer. I don't care what Diana or the Press think. I want you now – you're mine and I want the world to know it!'

Sarah turned in his arms. It was all she wanted, and yet she knew she couldn't do it – yet. 'Nick, I can't let people down,' she protested. 'I start the new Barbara Bentley in a couple of weeks. And anyway you'll be in South America or wherever for months, and you've already said you can't take me with you.' She could just see herself giving birth somewhere in the depths of the jungle where she knew his film was set!

'I know,' he sighed. 'I know all the sensible reasons. Well, at least put the flat on the market soon and start cutting the work down, then you'll be ready to slip away to the States the moment I get back from Brazil. Let Oscar and Seth work out all the ramifications of Equity and stuff for you – that's what Oscar is paid for, after all.' His hands were slowly driving her wild, to the point where her legs were trembling so much she could hardly stand, and she was finally clinging to him just to stay upright.

'I want to be with you too, Nick,' she whispered. 'Every day and every night.'

'So you will be, darling.' Nick lifted her into the bed, his own body eager for her, and Sarah pulled him down, her arms tight around his neck.

'Now, Nick,' she pleaded. 'I can't wait – please, I want you now!'

He was only too eager to acquiesce to her demands.

'At least come back out to LA for a few days after the Polka Dot shoot,' he suggested some time later, when all their pent-up needs had finally been met. 'A friend of mine is selling a property over in Palm Springs; I'd like you to see it.'

'Palm Springs? That's the desert, isn't it?'

'Partly.' He smiled. 'But it's also a luscious green oasis, and the house is in a stunning location with three acres of garden – far more space than Malibu. It would give us a chance for real privacy. At least let's look at it?'

'It sounds expensive,' she said, worried.

'So? You don't ever have to worry about money! It will be my wedding gift to you, darling.'

It all seemed so perfect. She agonized about the wisdom of the trip, knowing that in a week's time she would be four months pregnant. It would be impossible to hide her condition from him much longer, she was sure. But finally she decided she would take a chance and go, and sighing with contentment she wriggled herself into the warm comfort of his body.

Even in sleep Nick always held onto her, as if he couldn't bear to let her go, and she smiled happily to herself. Tomorrow, perhaps, she decided. Tomorrow she would tell him about the baby. She lay awake as Nick slept peacefully, his hand possessively about her breast, and she fantasised about living with him and their son – or daughter. In her dreams Nick welcomed and loved his new child, as he loved Charlotte – it *would* work out, she promised herself – it had to!

CHAPTER 22

But still she couldn't bring herself to tell him. She cursed herself for being so cautious, but Nick didn't notice anything different about her figure, apart from teasing her that she had put on a certain amount of weight. Now she was into her fourth month, the sickness had quite disappeared, and even *she* actually found it quite difficult to believe she was pregnant. Certainly no one else guessed, and she flew to LA with Nick thinking that perhaps *that* was the place to tell him, when they were relaxed in the sunshine of Malibu.

However, even that plan came unstuck. Nick was busy with the planning on his Brazilian film, and for the first few days he rushed off to the Waterston offices in Burbank every morning. There was very little time to relax together, and in the evenings they went out, as he seemed determined to proudly introduce her to most of Hollywood. In England they were still very careful not to attract attention, but in LA Nick didn't seem to care who knew about their relationship, much to Sarah's surprise.

She'd thought she would be lonely during the day, and half wished she hadn't come as she'd waved him off that first morning, but within a few minutes of his departure Miriam Waterston had arrived to whisk her off in her chauffeur-driven Mercedes for a day's shopping. She had finally persuaded Seth into marriage the previous autumn, and it was a state she highly recommended to an amused Sarah.

Enveloped in Miriam's warm friendliness, she had no time to think about much. She shopped and lunched as she was directed, and spent hours being pampered in Miriam's favourite health club before being returned to Malibu for the evenings with Nick.

'This is exhausting!' she complained a few days later as they dressed for the première of a Waterston film that Nick had felt obliged to go to. 'I thought we'd get a rest!'

'Not yet!' he laughed. 'Not just before a picture is due to start! God knows, I didn't want to do it, but now I am I have to give it my best shot. However, I *have* wangled a couple of days off. Tomorrow we'll drive over to Palm Springs to look at the house, as I promised we would, and we'll stay the night. Would that make up for it?'

'Yes, of course it would!' She sighed. 'I don't mean to sound whingey, Nick, really I don't.'

'I know, darling!' Nick hugged her. 'All I want is to spend time with you! I *certainly* don't want to spend the next three months in Brazil. Damn Seth and his silver tongue! I should have stuck to my guns and said no to him.'

'Well it's too late now; you're stuck with it. Maybe you'll win another Oscar,' she suggested. 'That will more than make up for it.'

'More likely I'll fall flat on my face! I'm about due for a flop, and this movie has disaster written all over it, I'm afraid. Seth has a mania for finding film scripts in turn-around and then expecting me to come up with a bloody miracle!'

'It happened with *King's Daughter*,' Sarah reminded him.

'That was a complete one-off. And they don't happen twice – at least not to me,' he complained. 'Come on, let's forget about it for the day. We'll concentrate on us for a change.'

He drove the Jaguar as fast as he dared, bearing the speed limit in mind all the time. He had been picked up too many times to ignore it, especially now he had an American licence that proclaimed his residency. But it gave Sarah time to view the spectacular scenery as they drew closer to Palm Springs, and to exclaim over the thousands of windmills that lined the desert road on the outskirts.

'A power experiment, I believe,' Nick said, casually as she questioned him. 'Amazing, aren't they?'

She cried out with pleasure at the sight of the immaculate state of the desert town too when they finally reached it. It was the perfect oasis, green-lawned and flower-filled along every street, each car they passed seemingly more luxurious than the one before.

'The grass is watered every evening,' Nick told her. 'Not the time to walk around town – you get soaked! We'll book into the hotel and then go over to Joe's place. The caretaker is expecting us.'

Even the hotel made her gasp, with most of its huge foyer taken up by a real lake. A luxurious motor launch ferried guests out through open windows to disembark at the restaurants on the edge of the outdoor part of it. 'Anything is possible in this town,' Nick laughed. 'It has some of the wealthiest citizens in the world. Bob Hope has a house up on the mountain that cost millions of dollars, and he only uses it for parties! The medical facilities are pretty fantastic too, and you can even get dried out.'

'Of course – the Betty Ford Clinic!'

'Not somewhere you'll need, I hope, darling!' Nick opened their room door and swung her into his arms. 'This is a cure for most ills!'

'Lovemaking?' Sarah giggled as he rolled her onto the bed. Nick was in holiday mood and she was loving it.

'Most of the time, but maybe not quite now,' he said regretfully. 'I really should learn to curb my baser instincts!'

304

'I'll tell you when that's necessary,' Sarah told him. 'But for now . . .' Somehow she manoeuvred him over her, and she found herself being very thoroughly kissed before he regretfully let her go.

'It's that or we'll never get to Joe's place,' he told her. 'I have only a certain amount of control, and I come very close to losing it every time you come near me! Now let's go!'

His friend Joe was a producer in commercials, and very successful, Sarah thought, if his house was anything to go by. She managed not to cry out with shocked delight as Nick drove in through the gates of the exotic, lush-looking development. How Maggie would love this, she decided with a wicked smile.

The house he aimed for was one of the largest. A huge and white-painted Spanish-style hacienda, with the soft terracotta curved tiles now so familiar to her, it seemed to ramble for ever with endless cool arched walkways and fountain-strewn courtyards.

'Nick! You can't be serious about this?' She stared at him in astonishment. 'It'll cost an absolute fortune!'

'If you like it, I'll buy it,' he said simply. '*I've* always liked it and if I'm really honest, I've coveted it for years. Now I can afford it, and at last I have someone to share it with.'

They were left to themselves to look around, and Sarah ran from room to room shrieking with delight like a small child on a treat. The whole house thrilled her almost senseless. There was nothing in it that she even remotely wanted to change, from the vast, immaculate kitchen to the wildly opulent master suite. Situated at the top of its own staircase it had curved walls, with huge French windows opening onto a balcony. The view of tall palm trees and mountains from it quite took her breath away – what was left of it.

'I'd want the house for this view alone!' she gasped. 'Oh, Nick, yes! I want it – desperately!' She leant perilously over the balcony rail to catch a glimpse of the obligatory California pool carved into the immaculate lawns, and thought of her child growing up in such beautiful surroundings, learning to swim in the pool, running and playing under the walkways, at home here. She turned to tell him about the baby – this time she would tell him, she decided – but, ironically, Nick was already halfway down the spiral staircase.

Slowly, Sarah walked away from the balcony and went back downstairs as the thought hit her. It was impossible to tell him about the baby. The time would never be right. And if she couldn't tell him that, where did it leave their relationship?

Ten seconds later, the reality of that horrible truth hit her. Nick paused in the doorway of what was obviously a nursery and laughed. 'Well, we won't need this room,' he said. 'But it might make a nice gym for you, darling.'

'Nick,' Sarah said, nervously. 'I know what you said about Charlotte, but don't you ever want more children?'

'No – no I don't!' Nick paused then at the look of pain that crossed her expressive eyes. 'Surely, darling, you must know that by now? Anyway, there won't be time – certainly not for a year or two. I want you to succeed in the business first. Does it bother you? Not having children? I've never made a secret of not wanting any more; I thought you'd accepted it?'

'I have – well, more or less,' she admitted, trying to sound casual. 'But I'm sure it wouldn't affect my career that much, Nick. After all, Demi Moore has children, and look where she is!'

'Perhaps later,' Nick acquiesced. 'When you're really established and we're *properly* married. Then I might be persuaded – though I think I'd have to be blind drunk for nine months to cope with it! I *certainly* couldn't envisage having a child out of wedlock. It wouldn't feel right at all. Sorry, does that make me sound old-fashioned?'

She knew then, miserably, that she would be taking her

secret back to England with her. There was no other way but to keep it from him until he was back from Brazil and they were finally together. It would be almost time for the baby to be born by then and Nick would have no choice but to go along with it. At least, she reasoned, he wouldn't have months to worry about her if he didn't know.

That thought was the only thing that comforted her on the interminable flight back. Knowing they were parting for at least three months made them both desperately unhappy, and at that point Sarah almost gave in to his pleas that she abandon everything and stay in LA with Miriam and Seth. Only her own strict sense of loyalty kept her from doing as he asked. It would be totally unfair to the cast and crew of the Bentley drama she told him gently, and of course he knew she was right. Nick, like Sarah, had a very strict code of behaviour when it came to work ethics. Nevertheless, she was close to tears almost the entire journey, and she was thankful for the luxury of being able to hide in the first class lounge at LAX before she boarded the plane.

Cress was livid with her when she met her at Heathrow. 'You can't do this, Sarah!' she stormed at her. 'It's not fair to Nick. He may have some funny ideas, but he has a right to know. It's his child, after all. You should have told him!'

'I'll do exactly as I please!' Sarah declared. 'Really, Cress, it's the only way.'

'And if Nick's film overruns, you'll simply present him with a bundle in a shawl, will you?' Cress said sarcastically. 'You're going the right way about losing him, Sarah. And it's not as if James and I will be around to pick up the pieces – for a while anyway.'

'Why? Oh, God, Cress, where are you going?'

'Australia! In two weeks' time,' Cress admitted. 'James has a fantastic new part and we'll be there for four or five months. I'm going with him, obviously. I couldn't bear to be apart from him for all that time.'

As she couldn't bear to be apart from Nick, and yet she

had to be. Without Cress around she would be really alone. She could hardly bear the thought of it, she relied so much on Cress. And it was Cress who, despite Sarah's misgivings about her own plight, went happily with her for the routine scan. She was as excited as Sarah as the radiologist explained all the lines and dots that made up the baby on the screen, and they went back to Hurlingham together both just as eager to show James the picture they had been given of the scan.

She roundly cursed her sense of honour on the journey out to Spain to start filming, and met up with the crew with a heavy heart. Yet it turned out to be her salvation. To be working hard again was exactly what she needed, and she didn't spare herself. Only the director and the costume designer knew she was pregnant, and, having worked with them both before, she trusted them with her secret. Anna, the designer, came up trumps with loose surcoats over her sumptuous medieval gowns that hid any trace of her thickening waistline, and the director carefully rear-ranged the schedule so that her more strenuous riding stints were at the beginning of the shoot.

She wrote long, anguished letters to Nick, as he did to her. At least his written words were some comfort in her unhappy state. She found herself carrying his letters around with her, reading and re-reading his beautiful prose. She realized then how limited her own education had been as she read the poetry he quoted, and eventually turned back to the classics she had long neglected to read the originals his letters gave hints of.

Daunted slightly by his knowledge compared to her own, her doubts began to plague her again. Anna laughed, and told her it was just her hormones playing up. As a young mother herself, she was the ideal person to have around – better in some ways than Cress. Anna was sensible and down to earth, and a fund of newly riveting information about babies!

Cheerfully, the two girls took a trip to Seville on a rare free day, and with Anna's help Sarah excitedly bought the first clothes for her baby – delicately embroidered outfits that she couldn't help looking at over and over again once they got back to their hotel. Anna taught her to smock in the long hours of hanging around that they had to do, and Sarah, always an enthusiastic needlewoman, took to it easily and was soon producing her own pretty garments. Even with the endlessly boring gathering she found it relaxed her tremendously.

By the time she returned to London she had quite a pile of clothes in the pale blue silk-covered box that Anna had given her, and she felt totally confident in her baby's reality. During the last few days on location it had begun to move inside her, a delicate fluttering that had terrified her for a few moments until the patient Anna had explained what it was. Then she had been thrilled, and had even more wanted to share it with Nick, and she had cried endlessly when she realized she couldn't.

He was in Brazil by then, and even if she had wanted to speak to him she knew it was almost impossible. He had already warned her of the problems. The unit was a good two days' travelling time from LA, way up the Amazon river in the depths of the thickest jungle the location manager could find, and living in remote native villages half the time.

The thrust back into her own world was sharp and painful, as George met her at the airport with the news that her flat was not only sold, but that the buyer, an American friend of his, wanted to move in very quickly. 'What the hell shall I do now, though?' Sarah wailed at him. 'I won't be going to the States for months, George!'

George frowned. 'Nick said you were to move into his flat, didn't he? What's the problem?'

'I can't do that!' Sarah gritted her teeth. 'George, don't you realize, I'm having a baby – Nick's baby. I can't move into his flat; it would attract too much attention. He isn't divorced yet, and if Diana found out he'd never get one. She would use it to make life even more difficult for him.'

'Well, you've really done it now! You bloody idiot, Sarah! Have you no sense?' George sighed with frustration.

'Not where Nick is concerned – not much,' she admitted.

'So what has *he* to say on the subject?' George asked. 'He's not much of a prospective father, I must say – swanning off to Brazil for months and leaving you to cope.'

Sarah had to admit then that Nick knew nothing about the baby, and suffered a furious tirade from her irate brother as he drove down the M4 towards Chelsea.

'Maggie will go mad,' he moaned. 'You know what she's like!' For all his high-powered business life, Maggie ruled her husband with a fierce power and her strait-laced upbringing coloured both their lives.

'Don't worry, George, I'm not moving in with you and Maggie,' Sarah reassured him. 'I couldn't take Maggie's fire and brimstone recriminations! I'll rent somewhere if I have to – perhaps in the country, away from the Press.'

'I can't believe thay haven't found out yet,' he groaned. 'It will be hell when they do. Perhaps it's a good thing Nick *is* so far away. Maybe they won't cotton on to his being the father!'

'Don't worry, George, I'll keep well away from the Press,' Sarah said loftily. 'They won't be interested in me – especially if I disappear for a while.'

'Don't be so sure, little one.' George looked worried. 'I think perhaps you should ask Charles for help; he *is* very fond of you – and Nick. I'm sure he'd do anything he could for you. You can't live completely alone in your condition.'

Charles! She has completely forgotten about him. Maybe, she wondered, he *would* have somewhere on the estate she could rent – but was it was really fair to ask him? He loved her, she knew and he would be devastated to find she was going to marry Nick. Since he and Nick had quarrelled over her they had almost ceased to communicate unless it concerned the business.

But once she had phoned the estate agents handling the sale if her flat she began to realize the urgency of the position she was in. The buyer wanted possession, and in less than three weeks she would be homeless. George had simply assumed she would move into Regent's Park – the one thing she knew she couldn't do.

With a heavy heart she drove down to Hastings Court, knowing by then that there was no other option. Panicked even more by yet another phone call from a newspaper columnist fishing about Nick that morning, she knew she had to get out of their way, somehow, before they really became suspicious.

Typically, Charles welcomed her with open affection, hugging her enthusiastically before he led her indoors. 'I was beginning to think you'd left me for good,' he told her, laughing. 'The whole day has changed for the better!'

'It may not have when you know why I'm here,' Sarah replied drily. 'You won't like it, Charles.'

She was as gentle as she could be in telling him and then almost wished she hadn't. He was indeed devastated, and for long minutes he said nothing as he struggled to get to grips with the news. He had always thought Nick was solidly trapped into his marriage to Diana, the fact that he was finally seeking a divorce hit him like the proverbial heat-seeking missile.

'He won't be able to divorce soon – probably not for years,' he said at last. 'You know that, Sarah?'

'Yes, I know.' Sarah picked nervously at the ruched edge of a cushion. 'It doesn't matter, Charles, really it doesn't. We can live with it. But Nick thinks all Diana really wants is money. She's just using access to Charlotte as a means to get it.'

'And she'll go on doing it, believe me!' Charles said. 'You'll never have a minute's peace. Do you really want to

311

live like that? Nick is hardly the super-faithful type; either. You'll have a dog's life with him.'

'He's faithful to me! Oh, I'm sorry, Charles, I *shouldn't* have come to you! It's really not fair! I should have known better.' Sarah got up, but immediately Charles reached out to her.

'No, don't go. Sarah, I can help and I will.' Charles could finally see a way to beat Nick. 'You can live here with me. I'll look after you, I promise.'

'Charles, I can't!' she protested. 'Nick would hate it, for one thing!'

'Nick's in Brazil,' Charles pointed out. 'And he's doing *nothing* for you. You could move into the pavilion for now. It's furnished and you'd be safe from the Press here. No one could get to you. The security here is very tight – as you know.'

The idea was tempting. Sarah thought rapidly. 'As long as you know how things are, Charlie,' she said, slowly. 'I'm asking you as Nick's friend – nothing more.'

'Nick's friend, but more yours,' Charles said. 'I would never let anything happen to you, Sarah, be assured of that. Leave everything to George and I to arrange. You needn't even go back to London if you don't want to. Let's go down and look at the pavilion, shall we?'

She had always liked the pretty little house in the grounds, and the thought of making it her home, albeit a temporary one, rather excited her. Charles seized on her enthusiasm and it seemed that within hours she had agreed to move in and he was making arrangements for it.

She went back to Chelsea feeling far more relaxed, and then freaked to find a couple of reporters on her doorstep. Luckily, she was wearing a loose sweatshirt and leggings, so her condition was easily disguised, but real panic set in then. She immediately phoned Charles. 'You were right!' she wailed at him. 'I'm going to pack tonight and come down tomorrow.'

'Bernard is at Dolphin Square tonight,' Charles said.

'I'll send him round first thing in the morning. He'll do it all for you, Sarah. Don't worry, you have me to care for you now.' He was careful not to use any endearment – that would come later, he decided – though it had never worried him before. This time – this time he was going to win the battle with Nick. Sooner or later Nick would play right into his hands.

It happened far sooner than even the optimistic Charles could have foreseen.

Sarah settled happily into the pavilion, and into the pampered lifestyle at Hastings Court. Within days she felt as if she had lived there all her life as almost every care and responsibility was lifted from her. She ate most meals with Charles, and consequently spent much of the day with him when he was at home, walking or even riding round the estate. She assured him she was quite capable of riding, but although he insisted on choosing the quietest mount she knew he was uneasy, and finally gave in to allow him to drive her instead.

Hastings quickly became her home, and Charles seemed only too happy to indulge her in any way he could. She itched slightly to have a telephone line installed in the pavilion, but when Charles suggested that it seemed a waste for so short a time she realized he was right, and settled for having calls put through from the house.

'It does at least screen out any unwanted calls,' he said sensibly. 'No one need know you're here at all, and the staff have been told not to say a word in the village.' It puzzled Sarah that Nick hadn't written since she had come to Hastings, but then she realized that her note about her move would not have reached him yet and she shrugged it off, writing letters to him almost daily for the faithful Bernard to post in the village when he went out.

She hadn't left the estate for a couple of weeks when Charles sauntered into the pavilion one afternoon. After a long walk that morning she was tired, and had flopped out on the sofa in front of the fire Bernard lit for her every morning. In her sixth month, she was finally beginning to feel pregnant!

'I think you should see this, Sarah,' Charles put a newspaper down in front of her. 'It doesn't make very cheerful reading, but . . .'

Sarah stared at the *Unicorn*. She hadn't seen a newspaper for ages – not since she had come to Hastings, she realized suddenly. It had become quite an event even to watch television somehow, and in any case the *Unicorn* was not her favourite paper.

'Why on earth should I need to read that rubbish?' she laughed lazily, sitting up and pushing her hair back from her flushed face. Really, she thought, she was getting almost too relaxed to move at all!

'Because it mentions someone we both know.' Charles opened it for her. 'I'm sorry, darling, but I think you should know the truth.'

'Truth? In the *Unicorn*? They don't know the meaning of the word!' Sarah picked up the paper and scanned the page. 'Oh, my God!' She dropped it again with a shriek and Charles reached out quickly, scooping her into his arms, frightened rigid at the sight of her ashen face.

Oscar-winning British film director Nick Grey frolics on a Rio beach with his latest love, Madeleine Miller. The randy director, not so long ago the lover of actress Sarah Campbell, is now said to be head-over-heels in love with his wife's best friend. Has he no shame? The couple are together in Brazil, where Nick is busy on his new film – but not too busy, it seems, for the beautiful Madeleine.

The text seared her eyes wherever she looked, taunting her with the photograph of a laughing Nick with Madeleine in his arms. She knew Madeleine vaguely from the Wardour Street office. She remembered Nick saying that she was in LA because her marriage was in trouble but she had thought nothing of it. Yet all the time Nick had obviously been seeing her. All the time she had been agonizing over telling him about his baby he had been seeing someone else!

'It can't be true, Charles!' she sobbed. 'It can't possibly be true! He loves me – only me!'

'Nick has never been the type to be faithful to one person,' Charles said. 'He's *never* believed in it. Look at the way he's deceived Diana all these years. He doesn't care, darling. Just be thankful you found out in time.'

'Charles! You surely don't believe all this rubbish, do you?' Sarah stared at him in astonishment. 'It's the *Unicorn*, for God's sake!'

'It's all true, Sarah,' Charles said quietly. 'I spoke to Jane this morning. Madeleine left her husband for Nick a few weeks ago. She went out to Brazil to join him. That's probably why you haven't heard from him. I bet he's too ashamed to write and tell you.'

'Oh, Charles, no! It can't be true! It can't be!' Sarah wept helplessly, hugged in Charles's arms.

For a few agonized moments he wondered if he had gone too far. But the photograph *was* genuine, and heaven sent. The sooner Sarah realized what Nick was like, the better, he justified piously to himself. She would soon get over him, and then he could ask her the one vital question he wanted to ask.

He quietly gave thanks to the persistent Maxie Moreton as he held Sarah tightly to him, revelling in the fact that for once she really needed him. Max had done everything he could have wished for, and, true or not, it was exactly what he needed at that point. He thought of all the letters he had intercepted in the last few weeks, and made a mental note to destroy them. Sarah wouldn't want them now, he thought.

'Charles, what am I going to do?' she agonized.

'Do?' Charles smiled down at her. 'I suggest you do absolutely nothing – apart from sending the bastard that ring back. Forget him, Sarah, he's not worth it!'

'I can't do that!' She wrenched away from him. 'He loves me. We're buying a house together, for God's sake!'

'So? Explain that, then!' Charles threw the paper at her. 'Photographs tell their own story, Sarah. Just look at it! Showing you a house is one thing, buying it is another thing altogether.'

'God! I wish I'd taken the chance and stayed in LA – even gone to Brazil with him.'

'You wouldn't be able to spend your entire life following Nick around just to keep him faithful,' Charles pointed out. 'And that's what it would entail. Face it, Sarah, he's no good for you.'

'I can't bear it, Charlie!' Sarah buried her face in the comfort of his soft pullover.

'I know, sweetheart, it's hard. But you have me, remember? And I won't let you down, I promise.'

'No, I know you won't.' Sarah wiped at her reddened eyes, and then tried to pull herself together – for the sake of the baby, she told herself as Charles quietly handed her a large linen handkerchief.

'Tonight we'll go out for dinner,' he suggested, surprised at his boldness. 'There's no way you're going to sit in here alone and mope about someone who doesn't deserve it. We'll drive over to the Manoir Quatre Saison, how about that?'

'Oh, Charles! Are you sure?' Sarah was doubtful. It would be a lovely treat, but she worried about her appearance in public far more these days. 'Someone might see me.'

'So what if they do? I'm single, don't forget, and so are you,' he reminded her. 'The papers have been trying to pair us off for months – what would be so unusual in our eating out together? Wear that pretty blue dress Catherine made for you; it would be a shame to waste it.'

'Are you sure I don't look too pregnant?' Sarah worried.

'My darling girl, you *are* pregnant!' Charles laughed. 'Maybe if the reporters find out they'll think it's mine –

316

that would teach Nick a thing or two about leaving you to fend for yourself!'

'Well . . . OK, then, I suppose it can't do much harm,' she acquiesced. 'But I'll need an age to get ready. I'm out of practice at the make-up.'

'Rubbish! Anyway you hardly need any. I'll pick you up at seven-thirty.'

Triumphant, he went back up to the house to make the reservation. A little more persuasion, he thought smugly, and Sarah would return Nick's ring – round one was definitely his!

CHAPTER 23

After that it seemed that life took on a different pattern, and suddenly Sarah went everywhere with Charles, even on short trips to the Continent, if he travelled there on business. It was as if he couldn't bear to leave her behind. Finally she began to realize just how caring and solicitous of her Charles was, and how pleasant his lifestyle could be.

She truly loved the peace and quiet of Hastings in between the trips to Geneva and Brussels – the birth of a new foal in the stud, going racing with Charles and Rupert, all interspersed with endless talk of horses. She was grateful that her height and well exercised body made her pregnancy seem far less obvious, and she became expert at hiding it for the social occasions she attended with Charles. Even at six months very few people guessed at it, and she had the energy of two most of the time.

Slowly, the thought of Nick receded from her busy everyday thoughts, though at night he came back to her very distinctly, invading her sleep, making her ache to her very soul for him. She said nothing to Charles about him, but each and every night she prayed that the paper had been wrong and that Nick would come sailing in through the door one morning and everything would be as it was before. But there were no letters from him, and gradually she began to realize that Charles was right. Nick had replaced her in his affections.

Finally she made the decision and wrote, enclosing the

ring she had loved so much. It hurt terribly for a while, as if she had cut herself in two, but she had the baby, kicking and very much alive inside her. Nick hadn't really left her, she tried to console herself when the pain got too much. He would always be with her in one way.

Charles deliberately filled her days and evenings with people and events until her head whirled – consulting her on dinner parties before he gave them, insisting that she was his hostess when he did. Her life was becoming Charles, she realized one morning as she strolled up to the house to swim in the pool, a daily habit now. He was even talking of joining her for the sessions with the childbirth teacher Richard Archibald had found for her locally.

'Why don't we arrange for you to have your baby here at Hastings?' he had suggested only the day before. 'It would guarantee privacy for you – you'd never get that in a normal hospital.'

A few weeks before she would have been horrified at the idea, now suddenly it seemed quite natural, and she had found herself telling him she would think about it. Maybe – now that Nick wasn't coming back for her – she *would* have her baby at Hastings, with Charles. He took so much care of her it seemed inevitable now.

Several times she was on the point of ringing Miriam Waterston, to find out what she knew, and then something always stopped her. It seemed so pathetic, somehow – to have to ask someone she didn't know that well about her own lover. Many times she longed for Cress – how much easier life would have been if Cress had been around to make her laugh, and simply just be sensible about things. Cress had a knack of putting things in perspective some-how. But she was away for a couple of months more, so that was right out of the question. Charles quietly filled the bill for all manner of things, even though his care was almost too claustrophobic at times.

It was still a while, however, before he subtly brought

up the question of marriage, and when he did, though she cheerfully laughed at the very idea, suddenly it wasn't *quite* so silly any more.

'Lady Sarah Hastings has a rather nice ring to it,' he said wistfully. 'I'd rather thought you were getting keener on the idea, Sarah?'

'Charlie, I'm just not ready for that yet,' Sarah stalled. 'Wait until I've had the baby, then perhaps I'll think about it.'

Despite her misery over Nick, Hastings itself was certainly growing on her. She loved the gracious old house and was always avid to hear the history of it that Charles imparted so well. They spent hours together in the library, poring over all the old family records that he got out to show her, and were soon exploring the older and forgotten parts of the attics and cellars in search of more.

In doing so they came across all Charles's old baby equipment – cots, toys, even clothes put away by his cost-conscious mother – and Sarah swooped on them in delight. 'We'll get them cleaned up!' Charles declared, excited by her enthusiasm. 'How lovely to be able to use them again! The baby will seem like a real Hastings baby then.'

A Hastings baby? Sarah stared at him. Less than two months she had lived there, and it felt like years. She was comfortable, and she was beginning to admit that it felt like home. She had done nothing for herself since she had come to live there, and the only time she left the estate she was with Charles in the car, or in his helicopter. Her own car sat unused in one of the garages. Her furniture, all but a few treasured pieces, was in store, and she was certainly spending far more time in the main house these days than she did in the pavilion.

Now she couldn't do any significant work she was completely idle. Oscar had been cutting back on her prodigious workload for some time in anticipation of her move to America, so her disappearance off the working scene had not caused too many ripples. The Press couldn't get to her at Hastings, and Charles's friends were so used to her visiting that her appearance at his side had caused very little comment locally. It was exactly what they expected to happen.

It was, on the whole, a very pleasant life, she told herself that late April morning as she gazed out over the lake and Hoover came chasing across the lawn to greet her with great lollopy licks. If only . . . she thought wistfully, her hands protectively over the curve of the baby . . . if only Nick hadn't betrayed her.

Two weeks into filming, and Nick knew he had made a terrible mistake. In over eighteen years of film-making he had never worked in such appalling conditions, and, physically strong though he was, his natural energies soon began to dissipate.

'Lord luv us, Nicholas, what the bleedin 'ell made you come all the way to this God-forsaken hole?' his faithful Lenny asked, in the mock Cockney he often used on American locations to annoy the Yanks. He had actually gone quite white with shock at his first sight of the impenetrable jungle they could see from the boat taking them up the river from the tiny town that was their main base. Coari itself was pleasant enough, built on a cool, silt-free lake, very unlike the river, and ringed with white sand and green jungle. Its streets hummed with life and it made a welcome change from the primitive conditions they endured elsewhere.

'I really can't imagine. I think I had a brainstorm and let Seth get the better of me,' Nick sighed. 'Cheer up, Lenny, it can only get better.'

But it didn't.

In fact it got a great deal worse, seemingly every day something else went wrong.

Nick could hardly believe how stoic his small cast were. All English, by his choice, and how wise he had been! The two lead actors were both products of good English public schools and the stiff upper lip bred in them was very much needed. Americans, he had told Seth firmly after his initial recce, would have been on the first plane home after half a day. Nick had little faith in the resilience of American film actors, cosseted as they were by the major studios and producers.

The jungle was relentlessly unforgiving to the invading film-makers, and consistently showed its worst side. They were constantly soaked by the endless rain, and eaten alive by the torrents of insects that never seemed to leave them alone, day or night.

Whole crates of equipment were still held up in Brazilian Customs, 'awaiting paperwork.' 'Bribes more like!' Nick grumbled, after yet another fierce argument over a crackling phone in a mixture of Portuguese and Spanish. Communications were, as he had predicted to Sarah, pretty well impossible, especially with Los Angeles. It could take hours just to get a call to Rio from the depths of the jungle.

'And we've got weeks more of this!' Madeleine told them cheerfully, when Lenny and Bud, the first assistant, were bending his ears yet again over their problems.

Nick swatted at a persistent mosquito and laughed. Every morning the one thing he thanked himself for was finally persuading Madeleine to come on location with him, after she had turned up unexpectedly in LA and looked him up at Jane's suggestion. She had proved to be an absolute godsend. Not just to him but to everyone on the crew.

She was wife, mother, girlfriend and father-confessor to everyone, and all without a sign of preferring one above another. Even Nick was treated in the same easygoing fashion, and it was a complete relief. Sexual hassle added to everything else would have finished them all. Most of the crew were too tired to even think of it, he decided thankfully. *He* certainly was! Lenny had christened her Florence Nightingale, and she certainly earned the title as they all preferred her to deal with all the cuts and bites that they all fell victim to, rather than the forbidding Portuguese nurse who was the unit first-aider.

Luckily, Madeleine had the same gift for languages that Nick himself had, having been brought up in a Spanish-speaking area, and she was almost as fluent as he was in Portuguese, so she was able to communicate easily with the natives who worked with them in the little village the art directors had built. From them she learnt of the plants they used for healing and was quickly following suit, frequently to amused laughter from a sceptical crew, which soon changed to gratitude when her potions actually worked.

Nick was troubled from fairly early on by a bite that swelled on his left arm and despite all Madeleine's efforts it seemed to remain, making him even more irritable, especially at night. Several times she begged him to let a local healer look at him, but Nick laughed her off. 'No old biddy is going to mutter incantations over me!' he told her firmly. 'It's only a bite, Maddy, it'll go down sooner or later. Otherwise I'll wait until we get back to Belem, and see a doctor there. Happy?'

'Stubborn sod!' Madeleine retorted cheerfully. 'Don't blame me if your arm drops off!'

Nick ruffled her cap of dark curls. 'Such a comfort you are, angel! Does that go as far as a beer?' Madeleine laughed back and reached into her ever-present pack. It contained pretty well every convenience.

'Warm, probably,' she warned, and tossed it to him. 'And the last one till we get back to base – make the most of it.'

Nick always seemed to be thirsty these days. He put it down to all the shots he'd had topped up before he came out to the Amazon, but at that moment he frowned. He had never had any effect from shots before, and he reasoned that he should be used to them by now. Working in often remote parts of the world meant that he always

323

kept his injections up to date; they were part of the medical checks insisted on by the film's insurers.

He decided he was making a thing about nothing. They were all feeling under the weather, indeed several members of the crew had already been sent back to Rio with various illnesses. Nick was determined he wouldn't be one of them. Though if he was, he realized one morning, when he felt particularly dreadful, then at least he would get back to the UK, and Sarah, that much quicker.

For a few minutes he was incredibly tempted to try it, until the next crisis arose and he automatically went to deal with it. Like Sarah, he knew he couldn't back out of a deal – too many people depended on him – and he finally shrugged it off.

He missed her desperately, missed her warm, chatty letters and the sound of her voice on the telephone. It seemed weeks since he had received a letter from her, and he cursed the situation he found himself in. His one consolation were the infrequent messages from Seth about the Palm Springs purchase, which was going ahead in his absence under the eagle eyes of Waterston's lawyers. The first thing they would do together, he told himself, was furnish their house, and the thought cheered him through many dreary days of foul weather and wading around in the endless sea of mud.

At night, as with Sarah, the longing was worse. Even if his body was exhausted it was difficult to sleep in the steamy humidity that never let up. Though their mock Indian village had a series of reasonably comfortable bungalows built onto it for the cast and crew to live in, there was certainly no air-conditioned comfort. It did save commuting back to the town every night, however, and with a small but efficient staff imported from LA it was preferable to stay there rather than face the horrible journey. They ate their own food, which was simple but edible, and even had a fairly well-stocked bar to call on. But they had quickly found that the picturesque thatched bungalows leaked like the proverbial sieves, and learned to sleep with buckets or bowls handy to catch the worst of them.

Nick lay awake night after night, his mind on Sarah, and Madeleine frequently heard him pacing the veranda early in the morning. But it was useless remonstrating with him, though she tried. 'Nick, you'll crack up at this rate!' she warned him in her motherly way. 'You need sleep badly, and you aren't eating properly.'

'I don't particularly feel like eating, Maddy,' Nick admitted. 'I hope I'm not going down with one of those bugs. I can't afford to be ill – not after all this battle to keep the schedule more or less on time, not now we're so close to finishing.'

'Is your arm bothering you still?' Madeleine caught at his wrist and quickly jerked up the cuff of his shirt that hung loose. She was too quick for him to stop her and she gazed at his swollen forearm in horror. 'For God's sake, Nick! This is a real mess! Why the hell didn't you say something?'

'It's only got worse the last day or so,' he lied. 'I thought it could wait until we go back to Coari or Belem.'

'Well, it won't! Let me get the village woman to look at it at least?' Madeleine coaxed.

Nick was in too much pain to argue with her by that time, though when half an hour later she returned with a middle-aged native woman with wizened skin and very black teeth he rather wished he had. With everything else to worry about he had tried to ignore the troublesome swelling. His apprehension grew as she clucked and muttered over it for long minutes before she finally dug into the straw bag she carried and began rubbing a cold-feeling salve onto it.

'What on earth is she doing?' he demanded of a fascinated Madeleine.

'Bad things in here,' the woman told him. 'They must come out.'

325

'I think she's going to lance it,' Madeleine volunteered. 'Get the swelling down.'

'What the hell with? Oh, my God, not with *that*?' Nick stared in shock at the curved knife that appeared in her hand. 'Get her out of here!'

'Very quick,' she told him, patting his arm.

'Shut up, Nick!' Madeleine put in. 'And don't be such a coward! I'm surprised at you!'

'It's all right for you!' he retorted, wincing as the knife touched his skin. Laughing, Madeleine took hold of his other hand.

'Come on, baby, I'll hold your hand for you,' she offered. 'It's poison, Nick, it has to come out.' She did her best to reassure him, having been told what it was likely to be and deciding that it was best Nick didn't know. 'Look the other way,' she advised.

But Nick didn't. He was riveted to the knife that slid through his distorted flesh, expecting the blood, and pain but to his everlasting shame he took one terrified look and fainted at their feet.

The treatment had been primitive, but it had had the desired effect. His arm was bandaged and in a sling, but for a week or two he felt far more able to cope. The weather improved slightly, and they even had several miraculous days without rain. Picking up shots he had thought he would have to do without cheered him enormously, and life took on a rosier hue altogether. Refusing to consider going back to Belem to recuperate, since finally he could get some work done, he battled on, convinced things were going his way at last. Even rest days on site were ignored in his push to keep to the murderous schedule he had set for himself. Anything to finish and get back to LA, he told himself, and pushed even harder.

Madeleine and Bud begged him to take it easier but he refused to listen. Without access to regular weather bulletins he had no choice but to keep working while the weather held, he told them firmly, and work they did. Nobody seriously minded the work; they were as anxious as he was to get the job finished and on time.

Actual money was in short supply, since all their currency had to be negotiated in Rio and cash brought up to them to pay their bills locally. Even, it was whispered amongst their native helpers, to pay off the rumoured bandits who were supposed to linger in the surrounding area. Nick doubted it, but he made sure they didn't take any more risks than they needed to, and the whole crew, native and American, guarded Madeleine and the one make-up girl as if they were rare and precious commodities when that particular rumour began to circulate amongst the already strung-out crew.

Elated by the fantastic footage he was getting, and the editor's enthusiastic reports, Nick decided to add more library shots to help the editing when they got back to the States. The sunset promised to be clear and perfect that evening, and he cheerfully bribed Lenny to forgo his evening drinking session and go out with him to shoot.

'I'll come too,' Madeleine decided. 'I could do with the exercise; I've been typing all day.'

'Well, don't moan if you can't keep up,' Lenny told her. 'I'm in a hurry, and it'll be no fun if we get stuck out there in the dark.'

'No chance.' Nick shrugged. 'We'll take one of the guides with us. Don't worry, Len, we'll get back in time for you to get a couple in!'

They rounded up a guide, a rather sour little runt of a man, and set off briskly, bouncing along the rough tracks in the battered Jeep they used as transport to the spot high above the river that Nick had noticed on a previous expedition. As he had hoped, the view of the river and the darkly encroaching trees made beautiful pictures, and they set up and took some stunning shots of the landscape before they finally got the sunset they were waiting for. It was magnificent, and Nick and Madeleine stood watching it in awe.

'God, I wish Sarah was here to see this,' Nick sighed. 'I bet she'd love it.' Madeleine, knowing the situation, squeezed his hand sympathetically.

'Cheer up, Nick only a few weeks to go.'

'Thank goodness,' Nick sighed. 'I'm not sure I can hold on much longer. Christ! I've got such a headache, Maddy. Do you have any aspirin with you?'

Madeleine pulled some out of her bag, laden as usual. 'That's the third headache in as many days,' she chided. 'Are you sure you're OK, Nick?'

'Nothing going home won't cure.' He grimaced, and swallowed the pills dry, choking slightly from the effect. Madeleine ran back to the Jeep and found a bottle of water to toss to him. He needed it desperately, and drank most of it in one go.

'You should have taken the chance to rest this evening instead of doing this,' she said crossly. 'You never learn, Nick.'

'Give me a break,' Nick snapped back. 'I can sleep all night! Come on, then, Lenny, get a move on.'

'Stop giving the girl a hard time, Nicholas,' Lenny warned as he packed the camera back into its protective bag. 'She only has your best interests at heart, and, frankly, you're beginning to look as if you have a permanent hangover or something. You look dreadful, mate.'

'If I want your advice Lenny, I'll ask for it,' Nick said. 'And that goes for you too, Madeleine. I feel fine.'

He didn't feel anything like it, but that was for his own thoughts only. He felt sick and cold, then hot and dizzy, and had been all day. He put it down to the wound on his arm playing up, and cursed the woman who had lanced it so crudely, convinced that she had made things worse, though the nurse, on dressing it, had commented favourably enough on the work that had been done. The native woman had even stitched it together, he had discovered when he had finally recovered consciousness, apologizing profusely to a giggling Madeleine. She teased him unmercifully about it, bringing forth all kinds of promised retributions from Nick if she dared to tell Sarah about it!

Slowly, he made his way back to the Jeep, and found to his amazement that he could only manage to climb into it with the greatest of effort, whereas he had sprung out of it only an hour or so before. 'Len,' he said, 'I think you may be right. I do feel really strange.'

'Nick!' Madeleine leapt at him as he swayed across the seat. She caught him just in time to prevent him falling back out of the cab, shrieking at Lenny to help her. Nick was so hot his skin seemed to burn her hands as she struggled to hold him. 'Lenny, he's ill – really ill. Feel his skin!'

'I'll be . . . fine . . . let's just get back . . .' Nick groaned, not wanting them to fuss.

His head hurt so badly that every bump and jolt of the truck made him want to scream with pain. Madeleine held him against her to try and cushion the friction, and eventually in desperation he buried his head into the curve of her neck in a fruitless effort to ease the pain. Lenny drove as carefully as he could, but in the darkening jungle it was a nightmare to try and see where they were going, even with their guide hanging out of the vehicle to tell him the way. By the time they finally made it back to the village Nick was almost delirious from the pain, and they had to summon help from other members of the crew to lift him out of the Jeep. Even though he had lost weight recently, he was still too heavy to lift easily.

Madeleine took charge automatically and made them take him to her own room. It was far more comfortable than Nick's, and she had her first aid equipment to hand. Not that there was a great deal she could do. 'Where's Erica?' she demanded as her first question, knowing that the nurse had been in the village that afternoon.

'Nothing for her to do,' Bud said. 'She went back to Coari.'

'Then radio for her and get her back up here fast,'

Madeleine ordered. 'And get a doctor, if you can, Bud. We sure as hell need one.'

Frantic now, she turned back to Nick, who was throwing off the blanket she had just put over him. His skin was burning, though his face was ashen under his deep tan. As Bud rushed to carry out her orders she ran to the tap that served for water and filled a basin under it. Wringing out a cloth, she tried to sponge his face to cool him, but he groaned at even the light the pressure of her hands and immediately tried to push her away, thrashing about the bed in an attempt to evade her.

'Get some ice, Lenny,' she decided. 'I'll try that. Nick, honey, don't fight it. Please, I want to help.' He was moaning unintelligibly, tossing on the bed, and she stood for a moment trying to think logically. Finally, and with a great deal of effort, she managed to get first his soaking shirt and then his shoes and chinos off him, before she tried to put the sheet over him again. He constantly threw it off, and she resorted to swearing at him as she tried to bathe his skin with cool water. Eventually, her somewhat crude efforts had an effect, and by the time Lenny came back he was a great deal quieter.

'I'll stay with him,' she told Lenny as she wrapped the ice in a cloth to put on his forehead. 'I can sleep in the chair.'

'We'll take turns,' Lenny offered. 'Until the nurse or a doctor can get up here – though I doubt that will be before morning; it's raining again.'

'I hope it will be.' Madeleine shuddered. 'He's ill, Lenny, far worse than any of the others were. They just had stomach bugs. This is far more than that. I can't get any sense out of him at all, and it happened so quickly.'

Lenny pushed his glasses to the top of his head. 'Fevers come and go quickly in these parts,' he tried to reassure her. 'He'll probably be fine in the morning. He's a tough bugger!'

'Not with this kind of thing,' Madeleine said, worried. 'He hasn't been well for weeks, Lenny.'

'Pining for that smashing bird of his, I wouldn't mind betting,' Lenny said sagely, and Madeleine stared at him.

'How did you know that?' she asked. 'No one is supposed to know.'

'It's common knowledge among the lads; he's only had eyes for her since the day they met!' Lenny grinned. 'You can't keep much from my boys! Stands to reason he's occupied, or he'd have had you in the sack pretty quick!'

'It takes two, Lenny.'

'Sure! But that's never been a problem for the boss!' Lenny settled into a chair. 'I'll take a quick kip, then it's your turn, miss. We don't want you sick as well, do we?'

Madeleine tossed him a blanket and then settled herself beside Nick, constantly sponging his heated body in a vain effort to make him more comfortable.

In the dark, quiet hours that followed the heat finally began to dissipate, but he then began to shiver violently. She tucked an extra blanket over him and then several of her jackets to keep him warm, but still long shudders racked him. Finally she lay down beside him, wrapping her own body around him to try and give him the warmth he needed. Surprisingly it seemed to calm him, though she knew from touching him that he was barely conscious, but he settled into a slightly calmer sleep in her arms.

She woke up with a start, finding Nick's arm heavy and hot across her waist and Lenny grinning down at her. 'Time I took over,' he said. 'He's hot as hell again. See if you can find some clean sheets. He'll be more comfortable if we can change these, they're soaked.' As Madeleine herself was too from the heat of Nick's body, and she slid off the bed to do as he suggested.

Between them they changed the bed and rolled Nick back into it. He had hardly stirred as they manoeuvred his limp body around, his only word was 'Sarah' as Madeleine leant over him.

'Time enough for that later,' Lenny told him, as cheerfully as he could manage, and settled down to sponging him as Madeleine had been doing, and trying unsuccessfully to get some liquid into his mouth. 'Tell you what, Maddy, Have you thought what the lads are going to do if the boss is out of action?'

'Carry on, of course!' Madeleine had no doubts on that score. 'Bud is a director in his own right – he's already done some second unit stuff – he'll have to take over. We can't afford to lose any time at all. You can use Nick's notes and guide him along, I'm going back to Coari with Nick. I'm not letting Erica take over; he loathes her.'

Despite Lenny's reassuring presence she couldn't sleep, and they finally both stayed awake, coping as best they could when Nick began to throw up even the water Lenny had tried to give him, until Bud appeared at five o'clock ushering in the nurse and a local doctor she had rounded up. By that time Madeleine was frantic, and she then had a stand-up row with Erica when Erica informed her she would not be needed in Coari.

'Where Nick goes, I go!' she announced firmly. 'I'll pack a bag for him and come with you!'

Erica recognized a formidable opponent and gave in. Madeleine packed a bag for both herself and Nick, gave Bud and Lenny the work list for the day and followed Erica and the doctor. The crew members they hustled out of bed managed to carry Nick to the waiting motor boat, and they finally started on the long trip down the river to Coari. Anxiously, Madeleine questioned the doctor at length during the journey, but to her fury he was totally non-committal. She had no faith in him whatsoever by the time they reached the little town and transported their patient to the tiny clinic the doctor managed.

'I'll give them forty-eight hours,' she threatened, after an infuriating wait with no results.

Nick was plainly deteriorating, his breathing laboured

and difficult as his body alternated between high fever and hideously racking shivering fits. A saline drip kept him from dehydrating but still he kept vomiting, and she was beginning to really panic, isolated as she was, miles away from the rest of the crew. Finally she could stand it no longer. In desperation, she found a telephone and managed to get a call through to Los Angeles and Seth Waterston.

'I've got to have the jet come for us!' she demanded of a startled Seth. 'Nick *has* to be in an American hospital! I'm afraid, Seth. He's going to die if we don't get him out of here; it isn't even clean!'

'Why the hell did you wait all this time?' Seth demanded furiously. 'We'll be with you in a matter of hours, I promise.'

'I thought he'd come round quite quickly,' Madeleine confessed. 'The others did.'

'He's obviously not suffering the same problems the other guys did,' Seth said. 'Hang on in there, Maddy, we're on our way.'

Rather like the cavalry, Madeleine thought with almost a smile as she hung up. And it felt a bit like that when eight hours later a solid and very comforting Seth arrived in his jet with a couple of reassuringly American doctors in tow and efficient, crisp-looking nurses to take over. Immediately hooking him up to drips and terrifying-looking bottles, they wasted no time in whisking Nick away to the plane, heading for the sanctuary of their Los Angeles hospital.

Tired out of her mind, and relieved at last of the responsibility, Madeleine fell into her seat on the plane and burst into tears of relief. She hadn't slept for three days and she was totally exhausted. 'Just let go and sleep,' one of the nurses told her gently. 'You've done everything you could; it's our turn now. He'll be fine.' She was given a sleeping pill to help her rest, and though she protested that it was hardly nessessary she took it and quickly fell into a deep, dreamless sleep, only waking as they taxied into their parking place at LAX.

'Nick?' was her first question on waking, and she was immediately reassured by the friendly nurse.

'He's stable,' she said quickly. 'Don't worry, I've seen worse.'

'But do the doctors know what it is?' Madeleine demanded.

'Some kind of virus, they think. His arm is crudely stitched, but not showing any sign of infection. They don't think the two are related, as the doctor in Coari thought.'

'He was an idiot!' Madeleine spat furiously. 'He would have let him die before he would admit he didn't know what to do.'

'Well, *we* are not going to let him die,' the nurse said. 'You can be sure of that.'

Miriam met them at the airport and stood no argument from Madeleine. She swept her off to the Waterston house with her as Seth took charge of all the arrangements. 'You can go see Nick later,' Miriam said in reply to her protests. 'First we must make sure his family know what's happening, and you need to help me with that. I don't seem to have a number for Sarah Campbell, and she should be told.'

'I don't think Nick has heard from her for weeks,' Madeleine admitted. 'He was getting quite anxious that something was wrong, but of course it was impossible to phone from the location.'

In vain they tried to phone Sarah's flat, and constantly got the number unobtainable tone. Finally Madeleine phoned Jane, and found that even Jane had no idea where Sarah was. She was quite *au fait* with the situation regarding Diana, and told Miriam in no uncertain terms that ringing *her* was out of the question. Perplexed, they tried Charles Hastings, at Jane's suggestion, but even Charles seemed to have no idea where Sarah was.

'Went on holiday, I think,' he said vaguely, when

Madeleine finally got hold of him. 'I'll ring his mother for you, though, Madeleine. She ought to know he's ill at least.'

'Thank you, Charles.' Madeleine sighed with relief. 'And you will let us know the moment you can locate Sarah, won't you? He really is terribly ill. She should be here.'

'Of course I will,' Charles said. 'Don't worry, Madeleine.'

CHAPTER 24

Charles put the phone down and gave a sigh of pleasure. With any luck, he thought viciously, Nick would die. What wonderful things unknown viruses were! Then he paused. How long would it be before they all realized Sarah was living at Hastings Court? Sooner or later someone in London would catch on. Oscar or George might let the cat out of the bag, though with the excuse of not letting the Press find out they had been sworn to secrecy. It was time to act, and act quickly.

It was quite casually that evening that he suggested to Sarah that they take a week or two for a holiday. 'A friend of mine has a villa in Provence,' he said as they lingered over dinner. 'Why don't we go there? It's lovely this time of year, just before the season really gets started.'

'It's hardly wise, Charles.' Sarah was doubtful. 'I'm over seven months pregnant. I could have problems, and then what would we do?'

'There *are* doctors in France – very good ones – and we'd only be a few hours' flying time from London if we needed to come back. I do own an airline, darling, remember?'

'Well, in that case . . .' She gave in. It was easier than arguing, and it wasn't as if she had anything better to do. France would be quite a treat, and warm too.

'We'll go tomorrow,' Charles decided. 'I'll make sure

everything is tidy here and we'll leave about midday. It'll be just what you need. We can even stop off in Paris for a few days. You can do some shopping.'

'Hardly!' Sarah laughed. 'I'm beginning to feel like a beached whale! I don't think it would be much fun!'

'You look absolutely wonderful!' Charles leant over and dropped a kiss on her forehead. 'All you need is a tan.'

For days Nick was deeply unconscious as the doctors performed test after test to try and determine which virus had attacked his visibly weakening body, trying several different antibiotics in the effort to find the right one. Madeleine had never been a religious person, but now she prayed desperately hard as she and Miriam sat together hour after hour watching the machines keep him alive in the Intensive Care unit. A deep bond began to form between the two women, who had been almost strangers until they had been thrown together in their joint worry over Nick.

Seth was mystified over not being able to contact Sarah, having badgered Jane constantly for news. That even Seth Waterston couldn't find her made Madeleine very suspicious that all was not well. 'It's as if she doesn't want to be found,' she said to Miriam as they took a short break and walked the short distance to a nearby diner.

'It doesn't seem possible anything could be wrong with those two; they're so much in love with each other,' Miriam puzzled. 'Nick would never have gone ahead with buying Joe's place if they were splitting – it's hardly a cheap bachelor's pad, after all!'

'I agree it doesn't make sense. All Nick talked about was Sarah coming out to LA the minute he got back.'

Five minutes later Seth joined them, a small padded envelope in his hand. 'This just came in from Brazil,' he told them. 'It was sent out to Nick on the last mail-run and

337

has obviously been returned as he's here. If I'm not mistaken, it's from Sarah.'

Both women stared at the package. Neither of them wanted to open it and intrude on Nick's private affairs. 'We'll hang on,' Miriam decided at last.

'Well, keep it with you, hon,' Seth told her. 'I have to get back. I just didn't want to trust it to a messenger.'

Madeleine stared at it for long minutes after Seth had gone. 'Maybe we should open it,' she said at last. 'It really is all we have to go on.' They hated doing it, but both were acutely aware that Nick might never know what they were doing. However, once it was opened, they both wished they hadn't done it.

'We can't tell him!' Madeleine moaned, turning the beautiful ring over in her fingers. 'If the virus doesn't kill him, this will!'

'Wait and see what happens,' Miriam advised. 'I'm certain Seth will find her fairly soon. She loves him. I'm sure it must be a misunderstanding. There's no other woman in Nick's life – that I know. I wonder what photograph she's referring to?'

'I can't imagine either.' Madeleine was puzzled. 'I've worked with Nick almost constantly since Sarah went back to England – there's been no one.'

'Maybe it's *you* she's referring to?' Miriam wondered.

'Me? Don't be silly, Miriam!' Madeleine was horrified. 'How could she think that? I *work* for him. Yes, I adore him – most women do – but that's a one-woman guy if ever there was one. I'd be on a hiding to nothing trying for him! Now Mark Winford, that's another story!' She had met the singing star the previous evening at the Waterstons, when Seth had insisted he take her back for a break.

'Well, honey, Mark certainly noticed you, so there's nothing wrong with *you*!' Miriam comforted her.

'Well, that I will certainly bear in mind! But I can't

think of anything but Nick at the moment. Oh, Miriam, he *is* going to get better, isn't he?'

'If there's a God, honey – yes! We can only hope that right now He's looking out for him!'

It was rather like floating in a sea of cotton wool. Sometimes he was aware of light . . . sharp, piercing light . . . other times it was voices . . . light, feminine voices. Sarah, his mind said . . .

Sarah, his voice wanted to say. But no sound came from his cracked, dry lips. Something blocked it. He wanted to open his eyes . . . to see Sarah . . . but they were too heavy. However hard he tried, nothing would happen.

Sometimes she was so near he could feel her . . . smell the warm scent of her. Often the drifting breath of the Chanel she wore brought him briefly up through the clouds of vapour that surrounded him . . . hampered his breathing . . . held him down. There were restrictions on his body, as if he couldn't move . . . something held him down. Ropes and ties . . .

He wanted to scream – let me loose – yet nothing happened. No one was listening.

It was almost midnight one night when he finally opened dazed blue eyes to stare uncomprehendingly at the tangle of wires and tubes around him. Still no sound would come as he tried to speak, and he gagged slightly on the tube in his mouth.

'Nick! Oh, Nick . . . at last!' He heard the relief in a female voice but it wasn't Sarah. Tiredly, he focused briefly on Miriam's face and wondered why she was in Brazil. He could hear her calling out, but nothing she said made any sense. Suddenly there were more people around him, noises and more voices. He was confused and woolly as faces blurred into his vision.

He was uncomfortable, flat on his back, he realized then, a position he had always hated, and he tried to move and couldn't, discovering the forest of wires that led to the monitors attached to every part of him, it seemed. The light about him was bright, too bright suddenly. One restless movement brought Miriam's hand into his, squeezing his fingers to calm him, and he clung to it, the one point of contact with reality in the confusion.

'Where . . .?' he managed, choking it out around the tube. A mammoth effort, but he had to know.

'You're in LA, darling.' Miriam leant over him. 'In the Cedars. Safe, I promise.'

'Sarah?' It was a difficult word to say, but he had to make Miriam understand what he wanted.

'Hush, honey, she'll be here soon.' Was Miriam crying? he wondered drowsily, but her words reassured him. A few seconds later he could feel the cotton wool overwhelming him again, but it was lighter this time – next time, he told himself he would wake up and Sarah would be there.

Miriam continued to hold his hand as the nurses and doctors checked the monitors and smiled at her. Things were definitely improving. Relieved, she finally left the room and went to phone Seth, weeping unashamedly as she relayed the news to him and then to an equally weeping Madeleine.

The next time Nick woke, it was for longer, and after that he was awake for more than an hour before the weakness overwhelmed him again.

Aware now of his situation, Nick began to fight, needing to be free of the tubes that nurtured and fed him and anchored him to the machines. He began to fiercely resent the ministrations of the patient nurses and loathed the utter humiliation of having absolutely everything done for him. When finally he could talk, he cursed fluently, and Miriam laughed happily.

'You, my darling Nicholas, sound almost normal!' she scolded him as the tears ran down her face, cascading mascara over her plump cheeks. 'And for once I'm just so glad to hear you swear!'

'Get me – out of here – Miriam!' he demanded.

'Patience, Nicholas!' she said. 'They'll let you out soon enough.'

He was restless and demanding now. As his health improved enough for him to be moved from the High Dependency unit to a room of his own his temper grew worse. He fought the sedation deemed necessary for the rest he needed, begged Seth and Miriam to get him out of the hospital, and constantly asked for Sarah.

When he was finally allowed out of bed he was appalled to discover just how frail he was. He could barely manage three steps before his legs simply gave out under him and he had to suffer the indignity of being lifted into a chair. Even then he could only cope with a very short time sitting up, before having to ask to return to bed again. 'I *have* to get out of here,' he begged Miriam continually, worrying about the film, – about Sarah – about everything but his own health.

'All in good time,' Miriam said, so frequently he wanted to kill her. 'The film is just fine. Seth has sent Madeleine back out to help Bud, and you'll be allowed out of here as soon as you are well enough. Believe me – they can't wait to get rid of you, you bad-tempered creature!'

'I can't bear it, Miriam!' he complained. 'I'm never ill.'

'That's obvious! Nick, you *have* to be patient. For heaven's sake, you can't even keep solid food down!'

'I did this morning! I'm better, I tell you!' he contradicted her. 'Which reminds me, Miriam. Why can't I have a telephone? I want to call Sarah – where is she? Do you know?'

'No telephone!' Miriam was firm. 'You'll never be off it, and your throat is not up to it – not yet. And Sarah is on location somewhere,' she lied. 'We *are* trying to find her, I promise.'

'Oscar will know,' Nick said. 'Ring him.'

Miriam had already tried that avenue, but Oscar, programmed by Charles, had denied all knowledge of

Sarah's whereabouts. 'He doesn't. But don't worry, Nick, we'll find her.'

It was another fretful and painful week for everyone before he was allowed out of the hospital and into Miriam's care. Kitten-weak, and lighter by almost a stone, nevertheless he was desperate to get back to normal life – and now he had access to a telephone. Finally Miriam knew she had to give him Sarah's letter. Predictably, Nick's reaction was enough to frighten her into calling her own doctor for help.

His grief was terrifying in its intensity. Endlessly he railed against the improbability of her rejection, until Miriam feared for his mental stability and the doctor agreed with her, immediately prescribing a sedative. At first Nick welcomed the oblivion sedation offered – a blissful release from the agony he was struggling with. In normal times he could have coped, but, weakened as he was, he simply collapsed. He woke every time to the anguish of his loss and it didn't get any easier to bear as time went on. Disorientated by his illness, he had no physical resources to cope with the stress generated by his loss.

'It's not true!' he wept in Miriam's motherly arms. 'I love her, Miriam – only her. How can she think otherwise?'

For several days after he began to refuse sedation he stayed in his room, unwilling to face anyone but Miriam. Overwhelmed by his grief, he ate little and threw up what pitiful amount she did manage to get him to eat. Miriam was frantic, knowing that every day Nick didn't eat his fragile health was suffering even more. She pleaded with Seth to try again to find Sarah, but even with his formidable resources he drew a blank, foiled by the careful plans Charles had made.

In the end, Nick made his own decision. 'I'm going to back to England,' he announced. 'Tomorrow. I must find her. I have to know why, Miriam.'

'Nick, you can't!' Miriam pleaded. 'For heaven's sake,

you haven't spent a full day out of bed yet! How could you contemplate a ten-hour flight to London and then driving all over England?'

'I'll sleep on the plane, and Bill can meet me at Heathrow,' Nick said. 'He can drive me anywhere I want to go if it's necessary.'

'Absolutely no way!' Miriam strode about the room and then finally turned to face him, recognizing at last that he was determined, as only Nick could be, and that there was no dissuading him from his purpose. 'Honey, if you really must go then go in Seth's jet. It will take slightly longer but I'll come too, and then we'll have a week or two at Cap Ferrat. That will certainly do you good.'

'The only thing that would do me good is to get Sarah back,' Nick said grimly. 'And I will, believe me! I love her to distraction – I won't give up! I gave up on Natasha and I lived to regret it. I won't let it happen again. Charles is at the bottom of this – I'm sure of it. She couldn't just disappear so thoroughly without help, and he certainly has the resources.'

'Charles has no idea where she is,' Miriam said. 'I've spoken to him several times.'

'Nevertheless, I'll tackle him first! I know exactly how devious he can be! He's not getting the better of me this time!' Nick was adamant.

He was slightly less sure the next day, when fatigue overwhelmed him within hours of setting off, and he was grateful for the care Miriam unfailingly provided. He slept through the refuelling stops, in the cabin set aside for that purpose which in the past he had scorned, but he emerged on landing in London with new resolve.

'I'm fine,' he asserted as they were driven to Regent's Park. 'Tomorrow I'll drive myself. I have to go alone, and deal with things my own way. I *won't* let you stop me. I promise to be careful and I'll keep in touch with you as many times a day as you dictate, my darling jailer! You can go off to Nice in the morning and I'll join you in a few

days. I need to spend a little time with Charlotte too; she'll
be wondering what's happened to me.'

He knew Miriam had his best interests at heart, and
despite his belligerence he respected her for it. In the
last few weeks her loving care had brought her far closer to
him than his own mother had ever been. Apart from a
couple of phone calls his mother had seemed almost
uninterested in him, he decided bitterly. But in some
ways it was a relief to be on his own again, making his
own decisions without having to ask anyone else's opinion.
It was good to be back behind the wheel of his Porsche,
feeling the challenge that the power of its engine presented
him with – and he responded to it, feeling some energy
flowing back at last.

It was a beautiful June morning and he was a great
deal more cheerful as he drove through the gates of
Charlotte's school in Ascot. A call the previous evening
had persuaded her headmistress to let him take her out
for lunch, and Charlotte threw herself at her father,
delighted at the surprise of being allowed out of school
midweek.

'But Mummy never said you'd been *really* ill!' she
protested as she finally released him from her bear hug.
'You look awful, Daddy!'

'Well, thanks for the welcome!' Nick laughed. 'But at
least Seth kept it out of the papers.'

'There was never a word – I'd have been out to LA like a
shot if I'd known.'

'I think your mother might have vetoed that,' he
commented wryly.

'She wouldn't have been able to stop me! I'd have
borrowed the fare from Uncle Seth if I'd had to!
Daddy, are you two *really* going to get a divorce?'

'I'm afraid so.' Nick hated the look of pain in her eyes. 'I
know it won't be easy for you, but I'm sure that in the end
things will be much better for your mother. Things are

hopeless as they are, it's no life for either of us, and it's gone on far longer than it should have done.'

'She wouldn't agree with you there,' Charlotte said. 'And Granny and Grandpa have forbidden her to even discuss divorce with you. They say she'll be in eternal damnation if she allows it!'

'What rubbish are they trying now?' Nick was furious. 'I've never heard such crap!' He thumped the steering wheel in frustration. 'Well, it won't make any difference, I'm afraid. I've put up with *enough* from them! God! I wish Diana could stand up for herself for once, instead of letting her parents rule her with their bigoted views! She's an incredibly intelligent adult – not a child! Oh, I'm sorry, darling! I shouldn't say all this to you. Forget it!'

'No, Daddy, I won't forget it!' Charlotte clicked her seat belt into place. 'I don't want you to divorce! It's just . . . well, Mummy says that if she lets you have a divorce you'll leave her and me without any money, and I'll have to leave my school and go to the local comprehensive, and it really is dreadful!'

'Charlotte! That's absolute rubbish! And your mother knows it!' Nick could hardly believe what he was hearing. 'For one thing, the courts would never allow it, and for another *I* wouldn't allow it! No way!' He thought with some amazement of the huge capital sum he had already offered and that Diana had summarily turned down. 'I would never leave your mother without money, and *you* have a substantial trust fund of your own anyway. You mean the world to me, Lotte, don't you *ever* forget that.'

'More than Madeleine Miller?'

'What on earth has Madeleine got to do with it?' he asked, puzzled.

'*Mummy* says you want a divorce so that you can marry Madeleine. It was even in the papers a while back.'

'Well, I don't! Let's get that quite straight!' The mists were beginning to clear considerably. If Diana thought that, why shouldn't Sarah? 'I'm very fond of Madeleine, and she probably saved my life when I was ill, but, no – I don't think of her in any other way, I assure you.' He wondered whether to tell her about Sarah, and his real purpose in coming back to England, and then realized that maybe there wasn't going to be a Sarah. Charlotte needed his reassurance, despite her seemingly calm acceptance of her parent's problems, not more to worry over.

He showed her the still livid scar on his arm and even made her laugh when he described the native woman's treatment of him. In entertaining her, he thought he'd make her forget her earlier questions – until he dropped her back at school. Then she clung to him as he kissed her goodbye. 'Daddy – Daddy – it *really* won't make any difference to us, will it?' she begged him. It was obviously still worrying her.

'No, darling – I promise.' He hugged her back, hating to let her go. 'I'll spend more time in the States, but you'll be able to visit whenever you like. Even study out there if you want to. Mummy can't stop you – I'll see to that.'

Mulling it all over, he drove on towards Hastings Court. He was desperately tired now, but somehow he forced himself onwards, steeling himself for the confrontation he knew was ahead.

Hastings looked so peaceful in the late afternoon sunshine, and despite his fears about Charles he smiled with pleasure at the beauty of the building that was so familiar to him. The forecourt was empty of cars as he pulled up, and he frowned. Charles, at least, always left his car out until early evening in case he needed it.

Frustrated, he pulled at the handle that operated the front doorbell and then with relief heard footsteps clicking across the stone floor of the hall. Too light for Mrs Johnson, and certainly not Charles . . . He hoped for a moment – but then he met the startled gaze of one of the cleaning ladies who helped Mrs Johnson.

346

'Iris? Is Sir Charles at home?' he asked as she recognized him and moved aside to let him in.

'No, Mr Grey.' Iris looked puzzled. 'They're away, Sir Charles and Miss Campbell, that is, but I can make up your room for you – it's no trouble.'

'That's OK, Iris, I'm not staying overnight.' Nick swallowed his apprehension. 'But I could do with some tea?'

'Of course! I'll bring it to the drawing room, shall I?'

'No, I'll come down to the kitchen and see Mrs J, since I'm here.' He was gambling on the kindly housekeeper being able to help him find Sarah, but he was in for a disappointment.

'Mrs Johnson has gone to her sister's for a few days,' Iris told him as she made tea, glad of a chance to put her feet up. 'And Bernard is at the London flat tonight.'

'And you don't know where they've gone?'

'No.' She shook her head. 'They've been away a few weeks now. Lovely lady, Miss Campbell – so kind. But then you'd know that, of course! Bernard thinks they're getting married and I wouldn't be surprised if Sir Charles has whisked her off to do it – so romantic, don't you think?'

'I'm sorry I missed them.' Nick fought to stay calm, wondering helplessly what he was going to do now. They could be anywhere in the world. 'Would anyone know where they are, do you suppose?'

'Well . . .' Iris thought for a moment. 'Mr Saunders might. He always comes over late afternoon to check the horses for Sir Charles; he might know.'

'Rupert! Of course! Charles would never go off without being in contact over the horses. I'll phone him now.'

'No need – he'll probably be over in a minute. He usually pops in for a cup of tea before he goes home. Put your feet up and wait for him. You look real tired, if you don't mind me saying so.'

He did mind, but he didn't dare tell her so and upset her

feelings. 'I'm fine, Iris,' he groaned. 'Look, I'll just go upstairs and collect a few things. I won't be long. Call me if Rupert comes in, will you?'

He went up to his room and tossed the clothing he normally kept there into the bag from the bottom of the wardrobe. He had left Regent's Park with only an overnight bag, and his practical side told him this would save having to go back to collect clothes. Then his emotional side took over, and as he sank down onto the bed in a weary gesture.

Just to touch the smooth silk of the bedcover reminded him of Sarah, and the number of times he had made love to her in this bed. He had used this room for years, ever since he and Charles had been promoted from the nursery, and everything in it was achingly familiar. He looked around with regret – there was no doubt in his mind now that this would be his last visit to Hastings, whatever the outcome of his search for Sarah.

At least Iris had confirmed the suspicions he'd had all along, that Sarah was with Charles – but in what capacity had she gone with him? Nick was tortured with the knowledge that he could well be too late, and almost at the point of being too weak to cope with it. Then he shook himself furiously. He would get nowhere behaving like a defeatist – he *would* sort things out. It was totally out of character for him to give up on anything. He *was* going to sort things out – get Sarah back – somehow.

'Nick! Nick, old chap, where are you?' Suddenly Rupert's booming voice intruded on his reverie and he jumped up in shock, calling back his whereabouts in as cheery a tone as he could manage.

Rupert, however, was not one to be fooled easily. 'Jesus, Nick!' he commented after one glance. 'At last your rowdy lifestyle has caught up with you. You look ready to drop!'

Nick was inclined to snap, but he needed Rupert so he held back and explained his illness and the reason for his visit to Hastings.

Rupert dropped his considerable bulk onto the window seat. Both Nick and Charles had been his friends since childhood, and his loyalties were very torn between the two of them. 'Charlie asked me not to tell anyone where they were,' he explained.

'But they *are* together?' Nick strode the room in frustration, realizing he had been right all along to follow up Charles.

'Yes, Nick, they are.' Rupert looked puzzled. 'I had no idea you and Sarah were still an item, though.'

'I intend to marry her,' Nick said. 'Once I can disentangle myself from Diana. We were just keeping it under wraps for a bit longer, until I finished in Brazil.'

'Well, divorcing Diana won't be easy.' Rupert certainly knew Diana's attitude to divorce.

'No, but whatever it costs I'll pay! I'm sure at the end of the day that's what will count the most with her! Now, where are they, Rupert? I have to know – I have to find out what's going on.'

'You may be too late,' Rupert said grimly. 'Charlie is determined to get Sarah to marry him.'

'Over my dead body! Tell me, Rupert, or so help me I'll shake it out of you!'

'You're in no fit state to do anything of the sort,' Rupert retorted drily. 'But – OK, Nick, if you must know. Charlie borrowed Liz's parents' place in the Luberon for a few weeks.'

'Provence?' Nick stared, first in confusion and then in fury. Miriam had flown to Nice only that morning – he could well have been with her, and far closer to Sarah than he was now. He had forgotten how casually his friends used each other's second homes; he had even lent his own Malibu house on occasions to Rupert and Liz. 'Then I'll drive down there tonight. I'll find them, Rupert, I have to,' he decided.

'You'll go nowhere tonight,' Rupert said firmly. 'You're out on your feet, for one thing, and I'm not about to have your killing yourself on the road with fatigue on my conscience. Come back to Lambourn with me, have a meal and sleep over. You can leave early in the morning. Then you'll have a better chance of making it in one piece.'

'No – I'm going now.' Nick gritted his teeth. Why were all his friends so determined to keep him from Sarah?

'The hell you are! See sense, Nicholas,' Rupert pleaded. 'You'll collapse at the wheel. Come on – let Liz feed you and then get an early night. It will make the drive far easier to deal with; it's a pig at the best of times.'

Reluctantly Nick remembered the promise he had made to Miriam, and, finally agreeing to his persuasion, followed the battered Land Rover back to Lambourn. He barely made it, and crawled willingly into the bed Liz had ready for him after Rupert's call to her, meaning only to take a short nap but instead sleeping for several hours. Liz finally brought him supper on a tray and sat on the bed comfortably chatting as she made him eat.

She was far more open about Charles than the more loyal Rupert, and had no compunction in decrying Charles's efforts to ensnare Sarah. 'He's crazily jealous of you, Nick, you should be really aware of that,' she said. 'It's quite worrying the way he's behaving over Sarah. I know he's in love with her, but it's become far too possessive a kind of love now for it to be really healthy. He's determined to have something he knew you wanted, and he'll go to almost any lengths to get it.'

'But surely Sarah can see through that?'

'No, Nick, I don't think she can – not in her state. He's got her tied to him in some way. She hasn't been well, according to Charlie. That's why he wanted to take her away. She certainly hasn't been working recently.'

'Oh, God, Liz, I really should go tonight! I can be halfway across France by morning.'

'No, you don't, sunshine! Rupert is dead right for once.'
Liz grinned. 'I took *all* your clothes away while you were
asleep! You'll get them back in the morning and only
then!'

Nick called her several nasty names, but he had no
choice but to obey her and finish the admittedly delicious
meal that he had been sure he didn't want. 'You're a worse
tyrant than Miriam,' he grumbled as Liz picked up the
tray. 'Women are all the same – all you want to do is bully
me while I'm down!'

'You're damn lucky to *have* us all to worry about you,'
she told him tartly. 'You're a ruthless sod sometimes,
Nicholas, but I'll give you your due. Even though you
knew you'd made a mistake with Diana, you stuck with her
a lot longer than most men would have done. She's a hard
one – always has been – and avaricious to the point of
lunacy.'

'Maybe that was my mistake,' Nick sighed. 'I encouraged her to spend money on herself and Charlotte. Maybe
I've turned her into the kind of person she is.'

'No, Nick. She was always like that!' Liz stood up. 'She
made no secret of the fact that she wanted you. Even at
university it was obvious you were destined for great
things, and she wanted part of it.'

'I should have listened to all of you,' Nick said. 'I was
far too arrogant to consider I could be wrong.'

'Well, we all have to learn by our mistakes; it's just taken
you a bit longer, that's all.'

'I'm not making a mistake over Sarah, Liz, believe me.
And I'll get her away from Charlie if I have to wrench her
out of his bed!'

'I doubt that will be necessary. Sarah was living in the
pavilion as far as I know – not in the house itself.'

'Thank God!' Nick's relief was enormous. 'Rupert
seemed to think they were on the point of marriage.'

'I doubt it!' Liz patted his arm. 'Rupert always was a
daft old romantic! Sleep well, Nick. I'll wake you early in

the morning, don't worry. Rupert has to be up at five. You can have your clothes back then.'

'That will teach me to worry about your sheets and not keep them on!' Nick returned. 'But you're right, Liz – I am lucky to have such good friends.'

CHAPTER 25

After manfully tackling what Liz considered a normal breakfast, Nick realized why she and Rupert were the size they were. He felt as if he had regained most of the weight he had lost in one overnight visit as he drove at his usual brisk pace to Dover.

He and Liz had tossed up over his route and he had opted for the shorter Dover crossing in the end. He spoke at length to Miriam in Cap Ferrat and then Jane as he drove, and felt far more like his old self as he did so. He was back in charge of his life, making decisions. Motivated now, he was full of energy at last, though he was still careful to conserve his strength, even catnapping during the Channel crossing.

Ordinarily, he would have made the drive to the south in one go, but he knew he still wasn't strong enough to do that on this trip, and reluctantly he found a hotel just outside Lyon for the night. But, unable to sleep, all he could do was toss around and think of Sarah. He was so close now, and in the early morning as he continued the journey south the air seemed warmer, even smelled different, and at last he relaxed a little, knowing he was nearing his goal.

He had visited the villa only once, at least five years previously, when he had brought Charlotte on a shared trip with Liz and Rupert, but he remembered the route with ease once he got within a few miles of it. The house was a typical Provençal Mas, low and stone-built, hidden amongst trees at the end of a narrow rutted track. It was an idyllic spot, nestled as it was into the hillside. Charlotte had loved it, and he smiled at the memory of that pleasant holiday without Diana fussing about wearing sun hats and eating at the correct times.

It was a little after twelve when he pulled onto the grassy driveway, swinging his car so that it faced the right way to leave and blocking the exit of the pale blue Jaguar he knew belonged to Charles before he strode across to the open front door of the house. They were here, and they could go nowhere without the car, he thought grimly, and reached into the open window of the Jaguar for the keys as an afterthought.

It was just as he remembered it; old stone-flagged floor, furniture painted in soft Provençal colours and, tossed on the hall table, the gaily coloured leather haversack he had bought Sarah in San Francisco at Christmas. For a moment he stared at it in confusion, then he could stand it no longer.

'Sarah? Sarah, where are you?' His voice sounded thinner – and strained, he thought irritably as he listened for a reply. But none came. Anxious, then, he made for the door that he remembered led to the sitting room and which in turn opened onto the garden. Suddenly he heard Sarah's laughter, and in the next second he saw her, laughing and pushing Charles playfully away from her as she sat at a white metal table in the sun. He couldn't help himself, and involuntarily he stepped forward.

'Sarah!' he said quietly. 'Sarah!'

She looked up, startled at an outsider's sudden intrusion on their solitude. Visitors had been rare these last few weeks. And then she gave a shriek of recognition. 'Nick! I don't believe it!'

Charles leapt up from his chair, his face a mask of pure hatred, and anger that Nick had found them so easily.

'How dare you march in without asking?' he demanded furiously. 'We want nothing more to do with you, Nick. You aren't welcome here.'

'Tough!' Nick swept Charles aside as if he were a small child. 'I've come to see Sarah, not you.'

Sarah rose slowly, her eyes never leaving Nick's face as she moved around the table. She had never seemed more beautiful to him as she did then, the cloud of honey-gold hair cascading down the back of her loose denim dress. Loose, he thought casually, very unlike Sarah . . . Then he realized, and his jaw dropped in astonishment. He suddenly remembered what Liz had said about 'her state'. Liz had obviously assumed he knew.

'You're pregnant!'

'Good God! Give the man a medal for observation!' Sarah said tartly. 'Yes, I'm pregnant, Nicholas.'

'Mine.'

'Of course it's yours! Do you think I'm like you? Off with someone else the minute your back is turned?'

Shock and horror at her announcement fought in his head for prominence over her accusation of his infidelity. 'How pregnant?'

'Eight months and a few days,' she said, holding his gaze firmly.

He calculated rapidly. 'The wedding?'

'The wedding,' she confirmed. 'Don't worry, Nick, I can cope with everything. You don't need to get involved. I know how you feel about babies.'

'Sarah and I are getting married,' Charles interrupted. 'Tell him, Sarah!'

'The hell we are. I told you no, and I meant it!'

'Then there's no discussion!' Nick caught her arm. 'Come with me, Sarah, *now* – this minute.'

'Don't order me around!' There was true fury in the wide hazel eyes that met his. 'I'm not a child, Nick. You can't tell me what to do.'

'No, but you are *carrying* a child,' he retorted, his

control reasserting itself as he tried to calm down and think logically. 'My child – and I have some rights.'

'You have none at all,' Charles snapped. 'Get out of here, Nick, we don't need you. Biological father you may be, but that child will be mine, not yours. I've looked after it – not you!'

Nick stood his ground. This battle was one he was not going to lose. 'Sarah, do you want to marry Charles? Because if you do I'll walk away, never see you again. I mean it.'

'I told you I didn't!' She was adamant.

'Then pack a bag – get whatever you need – and come with me *now*! I mean it, Sarah.' He was taking an incredible chance, but at that moment it was all he could think to do.

For a moment she hesitated, her expressive eyes going from one man to the other, both taut with their respective inner battles. 'I . . . I . . . Nick . . . Are you sure?'

'Do you think I've come all this way for nothing?' he demanded. 'The hell I have! I came for you, Sarah, nothing else. Believe me!'

'Then I'll come!' Sarah paused as Charles tried to grab at her and she shook him off impatiently. 'But Nick it means both of us – the baby and me. You have to accept that.'

'I can't do much else at this stage of the proceedings! Sarah, hurry – please, darling.' She heard the urgency in his voice and she moved then. Despite her pregnancy, she ran – back into the house to her room, hurling her few possessions into her bag, then carefully adding the outfits she had bought for the baby on their one expedition to the nearby town.

In the fragrant, sunlit garden the air chilled rapidly as Charles rounded on Nick, his fury unleashed completely now that Sarah had gone indoors. 'You bastard!' he snarled. 'You couldn't bear it, could you? That Sarah might prefer me?'

'Prefer *you*?' Nick laughed sarcastically. 'Is that why she went to pack? Face facts, Charlie. She was never yours to begin with. She's mine – my girlfriend – my lover – whatever you like to call her, and whatever game you're playing it's over! If I hadn't been ill I'd have been home much sooner – and, frankly, if I'd known she was pregnant I'd never have gone to Brazil in the first place.'

'Oh, you would,' Charles retorted. 'You've always put work first – all your life. Tasha gave up on you because of that. You're an out-and-out selfish bastard! You don't deserve a gorgeous girl like Sarah any more than you did Tasha. You managed to ruin her life – and mine.'

'I had nothing to do with that accident and you know it! I've told you often enough,' Nick said angrily. 'That part was all in your imagination. Tasha was hysterical that night over your treatment of her, but I thought I'd calmed her down. I told her not to come out. Obviously I was wrong.'

'It was you she wanted all along,' Charles said bitterly. 'Whatever I did for her it was never enough. When she got drunk, which was often, all she ever talked about was you! My marriage was hell, Nick, and it was down to you!'

'Don't give me such garbage!' Nick snapped. 'Your marriage was difficult because you were so obsessed with controlling everything Tasha did or said, and you were going to try and do the same thing with Sarah, weren't you? You don't want a wife, Charles, you want a puppet to manipulate.'

'All I wanted for Sarah was to keep her away from you!' Charles replied. 'To make *you* suffer like I did. Tasha was pregnant when she died – trying to get to you. I didn't just lose my wife, I lost my child too – and now I'm going to take yours!'

'Oh, my God! You never told anyone?' Nick stared at him.

'That was *my* grief, not yours. *You*, of course, already

had the perfect wife and an adorable baby to complete the picture of domestic bliss. Why should you have been worried about mine wanting you back?'

'Natasha chose to marry you,' Nick reminded him, horrified at the sheer venom in Charles's voice. 'Remember?'

'Only after a row with you! I hate you, Nicholas. I've hated you ever since the night she died, and I've waited all these years to get even with you! Sat back and waited for you to want something so badly that you were going crazy with wanting, and then I planned to take it from you! I really thought it would be the company, but when Sarah came along it was even better – especially when I found out you'd left her pregnant. Typical of *you*, I suppose! So touching those letters of yours were! Literary to the end! I really enjoyed burning those.'

'*You burnt my letters to Sarah?*' Nick roared at him. It was all he could do not to throttle him as he smiled smugly.

'And hers to you! Of course I did! She thought you'd deserted her. That's what I wanted her to think, and to make *you* suffer. I almost made it last summer – until you managed to get to her when my back was turned.'

'You hate me that much? I don't believe what I'm hearing!' Bewildered, Nick clutched at the table for support. 'All this time I thought we were friends, and you've hated me?'

'That's about the size of it! Oh, maybe sometimes the old childhood memories came back, but then I remembered Tasha and I hated you again. Since then, hating you has dominated my life. I've spent years trying to be like you, trying to be equal, and it never worked. Now, finally, I have something you want!'

'And I'm taking her back! Have no doubt about that, Charles.' Nick's voice had a dangerous edge to it. 'From now on leave Sarah alone. I never want to see you again, ever! I still can't believe you feel this way about our friendship, but I will never trust you again.'

'Don't think your threats can frighten me, Nick,' Charles said. 'I'll kill her rather than let you have her.'

'Keep away from her! I warn you, Charles. I warn you *now*. I won't tolerate you anywhere near her from now on. You so much as *breathe* a threat to Sarah and you will be the one in fear for your life. Remember that!'

He walked away before Charles could retaliate, striding into the hall as Sarah came down the tiny stairway. Quickly he reached for her bag and thrust her haversack at her. 'Let's go!' he said, more harshly than he had intended, shaken to the core by Charles's revelations and the fear that he would try and harm Sarah there and then.

'Nick . . . I . . .' Sarah hesitated momentarily.

'I want to get you out of here *now*, Sarah,' he reiterated, grabbing at her arm.

'I told you – stop ordering me around!' Sarah pulled herself away from him. She still had some pride.

'We'll argue about it later. You can shout all you want in the car,' he told her. 'Now, *get in!*'

Bewildered, she obeyed him, numb until he reached over for the seat belt, then she shook her head. 'It's uncomfortable,' she complained.

'Put it on!' He brooked no argument and did it for her.

For twenty minutes or so he drove without speaking, concentrating on getting his emotions under control before he could trust himself to speak, and in getting a fair distance between them and Charles before he felt safe. Finally judging that they were a far enough distance from the villa, he noticed a small bar/restaurant. On slowing down, he liked what he saw and pulled into the car park behind it.

'OK.' He turned to Sarah, still huddled in her seat. 'We need to talk, you and I.' Leaning across, he caught her face in his hands and kissed her, hard. 'I ought to strangle you for deceiving me like this, but instead I'm going to find out why! Come on.'

He led her to a vine-covered patio at the back of the inn, politely pulling out a chair for her before throwing himself into the opposite one. Briefly he acknowledged the young waiter who had followed them out and ordered a carafe of white wine, and then mineral water when Sarah grimaced.

'Hungry?' Sarah, not really caring, shrugged, but he turned back to the waiter. 'Omelettes – *fines herbes*,' he decided. 'And salad, please,' he added. 'OK! *Now* we talk. *Give*, Sarah – *everything*!'

'Such as?' Sarah feigned nonchalance. 'Why you deserted me for another woman the moment I went back to England?'

'What woman?' he demanded. 'I did no such thing! There has been no other woman in my life since I met you – you know that!'

'So why were you photographed carrying Madeleine along the beach? Why did the papers say that you and she were lovers? That she left her husband for you?'

'Madeleine? That's rubbish, Sarah, as you should know it is. Madeleine took over as my assistant since Jane didn't want to come out to Brazil. She left her husband for her own reasons, and it was nothing to do with me, I assure you. The only surprise was that it took her so long to realize what a boring old sod he was!'

'But the photographs,' Sarah protested. 'They were very – intimate. Neither of you had much on!'

'On the beach, you say?' Nick frowned. 'The only time I carried Maddy on the beach was at a unit party in Rio. We were having a race, if I remember rightly. There were probably eight or ten of us competing.'

'A race?'

'A race,' he confirmed, beginning to laugh with relief. 'Just a bit of fun, darling. That's all – I promise. Madeleine contacted me a day or so after you went home and I offered her a job since I couldn't persuade Jane to come out with me. Madeleine comes from LA, so of course she came home when her marriage broke up.

Since she'd worked for me in London, it was natural that she should get in touch. And Jane knew I would prefer someone I knew rather than a stranger. She was my PA, and nothing else – except that she probably saved my life when I got sick.'

He gave her the briefest outline of his illness, and Sarah listened in horrified silence, realizing how close she had come to losing him altogether.

'Charles,' she said at last. 'He told me it was all true, about Madeleine.'

'Charles, I'm afraid, has deceived us both very badly for his own ends. I never realized just how much he wanted revenge for Natasha's death. He only told me today that she was pregnant when she died, though I'm not sure Tash knew herself. I think she'd have told me if she'd known.'

'But it *was* an accident, wasn't it?' Suddenly she was hesitant.

'Yes, it was. But Charles has always thought that she was on her way to see me. She rang me in a dreadful state that morning and I told her that no, I didn't want to get involved in any quarrel between her and Charles. By that time I was married to Diana, and Charlotte was a baby. It broke my heart to refuse her, because I still loved her, but – well, my loyalties were to Diana. They had to be. I'd made my choice, wrong though it was.'

'And all this time Charles has waited for revenge? But I thought you were such good friends!'

'I did too, Sarah, and I'm still sure that a lot of the time we were.' He sank back into his chair in defeat. 'I've known Charlie all my life; I just can't believe he could hate me so much!'

'I think I can,' Sarah said quietly. Things were beginning to click into place. 'I think it was only when I came along that things really changed between you. You were like brothers, almost. After all, you knew he was in love with me long before I did. Perhaps it triggered his memory

361

about Natasha when you and I became involved?'

'It's certainly possible, and easier to believe,' he agreed. 'I always knew he could be obsessive about things, but I really thought he had accepted us. How wrong I was.'

'Maybe, but then remember, Nick, Charles resents the way so many things came easily to you – sports prizes at school, for instance. You even got the school captaincy that he coveted. I certainly know that from conversations with him recently in the last week or two. He can be quite frightening at times. Natasha was the only thing he won that you wanted, and in the end even she wanted you back. That's what he can't forgive.'

'Poor Charlie,' Nick sighed. 'I never meant it to be like that. I even tried to help him when his Lloyds syndicate got into financial problems.'

'Even that gesture probably rubbed salt into the wound!' Sarah picked an olive from her salad and chewed at it thoughtfully. 'Hastings is an expensive house, and he sinks every penny into it. Without that to drain him he'd be a very wealthy man.'

'And probably a great deal happier. But you're right, darling, the estate is at the bottom of it – his sudden obsessive need for a wife, for an heir just for Hastings.'

Sarah shuddered. 'And I was coming very close to giving in to him. I was feeling very vulnerable, and he was very persuasive, Nick.'

'I bet he was! Do you love him, Sarah? Because if you do . . .'

'No . . . no, I don't! And certainly not now – not after what he tried to do to us.'

'Us? So there is still an us?'

'You want there to be?'

'Would I be here if I didn't? Of course I want there to be an us! And you?'

'Yes – yes, I do, Nick. But . . . well . . . there is something else to consider. I want this baby and I intend to keep it.'

'You knew you were pregnant when we went to Palm Springs, didn't you?' he accused. 'You must have been – what – four months? Dammit, Sarah, why didn't you tell me then?'

'You know exactly why I didn't tell you!' Sarah jerked herself awkwardly from the low chair. 'All those stupid phobias about Charlotte's birth and never wanting any other children. You made it quite clear what your feelings were – and probably still are, for all I know. It was impossible to find the right time to tell you, and I did try – several times! I began to think there was something wrong with our relationship. If I couldn't be honest with you over that what chance had we?'

'Meaning I was so bigoted about it!' Nick sank his head in his hands. 'God! If ever a man's had his past come back to haunt him I have today! First Natasha, and now this! I've been such a fool! Oh, Sarah, you could at least have tried.'

'And let you worry yourself stupid over me while you were in Brazil?'

'I probably wouldn't have gone at all if I'd known! I had the right to know!' He grabbed at her arm as she swung away and Sarah immediately jerked free, aiming herself at a gate that led to an open, flower-filled meadow.

'You had no automatic rights!' she returned, swiftly. 'You would probably have told me to have an abortion, knowing you!'

'*The hell I would!* Sarah, come back!' Nick sprang after her, then remembered the waiter. Hastily he threw some notes onto the table and then raced after her. Despite his illness he was a great deal more agile than she was, and he caught up with her in seconds, grabbing her by the shoulders in a painful grip.

'*My* child!' he grated as he clutched at her. '*My* responsibility! Much as it terrifies me. I love you – you stupid woman. Can't you get that into your head? I love you whatever you do to me, and you seem to be doing

363

quite a lot at the moment.'

Sarah bit her lip, then finally met his eyes. 'Even when I'm making you a father against your will?'

'It does take two,' he reminded her, smiling at the memory of their reunion that October day. 'And I do seem to remember enjoying every minute of it! Diana will *have* to divorce me now, with this evidence.' Slowly, hesitantly, he put his hand over the bulge of the baby, and as if on cue the baby kicked, bringing an involuntary cry of surprise from him. 'It's moving!' he said, and Sarah smiled at the awe in his voice.

'Babies do – frequently,' she told him. 'It feels as if I have a rugby team in there sometimes!' Bolder now, she put her hand over his, guiding him. 'Feel, Nick. You can feel an elbow, and a foot.'

In complete wonderment, Nick stood very still, his sensitive hands absorbing the movements of his child. It was the wisest thing Sarah could have done. 'I've never felt that before,' he breathed at last.

'Not with Charlotte?' She was astonished.

'Good heavens, no! From the moment of conception, practically, I wasn't allowed near Diana in case it hurt the baby. The whole nine months was a complete nightmare.'

No wonder he was so anti-childbirth, she thought suddenly. His one experience of it had certainly not been a joyful one. 'This is different, Nick. *I'm* different. Our baby is perfectly healthy, and so am I. I can even show you the scan pictures.'

'Our baby!' Nick couldn't help the shiver of apprehension that ran through him. 'It's not at all what I wanted, but . . .'

'You still have the chance to walk away, Nicholas,' Sarah said quietly. 'I would never try to make you stay with me unless you wanted to.'

'But it *is* what I want – to be with you! Do you think I could leave you now?' he demanded. 'When I was ill, apparently the only comprehensible word I said for two weeks was "Sarah". You were the only thing that kept me fighting. And wanting this . . .'

He kissed her then, with all the pent-up need that had been imprisoned inside him for months, and Sarah felt his urgency as she responded to the hot, hard force of his mouth on hers, her arms tight around his neck as she clung to him. Every loving word he had wanted to say in those long months without her came tumbling out when he finally released her, until he felt the warm spill of her tears running over his fingers as he cupped her face in fiercely possessive hands.

'Don't cry, darling. I can't bear it when you cry,' he whispered. 'Whatever happens, we'll face it together.'

'I'm happy, Nick. That's all!' She smiled up at him as he wiped her tears away with his fingertips. 'But now you've effectively kidnapped me, what are you going to do with me? I can't fly to the States; the airlines wouldn't let me fly.'

'I realize that.' He smiled back. 'But Seth's jet is available, I only have to ask – I'm part of the company now. However, for the moment we'll go to Cap Ferrat and work out what we're going to do. I must admit my intentions were to whisk you away and spend weeks ravishing you, but in the circumstances . . .'

'Will you really stay with me?' she asked hesitantly. 'When the baby is born, I mean?'

Nick laughed. 'I'll probably do something totally stupid, like faint! But, yes, darling I'll be there if that's what you want.'

'It is! Oh, Nick, I thought I'd have to face that alone.'

'One thing . . .' Nick hesitated. 'No classes. I don't think I could stomach that!'

'Shame on you, Nicholas.' Sarah giggled. 'I've got a really nice teacher too – you'd like her.'

'Over my dead body!' he threatened. 'I'll read a book to get up to date.'

'Oh, I've got lots of those! Charles never stops buying . . . Oh!' Nick had put a hand over her mouth.

'I never want to hear about Charles again!' he said quietly. 'From now on he simply doesn't exist.'

Sarah could hear the firm resolve in his voice and she shivered. That such a long friendship could come to an end so abruptly saddened her. 'I still have all my stuff at Hastings,' she reminded him tentatively. 'I must get that back. It's all my parent's things.'

'Your brother would help over that, wouldn't he?' Nick knew how attached she was to the mementoes of her family.

'Yes, I guess so. I'll phone him this evening. And, whatever you say, Nick, I will phone Charles too.' She was standing firm on that. 'Whatever you think, he was very kind to me – I owe him that courtesy at least.'

'Knowing you, I rather expected you might.' He smiled. 'I'm being very selfish – of course you must. I just want you to myself now I've found you again.' He curved an arm around her waist to lead her back to the car. 'At least we have time to be together. You are obviously free to do as you please, and I'm under orders to rest.'

'Then I'll take care of you,' Sarah decided. 'You've certainly lost a lot of weight, Nick.'

'Almost a stone,' he admitted ruefully. 'But I dare say with your company to cheer me and Miriam's constant chivvying to eat I'll soon put it back.'

'Is Miriam at Cap Ferrat, then?'

'Yes. I was meant to join her for a few days. After she and Seth realized that I intended to come to England they insisted I went there for a rest. It was sweet of Miriam to come over, but I couldn't start to relax until I'd sorted things out with you. So now she'll have both of us to fuss over. Maybe Monte Carlo would be a good place to have the baby? Much safer than London as far as the Press are concerned.'

'More expensive, though.'

'The least of our worries! And from what little I know of

the procedure, France is a pretty enlightened place to have a baby in.'

'So I've read! But don't let's worry about it yet, Nick. There's almost a month to go.'

'A month to really worry over you,' he sighed. 'Maybe it *was* just as well I didn't know!' He handed her into the car with such care that Sarah laughed out loud.

'I'll make the most of it, I think.' She grinned at him. 'I certainly need some help rubbing all the oil into my skin.'

'That I will enjoy!' Nick picked up the phone to ring Miriam. 'We'll be there in about three hours, I hope.'

The Porsche had a hard suspension and, aware of it, Nick drove with a great deal more care than usual, reaching out occasionally to close his hand over hers as if to reassure himself she was there. Sarah smiled at his apparent insecurity, so unusual for the normally arrogant and self-assured Nicholas Grey!

To her surprise she grew increasingly uncomfortable. She had driven miles with Charles – albeit in the slightly more comfortable Jaguar – but this journey was causing a real ache in her back, and then her stomach. She twisted around frequently, enough to bring a concerned question from Nick several times. 'I'm OK,' she tried to calm him. 'Must have been something I ate at lunch. I keep getting the odd twinge, that's all.'

'You hardly ate any lunch,' he pointed out. 'Except olives, and you've always eaten loads of those. They're hardly likely to upset you. Perhaps it will be a bit easier on the motorway, we'll be on the A8 in a minute.'

'The Autoroute du Soleil – it always sounds so exotic somehow.' Sarah sighed. 'Do you remember going to Beaulieu?'

'I certainly do!' He smiled at the recollection. 'I think I *finally* fell in love with you there. I remember watching you sleep one night, and it was all I could do not to wake you up and tell you exactly how I felt. Which reminds me . . . reach over and get my jacket. In the inside pocket . . .'

Sarah reached for the navy jacket from the back shelf with difficulty, and then gave a shriek of pure pain.

Seconds later, as Nick turned in concern, she gave another cry of alarm. 'Nick! I'm bleeding!' The skirt of her denim dress was indeed soaked from the waist down. Hurriedly he aimed for the side of the road and stopped the car.

'It's not blood!' He touched her skirt tentatively. 'Look.' His fingers were clean, but definitely wet.

'Then what the hell is it?' Sarah was frantic.

'I rather think, my darling, that your waters have broken,' Nick said, struggling to contain his own rising panic. 'I guess we're going to become parents a little earlier than we expected. Don't worry, we'll cope.' He unstrapped his belt and got out of the car to go to the boot, pulling a towelling robe out of his bag and then reaching for the map tucked onto a side pocket.

'Nick, it's a month early!' Sarah blotted at her wet clothes. 'Oh, God, your car is soaked!'

'Never mind the damn car; it'll clean. Look, we should get you to a hospital, at least to get things checked out and make sure we can safely drive to Cap Ferrat.' He studied the map carefully. 'It's about five miles to Canville; that's a reasonable size – I'm sure we can get some help there. Hold on, darling.'

His driving was noticeably faster, his worried glances more frequent as he negotiated the winding uphill route. Frantic herself, nevertheless Sarah did her best to hide the sudden strength of the contractions she now knew were the real thing. They weren't, she knew, going to make it to Cap Ferrat.

The streets of the tiny town were deserted as the inhabitants took their normal long lunch break, and Nick swore violently as he realized their predicament. He was unable even to locate a hospital sign. Instead he aimed for the centre of town and finally breathed a sigh of relief. 'There's a police station.'

'Police? We need a hospital, not the police,' Sarah protested.

'Just stay in the car!' Nick pulled up, disregarding the parking restrictions, and raced into the police station. Sarah instinctively obeyed him, too frightened to move from her seat as she clutched Nick's robe around her, breathing the familiar scent of his cologne that clung to it. Within minutes he came racing back to her, with two very voluble policemen in tow.

'Nick!' she almost shrieked at him. 'What on earth – ?'

'Don't worry; they're only going to show me the way!' The two policemen swung onto motorbikes parked outside the station and gestured to Nick to follow them. They set a brisk pace, whisking through the narrow cobbled streets, and Sarah winced several times as Nick hit bumps in the road. The relief when they turned into the wrought-iron gateway of an impressive-looking building was immense to both of them. It looked more like a hotel than a clinic, and it reassured them more than a little.

One policeman bustled inside and seconds later a pretty young nurse came out to them. Remembering, then, Nick reached for the inside pocket of his jacket. 'Put this on,' he told her firmly, and promptly slipped her gold ring onto her wedding finger. 'I told them you were my wife.'

Somehow she felt much better with the familiar diamonds twinkling at her. 'I never thought I'd see this again.' She smiled at him as he lifted her out of the car. Despite her protests, he carried her up the short flight of steps into the cool white interior of the marble foyer before the nurse produced a wheelchair for her.

'I can still walk,' she argued vehemently.

'Do as you're told, Sarah!' Nick commanded as the nurse spoke in rapid French to him. His response was equally rapid and Sarah frowned.

'Nick, I don't understand,' she pleaded.

'Don't worry; I'll translate for you. I'm not leaving you

369

for any longer than I have to,' he said. 'They're getting an English-speaking nurse for you.'

'I need my medical notes – they're in my case,' Sarah realized. Nick cursed and went back to the car when the nurse was joined by another, who did indeed speak reasonably fluent English, and Sarah relaxed. However, it seemed an age before Nick was finally allowed to join her in the surprisingly unclinical room. Prettily decorated in pale blues and lemon, it had light curtains that drifted in the breeze from the open windows that led to a small balcony. Thanks to the policeman they had been directed to the best maternity clinic in the area, and Nick felt a great deal more confident as the doctor who had examined Sarah spoke to them.

'You will not be able to drive to Cap Ferrat today,' he told them. 'Your wife, *monsieur*, is most certainly in labour, and it would not be wise to leave here.'

'Is – is everything all right?' Nick reached for Sarah's hand.

'Everything is fine, *monsieur*.' The doctor smiled. 'All progressing normally. Help your wife to relax and don't worry. We won't be far away.'

'Relax! I'm a bundle of nerves!' Nick confessed, shame-facedly. 'Do you remember your exercises?'

'I didn't get to the end of the classes!' Sarah admitted with a grin. 'Cheer up, darling. Just think positive. If I have the baby today we can go to California that much quicker.'

'There is that, I suppose.' But at that moment it wasn't much consolation. Sarah went to the open French window and stood looking at the beautiful grounds, surprising him.

'Shouldn't you be in bed?' he asked, astonished.

'Don't be silly, Nick! It's much more comfortable to move around.' She was still wearing his towelling robe, thrown loosely over a Palm Springs T-shirt he remembered buying for her, and in the process she managed to

370

look about sixteen, with her hair still falling loose down her back.

'Well, if you're sure?'

'Of course I am. I got *that* far with my teacher!' Wincing, she reached out to him. 'Just hold me, Nick.' She soon found the most comfortable position in which to ride out the contractions, and Nick automatically curved his arms around her, holding her head against his chest as he stroked her hair. Concerned only for Sarah over the course of the long afternoon, he began to forget the long-abiding memories of Diana's frenzied reactions to the pain of childbirth. Eventually he could only admire what he perceived as Sarah's courage as she rode the increasing waves of pain that grew stronger as time went on.

Aware of his concern, Sarah calmly asked for pain relief from the midwife assigned to her, knowing exactly what she needed after her teacher's careful instructions. The sheer relief of having Nick with her, when she had been so certain she would be facing their child's birth alone, was in itself enough to give her the strength to cope.

Even with the help of Pethidine the pain was more than she had been led to expect. It hurt – she freely acknow-ledged and she clung to Nick unashamedly, but still practised the breathing techniques she had been taught.

Eventually it was a challenge that fully occupied them both. Though constantly encouraged by the sympathetic staff, and assured that everything was progressing quite normally, Sarah finally gave in to the pressure being put on her and yelled when she needed to. Even with Nick's translation of their instructions she knew things were rapidly getting out of her control. The contractions were coming one on top of the other. Barely had one faded when another started. It was too late for more Pethidine, and even the gas and air that Nick held out to her did little to help.

'Never again!' she told Nick through gritted teeth. 'I hate you, and your bloody baby!'

'I'm not translating that!' he told her with a grin. 'Behave yourself!'

'It's all right for you – you sadistic bastard!' she yelled right back at him.

The midwife laughed then. 'That needs no translation either. I've heard it many times before!' she commented wryly. 'Now, try sitting yourself up a bit; you'll be more comfortable.' At her instructions Nick lifted her up against him to support her as she leant back, trusting him to take her weight as they urged her to push – then stop – then push again. She needed no translation; the words were imprinted on her brain now. Her French was certainly improving! But she was tiring; they could all see that.

'I can't stand it!' she gasped in sheer exhaustion. 'I can't do any more, Nick!'

Nick exchanged glances with the doctor and midwife. 'You *can*, darling! It's so nearly here, I promise.' His own face was white with strain, the toll taken by his illness obvious as he leant over her. 'Try, please – just once more – please.'

'It *hurts*, Nick.' He heard the pain in her voice and his heart went out to her as he felt her grasp on his hand tighten. Sarah felt as if her whole body was being ripped apart as the next contraction tore through her.

'Push, darling!' he urged her in desperation. 'Push hard!'

She was beyond everything, sobbing and gasping with pain and the effort of responding to him. 'I'm going to burst!'

'Don't be so *silly*!' Nick laughed, and the atmosphere lightened immediately. 'Come on, Sarah, you can do it!'

Afterwards, she had no idea how she managed it, but with one last mammoth effort, as Nick urged her on, the baby slid out of her – and at once the pain stopped.

'It's a boy! Oh, Sarah, it's a little boy! Oh, well done, my darling. We've got a son!' Nick was crying as hard as Sarah was when the midwife wrapped the tiny wailing baby in a towel and put him into Nick's arms so that he could give him to Sarah. 'Oh, look at him,' he breathed. 'He's beautiful!'

They clung to each other and their baby as the staff bustled around them, voluble in their congratulations. It felt more like a party than a delivery room once the initial worry over the baby was over. He was almost six pounds, they discovered, and possessed the healthiest pair of lungs possible. The clinic believed in natural bonding after their deliveries, and once the baby had been checked thoroughly, and Sarah had taken the shower she'd demanded – to Nick's complete amazement – they were left alone with the baby.

Being France, champagne had appeared magically once Nick had asked for it, and, having shared it with the nursing staff, he held a glass out to Sarah. Leaning back in her nest of pillows, she was full of new energy. 'This will mix really well with all those painkillers!' she giggled after swallowing gratefully. 'Oh, Nick I'm so happy!'

'Happy it's over? Or about the baby?' He cradled his son in his arms as if he never wanted to let go.

'Both!' She hesitated. 'Nick, was I so awful?'

Nick compared the fear and drama of Charlotte's birth with the miracle he had just witnessed and reached for her hand. 'Of course not! And it was . . . well . . . something I'm just so glad I was here for.'

'I can't believe you were!' She sighed and stroked the baby's soft hair, drying now into a dark fluff.' At least you know it's your baby, with that hair!'

'I would never have thought otherwise!' Nick tensed as the baby suddenly started to wail. 'Oh, God! What's the matter with him? Is he all right?'

'I guess he's hungry.' Sarah took him from Nick and tentatively lifted him to her breast. 'Oh, Nick, I don't know what to do now!'

Laughing together, they coaxed the tiny mouth onto her

swollen nipple, and within minutes there was silence as the baby suckled hungrily. 'Just like his father!' Sarah giggled as Nick gently ran his fingers over his son's downy head.

'Not for a few weeks,' he joked. 'Darling, he's four weeks early! So much for getting ourselves together first!'

'We can get to know him instead,' Sarah pointed out. 'He's tiny, I know, but six pounds is a safe enough weight – we don't need to worry, Nick.'

'I just can't believe I'm a father again,' Nick admitted. 'It was all so sudden. Most fathers have nine months to get used to it.'

'And you had a few hours!'

'Traumatic ones. Darling, I was so frightened for you.'

'Nick, I'm only twenty-six, and very healthy,' Sarah assured him. 'Both Charles and I took a great deal of care over my health, whatever else you may think of him.'

'Diana was only twenty-five when Charlotte was born; they took her away from me to have the baby and she almost died.'

'Nick, I'm not Diana and I never will be! I don't quite know what you envisage for us, but let's get that quite clear. If we are going to stay together I will never be content with the kind of life you and Diana had.'

'I would never ask it of you.' Nick was horrified. 'I want to be married to you, Sarah. Live with you, go everywhere with you.'

'Live with the chaos that goes with a baby? Life will change for you – drastically!'

'Well, maybe we'll consolidate it and have another baby to go with this one! I think I'm getting the idea now!'

'Ouch! Not yet!'

'No, not yet. Let's get used to this one first.' Gently, he took the now peaceful baby from her arms. 'Get some sleep, sweetheart. I'll be back in the morning.'

'Nick, you look exhausted,' Sarah said, worried. 'Promise me you'll rest too? You've already had one night without sleep.'

It was typical of her to worry about him at a time like this, he thought as he drove to a nearby hotel. His body ached with fatigue, and he cursed the weakness that overtook him. He had to summon all his strength just to book himself in and make it to a room. Not even bothering to undress, he collapsed onto the bed and, clutching the pillow to his chest, was asleep as he hit the mattress.

He woke to bright sunshine and the cheerful clatter of a French town outside his window. Even as he surfaced his thoughts went to Sarah and his son, and he reached automatically for the phone. Refreshed by a few hours' sleep, she was incredibly chirpy as she filled him in on his son's progress.

'They say we can go to Cap Ferrat later today, if we are very careful and have medical care at the other end,' she told him, and Nick heaved a sigh of relief. The sooner he got her and the baby to somewhere safe, the better. Knowing the British Press as he did, he knew it would be only a matter of time before they discovered their whereabouts, and then all hell would be let loose.

'That's not a problem,' he said. 'Miriam will sort that out; I'll call her.'

'And George,' Sarah reminded him. 'Please? And in the meantime, Papa, you are going to have to do some shopping! Your son has only two babygros to his name at the moment, and he's soaked both of them!'

In a complete daze of euphoria, he phoned George and then sat with the phone in his hand as a dreadful thought struck him. How, he wondered, would he manage to tell his mother that her old-enough-to-know-better son had fathered an as yet illegitimate child?

Her reaction was all he expected it to be and worse. He wasn't, he discovered, too old to be thoroughly chastised by his mother! This was definitely his time for being brought down a peg or two. Having to go shopping for a tiny baby did very little for his ego either, when he realized he didn't know the first thing about a baby's needs. Luckily the assistant took pity on him, but seemingly sold him half the shop he'd been directed to by a sympathetic hotel manager.

He recalled all too clearly how closed off he had been after Charlotte's birth. Diana's mother had simply taken over, and for weeks he had barely been allowed near her. Charlotte had been three months old before life had resumed anything like normality. He couldn't help but compare that nightmare time with the present when, loaded with parcels, he strode into Sarah's room to find her standing at the window with the baby in her arms.

She glowed. It was the only word he could think of as he took in the picture she presented, with her hair loose on the shoulders of an unfamiliar flounced broderie anglaise dressing gown and just a touch of lipstick for make-up. Her eyes sparkled with life and her smile was the old familiar one, tilting her mouth up at the corners as she greeted him.

'My God! Shouldn't you be resting?' he demanded in surprise, dumping the bags on the floor.

'Don't be so old-fashioned, Nicholas!' Sarah chided. 'I've been up for hours. I had a bath at six o'clock this morning. I'm not ill, you know! I've had a baby, not a major operation.'

Carefully, Nick took his sleeping son and laid him in the crib. 'The first lesson you have to learn in this life, baby of mine, is that when I want to kiss your mother, you have to wait for her to cuddle you! And I do want to kiss her, so very badly.' He lifted her to him and kissed her deeply, feeling her trembling in his arms as she pressed tightly into them, and for a few minutes they were lost in their own sweet, sensual world.

A polite cough interrupted them finally, and they drew apart, both slightly embarrassed, to face a smiling young policeman armed with a huge bouquet of roses. 'André

Longueville,' he introduced himself with a little bow. 'I just came to wish you well.' It was one of the motorcycle policemen who had guided them the day before, and Nick shook his hand with pleasure after he had presented the bouquet with a flourish. 'A son is good news? Yes?' He beamed at Nick with an all-men-together smile. 'And such a beautiful mother too! You are a very fortunate man, *monsieur*!'

Sarah smiled enigmatically at his compliments, until he suddenly seemed to recognize her face, confident then that he knew her from somewhere. Things had been too frantic the day before for him to catch more than a quick glimpse of her. 'He recognized me, Nick,' she said, worried, when Nick came back from seeing him out. 'I'm sure he did!'

'I don't care!' Nick shrugged. 'I think I want the whole world to know how great things are! Except my mama!' Sarah roared with laughter when he shamefacedly confessed to his conversation with his mother. 'She told me to get my divorce sorted and make an honest woman of you forthwith,' he reported to her. 'And then had the nerve to say that if I *had* to behave so disgracefully, well, at least I'd managed to father a boy!'

'A very noisy one too!' Sarah walked across the room and lifted the crying baby from his crib. 'He's just feeling out of things; he can't be hungry.' Nick reached for him immediately, and to her surprise the baby settled in minutes as he soothed him before putting him back down.

'We can't go on calling him baby,' he said. 'Had you actually thought of any names?'

'Well, I wondered . . . perhaps . . . Sam? I've always liked it . . .' Sarah hesitated.

'Then Sam it is,' he decided. 'And Edward? It was my father's name, and it's my second name.'

'Samuel Edward! Do you hear that, Sam? You have a real name at last!' Sarah smiled. They both found it incredibly difficult to tear themselves away from the crib. Nick slid his finger into the tiny clenched palm and could have wept at the pleasure he gained from the way his son's little starfish hands clasped it.

'We must make some decisions, Sarah,' he said quietly. 'I have to sort out the paperwork here – get him registered and stuff. There are always reams of it in France. Do you have your passport, by any chance?'

'Oh, hell, no! Charles has it!'

Nick cursed. 'It may take more than a few days at Cap Ferrat, then! We certainly can't take him to the States without it. Maybe I can put him on mine, because he sure as hell is going to have my name, right from the start! But I'll have to organize a new one for you somehow.'

'George has all my paperwork; he'll do it if you ask him. After all, he'll be your brother-in-law soon.'

'If and when Diana divorces me!' he sighed. 'I want to marry you so much, Sarah Campbell!'

'To legitimize your son?' she teased. 'Just to please your mother? Shame on you, Nick! And I thought you were a big boy too!'

'If you weren't so fragile, I'd spank you for that! Now get some rest while I go and do battle with the doctors and the registration people.' He scooped her up and tucked her into the bed, accompanied by giggles from Sarah.

'Will you do this every day, Nick?'

'Try and stop me!' 'Now, rest!'

CHAPTER 26

Diana smiled, and, stretching lazily, felt pleased that she had remembered to tan her legs as she watched Paul pour champagne. He looked really distinguished, she thought, in the silk dressing gown she had bought him, and at least he'd *worn* it to go down to the kitchen for glasses. She had always been embarrassed by Nick's casual habit of wandering around without any clothes on, even when Charlotte was about.

She loved Paul's comfortable body, though, and the delightful things it could do to hers. It had been a revelation to discover how good sex could be with a man who truly desired her, and now she couldn't get enough of him. He gave her undemanding, thoughtful loving such as she had never known, and Paul never seemed to mind the fastidious precautions she insisted on – unlike Nick, who had always railed against them. All that and now added to it the news that Paul had been offered a knighthood in the Birthday Honours. Finally things were really looking up.

'Lady Miller!' she mused happily.

'Sounds good, doesn't it?' Paul brought the glass to her. 'When, Diana?'

'When, I've managed to screw enough cash out of that bastard I'm married to!' she told him with a grin. 'He is getting to the point of giving in, I'm sure. I'm going to be a very rich divorcee, Paul, you just watch!'

'Angel, you'll have this house – isn't that enough?' Paul had always envied the Greys their beautiful Georgian farmhouse. He could hardly believe his luck in knowing he would finally be living in it. 'We really don't need Nick's money. A dean's salary is pretty good, you know.'

'Oh, no, Paul, the house is not *half* enough! *We* are going to live in style, Sir Paul, mark my words. Mmm . . . do that again!'

Paul obliged, and pulled the sheet from around her and began his slow teasing of her breasts with his fingertips. Diana loved it, and was just reaching to pull him closer when the phone rang.

'Leave it,' Paul urged, but she laughed and picked it up despite his protests. She was glad she had, and was grinning broadly when she finally put it down.

'That was Maxie – Maxie Moreton!' she announced. 'And oh, boy, did he have some news! It appears my about-to-be-ex-husband registered the birth of a son a few days ago! In the South of France, of all places, and he's now holed up at Cap Ferrat with the child's mother.'

'Madeleine? Madeleine wasn't pregnant; I'm sure of that!'

'Not *Madeleine*!' Diana sat up and took a large mouthful of champagne. 'Remember all those rumours in the papers a few weeks ago about that little bitch Sarah Campbell being pregnant? *Guess* who the father is?'

'But he finished that months ago!' Paul stared at her, astonished that she could be so cheerful about it. Not so long ago she had been completely distraught about Nick's affair with Sarah Campbell. Mind you, that had been before he had decided to be truly bold and take her to bed – the day after Madeleine had walked out – he reminded himself smugly. He was delighted that she seemed to have completely changed her mind.

'Obviously not! The stupid fool has finally pushed me

too far! I've waited years for this moment, ever since he first started playing around. Oh, goodness, I can just see him buried under nappies and toys! Serves him right! Nick loathes babies! I think I'll send him Charlotte and her grotty moods for a week or two as well. That will really fix them! But he'll be desperate for a divorce now; the sky will be the limit financially, wait and see. At last I can take him for a fortune, and for that I think I can actually let my principles go hang. It might really be time I divorced him after all.'

'You've changed your mind?' Paul stared. Diana had seemed so determined not to divorce.

'You bet your sweet life I have! I never thought I'd say this, but I've *finally* had enough of Nick. Years ago I managed to palm Natasha off on Charles Hastings, and I married Nick because I knew he had talent and all the right connections. We all knew it. I got Daddy to back him at the right moment, and it worked! I did it all for Nick. But – now the time has come when I collect what I earned. The rotten bastard will have to pay for everything he's done to me over that bitch Sarah Campbell!'

'Hardly rotten, darling,' Paul pointed out. 'He has always been very generous, and he always seemed very fond of you.'

'When it suited him! He would never accept what I wanted in bed, though, as you always do. Mummy thinks he's a sex-maniac – the things he tried to make me do!'

Mummy, thought Paul, wryly, was going to be put straight on a few things fairly soon! 'So am *I* not allowed to make demands?' He raised enquiring eyebrows. He had already made love to her once that day.

Diana laughed. 'That's different! I could do it for ever with you!'

Paul savoured the thought and took a swig from his glass before he leant over her. Give the man his due, he mused, the absent Nicholas had very good taste in champagne – and women, come to that.

'To us, darling,' he toasted. 'And success for the lawyers!'

For two weeks, Nick and Sarah lived in a blissful cocoon of happiness. Both desperately needed the respite that the sanctuary of Seth's home provided them with. In the warmth of the Mediterranean sun they had the time to talk to each other, to walk in the spacious gardens and lie by the pool. They both took enormous pleasure in caring for their son, with the help of Isabelle, the young French nanny Miriam had found for them.

After only a few days Sarah had been astonished at the capable way Nick handled the tiny slippery baby in the bath, and he even changed the odd nappy, when she or Isabelle teased him into it – though he firmly drew the line at dirty ones!

Since he insisted that Sarah needed to rest, Nick did too, joining her in the huge canopied bed every afternoon for a couple of hours. Sometimes to sleep, often to lie in each other's arms and talk, and in doing so his own phenomenal energy began to resurface. In turn it gave him the strength to deal with the army of pressmen who, as they had dreaded, besieged the villa from the moment news of their presence leaked out.

'It's ridiculous!' Sarah protested, viewing the attendant hordes on the security monitors one day 'What on earth can they want with us?'

'Darling!' Nick laughed. 'Don't you realize what a furore you caused by disappearing?'

'Not really,' she admitted. 'I hardly saw a paper at Hastings.'

'Probably deliberate on Charlie's part,' Nick commented drily. 'And God help us when they find out about Sam – because they will! I still can't believe you managed to hide your pregnancy from them.'

'Clever clothes and a good figure!' Sarah grinned. 'I don't think even Mrs J. knew for certain!'

Restless, Nick strode the terrace. Now he felt better he was feeling the strain of the restrictions placed on their movements. 'Sarah, I really should go and see Charlotte, before the Press get to her. I can't tell her about Sam over the phone.'

'No, of course you can't. Why don't you go to London to see her? I'll be fine. Miriam is here, and Isabelle.'

'I think it might be for the best. I *am* worried sick about her, I admit. I could check on the office too, but I'll only be a day, I promise.'

He was as good as his word, but he arrived back with a truculent Charlotte in the car with him. He had seen the press cuttings Jane had collected up and, knowing it was only a matter of time before things began to get really heavy, he'd taken the decision to whisk her away. The only surprise was that Diana had made no objection, and in fact had seemed to welcome his request, according to his lawyer.

'Lotte is terrified that I don't love her any more,' he told Sarah, wary of her reaction. 'I couldn't leave her – especially as her exams are finished. We have to try, darling, please?'

'Of course we must.' Sarah swallowed her fears. 'Poor child, it must have been a horrible shock.'

'It wasn't the best half-hour of my life,' Nick admitted, remembering how his daughter had sobbed out her fears in his arms.

'Don't worry, Nick,' Sarah said softly. 'We'll cope – together.'

Nick sighed as he reached for her. 'I'm so lucky to have you. Come on, let's show her Sam together, then.'

Though she said very little, it was obvious that Charlotte was entranced with her baby brother. She continued to be wary of Sarah, however friendly Sarah was to her, but wisely Sarah never let her see that her coolness worried her. She maintained her serene attitude to the confused child thrust into their care and they began to

383

hope things were beginning to turn the corner when Charlotte started spending hours with Isabelle in the nursery.

When Nick's presence was again needed in London and he offered to take Charlotte back with him, she refused.

'I'll stay here with Sarah and Sam,' she elected. 'Isabelle said I could bath him tomorrow.'

'No problem, then!' Nick smiled at Sarah later that evening. 'I'll try and be back in a day, but my solicitor tells me there are an awful lot of problems to deal with – it may be overnight.'

'Is Diana being difficult?'

Nick sighed. 'You could say that! I had no idea how complicated divorce was! I'm certainly not going to make a habit of it, you'll be glad to know! But don't worry, we'll sort it out as quickly as we can.'

'At least we've got the Press off our backs for a while,' Sarah comforted him.

'At a price!' They had both hated having to invite them in for a photocall, but on the advice of his own PR company Nick had bowed to the inevitable and allowed them to set it up. Charlotte, surprisingly, had been almost enthusiastic.

'The girls at school will probably fall about laughing,' she had complained. 'But at least they'll know that *my* dad is not like the dinosaurs their dads are – at least he still *does* it.'

'I'm *so* glad you approve!' Nick had hugged her. 'And I think your dad needs all the moral support you can give him.'

'Well in that case, Daddy, let *me* choose what you're going to wear!'

'Over my dead body!' Nick had retorted, laughing. 'Ripped jeans and T-shirts are not my style! My wardrobe is my own affair! Go and advise Sarah instead, you cheeky baggage!'

Good-naturedly, Sarah had let Charlotte help her

384

choose a dress from the dozens Nick had bought for her on an expedition to Monte Carlo, and had even let her do her hair for her. Both she and Nick had congratulated themselves on the easing of the atmosphere after that event, and Nick left for London in the early morning, confident that things would be easier from now on.

Sarah wasn't quite so sure, after a few hours of Charlotte's company, although at first Charlotte was happy to bath Sam and wheel him around the garden with Isabelle. Her discovery of the powerful sound system in the family room had led to several sharp rebukes from Nick in the past couple of weeks, but with him absent, and Miriam calling on a neighbour, she took full advantage and played her very individual CDs at top volume.

Struggling with her irritation, Sarah tried desperately to put herself in Charlotte's place and ignore it, but it proved incredibly difficult. Mild requests had very little effect, and she was almost at screaming point before Miriam came back and immediately turned the music off with a firm hand. She had known Charlotte for many years and her bloody-mindedness cut no ice with her.

'Lotte, I'm surprised at you!' she said quietly. 'You'll wake Sam up with that racket!'

Charlotte was unabashed. 'Sorry, Auntie Miriam. I didn't think,' she said breezily. 'I'll go for a swim.'

'We'll have lunch by the pool, then,' Miriam said. 'I'm going into Nice this afternoon, do you want to come? Your father will be on the five o'clock plane after all; we can pick him up.'

'No, I'll stay here and sunbathe, I think,' Charlotte replied, surprisingly, and strolled out to the pool.

'Thank goodness you came in,' Sarah said. 'I have to admit that a few more minutes and Nick would have come back to find her floating in the pool!' she confessed.

'Honey, don't try and be too nice to her! She has to learn,' Miriam protested. 'Let her know you won't tolerate that kind of thoughtlessness, for heaven's sake! I know what it's like – I went through purgatory with Seth's kids. I know exactly what she's up to. Let her know where the limits are.'

'Miriam she's so young still.'

'And the little devil is playing on it! Nick won't allow it; he tells her and so should you. Stand up to her – believe me, it's the best way,' Miriam said. 'She already adores that babe, though at the moment she's shy of showing it to you both. She *is* coming round to the idea of you and Nick; I'm sure of it.'

'Oh, Miriam, I hope so – for Nick's sake,' Sarah sighed. 'I love him so much, and I know he loves me.'

'Yes, he does, and don't you forget it! I've never seen him so happy, Sarah, and it's all your doing. When he discovered you had dumped him, he was almost demented with grief.'

'He told me. Oh, Miriam, I wish I could come to the airport with you.'

'Hardly wise in the circumstances, is it? Cheer up, Sarah, he'll be back here by six, I promise.'

'Well, let's hope I can keep my hands off the little fiend till then!'

'Patience, honey, patience,' Miriam counselled wisely. 'Spend the afternoon resting, with earplugs in, if you can't bring yourself to discipline her!'

'I may have to! Oh-ho!' Sarah leapt up as a definite wail came from upstairs. 'Lunch-time for someone!'

Surprisingly, Charlotte was affable all afternoon, but she still seemed rather jumpy and was on the phone frequently. Sarah put it down to her looking forward to Nick coming back, as she was herself, and simply carried on with her normal routine – feeding Sam and playing with him for a while, before she went for the rest that Nick and the doctor still insisted on. It was still warm outside when she came down, and Charlotte was still spread out by the pool.

386

To hell with it, Sarah decided suddenly. A swim couldn't hurt her, she was sure. She had put on a swimsuit intending only to sunbathe a while, but it was almost a month since Sam had been born and her body felt back to normal. 'Coming in, Charlotte?' she asked, poised by the edge.

'Did Daddy *say* you could swim?' Charlotte drawled as she sat up, taking off her sunglasses to stare at Sarah. 'Hey! You look great!'

'I've been lucky, I guess.' Sarah looked down at her body. 'I'm a dancer, Charlotte, and my muscle tone *is* still good – and despite your papa I *have* been exercising. Surprise, surprise, I don't do everything he tells me to do; there's no fun in that!'

Leaving Charlotte staring in amazement, she slid into the warm water and swam lazily up and down, until Charlotte finally gave in and joined her. They were actually laughing together when they climbed out and sprawled on the loungers having tea.

'Do you really love Daddy?' Charlotte demanded, after lying in silence for several minutes.

Sarah rolled over and met her eyes squarely. 'Yes, I do, Charlotte. I really am sorry if your mother has been hurt, darling, but . . . well, things haven't been that great between them for a long time.'

'It worked until you came along!' Charlotte retorted. 'And trapped him by getting pregnant!'

'Believe me, Charlotte, I never intended to get pregnant.' Sarah stood up and reached for her robe. 'I knew only too well what Nick felt about that. But he's happy about it now; you must be able to see that?'

'Oh, yeah! And Mummy has that creep Paul hanging around her! Cosy, isn't it? Daddy never liked him.'

'Charlotte, is it Paul that's bothering you?'

'Not me . . . no, sir! I told you, everything is cosy. Now I'll have a stepfather, just like everyone else at school. Lucky me – an extra set of presents at Christmas!'

387

'Stop it, Charlotte!' Sarah was angry now. 'I'm not going to listen to self pity, and that's what it sounds like to me! Your father loves you dearly, probably even more than me, and that means he loves you *a lot*. I want us to be happy together because it means the world to him, and you are *not* going to spoil it, I won't let you, and that's an end to it!'

Leaving Charlotte stunned at her outburst, she stalked off, trembling with fear at what she had done, praying Miriam had been right and that she hadn't made things worse.

She looked in on Sam, asleep in his nursery as Isabelle sat calmly knitting, then went to shower and dress. Even the sight of her son didn't calm her quite as much as it usually did, since she was so worked up. He certainly seemed to look more like Nick every day, and he was growing at an amazing rate. Nick frequently laughed and demanded to know what on earth she was feeding him on to make him plump out so quickly.

Surprised by a sudden knock, she jumped, then called out cheerfully, hoping it would be Charlotte. It was a maid, telling her that there was a visitor in the drawing room with *mademoiselle*. 'Who is it?' Sarah demanded, annoyed that one of Miriam's friends should arrive just as Nick was due home. They would have to stay downstairs and be sociable, when it was the last thing she wanted. Then she shook herself and told herself firmly not to be so selfish. They were, after all, Miriam's guests.

'I don't know, *madame*, but *mademoiselle* seems to know him.'

'OK. Well, I'll be down in a second.' She pulled a brush through her barely dry hair and ran down to the drawing room. Easier to get it over with she thought, realizing from the fullness of her breasts that it was almost time to feed Sam. Normally he was yelling for his feed by quarter to six. Trust him to sleep on when she didn't want him to. She grimaced as she opened the door to the drawing room.

Charlotte was back in her jeans and a torn T-shirt, sprawled on one of the huge brocade sofas drinking Coke from the bottle – a habit she knew Nick hated. But opposite her . . . Oh, God . . . she thought helplessly, Charles sat calmly drinking tea. As neatly dressed as ever, in a pale grey suit, he even had his briefcase with him.

'Charles! How the hell did you get in here?' she demanded, and then the realization hit her. Charlotte had been on the phone constantly during the day. It must have been Charles she had been speaking to.

'Sarah, my dear!' Charles stood up. A different Charles, hard-eyed, and brittle-calm. 'What a greeting! Come and give me a kiss, darling.'

'The hell I will!' Sarah held the door open. 'Get out of here! I will *never* forgive you for what you tried to do to Nick and me! And neither will he!'

'Such melodrama! I told you the truth, Sarah, and don't you forget it! You look absolutely wonderful! Motherhood certainly suits you.'

'Stop it right there!' Sarah snapped. 'Just how did you get in here, anyway?'

'I invited him,' Charlotte announced defiantly. 'I thought he should have a chance to talk to you while Daddy wasn't on guard.'

'And your gateman wasn't going to refuse an old friend of the family, now, was he?' Charles was within a couple of feet of her, and she backed off nervously. There was something about him that she didn't like today. 'Not when Charlotte vouched for me!' he added smoothly.

'Stay away from me!' She tried to sound confident. 'Charlotte! Ring for Raoul. Tell him to come here immediately.'

'No, Charlotte!' Charles countermanded. 'You can go and fetch the baby. I'd like to see the results of all my care over the last few months. I think I have the right to that, don't you, Sarah?'

'No, I damn well don't!' Sarah was in a panic now. Any

389

moment Sam would be wanting his feed, and there was even a possibility Isabelle would bring him down to the drawing room. 'Do as I said, Charlotte.'

'She will do no such thing! This time I *am* going to do things my way.'

Charles reached for his briefcase, and Sarah began to shake with fear as she realized that there was indeed something very different about this man who had always shown her nothing but kindness. He appeared to have lost all control. And then she knew she was right . . .

Charles flipped open the case, and in the next second he had a revolver in his hand, pointing straight at her.

She froze, recognizing the gun. It was one of a pair he kept in the gun room. They had all used them several times, to shoot at tin cans in the garden, and she knew just how good a shot Charles was; far better than Nick or her.

'You are coming with me, Sarah. You and the baby! This time I won't let Nick cheat me.'

'He didn't cheat you before, Charlie,' Sarah managed in a strangled voice. 'You know he didn't. Natasha tried to go to Nick *despite* him telling her not to.'

'Oh, but he did! He wanted Natasha back and he would have stopped at nothing to get her! Charlotte, go and get that baby *now*!'

Equally horrified now, Charlotte stood up, and the Coke bottle slid from her fingers. Almost in a dream, Sarah saw the brown liquid soak into the Persian rug and thought casually how it would stain. Then her frantic eyes met Charlotte's.

'Don't, Lotte,' she begged. 'Tell Isabelle to take him to Miriam.'

'But Miriam . . . Oh . . .' Charlotte edged cautiously towards Sarah, her eyes glued to the gun.

'Miriam is out,' Charles said coolly. 'My little friend here was only too chatty this morning. Nice try, Sarah. Now *we* are going to take the baby and leave here together. Charlotte here will tell her daddy that you have changed

390

your mind about him and have decided to come back to me.'

'By force? Dream on, Charles Hastings! I'm not going anywhere with you!'

'But you are, Sarah.' Charles moved rapidly and caught her arm. 'We are going to be a very happy little family, you and I. Maybe we'll even manage to have a child of our own one day.'

'You have gone totally crazy!' Sarah tried to twist out of his grasp, but anger made him strong, and suddenly the gun muzzle was cold at the side of her throat. All the self-defence lessons she had taught on the programme were useless in this position.

'I've never been more sane in my life!' he assured her. 'This is going to be Nick's turn to suffer. Now get the baby, Charlotte, or I'll kill her now!'

'Uncle Charlie . . .' Charlotte pleaded, white-faced with fear. 'Please . . . don't.'

Charles whirled suddenly and the gun exploded, shattering a mirror close behind Charlotte's head, sending shards of glass everywhere as she screamed. 'Do it, Charlotte!' he ordered.

'Oh, God!' Charlotte fled, sobbing with fright, as Charles swung the gun back onto Sarah. In that split second Sarah heard the crunch of gravel on the forecourt and she realized Nick and Miriam were back – they would be walking straight into danger. If Charles would shoot at Nick's daughter, he would certainly shoot at Nick!

He was dragging her inexorably towards the door, the gun still pressed into her neck, his other arm trapping both hers. Now she had nothing to lose, as long as Charlotte didn't bring Sam. 'Nick!' she screamed, at a pitch only an actress could reach. This time it mattered that her voice carried. 'Nick! For God's sake . . . help . . .' Then Charles hit her with the butt of the gun, and her cry became a strangled scream as the pain of the blow stunned her for a moment.

Nick and Miriam, puzzled by the gateman's explanation of a visitor for Charlotte, were already alert as they reached the front door to be met by a sobbing Charlotte, hurling herself at Nick, almost incoherent with fear.

'Daddy! Daddy! It's Uncle Charles. He's got a gun. I think he's going to kill Sarah! Oh, do something, Daddy.' Nick thrust Charlotte aside, every sense alert.

'Miriam, get the men!' he ordered. 'Lotte, get Sam and Isabelle out of here. The pool house, next door – anywhere! Move!'

Charlotte raced upstairs just as Charles dragged Sarah out of the drawing room. Blood ran down her face from the blow on her cheek and Nick's heart stopped for a moment as he took in the horrifying scenario in front of him. It was a common enough scene in any of his films – but not in real life! Charles had the gun firmly at her throat and her arms pinioned by her side. That he was having to drag her, and having trouble doing so, was obvious to him. Sarah was almost as tall as Charles, and even having lost some weight she was still half a stone heavier that she had been.

'Leave her, Charles,' he said, as calmly as he could. 'Your quarrel is with me, not Sarah.'

'But it's Sarah I want, Nick – not you! You don't matter any more, because Sarah is going to be with me!'

'And how do you propose to keep her with you?' Nick taunted. 'Come on, Charlie, be sensible – let her go.'

'Never! I'll kill her first!' His grip on Sarah tightened, and Sarah couldn't help her stifled moan. Every tensioned muscle in her body screamed with pain as Charles wrenched her forward. Behind him, Nick was aware of other people in the doorway, and he heard the frightened cry of the maid as he frantically gestured them back. He, of all people, knew that when Charles was as cool as this he was dangerous. Charles rarely lost it, but when he did . . .

'Move over, Nick!' Charles snarled waving the gun at him, but Nick took a step forward instead, and then dared another. It was the one chance Sarah needed – and probably, she realized, her only one. With a hard jerk of her pinioned body she threw Charles off-balance, and the gun went off again, somewhere in the ceiling, bringing lumps of plaster down.

In that split second Nick lunged forward, hurling Sarah aside and launching himself on Charles in one almost continuous movement. A week or two earlier and he would never have been able to do it, but the rest and the adrenalin had brought his strength back in abundance. The three guards immediately sprang across the room to pull Sarah away from danger, and for a moment it was total chaos.

Locked together, Nick and Charles fought some macabre dance for long seconds, until suddenly Charles began to choke – long, heaving sounds that made Nick loosen his grip on him. Charles was going blue, grasping at his chest, until with a deep moan he slid to the floor.

For a moment Nick stared, stunned, as Charles shuddered and then lay still. Then he realized what was happening and dropped to his knees beside him, all animosity forgotten in an instant. 'Get some help!' he rasped at the men. 'And an ambulance. Oh, God, Miriam!' He was desperately feeling for a pulse and not finding one, ripping open Charles's shirt as he did so.

Miriam rapped out orders and joined Nick on the floor. 'Is he injured?' she demanded, puzzled.

'No! I think it's his heart; he's had an attack before. Try and find Isabelle, someone. Sarah?'

'I'll do it.' Sarah ran upstairs, hardly able to watch as Nick, in desperation, leant over Charles's prone figure and, taking a deep breath, began mouth-to-mouth resuscitation with Miriam's help. Charlotte and Isabelle had locked themselves in the nursery suite, and it was frantic seconds before Sarah could convince them that it was safe to unlock the door. Sam was howling with hunger and Sarah grabbed at him. 'I'll see to him. Isabelle, please, will you go down to Nick?'

'Daddy! Is he hurt?' Charlotte screamed, and Sarah stared at her. She had almost forgotten Charlotte.

'No – no thanks to you!' she snapped, and collapsed into a chair with Sam in her arms. Distractedly, she pulled the strap of her dress down and let Sam find his own way to her breast – which, like a little homing pigeon, he did. 'How could you have let Charles in?' she demanded, when silence had been achieved. 'After all you knew he had done to us?

'I didn't believe you, Sarah,' Charlotte admitted shame-facedly. 'I . . . I thought . . . you and Daddy were making it up, so that I'd forgive you about Sam. That's what Charlie said.' In floods of tears again, she almost fell across the room and buried her face in Sarah's lap. 'Oh, Sarah, I'm so sorry – so very sorry . . . I had no idea he was going to do that! Really I didn't! I didn't want any harm to come to you, or Sam.'

Sarah reached down and curved her hand over Char-lotte's dark curls. 'I know,' she said softly. 'Charlotte, even I had no idea Charles could be so . . . well . . . violent. And I know him as well as Nick does – better in some ways. Don't cry, darling, I think we all need to keep calm for a while.' She shuddered, realizing for the first time how close to death all three of them had come. Only the suckling baby kept her calm at that moment, and she went on stroking Charlotte's hair in a desperate attempt to get her to relax a little too.

They were still like that when Nick appeared in the doorway, fraught and dishevelled. 'He's breathing,' he said wearily. 'The ambulancemen are here so they have taken over. Isabelle was fantastic! Sarah, Charlotte – are you all right?'

'Oh, Daddy!' Charlotte hurled herself at Nick, her face tear-stained and red. 'Daddy, I'm so sorry.'

Relieved, Nick hugged her. 'It's all right, darling, *you* weren't to know. None of us were, but I guess I should have known he might try something like that – he threatened to.' With his arm still around Charlotte, he moved to Sarah, bending to kiss her cheek, only too aware, with some distaste, that his mouth tasted of Charles. 'I'll have to go to the hospital with them,' he told her gently. 'But as far as anyone else is concerned it was just a heart attack. We took the gun away and the staff will say nothing.'

'Nick! He nearly killed us!' Sarah protested.

'Yes, I know.' Nick looked grave. 'But I don't want it to get out – can you understand that? We've been friends for so long, darling, despite everything. Even if I never see him again – which I won't, believe me – I can't do it to him.'

'Nick!' Sarah disengaged Sam and pulled her dress back up. 'I think you are a far better friend to Charles than he ever deserves to have. But if that's what you want I'll go along with it; I promise.'

Nick went into the nursery bathroom and washed his face, then quickly rinsed out his mouth with antiseptic. He felt sick now the drama was receding, and he gripped the edge of the basin as nausea churned in his stomach. Finally, pulling himself together, he dampened a flannel and took it back to Sarah, to gently clean up the damage to her cheek where the blood had started to dry up. She had almost forgotten about it, and she looked at the blood on the flannel in surprise.

'I nearly had a heart attack myself when I saw that,' he admitted. 'But in actual fact it's little more than a graze. You were very lucky – in fact we all were. Look, I'll have to go. I'll be back as quickly as I can, Will you go and help Miriam for me, darling? I think she's as shaken as we are.' He was struggling to be matter-of-fact, when all he really wanted to do was grab Sarah in his arms and never let her go. The thought of the next few hours filled him with horror, but he knew he had to get through them. Hospitals were still part of Nick's nightmares.

When he had finally gone, following the ambulance in

his own car, Sarah pulled herself together and, after giving a repentant Charlotte strict instructions on how to look after Sam, went downstairs to Miriam. Somehow the two of them marshalled the bewildered staff into action, to clear up the broken mirror and generally make good the damage Nick and Charles had caused as they fought. Neither of them felt like eating, but when Charlotte came down, after handing over to Isabelle, Miriam poured them all a glass of brandy – including Charlotte.

'I think we all need this,' she decided firmly. 'Or at least, I do!'

Sarah smiled, for the first time in hours. 'I need it too, so Sam will sleep well tonight!'

Seth only bought good cognac, and it slipped down – the first alcohol Sarah had had since Sam's birth except for the champagne – and she relaxed in minutes. Tentatively, Charlotte crept up to her as she leant back on the sofa, still clutching her own glass, hardly daring to drink it. 'Sarah,' she whispered. 'Will Uncle Charlie be OK?'

'I honestly don't know. All Nick said was that he *was* breathing.' Sarah frowned.

'He worked miracles,' Miriam said in admiration. 'He simply wouldn't give up. Neither would Isabelle.'

'Daddy really is rather special, isn't he?' Charlotte said. 'Uncle Charles was very close to me with that bullet; I was so scared.'

'We all were,' Sarah admitted. 'But I'm sure Charlie only meant to frighten us, darling.' He was too good a shot to miss at that range.

Charlotte huddled close to Sarah, as she had done upstairs, for what seemed like hours, until Nick finally came back at almost midnight. He looked exhausted, and his face was pinched with fatigue as he slumped into a chair while Miriam silently handed him a glass.

'So far, so good,' he said slowly. 'He's still alive, but only just. We'll ring in the morning. We can only hope now.'

'In that case there's nothing else we can do,' Miriam said firmly. 'Come on, Lotte, bedtime.'

Left alone, Nick and Sarah clung together. 'It was a massive attack,' Nick said eventually. 'I really don't see how he can survive it, but I do want him to. I really do. I hope that doesn't seem disloyal to you, darling. I'm so confused.'

'It's not disloyal at all,' Sarah affirmed. 'I think over the last few weeks, Nick, I have learnt just how kind and thoughtful you can be. You hide your feelings most of the time, but with me and Charlotte, and especially Sam, you're so different.'

'I learnt long ago to keep my feelings to myself,' Nick mused. 'At home, at school, even at university, it really was frowned on to show them. It wasn't till Tasha came along that I learnt to say I love you. But when I lost her to Charles, I vowed I would never say it again. I don't think I ever told Diana that I loved her, yet I can't tell you enough.' He hugged her so tightly she thought her ribs would crack, but she knew then just how much he needed her and welcomed it. His pain was hers at this moment.

'Let's go to bed, Nick,' she begged. 'I need you to hold me.'

'That is something I've been longing to do all evening.' Nick lifted her to her feet with alacrity, and led her up the stairs.

When Sarah came out of the bathroom, wearing a long, floating white nightdress he had bought her in Nice, he was just putting down the phone. 'No change,' he said briefly, and strode into the bathroom. Sarah sat on the window-seat looking out over the subtly lit gardens and felt the tears of relief begin to slide inexorably down her cheeks. Frantically she wiped them away. She had no reason to cry for Charles, had she?

Nick came back into the room, his bare feet silent on the thick carpets. Since he couldn't make love to her, he had taken to wearing shorts to sleep in, but she felt the soft hair

on his naked chest rub against her own bare back as he slid
his arms around her, nuzzling her hair away from her neck
with his lips. They were gentle on the curve of her neck,
and Sarah smiled as she turned in his arms.

'I love you, Nicholas,' she said softly. 'More than
anything or anybody in the world.'

Nick laughed and nodded towards the crib where Sam
slept peacefully, his tiny fists clenched each side of his
dark head. He shared their room at night so that Sarah
could feed him – though the previous night he had slept
right through to their immense relief. 'Even more than
Sam?' he teased.

'Sam is part of both of us,' Sarah argued as he lifted her
up. 'A very precious part. You don't regret him, do you,
Nick?'

'Only when he's wailing at three o'clock in the morning! No – silly girl – I don't regret him I would never
regret him. I love him as you do, and *once* we're married
I'd like to have *other* babies! I've got over that stupid fear
now, thanks to you. In fact I have become a totally
different person because of you. Much stronger, in some
ways.'

'And protective,' Sarah added, as he slipped her into the
bed and then joined her.

'The next few weeks I'm going to need to be,' he sighed.
'Imagine what will happen now! The Press will be down
on us like the proverbial locusts they are – not to mention
Diana. No way are they going to believe that Charles paid
us a friendly visit and had a heart attack in the process.
And if he dies . . .!

'Oh, God! Nick what are we going to do?' Sarah buried
her face in the pillows as if to hide from the prospect. They
had suffered enough from the press harassment of the last
few weeks.

'Depends a bit on Charlie. It might seem a bit callous to
whisk you off to LA while he is so ill – but it would be safer
for us all. Charlotte should go back to Diana, anyway, so

she will be OK. Thank goodness she was upstairs when it happened; she was very fond of Charlie – even named after him.'

'Is,' Sarah corrected.

'Is,' he repeated, as if to reassure himself. 'We were so lucky tonight, Sarah. He could easily have killed both of us, the state he was in. There was no way he would have left without you, and if you'd continued to say no to him – he would have killed you rather than leave you with me; I'm sure of that. And I couldn't have contemplated a life without you. I know that now.'

'Thank goodness you came back that bit earlier, and didn't decide to stay in London overnight.'

'I couldn't bear to, though I should have done.' Nick sighed heavily. His solicitor was locked in combat with Diana's solicitor over the huge new claims she was making; and the situation was deteriorating rapidly. 'Just be glad that Miriam decided to collect me, and not the chauffeur. He drives at snail's pace, something you could never accuse Miriam of doing.'

Sarah shivered. 'Nick, do you think we'll ever be able to lead a normal life again?'

'Yes, darling, I do.' He was adamant on that point. 'LA is used to the film business, and the people who work in it. We'll be able to live and do as we please. Seth and Bob are delighted with *Emerald Isle*, so once that's out you'll have plenty of offers if you want to do other work apart from mine. Maybe I'll retire and let you keep *me*!' he added teasingly, and she laughed.

'That I doubt very much!' She knew Nick's capacity for work. 'But I'll make sure you stop working yourself into the ground from now on.'

'I won't have a chance to! Since with a son – or two – I'm going to need to find the time to play football, aren't I? And cricket – maybe even golf. I haven't played that for years.'

'More likely baseball!'

'Over my dead body! I think I'll put Sam down for Kings tomorrow!'

'I'm not sending our son to boarding school,' Sarah protested. 'Especially if we're living in the States.'

'By the time he's eight you may be glad to! My parents certainly were!' He cuddled her close to him. 'Wait till you've done the school run for a few years, with all the other Hollywood mums.'

'You can do that too.' She giggled, distracted now as he peeled the nightdress from her shoulders.

'*Me*?' He was appalled at the prospect.

'*You*!' she said firmly. 'You already bath and change him – why not that?'

'Nobody else sees me bathing and changing him,' he said, grinning in the dark. They both knew how much Nick enjoyed doing things for Sam. 'Or doing this, for that matter!' He caressed her breasts gently. 'Damn these doctors and their rules! I want you so much! Sarah, are you sure it's too early?'

'It's supposed to be, but – I feel fine, Nick.'

He was gentle, as she had known he would be; and afterwards, as Nick slept and she lay awake in his arms, blissfully contented, she knew. Everything was going to be all right.

CHAPTER 27

'Sarah! Sarah! Aren't you ready yet?' Charlotte bounced into the airy sun-filled room. 'Everybody's waiting!'

'Yes, I'm ready.' Sarah turned from the window, from where she and Cress had been watching the wedding guests assemble in the beautiful gardens of the Palm Springs estate she and Nick loved so much. Of their three homes it was the only one they had chosen together, and it had been the automatic choice for their wedding when Nick's divorce had finally come through – after three weary years of battling with Diana over money.

In those three years Nick and Seth had more than fulfilled their promise to Sarah. *Chrysalis* alone had made her a major box-office name, earning her an Oscar, as Nick had predicted from the outset of shooting. But despite her success, and the resultant attention from the media, as Nick had promised they persisted in living a normal family life.

Not for them the phalanxes of bodyguards. Sarah shopped in Malibu, with Sam singing and shouting in his buggy, like any other young mother, and Nick was frequently seen with a baby seat in the back of his car as he drove them all between houses or on frequent outings. Sarah Campbell was renowned for her cool attitude to the Press, and adamant in her refusal to allow them any access to her precious son whatsoever.

Isabelle had somehow stayed on with them. Devoted to

Sam from the very start, she had happily accompanied them to California and was now being ardently wooed by a young cameraman. From the window Sarah could see her trying to control an over-excited three-year-old, and Cress and James's little daughter. They laughed with amusement as the two children rolled together like battling puppies under the feet of other guests. A sophisticated wedding it most certainly was not, she thought, as Madeleine laughingly stepped in to grab at one child as Isabelle lifted up the other.

Despite her earlier suspicions, Sarah liked her. When Madeleine had fallen in love with Mark Winford, on the set of *Chrysalis*, Sarah had merrily promoted it – she and Nick helping it along by inviting them both back to Malibu, and then Palm Springs when they finally got it furnished. Madeleine was married to Mark now, and consequently travelled with him most of the time, but she still worked for Nick occasionally, and they both welcomed her. She was as efficient as Jane had been in London – though Jane was lost to the company now. Slowly, Sarah turned over the card in her hand, and looked again at the message on it. Simple, but heartfelt, she knew.

'With all our love on your wedding day, from Charles and Jane Hastings'.

That Jane had long nursed an affection for Charles had come as a complete surprise to them all. That she had flown out to Nice and taken charge of the situation astonished them – Nick most of all. She had simply refused to let Charles die, and six months later she had married him – to Sarah's private and intense relief. She put the card down and smiled at Charlotte.

'Is Nick OK?' she asked, reaching for the bouquet of delicate lilies that Cress held out to her.

'Poor Daddy! He's shaking like a leaf! I've never seen him in such a state!' Charlotte giggled. 'I'm sure he thinks you're going to change your mind at the last minute!'

'Since he and George dragged James out for eighteen holes of golf this morning, it's probably exhaustion!' Cress laughed. 'I know it's your wedding night, but I don't think you'll have much luck tonight, Sarah!'

'Rubbish!' Sarah retorted. 'He plays golf at least twice a week now. I swear it was half the reason he was so keen to buy this place! Even if he did insist it was years since he played, he soon got back into it.'

'Well, at least you know where he is on a golf course!' Cress joked.

'I have no worries there, Cress.' Sarah smiled. 'I never have had, and I'm sure I never will.'

'No, I don't think you will. I've never known a man as much in love with a woman as Nick is with you. I would never have believed it possible of him a few years ago. He's changed so much. I never thought he had the capacity to love anyone, yet to see him with Sam is a revelation!'

'Well, that's hardly surprising, is it?' Charlotte put in. 'Sam can charm the birds off the trees, and he's only three!' She adored her baby brother, and was constantly nagging them to have more babies – something they had steadfastly held back on until they could marry. Within months of their moving to California Charlotte had demanded to join them for every school holiday, and now planned to commence a Film Studies course at UCLA in the autumn.

'Well, we certainly know where he gets *that* from!' Cress said. 'He may be the image of Nick, but his personality is all Sarah's.'

'Apart from the odd flash of temper!' Sarah commented. 'Then he is pure Nicholas, I assure you! There – how do I look?'

'Absolutely gorgeous! As usual!' Cress made a critical adjustment to the coronet of white lilies that sat on Sarah's long hair and then smoothed out the floating layers of the delicate cream silk dress she had designed for her. 'OK, Charlotte, tell George he can come in now.'

Grinning broadly, George hugged his sister as she ran to him. At last he was free of Maggie grumbling about Sarah's appalling lack of morals. Down in the garden a beaming Maggie was fussing over Becky's bridesmaid dress.

Cress had calmly handed her own hoyden of a daughter to Madeleine, and just prayed that Daisy had managed to keep her bridesmaid dress *on* – never mind clean! Her favourite trick was to strip at any opportunity, much to James's amusement. Daisy was doubly precious to them after months of IVF treatment – a process Cress was considering again, since it had been discovered it was the only way they could have children.

Smiling now, she followed Sarah and George, scooping a hand from each little girl as George led Sarah forward to the flower-encrusted arbour erected on the terrace where an astonishingly nervous Nick waited with James grinning at his side. Charlotte was right. He had been terrified that Sarah would change her mind, and it hadn't helped being forced to spend the night away from the house at the Marriot, under James's care, and so being deprived of her overnight.

He looked so handsome, Sarah thought dreamily as George led her along the flowery path towards him, his white dinner jacket enhancing his tan and the deep, dark sheen of his hair.

He was smiling with relief as she reached him, but he said nothing, simply took her hand and lifted it to his lips in a silent gesture of his love. She barely heard the words of the service. All she was aware of was Nick beside her, his warmth and the light touch of his fingers on hers. He even laughingly needed to prompt her with her responses.

'First time Sarah's forgotten her lines, and it has to be now!' James quipped irreverently as they exchanged their rings.

Then the celebrant said, 'You may kiss the bride!' and she came alive, being swept into Nick's arms for a kiss that brought cheers from their audience for its length and fervour.

'At last, darling!' he murmured. 'At long last you're really my wife! I love you, Mrs Grey.'

'As I love you.' Sarah leant back in his arms and Nick lifted her up, spinning her round with sheer, exuberant joy.

'Tonight . . .' he whispered as everyone thronged around them. 'Tonight . . . we'll set about making Charlotte's wishes for another brother a reality, shall we?'

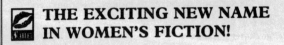

THE EXCITING NEW NAME
IN WOMEN'S FICTION!

PLEASE HELP ME TO HELP YOU!

Dear *Scarlet* Reader,

As Editor of *Scarlet* Books I want to make sure that the books I offer you every month are up to the high standards *Scarlet* readers expect. And to do that I need to know a little more about you and your reading likes and dislikes. So please spare a few minutes to fill in the short questionnaire on the following pages and send it to me. I'll send *you* a surprise gift as a thank you!

Looking forward to hearing from you,

Sally Cooper

Editor-in-Chief, *Scarlet*

P.S. Only one offer per household

QUESTIONNAIRE

Please tick the appropriate boxes to indicate your answers

1 Where did you get this Scarlet title?
Bought in Supermarket ☐
Bought at W H Smith ☐
Bought at book exchange or second-hand shop ☐
Borrowed from a friend ☐
Other _____

2 Did you enjoy reading it?
A lot ☐   A little ☐   Not at all ☐

3 What did you particularly like about this book?
Believable characters ☐   Easy to read ☐
Good value for money ☐   Enjoyable locations ☐
Interesting story ☐   Modern setting ☐
Other _____

4 What did you particularly dislike about this book?
_____

5 Would you buy another Scarlet book?
Yes ☐   No ☐

6 What other kinds of book do you enjoy reading?
Horror ☐   Puzzle books ☐   Historical fiction ☐
General fiction ☐   Crime/Detective ☐   Cookery ☐
Other _____

7 Which magazines do you enjoy most?
Bella ☐   Best ☐   Woman's Weekly ☐
Woman and Home ☐   Hello ☐   Cosmopolitan ☐
Good Housekeeping ☐
Other _____

cont.

And now a little about you –

8 How old are you?

Under 25 ☐   25–34 ☐   35–44 ☐
45–54 ☐   55–64 ☐   over 65 ☐

9 What is your marital status?

Single ☐   Married/living with partner ☐
Widowed ☐   Separated/divorced ☐

10 What is your current occupation?

Employed full-time ☐   Employed part-time ☐
Student ☐   Housewife full-time ☐
Unemployed ☐   Retired ☐

11 Do you have children? If so, how many and how old are they?

_____

_____

12 What is your annual household income?

under £10,000 ☐   £10–20,000 ☐   £20–30,000 ☐
£30–40,000 ☐   over £40,000 ☐

Miss/Mrs/Ms _____

Address _____

_____

_____

_____

Thank you for completing this questionnaire. Now tear it out – put it in an envelope and send it before 31 May, 1997, to:

Sally Cooper, Editor-in-Chief

SCARLET
FREEPOST LON 3335
LONDON W8 4BR

Please use block capitals for address.

No stamp is required!   SISAR/11/96

Scarlet **titles coming next month:**

WICKED IN SILK Andrea Young

Claudia is promised a large sum of money for her favourite charity if she will act as a kissagram at Guy Hamilton's birthday lunch. What she doesn't know is that his head-strong daughter, Anoushka, has arranged the whole thing. So when Claudia finds herself in Greece with Guy and Anoushka, anything might happen . . . and it does!

COME HOME FOR EVER Jan McDaniel

Matt and Sierra were lovers ten years ago . . . then she betrayed him by marrying another man. Matt hadn't married Sierra because he didn't want to bring a child into the world. What he doesn't know is that the child Sierra brings home for Christmas is *his*!

WOMAN OF DREAMS Angela Drake

Zoe has a secret which she finds difficult to accept . . . and when she falls in love with François, the gift seems to become a curse. To avert disaster, Zoe decides never to see François again . . . but *can* she survive a marriage without love?

NEVER SAY NEVER Tina Leonard

Dustin Reed needs a housekeeper . . . Jill McCall needs a job. What Dustin doesn't need is a single mother with a baby to care for, though that seems to be exactly what Jill is! Oh, of course, she denies the baby is hers . . . telling Dustin that the little girl was left on his doorstep! Whether he believes Jill or not, this is clearly going to be one Christmas Dustin will never forget.